"Maxi followed the doctor's gaze as it traversed long legs that traveled up to the hem of a skimpy, black leather skirt, up over the tight black chenille sweater, to the long, slim neck, and over the expertly made-up face. The mouth, open as if in disbelief. Bright red lipstick, still fresh. The softly rounded chin, the angular nose. The eyes . . .

The eyes! Maxi flashed. Partly open. Dusky, charcoal brown. The Gillian Rose Maxi and countless millions knew, or had seen pictures of in newspapers and magazines, print ads, and billboards, had eyes that were not dark brown—they were vivid, sparkling, cerulean blue.

more . . .

DEAD FILE

Other Books by Kelly Lange

THE REPORTER
GOSSIP
TROPHY WIFE

DEAD FILE

KELLY LANGE

WARNER BOOKS

NEW YORK   BOSTON

Copyright © 2003 by Kelly Lange
Excerpt from *Graveyard Shift* copyright © 2003 by Kelly Lange
All rights reserved. No part of this book may be reproduced in any form or by any electronic or mechanical means, including information storage and retrieval systems, without permission in writing from the publisher, except by a reviewer who may quote brief passages in a review.

Cover design and art by George Cornell

Warner Books

Time Warner Book Group
1271 Avenue of the Americas, New York, NY 10020
Visit our Web site at www.twbookmark.com
The Mysterious Press name and logo are registered trademarks of Warner Books.

Printed in the United States of America

Originally published in hardcover by The Mysterious Press
First Paperback Printing: June 2004

10 9 8 7 6 5 4 3 2 1

DEDICATION

for **BUCKY POOLE**
&
CHRIS POOLE

my fictional Maxi Poole's real spiritual brothers
. . . with love!

1

"Max, I found a new 'miracle pill,'" Wendy Harris said to Maxi Poole, holding up a white plastic container of dietary supplements. "Check this out—Zenatrex."

"What does it do?" Maxi asked her.

"Cuts your appetite." Wendy was a believer.

Wendy tossed the bottle of tablets over to Maxi. The two journalists were sitting across from each other in the newsroom at L.A.'s Channel Six in Burbank, during a rare lull in the usual bedlam that passed for business as usual. Maxi Poole—thirty-two years old, tall, angular, outdoor-girl fresh with short-cropped blond hair—was the station's highly rated anchor-reporter. Wendy Harris—thirty, pert, diminutive, with a mane of willful red hair and a sprinkle of freckles across her nose—was Maxi's longtime producer and close friend.

"Just what you need, Wen, an appetite suppressant," Maxi commented dryly, examining the container in her hand. Usually without bothering to leave her desk, Wendy might consume two shrimp with a wedge of lemon and call it lunch, or a cup of steamed rice with soy sauce and call it dinner.

Maxi unscrewed the cap and peered inside at the large brown tablets. "Whew!" she breathed, wrinkling up her nose. "This stuff stinks."

Wendy laughed. "Yah, the smell alone's enough to kill your appetite—you don't have to bother taking the pills."

Maxi read from the label. "Guarana extract, white willow bark, citrus aurantium, magnesium phosphate, ginger powder—"

"No ephedrine. That's the killer. Nothing terrible in it," Wendy interrupted. "And it works."

"How do you know it works?"

"I took one this morning with a cup of tea, and now I'm full."

"Placebo effect," Maxi pronounced.

"See, that's fine with me," Wendy countered, flashing the signature grin that reflected mischief in her eyes. "If it fools me into thinking I'm not hungry, then it works for me."

"Wendy, you eat zip as it is," Maxi said, glancing at her friend's petite frame.

"Yeah, but I *want* to eat the *world*. This stuff makes me not crave three jelly doughnuts on a coffee break. Especially this time of year, when everybody's bringing in cholesterol-packed Christmas goodies."

It was mid-December. Christmas in Southern California meant no ice, no snow, no freezing cold, but Yuletide music, gaudy decorations, and loads of food.

Wendy came from a family that made food an art form. Her dad was Tommy Harris, owner of Tommy's

Joynt, the world-famous San Francisco rathskeller on the corner of Geary and Van Ness Avenue in the city by the bay. All through her growing-up years, Wendy endured her ebullient Jewish mom and dad urging, "Eat, Wendy, eat." Until she ended up with—her term—a "humongous fear of food."

For Maxi's part, her father was a pharmacist who put in long hours navigating the small East Coast chain of drugstores he owned and had never been concerned with dinner being on the table at any special time, and her mother was a dance instructor who still maintained her dancer's lean body. Except on holidays, food was never much of an issue with the Pooles, and in fact nobody in the family was a particularly good cook, Maxi included. They joked about that. Takeout, both plain and fancy, had always been king at their New York brownstone.

Maxi twisted the cap back on the container of Zenatrex and handed it back to Wendy, who set it on her desk in line with an army of other bottles and jars labeled GINKGO BILOBA, DHEA, ST. JOHN'S WORT, MELATONIN, MILK THISTLE, GINSENG GOLD, SLO NIACIN, ECHINACEA & GOLD-ENSEAL, GLUCOSAMINE & CHONDROITIN, NATURAL ZINC, CHROMIUM PICOLINATE, and a dozen or so other purported health monikers.

Rob Reordan, L.A.'s longtime anchor patriarch who co-anchored the Six and the Eleven O'clock News at Channel Six, ambled down the aisle toward them. Peering down his nose with a look of disapproval at the vitamins and supplements Wendy was now doling out into her palm, he intoned in his resonant anchor voice that was familiar to all of Southern California, "Is there anything you *don't* take, Wendy?"

"Yah, Rob," Wendy flipped back. "Viagra."

Rob sniffed, tossing his generous head of white hair, and kept walking.

"Not nice," Maxi scolded, stifling a giggle.

"Oh, *please!*" Wendy blurted, rolling her eyes. "Eighty-something, and he's even *more* of a horn-dog since Pfizer foisted Viagra on the world."

"You don't know that he takes Viagra—"

"The whole newsroom knows he takes Viagra."

"That's gossip."

"Nope, that's Rob bragging to Laurel." Laurel Baker was a handsome, savvy, cynical, fortyish reporter who had become the object of Rob Reordan's romantic quest since he'd recently divorced his fourth wife. Laurel's response fell somewhere between disgust and disdain.

"Laurel told you that?" Maxi asked.

"Laurel told *everyone* that. She might as well have posted it on the computer bulletin board."

"Doesn't Rob know that if he actually did get involved with Laurel, she'd chew him up and spit him out to the coyotes in her canyon?"

"Doesn't stop him."

"Yeah, I guess it's his nature."

"Which reminds me, did you hear the one about the black widow spider?" Wendy asked, the impetuous grin lighting up her face again.

"No, but I'm about to, right?"

"Well, you know the black widow spider has sex with her mate, then she kills him. . . ."

"Yup—that's why she's called the black widow."

"Right. So imagine this conversation. The male spider says, 'Uhh . . . let me get this straight. We're gonna have sex, then you're gonna *kill* me?' And the female flutters her spidery eyelashes and purrs, 'That's right. It's my nature.' So the male spider thinks about it for a beat, then turns to her and says, 'But we *are* gonna have sex, right?' Well, that's Rob."

Maxi laughed. "It's his nature," she reiterated.

"The man can't help it. Meantime, each of his wives made a baby or two, then split and took half his money. Which leaves Rob with seven kids, more than a dozen grandchildren, and about eight dollars a month left over after living expenses, taxes, agents' fees, alimony, child support, college payments, new cars for the kids' graduations, et cetera, et cetera. Rob's gonna have to work till he's dead just to make his personal nut."

"And now he wants Laurel, the original black widow spider," Maxi said thoughtfully. "Men like Rob never learn. It's about their egos."

"It's about their dicks," Wendy shot back.

Maxi laughed. Wendy Harris was one of the few women Maxi knew who professed to actually understand men, and for Wendy, the explanation of all things male was simple. Not so for Maxi, who made no claims to fathoming the complexities of the male gender. Maybe someday, she thought, idly rubbing both her shoulders with opposite hands.

"Oh-oh, you've been lifting again," Wendy accused solicitously, watching Maxi knead her upper arms. "Are you supposed to be lifting weights this soon after surgery?"

Maxi had been badly injured not long before on a story that had turned deadly, and she was only a few weeks out of the hospital; she probably *wasn't* supposed to be lifting weights so soon, she knew. "I'm not supposed to be doing a *lot* of things," she said. "Neither are you, Wendy, now that you bring up the subject."

"What did *I* do?" Wendy protested.

"How about beating up on poor Riley just because he didn't get a crew to that second-rate garage fire in Pasadena before Channel Seven got there?"

"Really. Tell me, how am *I* supposed to beat up an assignment editor who's six-foot-four and weighs two hundred and forty pounds?" Wendy was four-foot-eleven and weighed ninety pounds.

"Oh, you beat him up, all right," Maxi reprimanded, smiling. "You beat him up verbally, mentally, emotionally, and bad. Now, unlike Rob Reordan, whom you've just informed me is our Channel Six Viagra poster boy, Riley will probably never be able to get it up again in this lifetime."

"If he ever did," Wendy tossed out of the side of her mouth.

Wendy didn't hate men, she just loved news, and she had a passion for getting it right. She *always* got it right, and she had a very low level of tolerance, or even understanding, for anyone in the news business who *didn't* always get it right. Which, of course, applied to every other mortal in the business at some time or other. Her ire was usually explosive, but fortunately it was never lasting. Still, it could have a lasting effect on the meek. But then, the television news business was not for the meek—only the tough survived for the duration.

A tinny *ding-ding-ding-ding* sounded through the newsroom, and both women's eyes immediately dropped to their computer terminals as, simultaneously, their fingers clicked on the wires. An URGENT banner scrolled across the top of the Associated Press file, followed by a story that was in the process of painting itself in print across their screens.

"Jeez," Wendy exhaled. "Gillian Rose—*dead!*" Gillian Rose of Rose International, the country's largest manufacturer of vitamins, supplements, and health foods, headquartered in Los Angeles.

Both women cast an inadvertent glance at the lineup of vitamins and supplements on Wendy's desk, most of which bore the familiar red-rose logo of Rose International on their labels.

Within seconds, a walla-walla of excited talk erupted in the newsroom, and managing editor Pete Capra came bounding out of his glass-enclosed office and leaped up on top of the desk nearest his door, scattering files and papers and startling the reporter who happened to be sitting there—no mean feat for a burly Sicilian who was fifty-something, who'd never grasped the concept of regular exercise, who cooked gourmet Italian for his family and ate most of it himself, washed it down with cases of Chianti, and chain-smoked Marlboros when he wasn't in one of his "I quit" phases, during which he was unfailingly, insufferably, cranky. Nonetheless, leaping up on a desk and barking orders was Capra's MO whenever a huge breaker hit the wires.

"Riley, get a crew down to Rose International," he roared, pointing at the assignment desk. "Maxi, you roll with the crew. Simms, Hinkle, hand off whatever you're working on and get on the horn—I want us all over this, *now.*"

Maxi waited a few seconds until the story finished scrolling, clicked on the PRINT button, grabbed her purse, and headed for the elevators, stopping only to snatch the story off the nearby printer she'd directed it to as she scooted by.

Her crew, in the person of cameraman Rodger Harbaugh, was already waiting in front of the artists' entrance when she got there, in the driver's seat of a big blue Channel Six News van, motor running, passenger door open for her. Maxi jumped in, yanked the door shut, and buckled up as Rodger slammed the bulky truck into gear and rolled toward the station's exit gates.

"What do you think's fastest?" Rodger asked. He knew, of course, but had the courtesy to consult with his reporter on the route they'd take. Rodger Harbaugh was in his late forties, medium height, medium build, dark hair beginning to thin on top, and a face liberally creased with sun and laugh lines. He was a toughened veteran of the L.A. news beat—fast, efficient, a man of few words, even-tempered in the clutch, and he always got the shots.

"I'd go up over Barham and south on the Hollywood Freeway—inbound shouldn't be too heavy right now," Maxi answered.

She liked working with Harbaugh. She especially liked what he was not: He was not a totally self-absorbed alpha dog, which prototype, she knew from long experience, was legion among competing shooters out on the street every day in the frenetic L.A. news "gang bang."

As the unwieldy van hurtled at seventy miles an hour on the freeway toward downtown Los Angeles, she clung to the grip bar while scanning the AP wire story she clutched in her other hand.

Gillian Rose had been found dead on the floor of her office, the copy said, in the glass-and-steel high-rise that housed the billion-dollar business she'd created and built with her husband. Gillian's body had been discovered at 1:36 P.M.—a little more than twenty minutes ago, Maxi noted, glancing at her watch. Besides the usual police personnel, detectives from the LAPD's elite Robbery-

Homicide Division had already arrived at the scene—a tip-off that foul play hadn't been ruled out.

The victim's longtime assistant, Sandie Schaeffer, had come back from lunch and found her body, the story said. In a preliminary report, none of the several employees in proximity who were questioned saw or heard anything unusual. The deceased's husband, the powerful Carter Rose, who had a suite of offices adjoining Gillian's on the penthouse floor of the Rose building, was currently away on business in Taiwan.

"What do you know about Carter Rose?" Maxi asked her cameraman.

"Not much," Rodger said.

"Me either."

As Maxi reflected on the fabulous Roses, she realized that while there often seemed to be a swirl of publicity revolving around Gillian Rose, very little was reported, written, or even spoken about Carter Rose. Touted as the business genius of the operation, he put up a very private front, leaving publicity and newsmaking to his stunning and articulate wife. And now, Maxi thought ironically, Gillian Rose had taken the spotlight again.

2

Kendyl Scott's beautiful eyes narrowed as she looked up to see her co-worker, Sandie Schaeffer, appear in the doorway to her office. Kendyl was Carter Rose's personal assistant, had been since the company started eight years before. Statuesque, with burnished skin the color of rich molasses and dark ebony hair drawn into a sleek knot at the nape of her neck, she was head-turning gorgeous. For eight years she'd protected Carter Rose and his inner sanctum with proprietary fervor, like the mythical Cerberus guarding the entrance to Hades.

And for nearly eight years, she'd been sleeping with him.

Sandie Schaeffer, the personal assistant of Carter Rose's now dead wife, was blond, sweetly pretty, five-foot-six, curvy, and quietly efficient. She, too, had been with the company since its inception. There had always been an unspoken air of rivalry between Kendyl and Sandie, heightened for Kendyl when she recently began to suspect that Carter Rose was also sleeping with Sandie.

Kendyl looked at the other woman without a smile and raised her eyebrows quizzically.

"Does he know?" Sandie asked.

"He knows."

"And . . . ?"

"And he's coming home."

"Did he get a chance to meet with Chen Shui-bian?" Chen was the new president of Taiwan, and Rose had gone to Taipei for meetings to initiate distribution of Rose International products in that country.

"Of course not. He's only been there a few hours."

"When will he get back here?"

"I'm not sure," Kendyl said with a hard look, which was code for *I'm not telling you.* It was not for any pressing reason that she withheld information from Sandie other than that from long habit, neither woman would easily give up a whit of control to the other. And Sandie knew the code; she knew there was no way she was going to get anything more out of Kendyl. She turned abruptly and exited the suite.

Kendyl resumed fielding phone calls—people reacting to the shocking news of Gillian Rose's death, which was just getting out on radio and television.

When the police talked to her after Gillian's body was found, she gave them Carter's cell-phone number and one of the detectives called him at once, used the phone on her desk to do it. Kendyl heard only the officer's side of the conversation. Heard him telling Carter that his wife was dead. Heard the questions he asked, could not hear Carter's answers. When the officer was finished, he handed the receiver to Kendyl. "He wants to talk to you," he'd said.

Carter sounded stricken. He asked her what she knew

about what happened. Nothing, she told him. He asked her to make a return flight reservation for him immediately. She did. He was in the air now, and she'd scheduled a car to pick him up at 5 A.M. tomorrow at LAX. She would accompany the driver out to the airport to pick up her boss. Her *lover*.

Lowering her eyes, she allowed herself a hint of a smile. Now that Gillian was dead, Carter Rose was going to be her *husband*. That was her plan.

3

As the Channel Six News van screeched to a halt outside the Rose building at Number One Wilshire in downtown Los Angeles, members of the press had already begun to gather around the entrance, dragging cable, planting lights and tripods, jockeying for prime position to shoot the comings and goings of personnel relevant to the story, and waiting for the inevitable press briefing.

The Rose building boasted twenty-six floors of prestigious office space in the heart of downtown, nine floors of which, the ground floor and the top eight, housed the offices, showrooms, conference rooms, and laboratories of Rose International. While Rodger Harbaugh hauled equipment out of the back of the van to set up, Maxi whispered in his ear, then quickly slipped around the building to the underground garage entrance.

She'd known Gillian Rose, had interviewed her several times for stories on the couple's business, their political activism, their philanthropy. She'd been to some of the lavish charity dinner parties the Roses had held at their Beverly Hills home, and she'd lunched with Gillian a few times when their schedules jibed. She'd never completely warmed to the woman, Maxi reflected as she darted between the phalanx of cars, trucks, SUVs, and such lined up in the dark parking structure. It wasn't that she'd disliked Gillian Rose, she'd just never counted her as a friend. Theirs had been a symbiotic relationship: For Maxi, the powerful businesswoman was a valuable contact; for Gillian, Maxi Poole was an effective conduit to the press.

Gillian had once given her the code to the building's back elevator, which was tucked in a corner at the far end of the parking structure on the street floor, an express that soared nonstop to the penthouse. Back then, Maxi and crew had come to Gillian's office to get a quick sound bite from her on a state bill to regulate dietary supplements, a bill that would greatly affect the Rose company's business. Gillian had been rushing out to catch a plane, but it was important to her to voice her opinion on the news that night, so she'd directed the journalists to the express elevator to save time. Now, at that same elevator door, Maxi had no trouble remembering the code, because it spelled out "Rose" on the keypad: 7673. She punched in the numbers and the stainless-steel doors parted immediately and soundlessly.

There was just one button inside, labeled PH. She pushed it, and the small, darkly mirrored car whooshed upward at high speed. In seconds the doors opened, and Maxi found herself on the penthouse level, which housed the upper-echelon executive suites. As working press, she was not authorized to be there.

Maxi put one of her personal aphorisms in play: Act like you know exactly what you're doing and people will *think* you know exactly what you're doing. She walked purposefully past desks and cubicles to Gillian Rose's suite, then brushed by the unoccupied desk of Gillian's assistant to the open door of the inner office, blocked off, now, by a double strip of yellow crime-scene tape. Although there'd been no specific mention of it in the wire story, the police were treating this death as a crime, Maxi noted.

She peered over the tape. A few feet to the right of a broad, black slate-topped desk, the body of Gillian Rose lay crumpled on the floor, police personnel working soundlessly around it. From her vantage, Maxi could see no wounds, no blood.

Gillian was dressed in her usual style—minimal but expensive, hip but offbeat. No uptight Laura Bush–boring nubby wool designer suits for her, Gillian had joked to Maxi once; she draped her long, lean, well-toned body in simple chic. But she did wear uptown jewelry, and loads of it, important, pricey pieces. Characteristic Gillian Rose, of the understated, skintight, thigh-high little black skirts and dresses, which Maxi had always seen as simple backdrops for her opulent jewels. Now Maxi took note of the gargantuan diamond earrings, the lavish gold necklace, the slim, gemstone-encrusted bracelet guards to the diamond-studded Patek Philippe watch, and Gillian's highly publicized ten-carat emerald dinner ring on the impeccably manicured hand that was splayed out in front of her.

Still, studying Gillian's lifeless body now, lying on her stomach, her face turned toward the outer office doors, her eyes half open, something about her bothered Maxi.

Something looked off, somehow. Out of sync with the woman's larger-than-life public persona. What was it about Gillian Rose in death that she was missing? Maxi asked herself.

Distracted by footsteps behind her, she turned to see the coroner approaching—not one of the many medical examiners who worked in the coroner's office, but Sam Nagataki, *the* Los Angeles County coroner, the top dog himself, in a well-cut black silk suit, crisp white shirt, gold cuff links, expensive shoes, designer tie. Big priority death scene, this one. There would be a lot of publicity.

As Nagataki approached the crime-scene tape, Maxi edged close to him. "Dr. Nagataki," she whispered, "may I have just a word—"

"Not now, Maxi—you know better," he said in terse undertones. Maxi did know better, of course, but that never stopped her from taking a shot. As Nagataki stooped under the tape, he slipped the reporter the slightest hint of a smile, which signaled to her that of *course* he'd talk, later. Nagataki loved the press.

Nobody had ordered Maxi out of the area yet. *Act like you know exactly what you're doing. . . .* Would be nice if she had Rodger behind her with his camera. But then they'd both be thrown out of there for sure.

The swarm of police personnel backed off as Nagataki knelt beside the body, touching nothing, his eyes slowly scanning the inanimate form, starting at the feet: black suede four-inch Manolo Blahnik heels, the right one still on, the other kicked to the side, revealing bright red polished toenails showing through sheer, dark gray hose.

Maxi followed the doctor's gaze as it traversed long legs that traveled up to the hem of a skimpy, black leather skirt, made even shorter because it had been forced upward underneath the body, presumably in Gillian's fall to the floor. Then up over the tight black chenille sweater, also pushed up, displaying a couple of inches of well-tanned, perfect midriff. Nagataki's eyes continued slowly upward to the long, slim neck, and over the expertly made-up oval-shaped face, its right cheek ground into the carpet—the face not classically beautiful, but exotically attractive. The mouth, open as if in disbelief, baring large, flawless white teeth. Bright red lipstick, still fresh. The softly rounded chin, the angular nose. The eyes . . .

The eyes! Maxi flashed. Partly open. Dusky, charcoal brown eyes. *That's what's off!* The eyes of Gillian Rose, eyes Maxi knew, eyes that for years had been photographed in newspapers and magazines, in the company's commercials and print ads, larger than life on billboards at times. The Gillian Rose Maxi Poole and countless millions knew, or had seen pictures of, had eyes that were not dark brown—they were vivid, sparkling, cerulean blue.

A voice just behind her ear uttered a low, raspy, "Yo, Max." She jumped and wheeled around, bumping into a grinning Rodger Harbaugh holding the big Panasonic DVCpro minicam down by his side, as if no one would notice it if it wasn't perched on his shoulder.

"Jesus, Rodg!" she whispered. "You scared the hell out of me."

"Sorry." Rodger was clearly pleased with himself.

"How did you get up here?"

"I was your shooter on the supplement legislation story, remember? I watched you punch in the secret elevator code that day."

He quickly hoisted the camera up and started

rolling—they both knew it would be a matter of minutes, maybe seconds, before he would be nicely but firmly asked to leave the building. And they knew that she couldn't get tossed out with him, or that would make news.

"Okay, I'm out of here," she said. "Get what you can. Of course we can't use it. This is private property—"

"I know, Max," Harbaugh pronounced in low tones, his eye pressed to the viewfinder. "We'll bring it in for the dead file."

4

Maxi was sitting in her study, laptop open, going through e-mail, when her dog bounded into the room. "Hey, Yuke, you're not supposed to be lifting weights either," she told the big Alaskan malamute as he came trotting over to her with a package in his mouth. Yukon had been slashed by the same killer who'd attacked Maxi several weeks before. It had landed them both in the hospital, she at Saint Joseph's in Burbank, he at the Eagle Vets on Robertson. He was doing okay now, though she could tell he was still a little sore. So was she. They were both still healing.

Yukon sat and lifted his chin, offering her the package. She hadn't seen it at her door when she came in from work a while ago; the mail carrier on her route was known to take items that wouldn't fit in her mailbox and tuck them down in the shrubbery next to her front door. Yukon, of course, missed nothing.

"Oh, boy," she muttered, absently giving his neck a

rub. The package looked suspicious. The size and shape of a big round loaf of bread, wrapped in scruffy, frayed brown paper and tied clumsily with string, it looked like a lot of the parcels she received from all manner of crazos out there who wanted to send "presents" to their favorite anchorwoman. Maxi routinely sent them down to the mail room to be X-rayed.

She took this one gingerly from Yukon's mouth and held it at arm's length. She didn't like that it had come to her home; in this age of technology, there were many ways a nutcase could get someone's home address, a growing danger.

Scrutinizing the label, she breathed with relief. *No wonder it looks dirty and beat-up,* she thought. The sender was her friend and colleague, reporter Richard Winningham, and the return address was somewhere in Pakistan. Richard was in the region on temporary assignment, but the prolonged war against terrorism was turning from "temporary" to "indefinite."

She reached into her WAKE UP WITH RICK DEES coffee mug and pulled out a pair of scissors. And, yes, she still woke up every morning with KIIS-FM's popular disc jockey—*listening* to him, that is, not sleeping with him. Maxi had been romantically unencumbered, as she liked to put it, since her marriage had ended in divorce more than a year ago. She and Richard Winningham were close, ever since he'd saved her life while she was covering the ill-fated story that nearly killed her. Between them there had been little sensual stirrings, small hints and flutters, but they'd never taken it to first base. Probably because both of them knew without saying it that an office romance was usually a bad idea. And now he was in the Middle East, sending her . . . *what?*

While Yukon looked on, panting attentively, she snipped the string and pulled off the paper, and a note fluttered to the floor. She scooped it up before Yukon did—her dog thought everything was delicious. It was handwritten in pencil on rough orange paper:

Hi Max—

A gift from the marketplace in scenic Islamabad—a reminder of just how lucky we are. I miss the station, I miss my Audi TT, I even miss Capra, and I miss you.

RW

She pulled out folds of a purplish blue fabric. *Oh Lord,* she gasped. A bourkha. Yes, she did know how lucky she was. And how lucky *he* was, she thought with a shudder. Journalists worldwide had been sobered by the murder of *Wall Street Journal* correspondent Daniel Pearl. Richard could have turned down the war assignment, she knew. He hadn't.

Her phone rang. It was her boss, Pete Capra—he never said hello. "Carter Rose gets in tomorrow," he barked. "You and Harbaugh are at LAX for his arrival— East Orient Air, Flight 20, 5:32 A.M."

Maxi scribbled the information on a Post-it pad. She glanced at her watch: 8:15 P.M. "Guess I'd better go to bed *now*," she said.

"Whatever."

"You have a nice evening too," she lilted, and put down the phone.

Capra's style of dealing with news and newsies was a lot of guff. Maxi knew that deep within that lumpy bear body of his he actually did have a heart, but she couldn't resist dishing up some of his own back at him now and then.

She sighed. She *could* go to bed now, but getting to sleep was a joke. Her schedule had been so erratic for so long that her body clock was on something like Venusian time—she could never get to sleep before two, three in the morning. But to be at the airport at five she'd have to get up at three. Fine, she thought. Good thing she *didn't* have a love interest. No time for a relationship.

When she'd got back to the station after covering the Gillian Rose story that afternoon, she'd ducked into an edit bay to view the tape Rodger Harbaugh had shot before he was politely ordered to remove himself and his camera from the premises. Most subjects of news stories do not beat up on television journalists in the same way they do the paparazzi. They do it, but without the cursing and the fisticuffs; it's in most of their interests to keep outwardly friendly relations with the legitimate press. Also, it looks bad when they're caught on camera acting like arrogant bullies, and you can count on any station that gets good shots of a bona fide fight to play up that footage on the news, with ongoing teases featuring the incriminating pictures and an anchor voicing-over something like: "Prominent CEO turns violent in company parking lot—on the news at eleven."

In the dark of the edit room, Maxi had labeled the cassette GILLIAN ROSE: BODY, dated it, then marked it DF with a broad circle around the letters, assuring that the tape would be put in the dead file so it couldn't accidentally get on the air. Any footage that was logged into the tape library, or put on the "Today" shelf, was fair game for writers, reporters, and editors to use in teases and cut pieces.

The dead file was a wall of locked cabinets back in the tape library where they stored any sensitive tape that couldn't be aired but shouldn't be erased, tape whose content was potentially valid but currently unsubstantiated, or too gory to show, or was deemed libelous, slanderous, or otherwise legally questionable but might be needed down the road if the story changed or in a possible lawsuit. In this case, they could not legally air tape that was shot on private property after a company spokesperson had specifically enjoined the journalists from continuing to shoot or airing what they had. The only pictures that could be shown with the Gillian Rose story that night had been shot outside the building.

Maxi had carefully reviewed her exclusive footage of the body of Gillian Rose lying on the floor in her penthouse office. Harbaugh had gotten close-ups of the deceased and wide shots of the police activity. Great pictures, but virtually useless. The tape could be aired only if Rose International, in the public interest, reversed the company's previous order and gave written permission, which was highly unlikely. And even if that should happen, showing a dead body on the news was always questionable. So the tape would remain in the potentially volatile dead file, to which only top news management had access.

Staring at the shots, even in the extreme close-ups, Maxi could not detect anything out of the ordinary about Gillian's eyes, and certainly not their color. What she'd seen, or thought she'd seen, must have been an illusion—perhaps the light was hitting Gillian's eyes in a way that made them look dark brown. Not that it mattered much, she mused—dead is dead.

In any case, there was no way she would be getting much sleep tonight, she knew. The tape that would be playing on both her waking and dreaming mind-screen long into the small hours would feature the dead body of Gillian Rose.

5

Maxi glanced at the digital clock readout on the dash, then floored her thirteen-year-old black Corvette; she was southbound on the San Diego Freeway headed toward LAX, with no time to spare. What else was new? Couldn't fall asleep nights; had trouble hauling herself out of bed in the mornings. After little better than three hours' sleep she'd foundered through her morning ritual, given each of her tired eyes a shot of Visine, and managed to get herself into a slim gray business suit and heels. She had the makeup thing down, thank the Lord and Max Factor—she could put on a camera-ready face in exactly six minutes.

It was 4:42 A.M. Very little traffic on the freeway at that hour. She had to get herself out to the airport, park her car in one of the high-tiered parking structures, and navigate across the congested eight-lane thoroughfare to the East Orient terminal, all much more time consuming now with heavily tightened security since 9/11. Then make the long walk down the busy concourse to the arrival gate and try to find her cameraman in the mass of media she knew would be milling about, there to meet Carter Rose's flight.

She heard the siren before she saw the lights behind her. A California Highway Patrol motorcycle loomed in her rearview mirror. "Damn!" Maxi said aloud. She was nailed.

Pulling over onto the shoulder, she came to a stop and yanked on the emergency brake. Then, keeping her seatbelt fastened, she reached into the glove box for her registration and insurance card, then into her purse for her driver's license, rolled down her window, then raised both arms up from the elbows so the officer could see them, her left hand holding the documents—all before the officer reached her window. She knew the drill: Make no sudden moves in his presence, no diving into a bag or compartment, give him no cause for alarm.

He turned out to be a *she*.

"Good morning," said the trim, fresh-faced CHP officer at her driver's-side window, the name BRAXTON shining on her brass nameplate.

"I hoped it would be, Officer Braxton," Maxi said with a chagrined smile, handing the woman her papers.

"Do you know how fast you were going, Ms. Poole?" Braxton said without having glanced down at the documents in her hand. Reporter Maxi Poole was high profile in Southern California.

"Uh . . . I'm not sure," Maxi answered. "I'm due at the airport on a story."

"I clocked you at eighty-two miles an hour."

"No! Really?" Maxi exclaimed with a sinking heart.

"I'll be right back," said Officer Braxton, who set off

toward her motorcycle, taking Maxi's documents with her.

Damn, damn, damn, damn! Maxi thought but didn't say aloud. It was her own fault, of course. This was going to make her even later. The officer had recognized her—did that mean she'd cut her a break? Doubtful, Maxi knew. Once in a while an officer would let her slide with a warning. She hoped this would be one of those times.

No such luck. Braxton reappeared at her window with the ticket written up. "Would you sign this, please, Ms. Poole?" she asked.

"Sure," Maxi said, resignedly taking the clipboard and pen offered. She signed and handed back the paper "confession."

"Be careful," Braxton said in parting. "Slow down, okay?"

Maxi sighed, and nodded, and rolled up her window. Two women doing their jobs. This meant a hefty fine, and another nine hours in traffic school spread out over three nights after work. And now she was really running late. And she didn't dare go a mile over the speed limit; glancing in the rearview mirror as she eased back out onto the freeway, she saw that Braxton was right on her tail.

Interesting, Maxi had to admit to herself, a woman officer mounted on the powerful, intimidating-looking CHP bike. Usually female officers used patrol cars and male officers jockeyed the motorcycles, the macho machines. Even though put in a foul mood from her encounter with Braxton, she considered contacting her through her badge number on the ticket and doing a profile on her for the news.

She watched as Braxton peeled off ahead of her into traffic, and tried to dismiss the idea. That little grudging, nasty part of her that she strove to keep in check wanted no part of glorifying this pretty, perky person who'd ruined her morning. But she knew that later in the day she would have to argue with that part of herself and effort a story on Officer Braxton. Professionalism would out. And, she would make sure, so would her better self.

"Plane's twenty minutes late," Rodger Harbaugh said when she skidded to his side in the crush of media waiting at the East Orient gate.

"Lucked out again," Maxi breathed.

"Nick of time," Rodger threw out as they saw the first of the passengers pouring down the ramp and colliding with a wall of reporters ten deep. Not one of the journalists would budge an inch to let the passengers by; the tired travelers were forced to squeeze against the walls around the edges of the media horde, wheeling overnight bags behind them, lugging backpacks, and hefting shopping bags, laptops, totes, purses, diaper bags, coats, jackets, umbrellas, some maneuvering cranky children in front of them.

"Here he comes!" somebody yelled. Cameras started rolling, flashbulbs popping, as the handsome Carter Rose surfaced in the crowd, squinting against the lights. Like the biblical Red Sea the media parted, making way for him to walk down the middle. The clearing suddenly presented was the path of least resistance and he took it before realizing that the hubbub was for him. If other passengers entertained the hope of following this man down the right-of-way, they were soon disabused of that notion as reporters pushed to close in behind Carter Rose.

Eyes straight ahead, the subject of all the media tumult made slow progress, doggedly moving forward through the pack, blinking in the harsh lights aimed directly at his eyes, muttering a few "No comment"s at shouted questions.

Then, inexplicably, he paused, made a right-angle turn, and headed straight for Maxi Poole from Channel Six. Maxi shot a glance at Rodger, who kept rolling as a somber and exhausted-looking Carter Rose, briefcase in hand, topcoat over his arm, approached the Channel Six News camera. Maxi seized the opportunity, raised her handheld microphone to her mouth, and spoke first.

"Mr. Rose, what do you know about your wife's death?" She thrust the mike under his chin.

"Hello, Maxi," Rose said. "I don't know anything except what the police told me."

"What did the police tell you?"

"That they found her . . . yesterday, I think. I don't even know what day this is. . . ." The man had been on an airplane for more than eleven hours.

"Where are you going now? To get some sleep?"

"No. I'm going to Parker Center. To talk to them," he said, with a nod over his shoulder, indicating two men in street clothes. Maxi assumed they were LAPD detectives who'd met his flight. With that, Rose moved off, and Rodger and the rest of the shooters followed with their cameras.

As she ran with the pack behind Carter Rose, Maxi made mental notes on how she perceived him. Tired. Seemingly not nervous. But not distraught, either. Good-looking, certainly: fortyish, about six feet tall, a hint of stubble on even features, expensively styled but slightly mussed light brown hair, well-cut business suit, polished Italian loafers, manicured fingernails. No surprises.

Rodger switched off the camera and picked up the pace. Carter Rose skipped the baggage-claim area—his chauffeur would probably pick up his luggage, Maxi figured.

For better vantage, the media gang pushed en masse in front of Rose and the two detectives, camerapersons still shooting as their subjects piled into an unmarked car. One of the detectives took the driver's seat, the other climbed into the backseat with the man of the hour. Their car slid quickly away from the curb and into traffic.

As the newsies scattered, Maxi whispered to Rodger, "What the hell was *that* about?"

"*What* that?" Rodger asked.

"Carter Rose giving me an exclusive. Even calling me by name, which will be great in the piece."

Harbaugh shot a quick look at Maxi's sculpted features, her glowing cheeks flushed from running, her full lips glimmering in smoky pink lipstick, the bright green eyes, blond hair shining in the lights, her long, trim body in the fitted gray silk suit, the spiky black heels, purse swinging from her shoulder, microphone in hand, her air of supreme competence overlaid with a look of vulnerability, like she really did need a man to slay dragons for her.

"Because he's a guy," was all he said.

"Oh, *please,* Rodg. He just found out that his wife is dead, maybe murdered, he's spent the entire night on an airplane from China—not that he said anything to me, really, but I'm sure the last thing he wanted to do was talk to the press. So, why?"

Harbaugh gave her a crooked smile and a palms-up shrug, not easy with a thirty-pound minicam on his shoulder. Clearly, he believed what he'd said, that it was a "guy" thing.

Maxi knew different. Carter Rose had an agenda, and she had a feeling she was going to find out what it was.

6

"Great get!" producer Wendy Harris called from the open door of the edit bay, where Maxi was recutting her morning piece for the Four O'clock News.

"Huh?" Maxi said.

"Your little exclusive with Carter Rose, of course, what else? What *planet* are you on, Maxi?"

"I'm walking and talking and doing, but I am actually asleep," Maxi responded. She'd been up and working for twelve hours, and still had three more hours to go before the Six O'clock newscast that she co-anchored with Rob Reordan. Between now and then, she had to do live reports on the set for the Four and the Five.

"Nobody else had him talking," Wendy went on. "Not at the airport, not at Parker Center, not all day."

"He gave me a dozen words and I've romanced them every which way since Sunday—I oughtta be ashamed."

Wendy cocked her head, calculating. "Thirty-seven words," she said after a moment. "I know them by heart—I've cut 'em up and danced 'em around for every tease and every show since you fed in at six this morning."

Maxi chuckled. "Since Carter Rose is my new best friend," she said, "what do you think my chances are of getting a real interview with him?"

"Nada. I've already called, and you gotta know that every media gang in the country is trying to get to him, but he has the palace guard up now. You caught him on some kind of groggy whim this morning. By now I'm sure he's wide awake and talking to his lawyers."

"Mmmm . . . I don't think this guy operates on whims, groggy or otherwise. He strikes me as way too cool."

"Maybe, but I'm betting we still can't score. Wanna give him a try yourself? Couldn't hurt."

"Got numbers?"

"Sure . . . his private at the office, his assistant, his home, his car phone, his cell, his mistress—"

"His *mistress?* Who—"

"Just kidding," Wendy sang with a grin. "Wanted to see if you were paying attention."

"Barely. I'm on autopilot. Would you leave the numbers on my desk? I'll give it a shot—nothing to lose."

"By the way, did you know that a few of our competition are so desperate on this one that they called here to get a statement from *you,* since you actually talked with the man this morning. Wanted your reaction, et cetera. We respectfully declined on your behalf."

"Thank you," Maxi deadpanned. Then, as an afterthought, she turned from the edit-room monitors and looked squarely at Wendy. "*We* would never resort to something that shabby, would we?"

"Sure we would," her producer tossed off. "If we had nothing else to go with."

"What a business," Maxi muttered with an edge of distaste.

"You *love* it."

"Ya, but . . . jeeesh, what a business."

Wendy went out into the newsroom, and Maxi turned her attention back to Jack Worth, her editor. She planned to cut a version of her Carter Rose story for the Four, another version for the Five, and run the entire piece on her Six O'clock News. Then go home, feed Yukon, do her forty-five minutes on the treadmill, and collapse.

The phone rang; Worth snatched it up. "For you, Max," the editor said, handing over the receiver. "It's Wendy."

"Hey girl, you don't get enough of me?" Maxi quipped.

"You're not gonna freaking *believe* this," Wendy said. "Carter Rose has called a news conference for tomorrow—it just moved on the wires. And you're on it—Capra put out the assignment sheet himself."

"So the mountain is coming to Mohammed," Maxi said.

7

In the news at the top of the hour—"

"Oh, *shut up*," Maxi groaned at the clock-radio. After her sixteen-hour workday yesterday, 7 A.M. came much too early.

". . . three people killed in a head-on collision on the Santa Ana Freeway in the city of Norwalk—"

Maxi put a pillow over her head and held it there with one hand while groping for the snooze bar with the other. Couldn't find the damn thing. She gave up, dropping her hand over the side of the bed. Until somebody started licking it.

"No, Yukon, *puh-leeeze,* give me a break. Five more minutes . . ."

No way. The boy wanted breakfast. Heaving a big sigh, she dropped the pillow on the floor, then dropped her feet to the carpet and sat up.

". . . business news: On the big board, stock in Rose International, the giant health-products company based

*in Los Angeles, took a big hit this morning, opening at
eighty-seven at the bell, now down to seventy-nine, and
the trading day is still young . . . Wall Street reacting to
the death yesterday of its co-founder and co-CEO, thirty-
seven-year-old Gillian Rose, the wife of—*

Maxi stared at the clock-radio. Whoa, a normal business reaction? she wondered. It wouldn't seem so, certainly not if the company was healthy. Maybe Carter
Rose would have something to say about the company's
stock dive at his news conference this morning; the press
would be all over him about that. Rose had to have taken
a hit in his own personal fortune, she considered. Then
again, he no longer had a wife he had to split that fortune
with.

Somebody was licking her ankle now. "Okay, Yuke, I
give up." She hauled herself off the bed. Had to take the
guy for a walk. Then breakfast, then suit up, race to the
office, check the wires, see what's doing, then team up
with her crew and drive back over to the Westside for the
Carter Rose news conference.

Odd, she mused, that the man had called a major press
conference at his Beverly Hills home instead of at the
company headquarters downtown. Even if he was in a
state of devastation over his wife's death, she couldn't
imagine why he would want to let a gang of rowdy news-
people invade his personal space and trample all over his
petunias. Oh, well, she'd find out soon enough—this
morning's parley was set for ten-thirty. Meantime, she
would surf the Net to find out anything that had made it
to cyberspace about the players, the policies, and the
stock drop at Rose International.

Yukon followed her to the bathroom, sat on his
haunches looking up at her while she brushed her teeth,

then followed her back into the bedroom and watched while she pulled on jeans and a sweater and laced up her running shoes. Another reason why she couldn't manage a time-consuming love relationship these days—her baby was a little vulnerable since their recent mutual life-threatening ordeal. Yukon couldn't handle the competition right now.

"Come on, snow-boy, we're outta here," she said to him. He padded happily after her out the door.

8

Rodger Harbaugh was assigned as her cameraman on the Carter Rose news conference. That was a break. You could never count on having the shooter of your choice on any story—it depended on the vagaries of availability. But since this conclave was called last night, Capra had seen the wisdom in assigning Harbaugh with Maxi, for continuity, and he'd had the lead time to do it.

When they arrived at Rose's white limestone mansion at the top of Carolwood Drive in Beverly Hills, the massive gilt and wrought-iron gates were open and an army of local and national media were already milling around on the immaculately groomed grounds. Harbaugh sussed out a spot, set down a folding two-step stool, and stood on it, making him a head higher than most of the gang staked out in front of him. He hoisted his minicam up on his shoulder and handed Maxi a wireless microphone. Palming it, she squirreled through the crowd up to the front of the ranks.

At 10:37 the massive, carved cherrywood front doors parted and Carter Rose stepped out onto the stone portico, followed by two detectives from the Beverly Hills Police Department, then two from the LAPD, since the Gillian Rose death happened in Los Angeles. Then, stepping out last, a big surprise to the journalists, was L.A.'s new chief of police.

Rose looked uncomfortable. Facing the media had always been his wife's role, and she had been a master at it. "Good morning," he said, which was met with some low mutterings from the rarely gracious massed press.

Then he lobbed a bomb.

"I've called you here to tell you that someone broke into *this* house yesterday, by *these* front doors," he said, turning to indicate the entrance to his home, "and would have tried to murder *me*, I'm sure, if I hadn't stopped it."

So that explained why he'd called his news conference here and not at the Rose building, Maxi noted.

To a gaggle of shouted questions Rose declined to give details, but he did say that it had happened in the afternoon, while he was in his bedroom trying to get some sleep after his all-night flight and the long morning session downtown with the detectives. He also told the press that he was going public with this to let his would-be assailant know that the police would be watching for him, and they would get him.

Rose went on to say that he had been issued a limited Los Angeles County Sheriff's Department permit to carry a concealed weapon, a permit given only to peace officers and to a very few citizens who demonstrated urgent need. He wanted this probable killer to know that he was carrying a gun now, he said, and that if he was threatened again, he'd use it.

"I'm convinced," Rose concluded, "that my wife was murdered, and that the person who tried to attack me yesterday is the person who killed her."

More shouted questions: "Was it someone you know?" "What did he look like?" "Was he armed?" "Were you hurt?" "How did he get through the doors?"

Rose put his two hands in front of him, palms forward, signifying that the news conference was over. He turned and headed back toward his front doors, which prompted the media horde to start gathering up equipment in preparation to leave. Then Rose abruptly turned back, caught the eye of Maxi Poole in the front lines of the throng, and beckoned her to join him on the steps. *Whoa, another little exclusive?* Maxi thought, moving to join him.

"Have dinner with me tonight," Carter Rose whispered.

Maxi's eyebrows shot up. In response to her unasked question, he answered, "Because you knew Gillian, Gillian liked you, and maybe you can help me."

When still Maxi hesitated, he added, "And maybe I can help you."

"I have to go back to work—" Maxi started.

"I know. And you anchor the Six O'clock News. Come back here after the show. My cook will make a light supper, and we can talk."

"Who's your cook?"

"Uh . . . her name is Angie," Carter Rose said, and his look asked why Maxi would want to know.

"Is she here now?"

"She's in the kitchen. Do you want something? A drink? A bottle of water to take with you?"

"Water would be great."

As the media made its straggly exodus from the premises, Rose led Maxi back through exquisitely decorated rooms to a gleaming stainless-steel kitchen where a bright-faced middle-aged woman was busily chopping vegetables and a younger woman was polishing cookware.

"This is newscaster Maxi Poole," Rose told them. "She's coming back for dinner tonight, I hope."

"You'll be here?" Maxi asked Angie.

"Of course." The woman smiled jovially, as if it were a silly question. *She doesn't seem to be mourning Mrs. Rose, her employer,* Maxi observed to herself.

"Then can I ask, Angie, that you not use any oil in my food? I'm not supposed to have oil of any kind," Maxi lied.

"I'll make sure. What time should we serve?" she addressed her boss.

"I can be here by about seven-thirty," Maxi offered.

"Then we'll have dinner at eight," Rose said.

"All right, then," the cook confirmed brightly, turning back to her vegetables.

Carter Rose walked over to a bank of four stainless-steel Traulson refrigerators, opened a door, and took out a small bottle of Evian. "Here you go," he said, handing it to Maxi. "So we'll see you at seven-thirty?" Accepting the water, Maxi nodded.

Back in her car, she weighed the odd invitation. Dinner with the point man on this story would certainly give her an edge. Still, she didn't know this man, and wasn't comfortable with the idea of being in his home with him. But that cheerful cook, Angie, would be there, and most likely other household staff as well.

Maxi thought a bit now before taking chances. In surviving the recent incident that could have killed her, she'd learned a painful lesson. Entering a house to get an interview on a murder story, totally unsuspecting, she'd found herself alone with a deranged woman who'd slashed her from the top of her sternum to her waist. No, the wound was not critical. Yes, it had been skillfully repaired by a top team of surgeons. Yes, she was healing well. But every day she was aware of the numbness from severed nerve endings along the slowly fading scar line, reminding her how lucky she was to be alive.

And reminding her not to go into a stranger's house alone.

9

"Poole . . . *in my office!*" Pete Capra bellowed across the newsroom with a jerk of his head toward his office door. Maxi was just walking in from the Carter Rose news conference.

"So what'd he say?" Capra blurted before she'd cleared his door.

"Good morning to you, too," Maxi said with mock sweetness.

"Yeah, yeah. So—*what?*"

"You haven't seen the tape?"

"Not yet. I'm up to my ass in crap."

Charming, she thought, but that was Pete. "He said he thinks Gillian was murdered. And that somebody broke into his home yesterday and tried to attack him. He said he's convinced it was whoever killed his wife."

"So who was it? A man? Woman?"

"A man, I guess, but he refused to elaborate. Wouldn't

take any questions. I talked to him after the press conference, off the record, and he still wouldn't give details."

"Well, guess what—the whole thing's turned into a non-story, anyway. The LAPD just issued a statement that the coroner's office found no evidence of foul play. The ME's still doing tests, but it's looking like Gillian Rose just keeled with a heart attack or something."

"What about Carter Rose? He says an intruder broke in, someone he thought was a murderous intruder."

"Could have been somebody trying to rob his house, figuring the man was still out of town, or at work in the middle of the day, and Rose surprised him. 'Course a mansion like that's bound to have help. Maybe it was some pissed-off nutcase employee who was jerked around too much—I hear that working for the Roses was no day at the beach."

"We're going to stay on it, aren't we?"

"Sure, if anything new breaks. But till then the story's relegated to the business news. Did you see what's going on with Rose International stock?"

"I heard, early this morning. It's still dropping?"

"Like deadweight."

"Isn't that unusual? I mean, Carter Rose is still at the helm, and the business seems solid. I see Rose vitamins, supplements, nutrition bars, and what-all in every drugstore and health-food store on the planet. And they sell it in catalogs and on the Internet."

"Who the hell knows with Wall Street? Anyway, go ahead and cut what you shot this morning for the Noon and for the early block, then you're off the story. I want you to start working on a series for sweeps. Wendy has my notes."

"You got it," Maxi said, and she left his office to cross to her own. A non-story? Maybe so, but she wasn't convinced. She'd decided not to mention to Capra that she was having dinner with Carter Rose tonight. At his house. Her boss would probably go ballistic, and that was never pretty.

In a small nook off the main dining room of the massive Rose villa in Beverly Hills, Maxi sat opposite her host over fillet of broiled red snapper and fresh baby vegetables, excellently prepared by Angie and elegantly served by two unobtrusive waiters. Pensively sipping a dry Balatoni Chardonnay, Maxi was appraising the man. She couldn't help being somewhat intrigued by the magnetic Carter Rose.

He told her he was devastated by his wife's murder. That he needed to find her killer. His seeming candor, his projected earnestness, his pained expression, his surprising shyness with her, his still boyish good looks coupled with a playful wit and keen mind, made for a deadly attractive package. She remembered, then, rumors of womanizing that had floated around the man from time to time, always deflected in the media with dignity and humor by his attractive and intelligent wife.

Startling her out of her musing, his metallic blue-gray eyes piercing hers, Rose said, "Maxi, I want you to help me find my wife's killer."

"The police are saying there was no foul play," Maxi said.

"The police are wrong."

"What makes you say that?"

"I could have been killed too. Somebody tried to get to me. I'm sure whoever it was got Gillian."

"Do you have enemies?"

"Everybody has enemies."

"I mean enemies that you know of."

"A few."

"Do the police know about them?"

"Of course. They questioned me for hours."

"Well, if Gillian's death does turn up suspicious, they'll be all over it," Maxi said, something she was sure he already knew. The case would be top priority. A veritable *crowd* in law enforcement had lost top jobs over the O. J. Simpson debacle. They were beyond cautious now. The Police Commission, the chief, the DA, the homicide detectives, and on down the line—all of them would need this one investigated meticulously, solved, tried, and won.

"The police are bunglers," Rose responded soberly to her comment. "They waste time, they contaminate evidence, they go down false roads, and meantime the trail gets cold. It's been two days now, and yesterday somebody tried to kill *me*," he said again.

Maxi continued to study him. His frustration seemed palpable. Was it feigned? If so, she decided, the man was good.

"If you want me to help," she said, "you have to tell me exactly what happened here yesterday."

"I can't. At least not yet."

"Then how can I help?"

"Tell me what you find out. And I'll tell you what I find out. That simple."

"And what do you propose to do with the information?"

"I don't know," he said, shaking his head slowly. "I really don't know. I just have to do *something*."

"Some kind of vigilante justice?" Maxi asked, tilting her head and looking at him askance. "Now that you're carrying a loaded gun?"

"Oh, no, no, no . . . that's for show. To scare the killer

off *me*. I really don't know what the hell I'm doing. I've been in a daze since it happened—first Gillian, then the break-in at my home. I don't even know how to *use* a gun—"

"Where is it?"

"I don't have one—I just have a *permit* for one." He laughed at that. He was charming in his confusion. Not at all the stony, reclusive business mogul she'd heard about over the years.

"Do we have a deal?" he asked.

"Deal," she said, and lifted her glass to his. She had nothing to lose, she figured, and definitely something to gain. Even if nothing else came of this pact, she'd have access—to him, to his company, to friends of his and his wife's.

Her boss had declared the death of Gillian Rose a nonstory, for now. If down the road it reared its head as a major murder case, she'd be on the inside. This, she concluded, was a propitious meeting for her. And besides, the fish was delicious.

10

Tell me what's going on with Rose International stock, Doug."

"It's in semi-modified free fall. Nothing like Enron, but it's in definite downward mode."

Maxi was sitting with Doug Kriegel, Channel Six's business editor. His office was clean, clear, and minimal, furnished only with two high-backed visitors' chairs along with his own leather chair and broad desk, on which rested three computers, all awake and streaming information, plus a printer, a scanner, a fax machine, three phones, and a photo of his wife and two boys.

"Because of Gillian Rose's death, do you think?" she asked him.

"No. Rose's downward spiral started about, oh . . . four months ago. Here, let's check."

Kriegel drew his chair up to one of his computer terminals and clicked through several screens until he found what he was looking for.

"Okay. Rose International—its history over the last year: a steady decline, but that was the entire economy. Then, in the first quarter of this year, Rose introduced a new line of what they called gym-bag nutrition products and saw a spurt in its stock that carried through most of the third quarter. In September the stock price leveled off, then started going down. Slowly, but definitely down. Then, with Gillian Rose's death on Monday, the last four days have seen a precipitous drop. Umm . . . twenty-two points. Down to sixty-five today."

"What do you think it means?" Maxi asked.

"No way to know. It could be just a correction. Profit-taking by investors after the stock's rise due to the infusion of new product."

"Or?"

"Or something's going on. Some inside thing. Whatever it could be, I have no information."

"If you had to guess?"

"There's no guessing, Maxi. It could have been triggered by any number of things. A sell-off by the principal shareholders, the Roses. Some outside activity by a takeover prospect, known or not known."

Kriegel was scanning computer files. "Nothing jumps out. Their expansion has been steady, but not inexpedient. Their profit projections are on track. So if something's going on inside Rose International, Wall Street is sniffing it, is reacting to it, but hasn't made it public. What did Carter Rose say about it at his news conference yesterday? I'm sure the newsies were all over him about his stock."

"He refused to comment."

"So that's why I didn't see anything about the stock dip in your story."

"Can we find out what's causing it?"

"By *we* do you mean *me?*" Kriegel asked with a grin. "You know I'd do anything for you, Max, but that would take legwork that I just don't have the time for and still get my regular business reports done for every show."

Maxi counted Kriegel as a friend. He was straightforward, right up front; you always knew exactly where you stood with him. "But Rose International is actually one of the stocks I've been tracking," he told her now, "partly because of Mrs. Rose's death, but mostly because of the big plunge since it happened. Tell you what—I'll print up any pertinent info on RI for you that surfaces on the business wires."

"That would be great, Doug," she said, giving him an air kiss as she got up to leave his office. "Just drop it in my mailbox."

11

Maxi's phone was ringing when she walked back into her office. She snatched it up, answered, "News—Maxi Poole."

"Ms. Poole? Kendyl Scott. Please hold for Carter Rose," said an efficient-sounding, chilly female voice.

"Okay," Maxi said. Then she was left on hold, listening to the taped voice of a woman extolling the health and beauty benefits of Rose International products. She tucked the phone between her ear and her shoulder and booted up her computer to check the wires. Half listening, she actually found herself mustering up a little interest in Rose's Hawaiian Kiwi-Banana facial mask as Carter Rose came on the line.

"Maxi, can you come down here?"

"Down where?"

"To my office. On Wilshire."

"No. I'm working. Why?"

"I have something to tell you."

"Well . . . tell me."

"Not on the phone."

Maxi mentally rolled her eyes. "Mr. Rose, I can't get out of here until after the Six O'clock News, and then I'm doing a shoot for the Eleven."

"Then can you stop by the house on the way to your shoot? Angie's making a shrimp salad. You could come by for a half hour, have a bite, and we'll talk."

Maxi hesitated. What if he really did have something to tell her? And maybe she could nudge some information out of him about why his company's stock was doing a nosedive. Not to mention that Angie was a terrific cook.

Bad idea. Too cozy, twice in a week. "I can't stay for dinner," she said, "but I could drop by after I do the story, on my way back to the station. Would that work for you?"

Maxi often did reports for the Eleven, usually live from the location, but tonight's piece would be on tape, which she would have to bring back and edit in-house. Then she'd do a live intro on the set. She still couldn't believe where Pete Capra had assigned her: to the opening of a club called Adonis in West Hollywood. It was a Chippendales wanna-be where nearly naked men danced and women stuffed money into their G-strings. Oh, *please*.

"Not me, boss," she'd pleaded. "Anybody but me. I won't be able to *not* put the whole scene down. No matter what I say on tape, the subtext, which our viewers won't miss, will be 'This is *way* too stupid.'"

"Wear something sexy," was his only response, then he was out of her office.

She made a mental note to have a private, woman-to-man chat with Pete Capra about his blatant sexism, and soon. She needed to tell him that one of these days he was going to get his ass sued for sexual harassment. It was amazing that it hadn't happened already. Given that he was in charge of a major market news operation, the employees of which were at least half women, was it possible, she wondered, that in today's highly charged politically correct climate, he was not *aware* of that?

The thing was, most of the staff got a kick out of Capra, recognized his status as a bona fide character on the local news scene. They also knew that he was arguably the best and most serious journalist in the city. Still, Maxi knew, it would take just one employee, disgruntled, or with an agenda, or one who was actually sincerely offended, to file a lawsuit. She intended to enlist Wendy's help to try to make him see that.

As she'd predicted, the Adonis club was tacky, tawdry, pathetic, and loud. She wore the same tailored black wool pantsuit with a white blouse she'd had on all day at work, the polar opposite of sexy. Her camerawoman tonight, Monica Drew, shot B-roll of the male dancers and the female revelers, pictures to lay over the sound, and Maxi interviewed the owners, a pair who could have come right out of central casting for this role, with the slicked-back hair, the tanning-bed glows, the gold chains and pinky rings, the drinks in their hands, the cocky swaggers.

She couldn't get out of there fast enough. While Monica headed back to the station to log in the tape, Maxi pointed her Corvette toward Carolwood Drive in Beverly Hills. She'd have a quick chat with Carter Rose, find out what was on his mind, then race back to Burbank to write her piece, edit it, intro it live on the Eleven O'clock News, and go home. And take a shower, she mentally added, blocking out mind-pictures of wriggling naked men slicked down with bronze-tinted oil, and women in polyester panting over them, while the greasy-looking owners pranced around looking like refugees from the seventies.

Hmmm. Was she turning into a prude? She'd have to look at that later, she thought as she pulled up in front of the pair of massive wrought-iron gates, each decorated with a giant gilt metal rose leaning toward the center.

The gates parted before she could ring the bell. A security camera, she saw, was mounted above and aimed directly at her, its red light aglow. She gave it a broad, exaggerated smile. She was used to cameras.

Rose himself came to the door. "I have a visitor," he informed her in low tones.

"Oh?" Maxi said. "No problem. We can catch up later."

She turned to leave and he took her elbow. "No, come in," he said. "You should meet this guy."

Curious, Maxi stepped inside the high-ceilinged foyer and followed Carter Rose under an archway and across the huge living room, its focus a towering, brightly lit Christmas tree decorated in silver and gold. They walked through a second pair of carved cherrywood doors into a well-appointed library. A slight man in a dark suit was seated at the far end of the room, by the warmth of a low-burning fireplace.

"This is Maxi Poole," Rose said to him, ignoring protocol dictating that one should introduce a man to a woman first, then the woman to the man. This subtle deference to his visitor signaled to Maxi that the powerful Carter Rose might be somewhat intimidated by this man, whoever he was.

For his part, the guest stood and extended a hand to her. "Goodman Penthe," he said.

Maxi recognized the name at once: founder and principal shareholder of the Penthe Group, an East Coast–based conglomerate made up of pharmaceutical companies, food makers, even a tire manufacturer, Maxi remembered. She nodded, and approached to shake his hand.

A woman materialized beside her and asked if she'd like a drink. Maxi asked for a cup of tea, then seated herself on one of the oversized leather club chairs in the book-lined library. Penthe resumed his seat on a matching chair, and Rose settled himself on a couch opposite the two.

"Goodman wants to buy my company," Rose directed at Maxi. "Whether I want to sell it or not," he added, letting out an awkward little giggle.

Maxi studied him for a moment. Could he be tipsy? Goodman Penthe, she noted, was cold sober.

12

"G uess who I just had a drink with," Maxi tossed at Wendy, who'd been tapped to produce the Eleven tonight.

"Umm . . . Hugh Grant and Divine Brown," Wendy deadpanned, not missing a click on her computer.

"Nope. I don't think they're a couple anymore."

It was quarter to midnight, the Eleven O'clock News was off the air, and the lights had gone out on the newsroom Christmas tree. At exactly 11:35 P.M., when the broadcast news day was over and viewers would no longer be seeing the Christmas tree on live shots from the newsroom, a timer shut off the holiday lights, one of the sillier management cost-cutting measures that the staff derided. Ebenezer must have hired on in Accounting. Sorry, no Christmas for the overnight shift.

The newsroom was quiet now, reduced to a skeleton crew, and Wendy was archiving the Eleven O'clock News show. Maxi was sitting at the computer next to her, sipping a Diet Coke and idly perusing the wires.

"So who'd you have a drink with?" Wendy asked.

"Goodman Penthe."

Without looking away from her computer terminal, Wendy's eyebrows shot up. "Of the Penthe Group?"

"The same."

"Wow! Because . . . ?"

"Because he was at Carter Rose's house."

"What the hell were you doing at Carter Rose's house?"

"Like I said, I was having a drink. Tea, actually."

"Maxi," Wendy said, looking over at her now, "you're off the Gillian Rose story. The truth: Why were you at Carter Rose's house?"

"Because I have a crush on him."

"Yeah, right."

"Well, if I did have a crush on him, I'd have been there on my own time, not company time, right?"

"First of all, you're too professional to get involved with the controversial subject of a news story. And second, as you well know, Capra would freak if he found out you went to Carter Rose's house."

"That's why we're not telling him," Maxi said with a twinkle.

"So what's up with Mr. Mysterious at Rose International?"

"I don't know. But something. Something weird's going on there, and I'd love to know what. I still think there's a helluva story buried deep beneath the tumbled marble facade of the Rose building."

"And where does Goodman Penthe fit in?"

"I have no idea, but I can tell you the man is strange. He looks like he died last month and nobody told him. Dyed black hair and not much of it, chalk-white face, grim black suit, emaciated, dour expression, and little wire-rimmed spectacles that pinch his nose so it looks like they hurt. He was drinking a glass of something sort of musty yellow, and he said no more than two words at a time." Maxi paused for a moment, then added, "And Carter Rose was acting like he was scared of him."

"I'd be scared of him too. He sounds like one of the grave dancers in Michael Jackson's *Thriller*."

"Well, something's going on with him and Rose International—Carter Rose made a joke that Penthe wants to buy his company."

Wendy picked up one of the containers of dietary supplements lined up on her desk and twisted off the cap. "Speaking of Rose," she said, "want some chewable vitamin C? A little immune-system boost?" She poured out a couple of big orange tablets and popped them in her mouth, then offered some to Maxi.

"No, thanks. But wait a minute—let me see that," Maxi said, taking the white plastic container bearing the familiar red rose out of Wendy's hand.

Maxi put on her glasses and studied the label. In fine print at the bottom were the words: ROSE INTERNATIONAL LABORATORIES, LOS ANGELES, CA. Then a zip code, a date, and a U.S. patent number.

"What?" Wendy demanded, still putting the Eleven O'-clock show to bed on computer.

"They patent this stuff. Did you know that? Come to think of it, there must be hundreds of companies putting out different variations of vitamin C."

"Must be something patentable in Rose's vitamin C," Wendy offered.

"Yeah, like something in the citrus flavor, or the coloring, or the chewable component—I guess it could be anything that makes *this* vitamin C uniquely *Rose's* vitamin C."

"It's not that hard to get a patent," Wendy said.

"No, but it has to be expensive developing products for patents."

"Okay, so getting a patent isn't hard, but it's expensive. Where are you going with this?"

"Nowhere yet—but as we know in this business, usually the best way to find out something is to keep your eyes on the money trail."

"Hey, on the subject of money, I could actually be making some," Wendy said with a big smile. "I finished *Don't Be Dumpy.*"

"Whoa! That's great!" Maxi trumpeted, leaning out of her chair to grab Wendy in an enthusiastic hug.

Diminutive Wendy Harris, who was obsessed with diet and exercise in order to stay that way, had been working for the past year on a how-to book targeted at short women like herself. The average height of the American woman is five-foot-four, which means half the women in this country are five-four or under, and those, Wendy reasoned, were her potential readers.

Maxi had helped with the book, offering suggestions and cheering her on from the day Wendy got the idea. Its message was that, although women see "tall" on the runways, although they see "tall" in magazines and television commercials, they don't have to *be* tall to look fabulous. Proportion is the key. Superstar Madonna, five-foot-four, plays tall. Actress Sarah Jessica Parker, five-three, plays tall. Paula Abdul is five-foot-two, Jada Pinkett Smith is an even five feet, and "this year's blonde," sexy Reese Witherspoon, looks tall on the big screen but is just five-foot-two. It's all about proportion.

"So now," Wendy said, putting the final keystrokes on her archiving and saving out, "I have to get myself a literary agent."

"What about the agent Sylvie put you on to?" Sylvie Tran was a Channel Six weekend anchor who wrote children's books.

"I'm all over it. It's a woman who specializes in self-help books, and I got the manuscript off to her today."

"You go, girl!" Maxi said, and she gave Wendy five.

Wendy responded with a whoop. "So now we just wait and see what happens," she said.

"Oh, it's going to happen," Maxi reassured her. "Your book is too good not to happen. When you get an agent, it'll be on the glide path. And we'll have a party."

Impromptu celebratory parties in the newsroom usually consisted of a couple of bottles of cheap red and a bag of pretzels.

"Can't wait! And let's put in a requisition to keep the Christmas lights on after the Eleven," Wendy quipped.

13

It was almost midnight. Sandie Schaeffer noiselessly approached her office on the penthouse floor of the Rose International building. Using her key, she quickly slipped inside the suite, then closed and locked the door behind her. As always, she'd left the reading lamp on her desk lit when she left work earlier this evening, and everything looked to be as she'd left it.

A pair of LAPD detectives had come by that afternoon, had taken a cursory look around, and had removed the yellow crime-scene tape from Gillian's office door. With the coroner's report that his office had found no evidence of foul play, the suite was no longer being treated as a crime scene, one of them said. The cause of death would be specified in the pending autopsy report, and initial indications pointed to natural causes.

Sandie walked quietly past her own desk to Gillian's inner office and unlocked the second door. Inside, she flipped on a bank of lights, then quickly depressed the dimmer switch to take the brightness down.

Sandie hadn't been in this room since the afternoon she'd found Gillian's body on the floor. Taking a slow look around, she kept her eyes averted from that particular area on the carpet.

The formula was probably somewhere here in Gillian's office, she figured. Her father's formula.

Dropping her purse on Gillian's desk, she decided to begin her search with the bank of file cabinets set beneath the broad, black slate countertop that lined the back wall of the office. These were Gillian's personal files. Business files were kept elsewhere throughout the company's nine floors in the Rose building.

On the expanse of countertop were pictures framed in silver: Gillian and Carter Rose on horseback; Gillian and Carter cutting the ribbon when the Rose International building opened; Gillian and Carter with Governor Davis; Gillian and Carter on the beach in the Caribbean, and dozens more. The Roses had no children.

Sandie was very familiar with Gillian's file system; she had set it up. She was pretty sure she wouldn't find the formula filed away in a marked folder. But she was also certain that her boss would not have kept it at the Roses' home, a fully staffed villa on the prestigious Westside. Where, then? A safety-deposit box? Then there had to be a key somewhere. If the key was here, she'd find it. Getting down on her knees, Sandie started with "A."

Over the next two hours, she came upon personal items that painted a picture of the business, social, and even secret life of the prominent and stunningly attractive Mrs. Carter Rose. A faded red rose pressed inside a file folder labeled BROSNAN, with a card attached that read . . .

a rose is a rose, but none so beautiful as you. A Music Center playbill from *Phantom of the Opera* signed by Michael Crawford, and a phone number scribbled under the actor's name. A photograph taken in the foyer of the downtown Museum of Contemporary Art of the mayor of Los Angeles and a smiling Gillian Rose in a slim, black-sequined evening gown. A letter from the director of People Assisting the Homeless thanking Gillian Rose for dedicating the health center at their facility. A man's white silk handkerchief with the monogram DJB, tucked down between the "B" and the "C" files.

A noise sounded in the stillness, the creak of a door, or the floor, perhaps. Who would be on the penthouse level after two in the morning? Not cleaning people; after 9/11, Rose International had changed its cleaning policy for security reasons. As in most of L.A.'s high-rise buildings, cleaning crews were now allowed on the premises only during regular business hours, and company personnel had to put up with the drone of a vacuum cleaner drowning out telephone conversations at times. Other than credentialed employees, the only people allowed in the building outside of business hours were the guard on the lobby floor and the team of four night watchmen making rounds.

Did she hear it again? Could be her imagination, Sandie thought. After-midnight jitters.

Having finished searching the files, she tried Gillian's desk drawers, still making a conscious effort to keep her eyes away from the spot where she'd found Gillian's body.

Inadvertently, her mind flashed back to that day, Gillian limp and crumpled on the floor, but still it had seemed impossible to Sandie that Gillian Rose was really dead. Even after the paramedics had arrived and pronounced her so, she'd found it hard to grasp. Not Gillian. Gillian Rose never lost control. Of anything. Certainly not her life. Looking long at the woman's lifeless body on the carpet that day, Sandie fully expected her boss to open her eyes, pull herself to her feet, and chastise her for wasting time standing and staring.

No sign of the formula inside any of the desk drawers; from the disarray she could see that the police had searched through them before her. Sandie had seen the formula—at least the outsized envelope it had come in, marked PERSONAL AND CONFIDENTIAL—when it was hand-delivered to Gillian by messenger from an outside lab. At the time Sandie had known exactly what it was, but she'd said nothing—just went inside and handed it to Gillian. Now she felt certain that it was still somewhere in this office.

She examined each desk drawer again, this time gingerly feeling underneath and around the back of each one. Her hand came upon something taped to the outside back panel of the lower left-side drawer. It felt like a large envelope.

She stretched down on the floor to get a better grasp on it. Wedging her thumbnail under the tape, she loosened it, then tugged at the paper beneath until she pulled it free. Bringing it out into the light, she saw immediately that it was indeed the envelope she was looking for. She didn't need to open it; she knew what was inside.

Sandie pulled herself up and reached for her purse on top of Gillian's desk. Taking a Kleenex out of it, she brushed away a layer of dust on the envelope, carefully stripped off the masking tape clinging to it and tossed it in the trash can, then tucked the envelope inside her big Fendi purse.

She was about to leave Gillian's office when, to her astonishment, the door opened. Sandie looked up aghast to see a person in a black ski mask wearing a tan trench coat that hung almost to the floor, pointing a gun at her.

"Who are you?" she demanded, with more bravado than she felt.

The person in the doorway said nothing.

Her heart thudding, Sandie gazed at the intruder. Something about the figure holding the gun seemed familiar. Just as she put it together and gasped a name aloud, she heard a shot, became aware of a stab of pain, grabbed at her wrist, and felt blood. That's the last she remembered.

14

"Max, hi. Where are you?" It was Wendy Harris on Maxi's cell phone.

"Ventura Freeway just east of Coldwater, on the way in," Maxi told her. She checked her watch: 8:43 A.M. "I'll be there by nine. What's up?"

"Listen, don't come in to the station," Wendy said. "Go right downtown to the Rose building—your crew's on the way. A woman was attacked there, sometime overnight. On the penthouse floor."

"Who?"

"Her name is Sandie Schaeffer. She was Gillian Rose's assistant. Shot in the head and left unconscious. One of the guards found her this morning when he was making rounds."

"I know Sandie—I've met her several times with Gillian. . . . Shot in the *head*? Is she going to be okay?"

"Don't know."

"Read me the wire copy."

"Hold on a sec. Okay, ready? Here's the AP:

Rose International employee Sandra Blaine Schaeffer, thirty-one, was found severely wounded this morning at the Rose building in downtown Los Angeles. Paramedics transported her to Cedars-Sinai Medical Center for treatment—her condition at this time is unknown. Preliminary reports say Ms. Schaeffer was shot by an unknown assailant. Police declined to speculate on how a gunman could have got inside the building. A spokesperson for Rose International said the building has tight security after business hours; only card-carrying staffers have access.

Schaeffer has been employed by the Rose company since its beginning, holding the same position throughout her tenure, that of executive assistant to co-founder and CEO Gillian Rose, who, herself, was found dead on the afternoon of December sixteenth. . . .

"And blah, blah, blah, all about Gillian, now," Wendy went on.

"Okay," Maxi said, sliding over into the right lanes and onto the Hollywood Freeway southbound, heading for downtown Los Angeles. "Skip down to the when, where, who found her, all that."

"Umm . . . discovered at eighty-twenty-two this morning when a guard was checking the penthouse level . . . on the floor, inside one of the executive suites . . . apparently comatose. . . . The ME is quoted saying she was shot once in the head. That same bullet grazed her left wrist . . . the theory being she might have raised an arm in self-defense."

"Anything else?"

"Nope. No witnesses. No clues mentioned in the wire story—doesn't say if there was an exit wound, or if the bullet was found. Schaeffer worked for Gillian Rose for eight years, and in her family's pharmacy in Westwood before that. A Los Angeles native. No husband. Father alive, mother deceased. No siblings. Investigation ongoing . . ."

"Robbery-Homicide Division?"

"I'd think so, because of the Gillian Rose case. A Detective Bill Murchison, LAPD, is quoted. I'll make some calls."

"Who's my crew?"

"Lemke."

"Bummer." Cameraman Alan Lemke was as lazy as he was arrogant, and seemed to care more about when he'd be sprung for lunch than getting the story.

"Yeah. Luck of the draw."

"If you find out anything else, call me on my cell."

"You got it, Max." They both disconnected.

She was southbound on the Harbor Freeway now, coming up on Wilshire Boulevard. She could see the Rose building rising over the trees at the bottom of the off-ramp. Déjà vu. It had been just four days ago that she'd approached Rose International on the Gillian Rose story. Now Gillian's personal assistant, shot. Maxi punched up Pete Capra's private number on her cell phone.

"Capra," came the abrupt response.

"Hi, boss. It's Maxi. I'm at the Rose building, just

pulling up. So I guess the Roses and company are back on the docket as a bona fide news story, huh?"

"Looks like it. Sorry you got Lemke. Push him."

"Yeah. I'll check in with you later." Maxi stabbed the END button as she pulled into the parking structure beneath the building.

The union that covered camera personnel was so strong that once a person was in, after the ninety-day trial period, there had to be impossibly strong grounds for termination. For instance, habitual drug or alcohol use did not constitute grounds. For that, the company was obligated to pay for rehab—once, then again, if the employee relapsed. Peddling drugs on the company premises—and there had been those who did that—didn't qualify for termination either. That was a transgression grouped with using. Stealing or embezzling was something that had to be proven by a union committee in order to warrant firing, unless there was a conviction in the courts. So a bad attitude definitely didn't qualify. And although almost all of the more than three hundred Channel Six News staffers made up a highly dedicated team, there were always a few who complained mightily about anything and everything while smugly expecting a free ride. Alan Lemke fit into that small group.

Maxi parked her car, then went off toward the front of the building in search of him. Knowing Lemke, she figured he wouldn't bother to get anything on tape until she got there. Even if Tom Cruise materialized at the scene, stood on a soapbox in front of the building, and publicly confessed that he did it, Lemke wouldn't shoot it.

She found him in the Channel Six News van, parked at the curb on Wilshire—he was sitting behind the wheel, stomach protruding from a stained gray T-shirt, one foot up on the front seat, hand resting on his knee, reading the *L.A. Times* sports section.

"Anything going on?" Maxi asked him. Not that he'd have noticed, she thought with chagrin.

"Nope. Whaddaya want to do?"

How about cover the damn story? "You get exteriors, and any relevant comings and goings. I'll run inside and see if I can find out anything."

"The vic's long gone."

"When?"

"Twenty minutes ago."

"Damn. Did you get the shots?"

"Nope."

"Uhh . . . why not, Al?"

"Didn't see 'em rolling out till it was too late. I wasn't set up."

Why the hell weren't you set up? Why aren't you set up now? Useless to ask, Maxi knew—she'd been there before with this cameraman. "Okay," she said. "Set up now. Please. I'll be back in ten."

Damn, Maxi thought. The media was out in force around the building; every station but theirs would have shots of the paramedics coming out the front doors and rolling Sandie Schaeffer into the ambulance, and she could count on Capra to hit the ceiling. Now there was probably nothing visual left of the story, except for the inevitable talking heads at the press briefing.

Maxi scooted back inside the parking structure. Might as well snag the bullet elevator to the penthouse again, she reasoned.

This time she made it no farther than two steps onto the penthouse floor. A tall, burly, African American uniformed police officer stood outside the elevator, facing the doors, both hands gripping the ends of his baton.

"Hello, I'm Maxi Poole from Channel Six," she offered.

"You can't come in here, Ms. Poole. This is a crime scene," the officer said with firmness and finality. Then he added, "They're planning to hold a media briefing downstairs outside the main entrance when the detectives finish up here."

Maxi checked his nameplate. "Officer Downey," she said, "I'm a friend of Carter Rose. I'm actually here to see him. No camera," she added, raising both arms, palms up.

"Is he expecting you?"

"Yes," she lied.

"Hold on . . . I'll check," he said, and he moved toward the nearest desk with a phone on it. LAPD patrol officers didn't carry cell phones.

The officer's response told Maxi that Carter Rose was in the building. She followed him, fingers mentally crossed, hoping that Rose would okay her to go in.

A hollow *ding* sounded, and the express elevator doors slid open again. Maxi and the officer turned in unison to see three people emerge, two men and a woman, all of them dressed in business garb. Maxi recognized the woman; she'd seen her a couple of times with Gillian Rose—a public relations exec, she seemed to remember. The workday was beginning—she figured the men to also be executives who worked on this floor. Officer Downey stepped quickly over to the three and asked to see ID cards.

Maxi took the opportunity to slip around one of the broad pillars in the reception area and stride briskly across the marble floor, expecting a heavy hand to fall on her shoulder at any second. Reaching the door marked CARTER ROSE, she opened it and ducked inside.

She found herself in a room done completely in cool shades of celadon green, from the carpeting to the plush upholstered furniture to the decorative mini-blinds at the six broad windows. A tall green vase of calla lilies was the only accent piece on an oval, celadon-green acrylic coffee table. On the matching translucent polymer desk there was a computer, a telephone, a mod halogen reading lamp, and a pale green Lucite nameplate that spelled out KENDYL SCOTT. Behind the desk sat a stunning mulatto woman in a chic, charcoal gray pin-striped gabardine suit, whom Maxi assumed was the so-labeled Ms. Scott herself.

Gillian's assistant Sandie Schaeffer's office was a mirror image of this one, down to the exact acrylic furniture and upholstered pieces, but all in shades of rusty orange. And continuing the contemporary theme, Gillian's huge inner office was decorated in rich woods with clean black slate surfaces. Maxi had never seen this side, Carter Rose's suite. Rose's assistant was looking at her now, her face devoid of expression.

"Hello, I'd like to see Mr. Rose," Maxi offered.

"Because . . . ?"

"I'm Maxi Poole, from Channel Six. He knows me."

"I know who you are. I don't know how you got in here. He's not seeing press."

Stone city. "Would you tell him I'm here," she said, more a statement than a question.

"He can't be disturbed."

Maxi pulled her cell phone out of her purse. "Tell you what," she said to the beautiful, icy Ms. Scott. "I'll call him, and you let him know I'm on the line."

"Really, Ms. Poole . . ."

But Maxi was already dialing, and a line on Kendyl Scott's phone lit up. With an air of peevish resignation, the woman punched the intercom button. "There's a reporter out here in my office, Maxi Poole from Channel—"

She stopped. Listened. And from the hard look in her dark, winter eyes, Maxi knew that she highly disapproved of what her boss was telling her. "Go in," she said then, without bothering to look up.

"Thank you, Ms. Scott. I appreciate it," Maxi returned brightly. No point in alienating this woman any further; she might need her later. But Carter Rose picked himself an icicle, she mused. She opened the door to the CEO's office.

Quelle surprise! Mr. Rose's office was a throwback to the twenties. Caramel-colored buttoned leather couches and plush club chairs; an old Green & Green onyx-studded coffee table; a bank of four-drawer oak file cabinets against a side wall—the real thing, Maxi noted, not reproductions; green Case lighting fixtures in the ceiling and authentic Tiffany lamps on surfaces; lush Oriental rugs throughout; and an outsized oak roll-top desk with a leather-padded oak desk chair, in which sat the man himself.

Maxi took in the ambience. "Wow!" she uttered before she said hello. "*This* is a retreat," was all she could manage.

"Hi, Maxi," Carter Rose said, getting up to greet her. "Sit down." He indicated the seating area, and they sat on opposite couches. "Coffee?" he asked.

"Umm . . . do you have tea?"

"Of course." He punched the intercom. "Kendyl,

would you order us a pot of coffee and some tea?" And to Maxi, "Is Earl Grey all right?"

"Wonderful," Maxi said. She was still nonplussed by the surroundings: original Louis Icart paintings on the walls, old leather-bound volumes in glass-fronted barrister cases, collectibles from the early past century everywhere, all of it arranged in a sort of artistically organized clutter. With Christmas five days away, she'd seen no holiday decorations in other parts of the building, but Carter Rose had a little Christmas tree set up on an oak side table, complete with lights, ornaments, and presents underneath.

"I can't get over your office," Maxi said when he turned his attention to her.

"Yeah, it's a hundred and eighty degrees from the rest of the nine floors. My wife and I didn't agree on decor."

"I see that," Maxi murmured. She wondered what else the Roses didn't agree on.

15

Kendyl Scott picked up the phone and pressed the speed-dial number for the cafeteria on the ground floor.

"Dennis? It's Kendyl."

"Hi, Ken-doll." The counterman's pet name for her. "What can we send up?" She ordered for Carter. And for the pushy blonde who was with him.

"It'll be just a few minutes," Dennis told her.

It was a good system. Someone on staff would hustle the order together and Dennis would send a waiter up on the express elevator with it. Kendyl had long since let Carter know that she didn't make coffee. Or lunch, or snacks, or drinks, or any of it, even though there was a full stainless-steel built-in kitchen between the adjoining executive suites.

Kendyl knew her boss well, knew his roving eye, and she considered every pretty woman with whom Carter Rose came into contact a potential rival. A threat, even.

Including this one, the reporter. She knew Carter had entertained the woman in his home. After his press conference at the house two days ago, he'd asked Kendyl to pull anything on Maxi Poole off the Net for him to review— she was having dinner at his house that night, he'd said. And yesterday he'd told her to send flowers to Maxi Poole at the station where she worked, Channel Six in Burbank. Red roses, of course, his signature flower. And he'd dictated a note he wanted sent with the flowers: "Here's to success with our new team effort. Warm regards, Carter Rose."

Kendyl never ordered the flowers. When he asked her if she'd sent them, she said of course she did. He was in there with her now, probably wondering when the woman was going to thank him for the damn roses. And Carter was a gentleman; he would never bring up the subject himself, because he'd know that would embarrass her if she'd just forgotten to say thank you. Eventually he would just have to think Maxi Poole was rude. Fine with Kendyl.

She wouldn't have to worry about Sandie Schaeffer being competition anymore. When Carter had asked her to call Dr. Wallace Stevens at the hospital for information on Sandie's condition, she was told that Ms. Schaeffer was still in a coma, still critical. Was she expected to come out of it? she'd asked. Sandie's doctor said there was no way to know, but he didn't sound optimistic. And if she did regain consciousness, Kendyl had asked, would she be . . . okay? "There might be brain damage," was all the doctor would say.

Kendyl was amazed that Sandie hadn't died from that gunshot to the head. A fluke, she figured. Lucky Sandie. Or maybe not so lucky. After her conversation with Dr.

Stevens, Kendyl wasn't worried about what Sandie would remember if she came out of it—it was looking like her brains would be scrambled. Even if she did remember certain things, and she talked about them, people would assume she was delusional.

The one beautiful woman Kendyl had never considered a rival was Gillian Rose. Carter had told her he hadn't had sex with his wife in years, that they were married in name only. But he could never divorce Gillian, because that would mean divorcing the company. Neither would have the means to buy the other out of the business, and they would be forced to sell it and split what was left. Which wouldn't be much, he'd said, because they were leveraged to the max. And everything they'd worked for, everything they'd built for almost a decade, would be wiped out. Well, couldn't they still run the business together, even if they weren't man and wife? Kendyl had asked him. "That's exactly what we're doing now," he'd said.

Carter was the business genius behind the company, while Gillian had been the creative prodigy. Gillian spearheaded the development of new product, while Carter jockeyed the contracts, patents, and funds. They were a brilliant business team, Kendyl conceded, but now that Gillian was dead, Carter would need a new creative force in the company. And in his life.

Kendyl didn't know much about the product side of Rose International, just the business side. Sandie Schaeffer knew everything there was to know about the company's plans for product development, because she had worked side by side with Gillian Rose since the company's inception. Kendyl had definitely considered Sandie Schaeffer a threat.

And certainly Sandie was pretty, in a soft, quiet way. Not dazzling, never dramatically beautiful, but still pretty, with that serene, blond, Grace Kelly kind of look that men seemed to go for. And just a few weeks ago, Kendyl had been confronted by the distinct possibility that Carter was sleeping with Sandie.

She knew because she knew the man, probably better than his own wife had known him. She took note of his several meetings with Sandie of late, either here in his own suite, or in Gillian's. Before, he rarely ventured over to "the other side," as they both jokingly called the adjacent suite of offices. Lately he'd become a habitual visitor, dropping in to see Sandie on what Kendyl considered one pretext or another. Or he'd call her and ask her to stop by his office, he had something to show her or to bring to her attention. Oh, sure. Kendyl knew the signs.

In Kendyl's mind, Gillian's death cleared the way for Carter to choose a new wife. Oh, not right away, of course, but at some point down the road. And if Carter was indeed sleeping with Sandie, she might have been a prime candidate. For two reasons. First, for her extensive and guarded knowledge of Rose International product development; Sandie could conceivably replace Gillian in that area. And second, for a man like Carter Rose, the best sex was new sex.

But Kendyl didn't have to worry about Sandie Schaeffer anymore.

There was a *tap-tap* on her office door. Then a waiter from the cafeteria came in carrying a tray. Kendyl wrote in a tip and signed the slip, thanked the waiter, and watched after him as he left the suite.

She considered the tray. A tall silver pot of steaming coffee and a round ceramic pot of tea that was still brewing. Along with a tray of miniature muffins.

If she were of a mind to do some damage, just think what she could do with this pot of scalding tea.

16

Maxi needed to ease the chitchat with Carter Rose into conversation about last night's attack on Sandie Schaeffer. She had a slug for a cameraman waiting for her twenty-six floors below, and the police would be holding a briefing for the assembled media down there that she couldn't miss—there was no trusting Lemke to shoot it properly without her, and besides, she needed to ask questions. Meantime, she wanted a statement on camera from Carter Rose on Gillian's assistant. Something. Anything he would deign to say. She'd have another exclusive; she was sure nobody else would get this far with him. And that might save her from the wrath of Capra for not getting the ambulance shots.

The door from the outer office opened and Rose's willowy, sloe-eyed assistant came in with the drinks. She put the tray down on the coffee table in front of Carter and Maxi, then set out cups, sugars, a pitcher of cream, and cutlery. Then, picking up the steaming pot of tea, she held a cup and the teapot, precariously, Maxi thought, directly over Maxi's lap. "Shall I pour?" she asked sweetly.

"No," Maxi said with an audible gulp. "Let it steep for a few minutes." She didn't trust this woman.

Kendyl set the teapot back down on the table with a prim little shrug, and poured coffee for Carter. "Is there anything else I can do for you?" she addressed them both.

"Yes," Maxi spoke up. "Can you give me a comment on Sandie Schaeffer? You two work closely together, and as I understand it, both of you were here from the company's inception. You must be devastated by what's happened to her." Maxi took a pen and her reporter's notebook out of her purse, opened both, and poised to write.

Kendyl straightened, and her face visibly sobered. "Sandie is wonderful," she said. "And she's a trouper. I'm sure she's going to get through this and be back with us very soon. And I'm certain that I speak for all of her colleagues when I say that we'll do everything we can to help her get back on her feet, and back on the job with her family here at the Rose company."

Maxi watched her. Pretty speech. But lying eyes, her intuition told her. Ice cream wouldn't melt in this woman's mouth. "Thank you, Kendyl," she said quietly, and equally as sincerely.

When Kendyl Scott left the office and closed the door behind her, Maxi poured herself a cup of tea, added a packet of sugar substitute and a squeeze of lemon, stirred the brew, and took a sip, then looked squarely at Carter Rose. "Well," she breathed, "I have a job to do. May I ask what *your* feelings are about this attack on Sandie?"

"Yes. Obviously it was the same person who killed Gillian," he responded with conviction.

"Why obviously?"

"Well, look at it. It happened in the same office. Four days apart. And Gillian and Sandie were joined at the hip."

"So you still think Gillian was murdered—"

"Of course she was murdered. And anybody who didn't think so before should certainly be convinced of it now, with Sandie almost killed."

"Who would do this?"

"I have no idea."

"Then why?"

"I don't know. Maybe Gillian and Sandie did something. Or knew something. Whatever the reason, I'm sure it involved both of them—those two used to finish each other's sentences."

"And what about the attempted attack on you?" Maxi asked. Carter Rose looked perplexed. "The break-in you told the press about at your house," she pressed.

"Oh, that. So much has happened that I actually forgot about that for a minute. . . ."

"You got a good look at the person, right?"

"Yes. In my bedroom."

On Wednesday Rose had refused to answer questions about the intruder. Maxi hoped to get something out of him now. "Was it someone you know?" she asked.

"I told you I couldn't talk about it," he said.

"Well, at least tell me if it was a man or woman. And if you still think that person is Gillian's killer, and Sandie's attacker."

"I can't, Maxi."

"Why not?"

"Because the police told me not to. You saw them that day, the chief as well as the detectives. They want to keep the details hushed so they can nail him with stuff that only he would know."

"Then it *is* a he."

"Okay, yes, it was a man."

"Just tell me if you think the person who broke into your house is the person who attacked Sandie Schaeffer and killed your wife."

"Yes. I do."

"How did he get in through your locked doors? And past the help, and upstairs into your bedroom?"

"Can't tell you that."

"This is exasperating. What about our deal?"

Carter smiled. "This was privileged information before we made our deal," he said. "Seriously, Maxi, the detectives warned me to tell nobody the answers to the questions you're asking. Especially not the media."

"Okay, then make it up to me. Give me a statement on camera about the attack on Sandie. Your thoughts about it."

"Sure," he said. That surprised her.

"Good. I'll call my cameraman up here." She reached for her cell phone.

"Wait on that," he said. "The police are going to let me know when they're ready to do the press briefing, and I don't want to miss it. Believe me, I'm as interested as you are in what they'll have to say. We'll go down to the lobby together when they're ready."

"Then afterward you'll give me a statement?"

"Yes, but not out front. I don't want the rest of the news vultures all over me. We'll go inside, into one of the ground-floor conference rooms, and lock the door."

"Perfect," Maxi said.

17

"And at this time we have no other leads on Ms. Schaeffer's attacker," Sergeant Carlos Salinger was saying. Salinger was one of the LAPD detectives who had been at Carter Rose's house two days ago when he held his news conference. Maxi threw out a question: "Is your investigation encompassing the death of Gillian Rose and the attempted attack on Carter Rose?"

"Yes," Salinger responded. "We've teamed up on the cases."

Maxi assumed that Salinger was the lead. "And have you come up with any evidence?" was her follow-up.

"On the Gillian Rose death, Ms. Poole, we have no indication of foul play, as you already know. And on the Carter Rose B-and-E there's nothing we can release at this time. As for the attack on Ms. Schaeffer, we're saying only that we believe it to be an inside event, perpetrated by someone she knew, someone with access to this building on a twenty-four-hour basis. We'll be canvassing the guards who were on duty through the night and checking their logbook to see who came and went, and we'll be talking to company personnel."

"Do you know who Mr. Rose's would-be attacker was?" piped up a reporter from Channel Four.

"We're not at liberty to divulge that," said Salinger.

"Why not?" came from several in the media crowd.

Salinger and his partner, Detective Donald Barnett, exchanged exasperated looks. They were never required to explain to journalists their reasons for withholding information from the press, and the reporters knew that. Salinger signaled an end to the briefing, which was remarkable only in its paucity of information.

Maxi turned to Carter Rose. "Shall we?" she asked.

"Okay," he said, and he turned and headed for the doors into the building. Maxi followed, with Lemke trailing her, lugging his equipment.

When they were set up inside the conference room and Lemke was rolling, Maxi warmed up with a softball. "Mr. Rose, your reaction to the attack on Ms. Schaeffer?"

"I'm devastated," he started, and he went on to extol the woman's virtues, her consummate skills, her many duties and accomplishments, her longtime loyalty to the company, the respect and affection for her held by all of her colleagues, and so on. Maxi patiently let him finish, knowing that she wouldn't use a frame of it on the air. When he wound down, she slid in the zinger: "Detective Salinger said they suspect that the intruder came from inside the company, somebody who knew her, and who had access to the building after business hours. That could describe you, Mr. Rose, couldn't it?"

Carter Rose gave her a look that said, *How could you throw that at me? I thought we were friends.* She returned his look with a stolid look of her own. Hers said, *Sorry, there are no friends when we're talking about a criminal investigation.*

"Yes, that could describe me," Rose answered then in measured tones. "But it wasn't me," he said. Then he waved his hand in front of his face to indicate that he was finished answering questions.

"We're done," Maxi confirmed to Alan Lemke, who turned off the camera and lifted it off the tripod.

"I can't believe this!" Rose blurted to Maxi. "What the hell did you expect me to answer to that?"

"I had to ask," Maxi responded, betraying no emotion.

"If you'll excuse me," he said curtly, "my wife's funeral is tomorrow and I have a lot to do." Services for Gillian Rose the next day were private, Maxi knew.

"Oh," Rose added, seemingly as an afterthought, "you're invited. Gillian liked you." With that, Carter Rose quickly exited the conference room.

Maxi stayed back with Lemke while he broke down and gathered up his gear. *Unbelievable,* she thought. *I just asked him on camera if he tried to kill an employee and he still wants to be my pal.*

That question, and his answer, was the sound bite that she would use on the Six O'clock News. What he said was not important, she knew; what made an impact was the look on his face when he said it.

18

Twelve minutes to ten, Saturday morning. The private funeral service for Gillian Rose was being held at Saint John the Apostle Episcopal Church on Sunset Boulevard in Beverly Hills, where the Rose family worshiped, at least on major holy days. The church was stately, one of the oldest in the city, rectored by the Reverend Lillian White, who would be assisting today. According to the program, Bishop James Bartlett had come from the diocesan house to conduct the services.

The high-ceilinged church was already packed to overflowing with family, friends, and colleagues of the deceased, company employees, and civic leaders, both local and national. Dozens of towering lit candles, three feet tall, adorned the elaborate, gilded altar, and the air was heavily perfumed with the scent of cut flowers displayed throughout the church. Conspicuous by its absence, the lack of a coffin had some of the people in the assemblage perplexed.

Another memorial service for Gillian, which would be open to the public, was scheduled to be held in a few weeks at the Globe Theater on Wilshire. That one would be attended by the press, Maxi knew, and by a lot of fans who felt they owed their quality of life to the woman behind Rose International's health-enhancing products, as well as the curious who had watched Gillian Rose ascend to celebrityhood over the last decade in Southern California.

Maxi was surprised to find her own name still on today's guest list, given the fact that she had aired her stunning question to the deceased's husband, along with the man's somewhat abashed answer, on the news last night. That would most likely be her last exclusive with Carter Rose, she figured.

She stood in the back of the church, hovering behind the glacial Ms. Kendyl Scott, who was seated at a table presiding over a large, open guest book. Kendyl was somberly asking arrivees to sign the book as they filed in, and Maxi intermittently peered over the woman's shoulder to read their names as they wrote. Kendyl more than once twisted around to level a sour look at Maxi, which Maxi returned with a tilt of her head and a sad, commiserative smile. In mourning, all. And she continued to steal glances at the names being written in the guest book.

No cameras were allowed in the church. The media gang were scattered outside, off the church grounds, on surrounding public streets and sidewalks, waiting to catch departing notables on tape and perhaps pick up an interview or two. Channel Six had Rodger Harbaugh out there.

It was Saturday; Maxi technically wasn't working today. She was tempted to take notes, but that would be tacky, since she was there ostensibly not as a journalist, but as a guest of the family.

She watched as a man who looked to be in his sixties maneuvered an electric wheelchair into the vestibule. While his physique was reed thin, his countenance was strong: long, narrow face, weathered but ruddy skin tone, alert blue eyes behind black-rimmed glasses, a thick head of coarse white hair, heavy salt-and-pepper eyebrows that almost met in the middle, and a full mouth set with an aspect of determination. He was dressed in a black suit with a blue dress shirt, accented by a conservative navy and red rep tie. On the wheelchair footrest his black leather shoes gleamed.

"Good morning," Kendyl Scott said to him. "Would you sign the guest book?"

Maxi watched the man divert his wheelchair over to Kendyl's table as he removed a fountain pen from an inside breast pocket. He signed with a flourish, *William Sanders Schaeffer.* Without saying a word, he placed the pen back in his pocket, wheeled around toward the church entry, and went inside.

William Schaeffer, Maxi thought. Related to Sandie Schaeffer, probably. And if so, what was he doing here at Gillian Rose's funeral while Sandie lay in the ICU at Cedars-Sinai Medical Center down the street, fighting for her life?

She walked over to the soaring entry doors and peered inside in time to see Schaeffer's wheelchair being guided by an usher over to the far right of the congregation. He rolled down the side aisle and settled himself beside the fourth row of church benches, taking care, Maxi noted, to allow those in the pew ample access to enter and exit. Apart from a physical disability of some kind, she observed, this man was vigorous, agile, thoughtful, and quietly intelligent. Her guess was that he could be Sandie Schaeffer's father, the pharmacist in Westwood who was mentioned in yesterday's Associated Press wire story.

The music prelude began and the congregants stood while Bishop Bartlett, Reverend White, and a third minister filed into the altarium, all of them solemn in white vestments. Escorted to the pulpit by the other two, the bishop ascended the steps and began the funeral liturgy: "I am resurrection and I am life, sayeth the Lord. Whoever has faith in Me shall have life, even though he die, and everyone who has life, and has committed himself to me in faith, shall not die forever. . . ."

Maxi slipped into a spot on the middle aisle at the rear of the church and looked around at the gathered. In the front row, to the left of the center aisle, she saw Carter Rose, flanked by two well-dressed older women, family members, Maxi guessed. The mayor was there—she'd seen him come in—along with several Los Angeles city councilpersons. The governor of California and an aide were also somewhere in the crowd, she knew; she'd heard people talking about them. A few rows in front of her, a beautiful actress who had recently appeared in an infomercial with Gillian as a high-profile endorser of Rose International products was audibly weeping. Maxi had the names of many more luminaries etched in her mind, having seen them inscribed in the guest book.

The voice of the presider intoned the collect, finishing with the refrain, "The Lord be with you."

"And also with you," responded the congregation, and the people were seated, signaling the start of the "Remembrance of the Life of the Deceased," the several scheduled eulogies.

One after another, friends and family of Gillian Rose stepped up to the microphone and spoke, extolling the woman's business genius, her philanthropic work, her social world, her love of people and her love of life. The final speaker was the deceased's husband, Carter Rose, who told of her beauty, inside and out, her front-and-center role in their global business, her loving kindness within their family—she was indispensable to him, he said, and he couldn't imagine his life without her. . . . With that, his voice broke, and he stepped down.

The bishop and his acolytes concluded the service, whereupon the ushers walked up the middle aisle to guide the mourners out of the church, starting with the family members in the front rows and working their way toward the back.

From her aisle seat in the second-to-last row, Maxi observed the passing procession. Carter Rose looked stoic. The family women were teary. Some people fanned themselves with their programs, others acknowledged acquaintances they spotted as they made their way up the aisle toward the exits.

She watched the man in the wheelchair slowly navigate the distance up the far right aisle, then around the back of the church and out into the vestibule. She slipped out of her seat and caught up with him as he rolled down the handicapped ramp that ran along the east rail down over the wide front stairs and was proceeding toward the adjacent parking lot. Coming around to the front of his wheelchair, Maxi stood in the gentleman's path and addressed him: "Excuse me, sir, are you related to Sandie Schaeffer?"

"I'm her father," the man said matter-of-factly. "And you're the newscaster Maxi Poole."

"Yes. How is your daughter doing?"

"There's been no change," he answered, his eyes clouding. He made no move to continue to his car.

Maxi lowered herself to one knee at the side of his chair and said softly, "Would it be possible for me to talk to you, Mr. Schaeffer? About Sandie?"

A beat; then he spoke. "All right, Ms. Poole. The police don't seem to be interested in what I have to say."

"I'll come to you. When's a good time?"

"I'm going to the hospital now. Then I'm going to work. Can you come to my store at around one o'clock? Schaeffer Pharmacy. It's in Westwood, on Glendon."

"I'll be there," Maxi said, and she stood to let him pass.

19

Carter Rose was pensive when he left the church. He steered his black Mercedes S500 sedan east on Sunset, heading for Cedars. He would check on Sandie, see what he could find out, then go home. To a weekend alone in the sprawling manse that he'd shared with his wife of fourteen years. His life was now forever changed; it would take some getting used to.

The service for Gillian had been everything it should be, but he certainly hadn't taken away from it any sense of closure. After the near fatal attack on Sandie Schaeffer yesterday, the police rescinded the order to the coroner's office to release Gillian's body, pending further investigation, they'd said. By that time it was too late to cancel this morning's service. Everything was scheduled, the invitations had been phoned, faxed, and e-mailed, the bishop had committed, and people were already en route from different parts of the country, some even coming from abroad. So he had gone ahead with her funeral this morning. Without her.

Next week he and Gillian had been scheduled to attend a worldwide anabolic biology conference in Maui. A paradise. He decided not to cancel—friends even told him it would do him good to get away. He had intended to bring his assistant Kendyl with them. It occurred to him that if the LAPD released Gillian's body in time, he would immediately have her cremated, tuck the urn in his carry-on bag, and discreetly scatter her ashes somewhere off that beautiful Hawaiian island. No service, no ceremony, no checking in with authorities there. He would just drive out somewhere and do it. And that would be the end of his life with Gillian Sevier Rose.

He would sell the big house on Carolwood. No point rattling around in it anymore, along with the nine people on staff. He was actually looking forward to getting rid of it, and everything in it. He would buy himself a penthouse apartment in downtown Los Angeles and give it a touch of the style *he* liked, twenties retro.

The company was yet another consideration. He intended to unload it, too, before all the company skeletons seeped out of the closet and did a Mardi Gras dance on Wall Street and the stock plummeted even more. Sell off and get out. Take the profits and start another business. If everything went according to plan, he would be out from under the barely manageable structure of Rose International in a matter of months, with cash secretly amassed in several bank accounts in different parts of the world to get him launched again. His patsy was Goodman Penthe, an underhanded creep, but *his* underhanded creep. As long as he could control him. Not easy, but he seemed to have the upper hand: Penthe wanted the Rose company very badly.

Then there was Kendyl. She was meeting him at the hospital now. So much of his plan depended on her, he reflected. In the past few weeks, Kendyl had become even more indispensable to everything he was doing. *Too* indispensable, and that was a problem.

William Schaeffer wheeled into the waiting room outside the Intensive Care Unit at Cedars-Sinai, where Sandie's primary-care doctor was to join him. Schaeffer had called ahead to the hospital; he had already been told by Dr. Stevens that his daughter was still comatose. But stable. Her vital signs were holding, the doctor said.

The card posted in Sandie Schaeffer's chart said that only next of kin were allowed in to see the patient, and on the card only one name was typed in, his own. They had lost Sandie's mother to cancer three years ago—this hospital brought back all those memories now. The couple had always wanted a big family, but Jo could never conceive after Sandie. And now his only daughter, all he had left of family in the world, was teetering between life and death within these walls.

He steered his wheelchair over to a corner table and picked up the phone to call Dr. Stevens. The duty nurse told him she would page the doctor and let him know that Mr. Schaeffer was in the waiting room.

As he put the phone down, the front door opened and Carter Rose came in. Rose walked right to him and offered his hand. Schaeffer took it, then said quietly, "I'm sorry for your loss, Mr. Rose. Gillian was wonderful."

"And I'm so sorry about your Sandie. *Our* Sandie. How is she?"

"There's been no change."

The door opened again, and Kendyl Scott walked into the waiting area. Carter Rose introduced the two.

"We've talked on the phone," Schaeffer said to her.

"We have? I don't remember."

Schaeffer remembered. He had called Kendyl Scott one afternoon looking for Sandie, thinking perhaps his daughter was on that side, or that Kendyl would know where to find her. He remembered that Ms. Scott had been distinctly unpleasant to him. And looking at her now, he was sure that Kendyl Scott remembered that conversation too.

Dr. Stevens entered the room from a side door. Schaeffer briefly introduced him to Carter Rose and Kendyl Scott. It was the doctor's turn to say, to both of them, "We've talked on the phone." And to Schaeffer, he said, "They've been calling to ask about Sandie."

"And that's why we're here," Rose said. "May we see Sandie, Doctor?"

"That's up to her father," Dr. Stevens said. "He's the only person authorized in the ICU right now."

Rose and Kendyl looked down at Schaeffer in his wheelchair. He looked back at them, paused for a beat, then said, "I think it's too soon. There's nothing to be gained—she's in a coma." With that, he wheeled around them toward the entrance to the Intensive Care Unit. Dr. Stevens gave the two a look that said *Sorry,* and followed Schaeffer through the doors.

Wheeling down the white-tiled corridor of the ICU, William Schaeffer considered what had happened to his daughter. Someone had shot her, in her office, well after business hours, in the early morning, in fact. Someone who knew her, the police speculated, someone inside the company. Someone high up, Schaeffer reasoned, to have access to the top executive suites at that hour, or any hour. Instinctively, he didn't trust those two.

20

Schaeffer Pharmacy in Westwood. William Schaeffer, in a white lab coat over the blue shirt, rep tie, and black trousers that Maxi had seen him in at the church that morning, greeted Maxi from behind the prescription counter.

"Hello, Mr. Schaeffer," Maxi returned. "Is there someplace where we can talk?"

"Come back to my office," Schaeffer said. "Benny will tend the store."

A tall, lanky young man in large black-rimmed glasses, wearing a white coat over a yellow V-neck sweater and jeans, responded to the pharmacist with a nod.

"Is he a student?" Maxi asked when they were inside the office.

"Of pharmacology," Schaeffer said. The sprawling UCLA campus was just down the street.

Schaeffer rolled his wheelchair behind a cluttered

desk, and Maxi settled into a metal folding chair, one of two in the tiny office.

"May I ask what brought you to Gillian Rose's funeral?" Maxi asked.

"I knew Gillian. I liked her. And she was good to my Sandie."

"You said you were going over to Cedars to visit your daughter after the funeral—"

"I did. She's still in a coma. It's distressing. They're worried about infection now."

"Do you know anything at all about what happened, Mr. Schaeffer?"

"No. But I have my theories."

"Which are?"

"I think it must have had something to do with business. Gillian was the brains behind Rose's product output, and Sandie was her right hand—maybe the two of them knew something."

"About . . . ?"

"Well, Gillian was testing some innovative formulas, some of them for products that would classify as drugs, so typically they would be outside the parameters of Rose International's business model."

"How do you know that?"

"Gillian talked to me from time to time about things she was developing, because of my drug expertise."

"What made her consult with you? I'm sure the Rose company has its own labs."

"Sandie told her about something I've been working on. Gillian got interested and came over to see me about it."

"Can you tell me what it was?"

"No. But Gillian and I met several times about it, and

eventually we both signed a letter of intent for her to purchase my formula. We were going to collaborate on its development; then she was going to market it. We signed a confidentiality agreement—Gillian didn't want it public until we were ready to go with it."

"I promise what you say will stay right here."

"But you people put everything on the news—"

"Not if you tell me not to, Mr. Schaeffer."

"Then why do you want to know?"

"Because Mrs. Rose is dead—and maybe it *wasn't* natural causes. Maybe something you tell me will give me some insight into the reason why she died. And why someone tried to kill your daughter. None of this will go on the news, I promise you."

"All right, then I'll hold you to that, Ms. Poole. It's a drug I'm working on for glaucoma. I've had glaucoma for years, and I've been developing an eyedrop for glaucoma relief. And I think I'm on to something. Something that not only effects relief, but reversal as well. Gillian was very interested—she was going to finance the FDA-required double-blind studies."

"So you were going to sell your formula to the Rose company?"

"No. As I said, Rose International is not licensed to develop or distribute prescription drugs, just over-the-counter vitamins and dietary supplements. This is a pharmaceutical product that I tendered my intent to sell solely to Gillian Rose. She was going to start up a separate company to market it."

"Why would she want to do that? Bother to develop and market one prescription glaucoma remedy when her company makes millions manufacturing over-the-counter dietary supplements."

"She never said. Maybe there was a history of glaucoma in her family and she wanted to help get this drug to market. Glaucoma is hereditary, you know."

"Well, I'm sure Carter Rose is Gillian's sole beneficiary. Now he'll be in possession of your intent document, right?"

"No. That deal is now null and void. But I'm still perfecting the product, and I'll look for another company to test and distribute it."

"I don't understand," Maxi said. "Even though Gillian is dead, the Rose company is still very much in business."

Schaeffer looked away, studying the wall for a beat as if contemplating whether to answer. Then he said, "Gillian made it clear in the wording that the agreement was exclusively between herself and me. She told me that her husband wasn't interested in the product, so she was going to pursue this venture on her own. Distribute it under the aegis of a new company she would form, as I said, apart from Rose International."

"Could this formula be something that someone would kill for?" Maxi asked with a note of incredulity. That strange meeting that she'd happened on between Carter Rose and Goodman Penthe had come to mind.

"I can't imagine it," Schaeffer said.

21

Blessed Sunday. *That can't be the phone ringing,* Maxi wailed silently. She glanced over at the digital clock by her bedside: 6:12 A.M. Let it ring, she told herself, pulling one of the down pillows up over her head and covering both her ears. Unless all hell was breaking loose at work—earthquake, fire, Britney Spears was back with Justin Timberlake—she was going to ignore it.

The answering machine clicked on, and she heard her own muffled voice instructing the caller to leave a message at the sound of the tone. Then she heard the sound of the tone. It was followed by a grainy voice shouting over static, "Maxi, hi . . ."

"Omigod!" Maxi screeched, bolting straight up in bed and pouncing on the phone. It was her good friend and pre-sexual somewhat-significant-other, reporter Richard Winningham.

"Richard! How are you?"

"I'm fine. What time is it there? What *day* is it there?"

"Uh . . . Sunday morning . . ."

"Are you free for dinner Tuesday night?"

"Richard! You're coming home!"

"Yes, but just long enough to get my dry cleaning done. Capra's sending me to Israel."

"Oh, I can't wait to see you!" Maxi shouted into the phone. "When are you getting in? I'll pick you up at the airport—"

"You don't want to do that. My flight gets into LAX at 3:52 A.M. Tuesday morning. The station's sending a courier to pick me up."

"Okay," Maxi said. "And really, how long will you be here?"

"I leave for New York on Friday to spend a few days with my mom, then on to Tel Aviv. We'll get all caught up, Maxi. But I have to hang up now. I found a phone that actually works, but there's a line of raucous journalists behind me waiting to use it."

"Wait! Wait! Where *are* you, Richard?"

"In a bar in Lahore—with a CBS correspondent literally pounding on my back waiting to call home—see you Tuesday, Max." Before she could respond, the line went dead.

Maxi fell back on the pillows, smiling. She lolled in wakeful dreamland for about twenty seconds, then she felt the covers rustling. Opening her eyes, she twisted her head to the right and saw two gray paws that had claimed purchase on the side of her comfy feather bed.

"No, Yuke," she mumbled to the paws. "It's Sunday. Sleep-in day, remember? Go back to sleep. We'll go to the dog park later. Much later. Okay?"

Evidently that was not okay. Yukon dropped back

down to the floor and emitted a stream of small, cranky whines.

"Don't sulk, Yukon," Maxi said, sternly now. "That'll get you nowhere."

That remark was apparently lost on the big, furry malamute, who started pawing the carpet beside Maxi's bed. *Just like a man—he wants what he wants when he wants it,* Maxi thought to herself, all the while staying perfectly still, her eyes tightly closed. Maybe she could fool him into thinking she'd gone back to sleep.

Wrong. Keeping up his restless noodling, he was not to be ignored. With a sigh of resignation, Maxi sat up, swung her legs around, hit the floor, gave the guy a quick rub, and headed for the bathroom, with Yukon padding after her, a big smile on his face.

Christmas was three days away. She'd already sent off gifts to her family in New York, and today was her last chance to do some fast shopping for friends here. But first to the dog park for an hour with Yuke, their Sunday-morning ritual. Now that she was up, might as well get an early start.

At the grassy public park at the corner of Laurel Canyon and Mulholland Drive, the city allowed dog owners to let their animals off the leash. Of course you had to hang with them every second, and even then an occasional fight would break out. Angelinos called the place the showbiz pooch park, because on weekend days you would catch any number of celebrities supervising any variety of dogs. For Maxi, there was the added perk at times of nailing down interviews with dog-owner celebs. Dog-park camaraderie was infectious. Stars who ordinarily would have their "people," the layers of staff they maintain between themselves and the press, routinely turn her down through regular channels would happily acquiesce at the dog park. Maxi would schedule her interviews first thing Monday morning, while the mutual doggie glow was still in the air. The most fun interviews were when she got the celebs on camera with their dogs. Jack Lemmon and Chloe, his big, beautiful, black standard poodle, did many interviews with her—Chloe would sit up in her own chair next to Jack's.

This morning the dog park was less crowded than she usually found it, probably because it was not yet seven o'clock. And not a celeb in sight. *They're all sleeping in,* she thought, just like she should be doing. But at least it gave her and Yukon loads of room to do their Frisbee thing, and she felt her body waking up with the exercise. Still, every movement was circumscribed by her recent injury. With each jump, sprint, reach, and stretch, she felt twinges of pain, and she knew Yukon, game though he was, did too. They were both a lot slower than they were two months ago, but getting stronger every week. Today's workout had been a little less painful than last Sunday's.

Rolling out of the dog park at a little after eight o'clock, it occurred to Maxi that this might be a perfect time to drop by Cedars and check on Sandie Schaeffer— Sunday morning, early, no traffic, and quiet. It was a fast six minutes across Mulholland Drive to her small house in Beverly Glen. She settled Yukon in the backyard, put a tub of water next to his Home Depot "designer" dog house, then jumped back into her weekend junker, a beat-up Chevy Blazer, and zipped down to Cedars at Beverly and San Vicente.

Turns out this *was* a good time for a hospital visit— she even found free parking, no charge on Sundays, at one of the meters around the rambling medical center.

In jeans, T-shirt, and running shoes, she skipped up the concrete steps to the entrance at Cedars, and without stopping at the desk she made her way directly to the Intensive Care Unit on the eighth floor. *Act like you know exactly what you're doing . . .*

When she got to the entrance, three white-coated doctors were walking out of the steel-and-glass doors of the ICU, engrossed in conversation. As they rushed past her, Maxi managed to slip inside before the double doors closed behind them. Maybe she should have asked Mr. Schaeffer for permission to visit his daughter. Then again, maybe not. When you don't ask, nobody says no.

She hoped she'd be able to recognize Sandie Schaeffer in this sea of ailing patients. Walking briskly past the nurses' station and down the corridor that bisected rows of separate small patients' rooms, she glanced right and left into each space as she passed. She found Sandie in a room about halfway down the hall, and she ducked inside.

Sandie was alone, lying perfectly still on the hospital bed, her lips dry and bluish, her head swathed in dressings, her arms, neck, and side hooked to tubes running from IV bottles and pouches. She looked pale, frail, and very small.

Maxi was about to say something to her when a white uniformed nurse bustled into the room. Above her left pocket she wore a plastic name tag, white letters cut into royal blue that read JANELLE ADAMS.

"Hello," Nurse Adams said brightly. Which was not what Maxi expected her to say. What she expected to hear was "Get out."

"How's she doing, Ms. Adams?" she asked the nurse in a quiet voice.

Not so quiet, the bright-faced nurse said, "Actually, she stirred for the first time. This morning. She was trying to speak. Her doctor was very gratified. Are you her sister?"

"No," Maxi said. "I'm a friend of hers, and the family. Her dad keeps me posted, of course. Bill."

"Oh." The nurse beamed. "Bill is wonderful. He's here every day, most of the time twice a day, as you probably know. He was here this morning, talking to her—that's when she tried to speak."

"Yes, Bill is an early bird," Maxi said, like she knew what she was talking about. "I'd like to try speaking to her a bit, tell her I'm here, and I love her. Is that okay?"

"Sure. That kind of stimulation is good for her, Dr. Stevens says. Let me get her pulse first."

The nurse reached under the covers and lifted Sandie's wrist, eyeing her watch as she did. "Strong," she observed aloud. Then, "Y'know, you look like that newswoman—anybody ever tell you that?"

"All the time," Maxi said.

"Well, don't stay too long, now—don't want to tire her out."

"I won't."

When the nurse was gone, Maxi went around to the front of the bed and lifted the medical chart out of its metal holder. The inside cover had a card clipped to it; on it was a typed notation stating that only the patient's father, William Schaeffer, was allowed to visit. Guess Ms. Adams wasn't familiar with that order in the chart.

Skimming quickly over Sandie Schaeffer's medical information, she noted procedures, medication, prognosis, and the rest of it, then closed the chart and dropped it back into its holder. Amazing that the woman was even alive, having sustained a gunshot wound to the head. Her chart recorded that the bullet had been removed in surgery. It would now be in police custody, Maxi was sure.

Coming back around to the side of the bed, she reached down and took Sandie's hand in hers. Leaning close to her ear, she spoke softly. "Sandie. How are you? It's Maxi Poole. Do you remember me?"

No reaction.

"It's Maxi, from Channel Six. . . . I met you with Gillian, several times."

She thought she felt the slightest pressure from Sandie's hand.

"Can you hear me, Sandie?"

She felt another bit of pressure, a little stronger this time. Then, to Maxi's astonishment, Sandie's lips parted. Then closed again.

"Do you want to tell me something, Sandie?" she whispered.

The two words, from the patient on the hospital bed, were barely audible. "Help . . . me."

Maxi looked up to see if anyone had heard, then bent her head back down to the patient. And again she became aware of the barest pressure on her hand that held Sandie's, so slight that she wasn't sure she'd really felt it. Then came more halting but unmistakable words from Sandie Schaeffer: "He tried . . . uhh . . . to kill me."

"Who?" Maxi said in an intense stage whisper. "Who tried to kill you, Sandie?"

No reaction.

She tried again. "Sandie, tell me who tried to kill you. Who shot you, Sandie? Do you know who it was? Talk to me, Sandie. I'm here to help you. The person who—"

She was cut off by the brusque re-entry of Nurse Adams into the cubicle. "I've just been told by the duty nurse that you are not authorized to be in here," she said briskly. "You'll have to leave, Miss—"

"She spoke," Maxi said to her. "Sandie said some words."

Adams jumped to the bedside, crowding Maxi out of the way. Gently, she rubbed both the patient's wrists as she spoke to her. "Sweetie?" she said softly. "Sandie? Can you talk to me, honey?" She kept it up for several minutes as Maxi silently stood by.

Nothing.

Finally, she ceased trying. Turning, she looked surprised to see Maxi still in the room.

"I was just leaving—" Maxi started.

"What did the patient say?" the nurse asked, all business.

"She said . . . she said . . . I'm not sure what she said," Maxi responded.

22

Monday morning, ten to nine. Maxi waved her ID card in front of the security panel to the right of the Channel Six newsroom door, triggering access. The cavernous work space was chaotic and noisy—business as usual.

"I've got news," she called over to Wendy as she approached her producer's desk.

"Me too," Wendy said while batting out a story on her computer. "What's yours?"

Maxi dropped into a chair next to Wendy's desk and lowered her voice. "Sandie Schaeffer talked to me."

"Uhh . . . in your dreams?"

"No. In the ICU at Cedars. Yesterday."

"How did you—never mind," Wendy said, knowing that Maxi had a way of getting in anyplace when she had a mind to. "What did she say?" she asked.

"I think she said, 'He tried to kill me.'"

"Well, we *knew* somebody tried to kill her," Wendy said.

"Yeah, but we didn't know it was a *he*."

"True. Did you call it in to the LAPD?"

"Of course. And I told her doctor. Dr. Wallace Stevens. He said Sandie actually talked a little bit a couple of times, later in the day."

"A *coherent* little bit?"

"I don't know. But she sounded semi-coherent to me."

"Wow. If she can finger the person who attacked her, that could crack the Gillian Rose murder."

"The police are still not saying Gillian Rose was murdered."

"Yeah, right. What do *you* think?"

"My uneducated guess? I think she must have been, but it seems the LAPD have no wounds, no weapon, no evidence of foul play, no nothing."

"What was the cause of death, do we know?"

"Just what the wires reported. Heart failure."

"Yup, well, that's what death is. Your heart fails, you're dead."

"Can't argue with that. What's *your* news?"

"I've got myself a literary agent! She loves my book, and she's already got a marketing plan, she says. Can you believe it?"

"Oh, that's wonderful, Wendy!"

"First, she wants a doctor's validation, a doctor who'll collaborate with the nutritional information and put his name on the book. That'll be easy; we've interviewed a zillion nutritionists—I've got a file full of them. Then she wants some rewrites, and some adds. More of my quick-fix low-fat, low-carb menus, and two additional chapters: one chapter on famous short women in history, and one on clothes that add the illusion of height. And she wants to include photos along with the diagrams."

"Oooh, very exciting," Maxi said. "Time to have a party, don't you think?"

"Sounds good to me. I'll bring the wine."

"No way," Maxi said. "It's your party; I'll get the wine. And some goodies from Bristol Farms. I'll bring it all in tomorrow morning and we'll party tomorrow after the Six. I'll post it on the computer."

"Okay. And pick up some more plastic wineglasses, will you? We're almost out."

"You got it," Maxi said, and she gave Wendy a hug.

"Hi, Charlie. I need a favor." Back in her office, Maxi was on the phone with Charles Strand, a longtime friend and contact in the coroner's office.

"Let me guess," he said. "You want me to purloin a copy of the autopsy report on a certain high-profile dead woman."

"Can you do it?"

"I can. The question is, *will* I? Or, more precisely, the question is, are you buying lunch today? Long time no see, Maxi."

"I can't do lunch, Charlie. Would you settle for a glass of wine and some trail mix after the Six O'clock News tonight?"

"Sure. Let's meet in the middle." Charlie worked at the county morgue east of downtown L.A., and he lived in West Hollywood. Maxi would be coming from Channel Six in Burbank. Traffic all over would be a bear at that hour.

"Sullie's at seven?" she asked. Sullivan's was a popular bar and restaurant in the Silver Lake district.

"I'll be there."

"Bring a printout of the autopsy report," she said.

Maxi had crossed the newsroom to Pete Capra's office. She could see through the glass that he had a phone in his ear. As usual. She let herself inside and sat on his couch. Capra shot her a look of annoyance and turned his body away from her. Another Capra-ism: He got annoyed when the mail guy came around.

He hung up and squared himself toward her. "What?" he bellowed. His phone started ringing again. At least he had the grace to ignore it.

"Good morning to you, too, boss," Maxi said sweetly. "So, Richard's coming home."

"Yah. So?" his usual charming self replied.

"So how come, and for how long?"

"I'm reassigning him. And he'll be here for fifteen minutes."

"Richard saved my life," she mused.

"I was there, remember? The lesson is, don't back yourself into that kind of stupid situation again," he said. "So what do you need, Maxi?"

A civilized word. "Wendy just signed with a literary agent for her book, so we're having a little wine-and-goodies thing to celebrate. Tomorrow, after the Six. I thought if you could reach Richard, you could tell him to come in to the station—"

"Of course he'll come in to the station."

"I know, but I mean if he could come in after the Six tomorrow, while everybody's gathered, then we can toast him as well, and he can see all his pals at once." She neglected to mention that she was having dinner with Richard tomorrow night. You could never tell what would majorly agitate Capra.

"Can't reach him now. He's on a plane. I can get ahold of him tomorrow morning. But he'll probably be beat."

"Okay. Thanks, boss." He hadn't told her anything she didn't already know, but she wanted to include Capra in her plan to get Richard in to see everybody. Capra was weird about being left out of the loop on anything that went on at Channel Six News.

"Maxi—over here!" Charlie Strand called over the din. Sullivan's Bar in the newly trendy Silver Lake district of Los Angeles was jammed three deep with the after-work singles crowd, and Maxi was jostling her way through it. Charlie was at the end of the bar; she saw that he was actually perched on a bar stool, a prime piece of real estate during happy hour at Sullie's.

"How many phone numbers did you pick up while you were waiting for me?" Maxi asked when she got there, eyeing the plenitude of attractive young women in his immediate area. Charlie was in his mid-twenties, tall and rangy, with dark, spiky hair, crinkly blue eyes, and a killer smile. And single. And yes, Maxi noted, women were definitely checking him out.

"None," Charlie answered, reaching out to give her a hug. "You know I'm saving myself for you, Maxi. We're going to get married and have two-point-four kids. What are you drinking?"

"Cabernet. And that's exactly what I dream of. Being

married to a guy who works at the morgue and comes home smelling of formaldehyde."

"We don't use formaldehyde—we don't embalm them."

"Well, what *is* that smell at your workplace, sir?"

"Death. I'll shower before I come home."

"Did you bring it?"

"Wait, we're not finished with the small talk. And we haven't even started with the hot talk."

Charlie got up to give Maxi his stool and the bartender slid her glass of wine across the bar. "Nice to see you again, Ms. Poole," he said. "This one's on Sullie."

"Aha!" Charlie piped up. "The first one's free. Just like drugs." Maxi and the bartender laughed, and she tipped her glass to Charlie's beer bottle.

"So," she said again. "Did you bring it?"

"Yah, I brought it." He patted the pocket of his loose-fitting corduroy jacket, then lowered his voice so Maxi had to draw closer to hear him over the bar din. "Listen," he mumbled, "you never got this from me. I would be in exceedingly deep shit if I got nailed giving you this."

"But isn't it a matter of public record—"

"Not this one," he interrupted, his eyes narrowing. "This one has a note attached. Which means it's not completed, and not released yet."

"What kind of note?"

"A standard 'cause of death deferred pending tox and micros' note."

"Which means further toxicology testing is being done, right? But what's micros?"

"They take very thin slices from multiple organs, thin as paper. Kind of like slicing a turkey. They slice up the heart, the liver, the brain, a bunch of organs, then they lay the slices out on micro slides, and—"

"Okay, *okay*. That's *way* too much information, Charlie. So how long does all this take?"

"About six weeks."

"That's why they haven't released the body yet."

"Bingo."

"So if the autopsy report hasn't been completed what did you bring me?"

"A work in progress. Didn't know that till I went in for it. But my ass is majorly chopped grass if—"

"Don't even say it," Maxi jumped in, putting a reassuring hand on his arm. Then, as if they'd never had the conversation, she sat back, took a sip of her wine, and smiled. "Wonderful to see you, Charlie. How have you been?"

He smiled back. "Hmmm. Is this the end of the small talk, or the beginning of the hot talk?"

"Both," she said. She liked Charlie a lot.

"I've been great. My Forty-Niners are winning. And I'm dating a flight attendant. She's marginally hot, and she gets us free tickets on American."

"And how's the job?"

"Oh, fabulous. I can swab down an autopsy room in four minutes flat now. You know I only work there because you call me three times a year. When are we gonna have a real date?"

"I'm old enough to be your mother."

"Sure, if you had me when you were twelve."

"Eight, actually."

A pretty young woman in her early twenties with short-cropped magenta hair, big gold-flecked hazel eyes, and a wide, cheerful smile was making her way toward them.

"Heads up, Charlie . . . incoming! Redhead at two o'-clock," Maxi mouthed.

"You're dreaming," Charlie muttered.

The woman stopped squarely in front of Maxi. "Ms. Poole, I'm a big admirer of yours," she said, extending her hand. "My name is Lonny Haines. I'm a law student at Loyola. You are truly a role model for women."

Maxi accepted her hand. "Thank you," she said. Then Ms. Haines turned her thousand-watt smile on Charlie. "And who are *you?*" she asked him pointedly.

"I rest my case," Maxi mumbled to Charlie.

23

Settle down, Yukon," Maxi murmured. She'd been away since early morning and her big pup wanted some attention. Curled up on the couch in her study in black-watch-plaid flannel pajamas and fleece-lined slippers, a cup of steaming herb tea on the side table, she was reading over Gillian Rose's autopsy report for the fifth or sixth time.

She and Charlie Strand had left Sullivan's and gone over to the Sonora Cafe on La Brea for a light dinner. They talked and laughed a lot. When they were about to part in their separate cars from the restaurant parking lot, Charlie tried to kiss her, as usual. And Maxi wouldn't let him, as usual. They both giggled and said good night. And Maxi had the autopsy-report printout in her purse.

She couldn't wait to read it, was sorely tempted to pull over on Beverly Boulevard on the way home, park under a streetlight, and scan the report. But she didn't. Since covering that seminal story six weeks ago that almost got her killed, she'd been working on curbing her obsessive personality. Not altogether successfully, but now and then she was able to squelch an urge to leap before she thought. Only now and then. Waiting to read the printout until she got home, like a normal person, was just an exercise in self-control. Sadly, she had actually been backsliding in this area over the past few weeks. Kind of like a diet: you start out in a blaze of glory. . . . Oh well, this time she'd made it.

At home, now, she was devouring the report. Trying to read the subtext, trying to find things that weren't actually there in print. Like a definitive cause of death. Like what it was, exactly, that *caused* Gillian Rose's heart to stop. Nothing in the report cleared up that question.

As Charlie had told her, the thirty-two-page report was not yet signed and dated by the Los Angeles County Coroner's Office deputy medical examiner who was working on the autopsy, but all organs had been weighed, measured, and examined, their condition noted, and all pertinent descriptions, numbers, and status positions were documented. The cause of death was listed as cardiac arrest, and the time of death given a range of from noon to 1:30 P.M. on Monday, December 16. Maxi remembered that day well. She assumed that window was settled on because Gillian would have been seen alive by colleagues at least up until noon, and her body was discovered by Sandie Schaeffer when she got back to the office after lunch and called the paramedics, who had arrived and pronounced Gillian Rose dead at around 1:30 P.M.

Gillian's personal statistics were listed. Gender: female; height: 5′ 7½″; weight: 124 lbs., color of hair: dk. brn; color of eyes: blue.

Blue. No surprise, really; everybody knew Gillian's eyes were blue. Blue as the October sky, as one writer had poetically reported in *People* magazine. But when Maxi saw her body on the day she died, the body lying on the carpet next to her desk in her penthouse office, Gillian's eyes were partly open, and they were brown. Deep, dark, dusky, unnatural brown. Was Maxi imagining that? Was it the lighting? She didn't think so. Her journalist-trained powers of observation would never have failed her to that extent. Would they?

She put down the autopsy report. It contained more questions for her than answers.

24

W hoa! You look terrific, Maxi. Hot date?"

Tuesday morning in the newsroom. Wendy was already at her computer terminal and Maxi had just come in, wearing a short, silky, printed skirt with a soft sweater in shades of what her grandmother used to call ashes of roses. She was hefting three shopping bags full of groceries.

"Yup. Dinner with Richard Winningham."

"Oh, great! I heard he was coming home. What's up with him?"

"Capra pulled him out of Pakistan and he's sending him to Israel."

"By way of *Los Angeles?*"

"He's giving him R and R for a few days to bond with his house plants."

"Generous. I'm amazed Capra didn't just shuttle him across the Persian Gulf, save the airfare."

"Well, of course that's what he *wanted* to do. I talked

to Richard this morning. He said he begged Capra for some home time."

"How'd he get it? Newsies don't do Christmas."

"Oh, he knew asking Capra, the Italian Scrooge, if he could come home for Christmas wouldn't fly. He told him he needed to go through his mail, take care of bills, get his life up to speed. This, Pete could understand—he gave the guy seven whole days."

"Big heart, our boss."

"Richard is actually grateful. He'll leave here on Friday and stop off in New York to spend part of the holidays with his mom. Today he was planning to just zonk out. Says he hasn't had more than a few hours' sleep a night since he left here. But he's coming in for our party after the Six."

"Cool," Wendy said, beaming, still typing. "We'll entertain him royally. At least it'll *seem* royal to him after Afghanistan and Pakistan. What'd you bring?"

Maxi rummaged through the shopping bags. "Totally royal stuff. Chips, dips, water crackers and two different cheeses, dippable veggies, peanut-butter pretzels, napkins, plastic glasses with actual stems like you ordered, and six bottles of a nice Pinot Grigio and an okay Cabernet. And some fabulous homemade chocolate-chip cookies from Bristol Farms."

"Fancy," Wendy said approvingly.

"Hey, it isn't every day that we snag a literary agent."

"Or a drop-in from our man in the Middle East."

"And it's Christmas Eve," Maxi added, giving Wendy a peek at a few wrapped presents in one of her shopping bags. Holidays, even major ones, went largely ignored in the television news business, because whatever the day, the news went on the air as usual and the work had to get done as usual.

Although the commercially decorated newsroom Christmas tree, placed behind the live set to be seen on air, was strictly for show to viewers, rebel Channel Six newsies did their own decorating when the bosses weren't looking. With typical newsroom gallows humor, they impaled particularly grisly wire stories on the Christmas tree's branches: the twin nurses whose bludgeoned torsos were found in separate freezers in a meat-packing locker in Chicago; the skeletal remains of a priest who'd evidently hung himself deep in the catacombs of a Boston cathedral; the man in Macon, Georgia, who slipped while high up in a tree on his property and cut off his own head with his chain saw. Merry Christmas. Management types would routinely strip the wire stories off the Christmas tree when they saw them, but they never put out memos to cease and desist. Most of them were at one time rank-and-file themselves, and it was tradition.

"I'm going to stow this stuff," Maxi said, and she set off for her office with the shopping bags.

The light on Maxi's phone was blinking. She dropped the munchies, paper, and plastic goods on top of a file cabinet and put the perishables in her small fridge. Then she sat at her desk and listened to her messages.

There were eleven of them. The first one was intriguing, from Goodman Penthe in Baltimore.

She dialed the return number; got an operator who put her through to Penthe's assistant. "Yes, Ms. Poole," the woman said, "Mr. Penthe will be on the coast the week after Christmas, and he wants to meet with you."

"And the purpose of this meeting would be . . . ?"

"Well, I don't know," said the assistant, as if astounded that anyone on the planet wouldn't jump to meet with the important Mr. Goodman Penthe, no questions asked.

"Would you find out and call me back?" Maxi asked sweetly.

"Umm . . . okay. Meantime, can you give me some dates and times of your availability?" The woman was evidently not used to having Mr. Penthe put on hold.

"Well, there's no point, is there, if we don't in fact intend to meet. So call me back, tell me what this is about, and we'll go from there. Thank you," Maxi said, and hung up. Arrogance on any level got her back up.

She pressed the MESSAGE button on her phone again to continue listening to her unplayed messages. Two were potential news stories. Then a callback from Jenny Braxton, the CHP officer who had given her the traffic ticket last week; Maxi had connected with her and was shooting a profile on the spunky, ash-blond "Chippie." Turned out Braxton had had one of those Is-this-all-there-is? epiphanies one day while she was bagging groceries at Gelson's, so she took all the courses, passed all the tests, and, at twenty-four years old, she was now jockeying the freeways on a big, brawny white-and-black BMW motorcycle displaying the colored star seals of the California Highway Patrol.

The next message was from Maxi's mom in New York reminding her to call her aunt Beth in Boston tomorrow, Christmas Day. Then a viewer from Arcadia wishing her happy holidays. Then . . .

Maxi's heart jolted. The next message was just one

short, cryptic line, a raspy, whispered threat from an anonymous voice: "If you want to stay healthy, news-bitch, don't try pumping Sandie Schaeffer for information again."

She pressed the REPEAT button to replay the message. Was the voice male or female? She couldn't tell.

Pressing the button for her second line, Maxi punched in Pete Capra's number. He picked up, harried as usual.

"Capra."

"Pete—I need you to come over to my office right away."

She hung up before he could argue with her. Then she listened to the message again. During its transmission, the LCD readout on the phone read PRIVATE CALLER. That meant the caller either had an ID blocking feature or had punched star-67 before dialing her number. Maxi wasn't hard to find. The station was listed, and operators routinely put callers through to the people who worked there.

In less than a minute Capra was at her door.

"What?" he barked, with his typical economy mixed with annoyance.

Maxi beckoned him inside and played the message for him. Then she told him about her short sojourn with Sandie Schaeffer in the ICU at Cedars on Sunday morning. Capra listened to her account of the hospital visit without saying anything, then he hit the REPEAT button on her phone.

"'Private caller,'" he muttered, looking at the readout. "No way to put a police trace on it." Then, "Who would know that you tried to talk to Sandie Schaeffer in her hospital room?"

"That nurse I told you about. Janelle Adams."

"And who would she have told?"

"Somebody at the nurses' station on the floor—whoever had me thrown out."

"Did anyone else see you?"

"Sure. Lots of people. It's a busy place." That was no help, she knew. Maxi Poole was highly recognizable throughout the Channel Six coverage area, which stretched from Santa Barbara down to the Mexican border.

"Get a tech to lift the message and give me the tape," Capra said. "I'll send it over to Henders." Detective Skip Henders was one of Capra's contacts and buddies at the Burbank PD.

"Thanks, boss," Maxi said. It was all they could do.

Capra left her office. Maxi thought about his question: Who else knew? More important, who would care? Obviously, anyone who knew something about the attack on Sandie Schaeffer. The answer to that could be the key to an attempted murder.

The implication set in. Had somebody besides the nurses seen her in Sandie's room in the ICU? And if so, what would that somebody have been doing there? The biggest question, of course: Was Sandie Schaeffer in danger?

And where did Maxi Poole figure in this? *Watch your back,* she told herself.

She picked up the phone and called for a technician.

25

"Attention! Merry Christmas, everybody! We've got wine! We've got goodies!" Maxi called out over the cacophony in the newsroom. The clarion call for food and booze was never ignored in this crowd. It was 6:45 P.M.; the early block was off the air. Gone to Mars, as the newsies liked to put it. And the party was on.

Staffers were buttoning up after the Six O'clock News and drifting over to the area where Maxi and Wendy were setting out snacks. Wendy already had a glass of white wine in her hand as she filled a plate with crackers and wedges of Cheddar and Brie.

Sunday Trent, the station's new, very young, very blond, very eager intern, came over and asked what she could do to help.

"Thanks, Sunday," Maxi said.

"How did you get the name Sunday?" Wendy tossed out.

"I was born on Sunday, and Sunday is my mom's favorite day of the week. But now she calls me Sunny."

Sunday Trent had just recently stepped nimbly onto the north side of twenty. She was one of the most delectable young beauties the sweaty Channel Six news troops had ever seen. A communications student at USC, she'd started her Channel Six internship a week ago. And when Sunday walked across the newsroom, many pairs of eyes followed her. Eyes that lusted, almost to a man. Some women, too.

"What do you like to be called?" Wendy asked, pouring a bag of potato chips into a bowl.

"Sunday. Because it's different, don't you think? Because *I'm* different."

"You are definitely different," Wendy acknowledged. "Why don't you put out these pretzels and corn chips."

Wendy Harris was known in the business for mentoring young people, even those from other stations. She would sit them beside her for hours and explain everything she was doing as she produced a newscast. And if they showed promise, she would use her wide contacts to help them get entry-level jobs.

Sunday Trent had potential, Wendy thought. She wasn't a strong writer, but she was smart, she was willing to work, hungry to learn, she stayed all hours, and she was devastatingly lovely. Nobody made it to reporter or anchor on looks alone, although being pleasing to the eye didn't hurt, and Sunday Trent was surely that. Wendy had been trying to help her with her newswriting, which was bedrock basic to the job.

Now Sunday was talking to Rob Reordan. Maxi and Wendy overheard her asking if she could follow him through a typical day, see how an important anchor prepares. They could see Rob's face lighting up. Yes, this girl was a mover.

Maxi called for attention again. "We have some great news," she announced to her colleagues. "Wendy has just signed with a big-time book agent, and *Don't Be Dumpy* is gonna fly!"

A cheer went up; glasses tipped toward Wendy. Questions were tossed her way. Who's the literary agent? From here or New York? How did you find him? What, it's a woman? What happens now? What kind of advance do you think she'll get you? Is there a timetable? And on and on. Most journalists think they have a book in them.

When the initial hubbub died down, Sunday Trent came over to Wendy. "I'd like to help you with the book," she said.

"Help me how?" Wendy asked as Maxi looked on.

"Oh, I know I can't write like you two, but I could do legwork. Research. Line up interviews. Proof your pages, Wendy. I'll do it on my own time. I'd like to."

Maxi and Wendy exchanged skeptical glances. Why would a young beauty like Sunday Trent, who carried a full load of courses at USC and who worked in the newsroom two nights a week as well as on weekends, want to take on anything more? Didn't she have a boyfriend? A life?

"I couldn't pay you," Wendy said.

"Oh, I wouldn't be doing it for money."

"For what, then?"

"For the experience. I think it'd be terrific to work on a book. And I could use it on my résumé."

"Well, if you mean it, maybe I actually *could* use some help. My new agent wants the changes yesterday. The sooner she gets them, she said, the sooner she can bring the book to market."

The next day was Christmas. That meant turkey and

trimmings spread out on the long conference-room table for everybody who had to work the holiday. Nice touch, except after the spread was delivered and laid out on Christmas morning, it would be left out there with nobody tending it during all the shifts, and after the first few hours you'd have to be really hungry to partake—the turkey would be cold, the stuffing congealed, the mashed potatoes would be like rocks, the gravy would have a layer of congealed fat on top, the salad would be wilted, and the bread would be hard. A gamey smell would permeate the room, and there'd be a greasy mess of cranberry sauce and gravy spills all over the slick mahogany conference table. Still, it would be festive—as festive as it gets on Christmas Day in the newsroom.

Wendy made an appointment to meet with Sunday on the day after Christmas, right after the early block got off the air, to determine what, if anything, Sunday Trent could do to help with her book project.

There was a whoop in the party crowd as Richard Winningham came in the door. Looking thinner and more rugged than when he left, Maxi observed, feeling a little flutter in the pit of her stomach. Interesting, the flutter, she thought, ever the objective analyst of her own libido. Richard walked over to Maxi and whispered in her ear, "I saved your life—that means I'm responsible for it, right?"

"So say the Chinese," she whispered back. His warm breath stirred up the flutter again, she noted.

He turned from her and circulated, shaking hands with colleagues, telling war stories. Somebody handed him a glass of wine, and Pete Capra emerged from his office and gripped Richard in a bear hug. The party was jumping. They ate, they drank, they schmoozed, they congratulated Wendy, and they welcomed Richard home.

Maxi milled about with her bag of Christmas gifts. A signed copy of Tom Brokaw's latest book for Pete; a new robin's-egg-blue Kipling gym bag for Wendy. Small presents for reporters and staffers—soaps, candy, scented candles. Until there was one gift left in the bottom of the bag. For Richard.

After a little more than an hour, Richard cycled back to where she was standing and said, "Let's go." She grabbed her purse and followed him toward the door.

26

Carter Rose thought it would look unseemly, just eight days after his wife's death, but Kendyl insisted on going to Spago, Wolfgang Puck's trendy, celebrity-packed restaurant in the flats of Beverly Hills. "We could never go anywhere because of your wife. Well, now she's dead, and we can go to Spago. I've waited years for this," she'd told him. Nagged him, really. Carter wasn't liking this new Kendyl.

They were scheduled to go to Maui on Thursday, the day after Christmas, for the annual four-day industry conference that would mix business with festive fun, but without Gillian, taking Kendyl to Maui was out of the question. Carter had grudgingly agreed to take her to Spago tonight, but he was going to use the opportunity to tell her at dinner that Maui was off.

Kendyl wanted him to pick her up at home, like a real date, she said, but he'd held his ground on that one—they would meet at the restaurant. Heading south on Cañon

Drive in his dignified black Mercedes, he made a silent note to himself to trade it in for a sports car in a few months. Something like a red 360 Ferrari Spider. Yes!

The street outside Spago was jammed, as usual, with limo pickups and dropoffs, diners meeting and greeting, and paparazzi in wait to catch celebs whose photos would sell to *People*, *Us Weekly*, *Self,* the tabloids, or any rag that would cough up a few bucks.

Carter pulled up behind the row of cars waiting for valet parking. As he climbed out of his Mercedes, he was astonished to see the gang of photographers suddenly bearing down on *him* in a blast of popping flashbulbs. To shouts of "Over here, Mr. Rose!" "Sorry about your wife, Mr. Rose!" "What do *you* think happened, sir?" he presented just a sad, resolute, tight-lipped half-smile as he moved politely through the crush. These damn pictures would show up *somewhere,* he knew, so he did his best to keep his temper in check until he escaped inside the restaurant. Stupid idea, Spago.

He'd made it a point to get there early. Dropping a twenty on the bar, he ordered a martini, then stood with it, facing the door, waiting for Kendyl to come in; he intended to head her off before she made a big announcement to the chic hostess that she was there to join Mr. Carter Rose.

Sipping his drink, he thought about things. The police hadn't proved that Gillian was murdered. Nor would they ever find his own would-be attacker, he knew. As for Sandie, that depended on whether she came out of it, and if she did, what kind of mental shape she'd be in.

And Kendyl. Kendyl had to go. Their affair worked well for him for nearly a decade while he was married to Gillian, but she'd been getting increasingly clingy over the years. Complaining that he was cheating on his wife with her, and cheating on her with other women. He'd always managed to deflect her accusations handily, but with Gillian dead she'd been acting as if she owned him now. Conversely, his wife's death seemed to signal a sea change for him, a hundred and eighty degrees. Though he wouldn't admit it out loud, he was looking forward to embarking on totally new experiences, and that included the area of his sex life.

Kendyl came in the door, tall, golden, sleek, and stunning, in a black silk pantsuit with silver pinstripes and five-inch strappy silver heels. She looked around, caught Carter's eye, and broke into a dazzling smile that lit up even the glittering Spago bar. Kendyl Scott turned heads, no question, but Carter mentally recited to himself the ages-old locker-room cliché: For every beautiful woman, there's a guy who's tired of fucking her. Smiling to himself, he walked over, took her elbow, and guided her to the reception desk, where he didn't introduce her.

"Your table is ready, Mr. Rose." The attractive, leggy, brunette hostess beamed.

Carter smiled back at her. *So many women . . .*

"Really, Richard, Spago!" Maxi said. The two were seated in a far corner booth that looked out on the wide expanse of the holiday-bedecked main dining room.

"Tonight is special, Max—who knows when I'm going to get another one like this?"

Their waiter came over and poured more champagne. The two tipped their glasses to each other. Again. Maxi felt thoroughly warm and fuzzy.

"I've missed you, woman," Richard said.

"How have you had time to miss anybody?"

"Trust me, between filing stories and ducking trench mortar, there's time. Not a whole lot of good theater in Kabul or Karachi."

"Do you hate it?"

"Actually, no. It's the most interesting assignment I've ever had. The most humbling, too. We're so lucky here."

"I know. I've hung the bourkha you sent in my office. To remind me that the newsroom isn't the real battlefield, even though a lot of times it seems like one." She didn't mention that she'd also hung it there to remind her of Richard.

She hadn't had time to really get to know him before he was assigned to the Middle East. Assigned there because albeit he was the newest reporter at Channel Six, he was arguably the best. So when the United States went to war, Richard went to Afghanistan then Pakistan.

He'd moved to Southern California after ten years as a crime reporter at the ABC station in New York, and he'd been on staff at Channel Six for just a few weeks before she'd gotten herself into that terrifying situation with a deranged drug addict who most certainly would have killed her if Richard and Pete Capra hadn't shown up when they did. Then, before Maxi had had time to recuperate fully, Richard had left the country.

Maxi reached into her purse and brought out a small package wrapped in bright red paper and tied with black satin ribbon. "Your Christmas present," she said, and she handed it to Richard. His face lit up in a wide, boyish grin. *Like a kid at Christmas,* was the phrase that came to Maxi's mind. She loved that he didn't ward her off with the usual "Oh, no, you shouldn't have!" business. "For me?" he exclaimed with obvious delight.

"For you," she said, "because I'm sure you haven't had time to pick one up yet, and the new year starts next week."

He untied the ribbon and removed the wrapping paper. It was a small, black leather agenda book for the new year.

"Oh, I *need* this!" Richard said, caressing the rich leather and the gilded pages. "You're right, you can't get one of these where I've been. Not a priority item at the bazaar in Mazar-i-Sharif."

"Small enough to take with you on shoots, and there's room each day to keep a limited journal," she pointed out.

Richard opened the book to a place marked by a woven gold ribbon. There was handwriting on the page, Maxi's writing. He checked the date: October 30. *My everlasting thanks,* the message read. And it was signed, *Maxi.*

"Our anniversary," Richard said, and smiled. October 30, almost two months ago, was the day Richard Winningham had saved her life.

"I'll be thinking of you on that day," Maxi said, expecting him to say something like "We'll spend it together." What he said was, "Wow, beautiful leather." Men.

"I have a gift for you, too," Richard said then, reaching into his pocket and taking out a small cardboard box tied with string.

"You do? When did you . . . How . . . ?"

"Oh, we have ways," Richard said. "And coincidentally, my gift is a continuation of the theme."

Maxi opened the box. Inside, wrapped in coarse, yellowed Arabic newsprint, was a tiny, sterling silver whistle on a chain. "In case you ever get dragooned again,"

Richard said with a smile. "Try it. It's small, but it really shrieks."

She felt her eyes burning. For all they had been through, and for this lovely night. Handing the amulet to Richard, she turned away from him on the leather banquette so he could fasten the clasp. And so he wouldn't see her misty eyes.

They toasted again. "To a terrific year," Richard said. "For us, and for the state of the world."

"Good thing I don't have a story for the Eleven tonight," Maxi said with a grin, and they drank.

Maxi turned to look at an attractive couple who were being led to a table in the middle of the floor. When the woman looked their way, she recognized Kendyl Scott from Rose International. And the woman's escort was her boss, Carter Rose.

The mogul and his assistant, unremarkable enough, certainly. So why did it strike Maxi as wrong in some way? Maybe because the restaurant seemed too fancy, and the time too short since Rose had lost his wife. This Christmas Eve date just didn't look like business to her. She filled Richard in on who the two were, and the ongoing story involving the man, his wife's recent death, and her assistant's subsequent attack.

Carter Rose shifted in his chair. "Wine?" he asked Kendyl.

"Wonderful," she answered, with a loving smile that reached her eyes.

"White or red?"

"You know I like white, darling."

"How about a nice champagne tonight?"

With a puzzled look, she said, "You also know that I'm not fond of champagne, Carter."

"Sorry."

Carter felt enormously uncomfortable in this high-profile restaurant with Kendyl. As he'd known he would, especially after the unexpected media assault at the entrance. "Listen," he said to her, "I can't take you to Maui." Might as well get that out of the way, he reasoned.

"Wha—why not?" she asked, her exotic, blue-black eyes darkening even more.

"Because it isn't right."

"I don't understand. It was right to travel with you when Gillian was alive, but it isn't right now that she's dead?"

Their waiter came to the table. Relieved at the interruption, Carter made a ritual of ordering a bottle of 1982 Chateau St. Jean Chardonnay. When the waiter left, he took a deep breath and tried again.

"Look, Kendyl, be reasonable. We have to stay away from each other for a while. Let some time go by."

"I let eight years go by, Carter. I want a life. I want children. I want to marry you. I've always wanted to marry you. And you've always known that."

Carter was not happy with the way this conversation was going. Clearly, he and Kendyl wanted very different things. "The timing is wrong," he said.

"When will it be right?" She leveled her gaze at him. "When can we be a real couple?"

Never, he said to himself. This was over. What he said aloud was, "I don't know. I can't handle any more pressure right now. All I know is I need time to adjust to everything that's happened. That's still happening. This ugly mess is far from over." And again he said, "I need time."

Kendyl looked incredulous. "But I don't have any more time to waste, Carter. I've given you nearly a decade of my life. And I can't wait another decade. Or a half a decade. Now I want what you promised me over the years. Legitimacy. A baby, maybe two. It's what we've always dreamed of, darling."

"Things have changed—"

"What do you mean, changed? Gillian's gone, yes, but nothing's changed between us."

"It looks bad."

"Listen, people don't really care what other people do. They forget. It doesn't matter what they think, anyway. I'm listening to my biological clock, Carter, and I want to start a family. You always told me that you'd leave Gillian. Now you don't have to. Now we can be together, *really* together. I'm not saying tomorrow, but we can make plans. We can get married quietly, maybe in June—"

Carter put a hand on her arm to stop her. "Kendyl," he said, "I can't think about this now."

She softened. "We'll think about it in Maui," she said. "We'll get away, walk on the beach, clear our heads of all this, figure out our future—"

"I'm not taking you to Maui," he interrupted, his eyes determined. "I told you that. I can't take you to Maui."

In that instant, Kendyl grasped his subtext. He wasn't taking her to Maui. He wasn't going to marry her. She was becoming less important in his life, not more important. She'd wasted half her twenties and thirties, her best years, waiting for a man who had no intention of giving her what he'd always promised, what she'd hung in for.

Their waiter came back with the wine. With a smile

and a flourish, he presented the bottle, label up, to Carter, who nodded perfunctorily. The man uncorked the wine and poured a half inch into Carter's glass for him to sample.

"Yes, yes, pour it," Carter said irritably without tasting it. The waiter quickly filled both glasses. Then, sensing the tension between the couple, he mumbled something about coming back in a bit to tell them the specials and backed away from the table.

"You don't want me anymore, do you?" Kendyl said then in a fierce whisper. Rose looked at her, not sure how to respond. After a long moment of silence, Kendyl slapped her napkin on the table, pushed her chair back, and stood. Then she picked up her wineglass, slowly took a sip, and hurled the rest of the liquid in Carter's face. Calmly, then, she set the glass down on the table, picked up her purse, strode purposefully through the packed dining room, head held high, all eyes following her, and gracefully pushed out of Spago's front door.

27

Yikes! What just happened over there?" Richard mouthed, his eyes, along with most of the diners', still turned to the door where the stunning Kendyl Scott had left the building.

Maxi giggled. "High drama."

"A lovers' quarrel? But you said she was his business associate."

"Who knows, but you can bet it'll be all over the columns. Not tomorrow; there're no papers on Christmas Day, but we'll read all about it on Thursday, if we care."

"Do we care?"

"Absolutely. I happen to be hip-deep in the Rose International story, which gets curiouser and curiouser."

The waiter came by to take their order. "So, what went on at the Rose table?" Maxi asked him offhandedly. It never hurt to ask; you never knew what you might find out. And discretion didn't happen to be a priority among the young wait help at Spago; most of them were aspiring actors who loved to dish.

"I don't know—it's not my table. But I'll ask Jason when I get a minute."

Maxi looked over at the scene of the spat. Carter Rose still sat there, alone at the table, sipping wine. Any other night she'd have invited him to join them for dinner, appear to extricate the man from an embarrassing situation and see what she could find out, but this was her very limited time with Richard and she was not anxious to let work intrude, no matter how intriguing the story.

"Are those two regular customers?" she asked the waiter.

"Mr. Rose came in a lot with his wife. She . . ."

"I know," Maxi said. "What about the woman he was with tonight?"

"I've never seen her in here before. And believe me, I wouldn't forget that body."

"How's the lemon chicken?" Richard asked.

"Fabulous," said their waiter. "It's a house specialty."

After about ten minutes, Carter Rose summoned his bill, settled up, and quietly left the restaurant. He didn't see Maxi, and she decided it was probably better that way. She and Richard had a glorious dinner, capped by Wolfgang's sinful double chocolate hot fudge sundae, which they'd ordered served with two spoons.

While they waited for the scampering valet guys to fetch his car, Richard breathed deeply of the crisp Southern California night air. "It's still early, Max, and you don't have to get back for the Eleven," he said. "How about a drive out to the beach? I'd like to see the ocean while I'm here, get my feet wet."

"Sounds nice," she said.

Actually, it sounded particularly divine. She was so enjoying this evening with Richard Winningham. Lovely Christmas present, she thought to herself.

They cruised up Cañon to Santa Monica Boulevard, then took a left toward the ocean. It was a beautifully clear, crisp night, as chilly as it gets at Christmastime in Southern California. They had the top down in Richard's Audi TT convertible, and he'd slipped his jacket over Maxi's shoulders.

"I was half afraid my car wouldn't start up after sitting idle while I was away, but I lucked out," he said. "She needs to take a run, charge up the battery, blow out the engine."

He pushed the speedometer past the speed limit on the thirty-minute drive to the beach, then angled to a stop on Pacific Coast Highway just above the Santa Monica Pier. The area was a festive jamboree, the pier jumping with nightlife, people strolling, sitting on benches eating popcorn and cotton candy, standing at the railings looking out at the ocean while lights from its restaurants and bars lit the broad stretch of sand below. The merry-go-round clanged around and the giant Ferris wheel revolved, their kaleidoscopic lights joyous against the night sky as salt winds blew their tympanic music into the air, mixed with live jazz and rock 'n' roll, buoying the spirits of a thousand revelers.

On the other side of the highway, more people crowded the walkways around the several busy restaurants, while just north of the pier, down on the sand, the colorful, wide-striped tents of Cirque du Soleil rose like a gypsy bazaar. Off the coast scattered white sails caught the light from their yachts, while rhythmic, roaring waves breaking on shore glinted silvery white in the moonlight.

Christmas Eve in Southern California.

"Shall we walk on the beach?" Richard asked.

"Okay. I'm going to take my shoes off."

"Good idea," Richard said.

They crossed over the boardwalk and went down a flight of stairs that led onto the strand. Richard bent over and rolled up his pant legs, then led Maxi down to the water's edge, her flirty silk skirt floating up over her knees. Music from the pier drifted around them, and the heady salt air invaded their senses.

Richard put an arm around Maxi's shoulders as they walked along the surf line, waves rolling up over their bare feet. Above was a sky full of scattered stars and low-flying seagulls whooshing overhead, while a hundred yards offshore, dark pelicans in silhouette bobbed atop the waves.

"Perfect, isn't it?" Maxi said, drawing Richard's jacket around her.

"Beyond perfect," Richard murmured. "This night's going to last me for a long time."

"How long will you be in Israel?"

"For as long as it takes, I guess," Richard said.

He stepped in front of her then, and put both arms around her. And gently drew her close, and kissed her.

"It's midnight," he said. "Merry Christmas, Maxi."

28

Christmas Day. Just like any other day in the newsroom. Except for the tired spread of turkey and trimmings in the conference room. Like every other Christmas Day probably in every other television newsroom in the country.

You can always count on what the newscasts will look like on Christmas Day. Very little crime—seems robbers and burglars and muggers and car thieves take Christmas off too. There'll be the montage of Christmas morning services, ranging from Roman Catholic and various Protestant denominations, to Greek Orthodox, Church of Religious Science, New Age outdoor religious celebrations in the parks and on the beaches, and more. There'll be interviews with Salvation Army bell-ringers on city sidewalks and stories that embody the particular magic of Christmas in L.A., like a profile that was cut and ready to roll on Los Angeles songwriter Ray Evans, who wrote the enduring *Silver Bells* for a Bob Hope movie half a century ago. There's always a story about some adorable kids in a family subsisting below the poverty level who'd been majorly gifted by some private or corporate benefactor this season. And, sadly, there were always the Christmas tree fires that burn up the presents, sometimes injuring family members or destroying homes at Christmas.

This year, the traditional Christmas services at Bethlehem's Church of the Nativity would be interspersed with stories of the ongoing violence in the region. And in economic news there'd be the sum-up of holiday shopping sales for the season, locally and nationally.

Maxi was scheduled to cover the downtown mission today, where volunteers would be dishing up the annual Christmas dinner for the city's homeless. She requested that assignment every time she worked on Thanksgiving or Christmas Day, because she would be able to take a couple of hours to help out at the tables before coming back to the station to edit her piece for the early block. She and her crew were set to leave in thirty minutes. While waiting she sat in her office, chatting on the phone with her mother in New York.

"I'm so sorry I couldn't make it home for the holidays this year—you know that, Mom," she said. After taking three weeks off last month to recuperate from her injuries, she'd felt she couldn't leave the station again so soon. "Next year," she promised Brigitte.

Her mother told her the whole family missed her. Her sister, Ellie, and her husband and their three kids were there, doing Christmas stuff and having fun in the Pooles' spacious Manhattan brownstone. A dozen or so guests were coming over later for Christmas dinner, her mother told her.

"And you've got snow!" Maxi said.

"And we've got snow," Brigitte echoed with a big smile in her voice. "It started yesterday morning, and it's still coming down. The city is a fantasyland."

"Who's cooking?"

"Chef Harry's doing dinner again. Ever since Mortimer's closed. But Harry does a great job. The turkey's in the oven; the mincemeat and pumpkin pies are on the sideboard, ready to bake."

"Mmm, I can practically smell it."

"What are you going to do today, sweetheart? Besides work, I mean."

"I've got a story for the Eleven, Christmas Day at the White House. I just have to write and voice over network footage, piece of cake. So between shows, I'm going to take a run down to the beach and have Christmas dinner with Debra and Gia. Debra's having some people in." Actress Debra Angelo was Maxi's close friend; they had married and divorced the same man.

"That'll be fun, dear. Drive carefully—a lot of people will be on the roads tonight, after too much Christmas spirits, if you know what I mean. Do you want to talk to Dad?"

"I sure do. Thanks, Mom. And Merry Christmas."

Her father came on the line. Christmas was the one day of the year when Maxwell Poole closed his successful East Coast chain of boutique drugstores. After some small talk, her dad brought up Richard Winningham, whom he and her mother had met in Los Angeles last month when Maxi was recuperating. Maxwell Poole would always be indebted to Richard for saving his daughter's life in a deadly situation. "So what's happening with you two—anything?" he asked.

We had dinner last night and I thought my heart was

going to explode out of my body and do a jig beneath the Santa Monica Pier, was what she thought. "Dad, we work together," was what she said.

"Well, sure, but isn't that where most young people meet someone? At work?"

"He's assigned to the Middle East. Maybe for a long time, Dad."

"Hmmm. Well, he's a terrific guy. Don't you think so?"

Way past terrific—I've been thinking about him non-stop all day. "I hardly know him, Daddy. He'd just started at the station when you met him."

"Just in time to save your life, thank God."

She needed to change this subject. She told her father that she was working on a story and she wanted to pick his pharmacist brain.

"What do you need, honey?"

"Dad, do you know of anything in medicine that would turn a person's eyes a different color?" she asked him.

"Actually, yes," he said. "Look up a drug called Xalatan. Spelled with an X, but pronounced *za*-la-tan. It's an eyedrop medication, used for persistent high pressure in the eyes. There are a host of unpleasant, even dangerous side effects, so it's only prescribed when all other medications have failed."

"Pressure—does that mean glaucoma?" Maxi asked him.

"Specifically, a rare condition called open-angle glaucoma. And it can turn the iris brown. Does that help?"

"Maybe," Maxi said. "I'll check it out."

"One reason why it's a drug of last resort, even though it's extremely effective: Xalatan is very easily contaminated. You have to keep it refrigerated. You can't even let the *bottle* touch something else on the refrigerator shelf or the solution can become contaminated and cause serious eye damage, even blindness. This drug can be very dangerous if not handled carefully. I never keep it on hand. When we get a prescription for it at any of the drugstores, we special-order it from the maker."

"Can it kill you?"

"No. It can destroy your vision. But Xalatan won't kill you."

29

Maxi lifted her jacket off one of the hooks in her office and slung her purse over her shoulder. It was cool out, even for Christmas in Los Angeles. Or maybe she was reacting to the images of snow falling at her mom and dad's place in Manhattan. Thinking about that made her smile. Thoughts of her parents' home at Christmas, the home she grew up in, always gave her the feeling that all's right with the world.

The phone on her desk lit up. Her crew would be waiting for her on the midway—the wide private lane that bisected the network complex; she didn't have time to get involved with anyone or anything right now that could wait. Without picking up the handset she glanced at the caller ID LCD readout on the telephone. CEDARS-SINAI MEDICAL CENTER. She picked up the handset.

"News, Maxi Poole," she said briskly.

"Ms. Poole, this is Dr. Wallace Stevens at Cedars. Sandie Schaeffer's doctor. So you're working on Christmas?"

"You too, Doctor."

"Yes." Then his voice darkened. "We have a problem here, Ms. Poole. Somebody got into Sandie's room in the ICU and ripped out her IV tubes."

"Omigod! When?"

"Sometime during the night. The night-duty nurse found all the tubing lying on the floor, yanked out of the pouches—"

"Is Sandie okay?"

"Yes, there was no serious harm done. The drips contained only painkiller medication, and saline with dextrose and electrolytes. And they weren't detached long enough for Sandie to dehydrate. But it's obvious that whoever did it tried to harm her."

For a beat Maxi was nonplussed. "Who . . . who could get in there?" But even as she asked the question she flashed on how easy it had been for *her* to get in there on Sunday morning. And there was the threatening message on her answering machine. Somebody did not want Sandie Schaeffer talking.

"Did you call the detectives, Dr. Stevens?"

"The staff immediately called nine-one-one and they alerted the authorities involved with the case."

"The detectives came?"

"Yes. I have their cards. Detectives Murchison and Black. They had the police post a round-the-clock armed guard at the door to Sandie's cubicle."

"Were they able to talk to Sandie?"

"No. I couldn't allow them to try to question her. My primary concern is not who did this to her; as her physician, my concern is her physical and mental recovery. It wouldn't be helpful for her to have the police grilling her at this point, perhaps invading her subconscious. It could actually set her back."

"What can I do, Doctor?"

"We thought if *you* spoke to her, maybe—"

"But . . . couldn't that set her back as well?"

"She seems to want to talk to you. She's been asking for you."

"For *me?*" Maxi asked incredulously.

"Well, she's been saying your name. She's not altogether coherent, but we recognized your name a couple of times. That's why I'm calling you. I think it might help if you came over here and talked to her. Maybe hearing your voice will trigger something more from her."

Maxi paused for a beat, processing the information. "Does the media know about the break-in?" she asked.

"No. The detectives asked us to keep it quiet. But as I told them, I can't guarantee how long that embargo will last, with all the people who work here—"

"All right, Doctor," Maxi cut in. "I'll find another reporter to cover the story I'm assigned to and I'll come over to the ICU. As soon as I can."

Maxi had a question for herself: *How did I manage to get myself on the inside of this story?* Oh, well, you know what they say about a gift horse.

"Thank you, Ms. Poole," Dr. Stevens said. "I'll be here. And Mr. Schaeffer will too. He says he knows you."

Hurrying down the central corridor of the Intensive Care Unit at Cedars, Maxi spotted the uniformed LAPD patrolman posted outside the door to Sandie Schaeffer's small ICU cubicle. Anticipating him, she had her press credentials in hand.

"Hello, Officer Ricklaus," she said, glancing at his name tag. "I'm Maxi Poole. The patient's father is expecting me."

The officer took her ID cards and studied them for a beat, then studied her face. "That's you, all right," he muttered without a smile and handed the credentials back to her. "They told me you were coming. Go on in."

"Is everything okay?" she asked him.

"Fine," he said noncommittally and looked away from her.

"Well, Merry Christmas," Maxi offered, attempting, as always, to make a friend who might be helpful on the story later. This officer was having none of it—he didn't respond.

She stepped into the room and said a general hello to the people inside. A tall, thin man in a white lab coat, fifty-something, with rimless glasses and receding blond hair tinged with gray, offered his hand. "We spoke on the phone," he said. "I'm Dr. Stevens." Maxi saw that his eyes looked tired.

Turning to another white-coated man by his side, Dr. Stevens introduced his colleague, Dr. Ari Hamatt, a brain-function specialist. A female nurse in white uniform and surgical mask, holding a clipboard, stood at the foot of the bed. And William Schaeffer sat in his wheelchair on the far side of the bed, watching his daughter solicitously.

Maxi turned to the patient. "Sandie," she said quietly, "it's Maxi Poole. I'm here. And your father's here. And your doctors. It's Christmas, Sandie. Can you hear me?"

She slipped into the one vacant chair by Sandie's hospital bed and bent low over the patient's ear.

"Sandie," she said again, louder this time. "Can you

hear me? It's Maxi Poole. You asked for me, Dr. Stevens said."

She took one of the patient's hands in hers. "Can you hear me, Sandie?" she repeated, putting pressure on Sandie's hand. And in that instant she felt a little pressure in return.

Seeking Dr. Stevens's eyes with hers, Maxi lifted Sandie's hand a few inches off the bed, indicating that she'd had some reaction from his patient. Then she said, "Good, Sandie. I know you can hear me. Squeeze my hand again." And she felt more feeble pressure.

Maxi nodded to the doctors. "She hears me," she said. "She understands. She squeezed my hand again, lightly, but definitely."

Then Sandie opened her mouth. With what looked like a great deal of effort, she whispered a few words. It sounded like, "He tried to kill me. . . ." The exact words Maxi thought she'd heard Sandie say the last time she'd come into the ICU and tried to talk to her.

"What did she say?" asked an anxious William Schaeffer, never taking his eyes off his daughter's face.

"I think . . ." Maxi began. "I think she said, 'He tried to kill me.'"

"That's what I heard too," the nurse offered.

They spent the next half hour in Sandie Schaeffer's room, taking turns talking to the patient, but got no more reaction from her. Maxi stood up then, walked around the bed, and knelt beside Bill Schaeffer's chair. "She's getting better," she said to him.

"I think so," he returned, his intelligent eyes warming to Maxi's concern. "At least she seems to be coming out of it. The real question is, how will she be then? How will she be for the rest of her life?"

"I'm thinking good thoughts for you and your daughter," Maxi told him. "That she reacted this much today is a real holiday gift for you, isn't it, Mr. Schaeffer?"

"I hope so," Schaeffer said.

"She's tired now," Dr. Hamatt put in. "It's very common that after the kind of activity she showed earlier, the patient will be very tired. But she's had a productive day."

Maxi gave Mr. Schaeffer's arm a solicitous pat and stood up. "I've got to go back to the station for the Six O'-clock News," she said. "Call me if you need me again. I'll do whatever I can to help."

"That means a lot to me," Schaeffer said. "Sandie seems to respond to you."

Maxi hesitated a beat, then decided to level with the patient's father. "Mr. Schaeffer, I'm going to report what Sandie said on the Six O'clock News tonight. Both her progress and her words today are news. You and I have no source confidentiality agreement, and I'm actually working right now; I dropped a story assignment to come here. I want you to know that I've come to care about you and your daughter, but I also have a job to do."

"I understand, Maxi," Schaeffer said. "In fact, I'm hoping that whatever you report will help bring Sandie's attacker to justice."

Good, Maxi thought as she hustled out of the ICU. She had established that henceforth, any "personal" visit was also business.

Back in her office, Maxi had several messages waiting, most of them holiday greetings. One was from Richard. "Call me, Maxi," he'd said on her voice mail. She dialed the number for his apartment.

"Hello," he said, and Maxi's heart jumped a little.

"Merry Christmas," she said.

"Back atcha. I've been thinking about you."

"What have you been up to?"

"Exactly what I told Capra: I spent the day going through a ton of mail, writing checks, catching up, trying to clear the decks before I have to leave again."

"Did you accomplish a lot?"

"I did. For some reason I was in a good mood all day."

"Probably because it's Christmas."

"Probably because of Christmas Eve."

Maxi smiled. "What are you doing tonight?"

"That's why I'm calling. Are you doing a story for the Eleven?"

"Yes, but I'm just recutting a network piece."

"How about having a bite?"

"Well, I'm going to the beach between shows. To Debra's house, for Christmas dinner." Richard had met Debra Angelo before he left for Afghanistan, at St. Joseph Medical Center in Burbank where Maxi was recovering.

"She's fun," Richard said.

"Wanna come?"

"Really?"

"Of course really." She laughed.

"You're on. I'll pick you up in the newsroom after the Six."

Maxi hung up. Smiling. She called Debra to ask if she minded setting another place, then went out to the assignment desk to pick up her network tape on Christmas at the White House, to cut her story for the late news. Might as well get it out of the way before she left for dinner, she figured, so she wouldn't have to hurry back. She was looking forward to seeing Richard.

30

Thursday morning, the day after Christmas. When Maxi got in to work, there was a message on her voice mail from an Adrienne Gray asking her to get back to her as soon as possible. Maxi recognized the humorless voice: Goodman Penthe's assistant. The time code on the message was 4:36 A.M. That was 7:36 A.M. in the East. Ms. Gray had promised to get back to Maxi after Christmas. What took her so long? She dialed the number.

"Oh, Ms. Poole, thank you for returning my call," said Ms. Gray. *Good,* Maxi thought, *she's a step or two down off her lofty horse.* Then it occurred to her what a drag it must be to work for a creep like Goodman Penthe and she melted a bit. "What can I do for you?" she asked the woman.

"Mr. Penthe is arriving in Los Angeles this afternoon, and he wants to know if you're free for lunch tomorrow."

"And again—" Maxi started.

"Yes, I know, Ms. Poole," the woman jumped in. "He wants to discuss Carter Rose and the Rose company."

Big surprise—what else did they have in common? Could be interesting. "I can't do lunch," she said. She didn't want to look at this guy over tuna salad. "I could see him before lunch. Late morning, say, eleven o'clock? Here at the station."

"I'm sure that'll be fine with him," Penthe's assistant said. "Give me an address, if you would. And unless you hear from me, he'll be there at eleven."

Maxi entered the appointment in her agenda book, then thought a little about last night. For about the twenty-fifth time today. And it was only nine in the morning. Richard had collected her in the newsroom after the Six, and they'd driven to Malibu for Christmas dinner with Debra and her guests, mostly interesting people from the movie world. And Debra's beautiful daughter, Gia. Maxi had been Gia's stepmom during the five years she was married to their mutual, now dead ex-husband. Couldn't have happened to a nicer guy, as Debra always said.

Dinner was fabulous, and fun. Maxi had brought an armful of presents for Gia, and a bottle of Dom Pérignon with a tin of beluga caviar tied to the neck with Christmas ribbon for Debra—to save for a night with a special guy, she'd told her. Debra gave her a see-through negligee that was way too risqué, but that was Debra. "You too, darling—for a night with a special guy," she'd said, with a pointed look at Richard.

When they got back to the station, Richard parked in the lot and came up to the newsroom with her. To prowl through the mountain of mail that had come over his transom while he was gone, he'd said. Maxi looked over the piece she'd written earlier, then went downstairs to Makeup, then onto the set to intro it. When she came back upstairs, Richard was still in his office going through paperwork. She stood in his doorway and looked in.

"So, can I come over to your house?" he'd asked without looking up. His aspect, in fact, just a little sheepish. Which was *so* not Richard. Which was enormously endearing. And she felt that annoying, delicious flutter in her stomach again. Or was it her stomach? Hard to know.

"Way too dangerous." She grinned.

"Yeah. Okay, tomorrow night. Dinner."

When she hesitated, he went on: "It's my last night in town before I go to war."

"You're going to your mother's, Richard."

"Ya, but . . . then I'm going to war. I may never come home."

"You're shameless."

"It worked during World War Two. And Korea, and Vietnam, and the Gulf War. Women worldwide—"

"Shameless!" Maxi said again. Then, "Okay. Tomorrow night."

"Great. Meet me at Mimosa at seven."

"For a guy who's only lived in L.A. for fifteen minutes, you sure know all the good restaurants."

"Guy's gotta eat," he said. He got up from his desk and started toward her, whereupon she turned and headed back to her office. She felt a newsroom clinch coming on, a very bad idea. "Tomorrow at seven," she tossed over her shoulder. "Mimosa on Beverly."

"Come on," he said with a grin, "I'll walk you down to your car."

There was no parking-lot clinch, either, Maxi thought

back dreamily. Not that she wouldn't have liked it. But they both knew better.

She was looking forward to dinner tonight.

Carter Rose sat on one of the plush leather couches in his office at Rose International, drinking coffee and reading the *L.A. Times*. Kendyl hadn't come in to the office this morning. Nor had they spoken at all yesterday, Christmas Day. He still had the little package for her that he'd intended to give her at dinner on Christmas Eve, until she blew out of Spago in a huff: a pair of very expensive diamond earrings. Three carats each. A token of his professional appreciation. And maybe a little personal appreciation. After all, they had a history. A steamy history. But it was over, the steamy part at least.

He finished reading the sports section, folded the newspaper and set it down on the coffee table in front of him, took his cell phone out of his pocket, and dialed her number. Her answering machine picked up.

"Kendyl, come to work," he said. "All is forgiven. I sat at our table in front of God and Wolf and everyone and finished the bottle of wine. Like you said, who cares what people think? Livened up Spago, what the hell. I'm going to Maui this afternoon. And you have to understand why I can't take you. But I need you at work while I'm gone. There's a lot happening. I'll be home Monday night, and I have your Christmas present for you. Okay? Call me. Please."

He hung up. Hoped that would work. Their affair was over, but he couldn't let her know that yet. He had some loose ends to tie up with Kendyl. Big, dangerous loose ends. He couldn't afford to let her stay furious with him.

Sunday Trent came over to Wendy's desk in the Channel Six newsroom and pulled up a chair beside the producer's computer terminal. "I'm here for our meeting," she said. "About your book." Classes at USC were out for Christmas week.

"Okay," Wendy said. "I've given this some thought, Sunday, and I'm going to tell you exactly what you could do for me. Then you'll tell me if that works for you. Don't forget, I can't pay you. I'll take you to lunch when my literary agent sells the book."

"No, I'll take *you* to lunch. This is very exciting," Sunday responded.

Wendy started taking her through the procedure that connected her office terminal to her computer at home where *Don't Be Dumpy* was stored, and Sunday took notes. After about a dozen steps, several of which were passworded, the directory for the book files came up on Wendy's screen in the newsroom.

"That's amazing," Sunday said. "I didn't know you could access home from here."

"Not everybody can. I have a special setup. Now, don't ever let anyone else see these files," Wendy said. "Or know my passwords."

"Of course not."

Wendy clicked on file after file, briefing Sunday. After about forty minutes she'd walked the intern through the book chapters and carefully explained everything that needed to be done.

"Got it?" she asked Sunday.

"Absolutely. I know exactly what to do. I can work on the book for a couple of hours most days I'm here. Okay?"

"Sure, okay. Better than okay," Wendy said. "But what can I do for you?"

"Help me get a part-time job when I've finished my internship. You know everybody in the business."

"Deal," Wendy said, and they shook on it.

31

Mimosa. A small, charming bistro on Beverly Boulevard in West Los Angeles. Mostly couples paying attention only to each other. Richard and Maxi sat at a table tucked in a corner of the heated, outside patio lined with ficus trees studded with tiny white lights, not only at the holiday season but all year round. Their waiter was pouring French Merlot.

"I'm glad you don't have a story for the Eleven," Richard said. "We don't have to rush."

"What time is your flight tomorrow?" Maxi asked.

"I changed my mind. I'm not going."

"Ahh. And have you mentioned this to Capra?"

"Sure. He had no problem with it. He said, Stay home, Richard, relax. Take a month off, with pay, for that grueling stretch in Afghanistan and Pakistan. He also said he's gonna give me a big fat raise."

"Right. So what time does your flight leave?"

"Four-fifteen. In the afternoon. LAX to JFK. I have to be at the airport two hours early."

"Want me to drive you?"

"What if you're on a story?"

"Capra told me I could take you. He said it'll save him sixty-five bucks on a courier."

"That's Capra. What are you having?"

Maxi perused the menu. "How does the sliced steak for two with pommes frites sound?"

"Perfect," Richard said. "Medium rare?"

"Perfect," Maxi echoed.

It *had* been a perfect Christmas, she reflected. Thanks to Richard. Had it only been three days? A relationship in a microcosm—easy to be perfect when it was only three days long, she knew. She also knew that they would never have allowed themselves to feel what they were feeling if they'd had any more than a fleeting three days. If they were looking at a normal, ongoing working relationship stretching out ahead of them, they never would have let this happen. They were both too smart to let this happen. She smiled.

"What?" Richard asked.

"The wartime syndrome," she said.

"Yes. This is our last night before—"

"Stop it."

He stopped talking but couldn't shut down the mischief in his eyes. "I *am* coming to your house after dinner tonight," he avowed. "Just to make sure you get home okay."

"I'll be fine, thank you. I have my whistle," Maxi said, fingering the silver talisman around her neck.

"Yes, but . . . I have to be there in case you blow it."

*　　　*　　　*

Richard had indeed insisted on following Maxi home. She'd protested vigorously, of course, but as she steered her Corvette up the canyon toward her house in Beverly Glen, now and then glancing in the rearview mirror at his small silver Audi behind her, she felt her blood race. *Oh, God,* she thought, *what am I doing?* Nothing, she told herself. They would have coffee. And talk. He was leaving tomorrow, on an extended assignment.

She zapped open her garage door and pulled her car inside as Richard pulled to a stop at the curb. Sprinting, he came up to her driver's-side door and helped her out of the low-slung Corvette. And took her in his arms, and kissed her. She felt herself melting into his long, dizzying kiss.

"Cof-coffee," she mumbled feebly, finally.

"Right. Coffee," he returned, and he allowed her to lead him through the door into her kitchen. He stopped her hand as she reached to switch on the lights and took her in his arms again. And kissed her again. Until they were interrupted almost immediately by the sound of paws skittering on the travertine kitchen floor. "Yukon," she murmured.

"Hi, buddy," Richard pronounced, and he snapped on the lights and stooped to roughhouse with the big, friendly malamute. "Jig's up," he said with a laugh. "Might as well make coffee."

There was coffee. And there was talk. A lot of talk at the kitchen table. Until there was a lull. And the two of them locked eyes. And Richard stood up, took her hand, and said, "I'm sorry, Maxi . . . but I'm only human. Where's the bedroom?"

* * *

Later, much later, Maxi sat curled up on the love seat in
her master bedroom, wrapped in a thick white terry-cloth
robe, watching Richard scramble for his trousers, shirt,
socks, shoes.

"I can't believe we did this," she said.

"Uh . . . will you respect me in the morning?"

"I'll pick you up at one o'clock for the airport. And I'll
let you know then."

32

Friday morning in the newsroom, 10:55 A.M. Maxi's dreamy personal reverie involving scenes from the night before was interrupted by a page over the loudspeaker. A Mr. Goodman Penthe to see her, the assignment editor blared. "Should I let him up?"

Picking up her phone, she punched in the number for the desk. "Yes, Riley, let him up. He has an appointment."

Get your mind on business, woman, she chided herself as she waited in front of the assignment desk for an intern to bring in her guest. As the two walked toward her, Maxi scrutinized the man with the bright yellow visitor's pass pinned to his suit coat. Same short, slight build that she remembered, same thinning, dyed black hair, same chalk-white face, same dour black suit, same prissy little wire-rimmed glasses. Same guy. But this very prominent man, this East Coast industrial bigwig, looked somehow even smaller here in the newsroom, on uncharted turf, than he had the night she met him at Carter Rose's house.

Maxi thanked the intern, then led Goodman Penthe into the conference room. She could still smell the damn turkey in there from two days ago. If Penthe noticed it, he didn't say anything. The two settled across from each other at the long table, and Maxi took her tape recorder out of her purse and set it on the glossy surface between them.

"Mind if we tape this?" she asked.

"Yes. I do. What I have to say has to be off the record."

Maxi pointedly glanced at her watch. "I didn't know that," she said. "We don't have a lot of time here for conversations that are off the record, Mr. Penthe—we're a news organization. Ours is a business that's *on* the record."

The reprimand was lost on Penthe, or he chose to ignore it. But Maxi didn't turn on the tape; privacy was his prerogative, after all. She just silently regretted what was probably going to be a chunk of wasted time. She'd find a way to cut it short.

"So," she said, "what's this about?"

Penthe looked around the spacious conference room, occupied at the moment by just the two of them. "Is this room private?" he asked.

"Of course. We don't bug our meetings, Mr. Penthe. And as you can see, you and I have the room to ourselves right now."

"All right," he started, though he still looked uncomfortable. But he seemed like a man who wouldn't be really comfortable anywhere, Maxi observed as she sat quietly, keeping her gaze leveled at him.

"I'm in town for due diligence on the Rose company," he said.

"Oh? Is Rose merging?"

"No. Selling, perhaps. If Carter Rose and I can come to terms."

"And this is off the record?"

"No, no, that's a matter of public record, of course, even though it hasn't been widely publicized. I've been looking at acquiring Rose International since well before Gillian Rose's death."

"And what does this have to do with us at Channel Six?"

"It has to do with you, Ms. Poole. The night I met you at Rose's home, Carter talked about you after you left. He told me you were the best investigator in the city."

"Really. With all due respect, what was Mr. Rose smoking that night? I'm a journalist, not an investigator."

Penthe actually smiled. "Well, I don't know about smoking, but he *was* drinking, I remember," he said. Maxi remembered that too. She remembered being surprised by that. She remembered thinking that the unflappable Carter Rose seemed somewhat intimidated by Goodman Penthe.

"He told me that you two were going to exchange information on his wife's death."

"Mr. Rose never gave me any information I could use, and I never had any for him that we didn't put on the news. As you probably know, there hasn't *been* much information on his wife's death."

"Well, in any case, I'd like to make that same arrangement with you. I'll tell you what I know, and you tell me what you find out."

Maxi gave an audible, slightly exasperated sigh. "Again, Mr. Penthe," she said, "I'm not an investigator. I have no interest in information about anything at all unless it's something I can use in a story for broadcast. Do you understand that?"

"All right, yes, I do—"

"Well, then," Maxi stopped him. "If that's what you came to say—"

His turn to interrupt. "Let me tell you what I think," he said. "I think Gillian Rose was murdered, and I'd like to see the murder solved. I'm in negotiations on the company, and I don't want to buy any skeletons with it, no pun intended."

Maxi mentally groaned. "What makes you think Gillian was murdered?" she asked.

"Gillian was going to divorce Carter. He cheated on her right under her nose—he's been having an affair with his assistant for years. And he has other women everywhere, in different cities, different countries. Gillian was humiliated. But she wanted to get her ducks in a row before she left him."

"What ducks?"

"Specifically, a formula that she was developing with a pharmacist she knew, her assistant's father, William Schaeffer. Gillian came to me about it. Told me she was going to leave Carter, and that the divorce would force a sale of the company in order to divide their assets."

"Why would she go to you with this?"

"Because, as I said, I was interested in purchasing Rose International. I had come out here to talk to the Roses about it a couple of times over the past year. I offered them an inflated price on the stock. Carter wouldn't hear of it; he had no interest in selling. Which didn't surprise me, of course; the Roses were young, and the company was building. I just took a flyer, as it were. Nothing ventured . . ."

"And Gillian?"

"Gillian *did* surprise me. She said nothing during our meetings; Carter did all the talking. But later she flew to Baltimore to meet with me, alone. She had me sign an affidavit of confidentiality, then told me about her plan to divorce Carter. Let me know that there definitely *would* be a sale of the company, even though her husband didn't know it yet. And she went on to tell me about a product she was developing."

"That Carter also didn't know about?"

"That Carter didn't know about. She didn't want him to know about it. After Rose International was sold, she planned to launch a new company with this product. She was convinced it was going to be a gold mine. But start-up costs—developing it and bringing it to market—are always very expensive. Her plan was to move back east, she said, leave this part of her life behind her. And she wanted me to be her partner. She wanted to use my company, my bricks and mortar, my distribution machinery, to get this product to a worldwide market. And in return, I would be half owner."

"And you were interested?"

"Very. We entered into an agreement that was to go into effect upon the sale of Rose International. And I told her that I was, of course, still interested in purchasing the business, and keeping her, without Carter, at the helm for a period of time. That was fine with her. The company would need a buyer for Gillian to realize her half of the Rose assets, and I was a viable prospect. So here was an opportunity for me to accomplish two objectives: to buy Rose International, which was my initial aim, and to enter into a promising new venture with the creative half of the Rose company, Gillian Rose. But as you can imagine, at that point in our planning, secrecy was imperative."

"How could a contract of that nature be kept secret from a man she was wed to both in business and in life?"

"Well, Gillian purposely had nothing concrete signed with William Schaeffer, just a letter of intent that she assured me wouldn't surface. She said she needed to wait until her divorce was final before formally structuring the deal with Schaeffer, because when the lawyers did the forensic assets search as part of the divorce proceedings, any and all legal contracts would certainly turn up, as you suggest. And Carter would automatically become half owner of the project."

"And what about *your* contract with Gillian? Wouldn't that show up?"

"That didn't matter. It was a simple agreement to partner on product development and production after Rose International was sold. There was no specific mention of the Schaeffer formula."

"So, now?"

"So now, with Gillian dead, there's no partnering in the offing, obviously. But I'd still like to buy Rose International. And I'd like to know who murdered Gillian."

"Why? If it *was* murder, what would it have to do with you buying the company?"

"Strictly business, Ms. Poole. I happen to think that Carter Rose murdered his wife. Maybe he found out that she was planning to leave him—if she was conveniently dead, he wouldn't have to split his assets. In any case, if Carter was facing prison, the price of the stock would plummet even farther."

"And the company would go cheaper," she said.

"Rock bottom. And I happen to be in the post position.

We have a stock sale purchase agreement in place, pending due diligence."

"Then wouldn't you be locked in to that stock price?"

"We have contingencies. Wall Street would certainly pay attention to a CEO who murdered his wife and business partner. Don't you think a consumer who's up on the news would think twice before picking up a bottle of Rose multivitamins in a health-food store?"

"Okay, so sales would dry up and the stock would plummet. Then what good would the company be to you, at any price? It could be years before—"

She stopped herself, the answer to that becoming suddenly clear. The *formula,* again! Whatever this mystery formula is, Penthe thought it was worth putting money into a fatally damaged company to get his hands on it. And evidently he thought he could get it.

Whether Penthe saw enlightenment dawn on Maxi's face or had no intention of answering that question anyway, he put both hands on the table in a we're-finished-here gesture.

And how do you know I won't run to Carter Rose with this? Maxi thought, knowing she would if it moved the story forward. She owed no loyalty to either of them. "Why are you telling me this?" she asked, just to clear the air on that point.

"Because the meter is running. I want Gillian Rose's murder solved, and Carter Rose put away."

"Does Mr. Rose know you feel this way?"

"There's no reason why he should. And I would prefer that he didn't know my theories. That said, if he finds out, it changes nothing between us. It's only business."

No wonder Carter Rose had seemed afraid of him,

Maxi thought. It occurred to her that she wouldn't want this man for an enemy. He had ice water for blood.

"And you think I can help. Why?" she asked.

She already knew the answer to that one, too. Why would somebody like the inscrutable Goodman Penthe suddenly become Mr. Loquacious in the Channel Six conference room? Why would this business magnate personally come into the station two days after Christmas to tell her his story? Why did most strangers tell her their stories? To influence what she put on the air, of course, in the second-largest news market in the nation.

"Because the police aren't doing anything," was his answer.

"Have you told them any of this?"

"I tried. Couldn't get their attention."

"Carter Rose thinks Gillian was murdered too. And he wants to find the killer."

"Tell him to look in the mirror."

Maxi said nothing.

"It's a helluva story for you, Ms. Poole," Penthe summed up. And with that—no good-bye, no nice to see you, no happy New Year, no go to hell—he got up and exited the conference room.

Don't let the door hit you in the ass, Maxi thought as she watched his back sail out of there. Creep. *And with Gillian Rose dead, you've got the inside track for a shot at William Schaeffer's solid-gold formula, whatever it is.*

"What was *that* about?" Wendy asked Maxi after, as she put it, an abbreviated dervish blasted out of the conference room, stormed across the newsroom, and slammed out the door.

"A man who isn't used to people not toadying up to him: Goodman Penthe," Maxi told her. She'd stopped over at Wendy's desk and pulled up a chair beside her.

"Oh, I heard Riley paging you that he was here. So what did your nervous visitor have to say?"

"He said he's convinced that Gillian Rose was murdered, and that Carter Rose did the deed. He says he told the detectives but they didn't care."

"So he probably has nothing to back up the yarn he's peddling. Does he have any reason to want Carter Rose to go down?"

"Bingo. It has to do with grabbing up Rose International cheap. This guy is a consummate conglomerate shark."

"Did he give you anything that moves the story forward?"

"Nothing he'd go on the record with. But some anecdotal stuff that's maybe worth a little digging into. What have we got archived on the Rose story?"

"Let's look," Wendy said, and she clicked over her computer keys to call up the directory of all tapes that were slugged ROSE.

"Umm, a bunch of news conferences: one with Carter Rose, one with the ME, several with the Robbery-Homicide detectives, one with the LAPD on Sandie Schaeffer. Your updates on Schaeffer's attempts to speak in the hospital. Some tape featuring exteriors of the Rose building, including an aerial from the chopper. Also, Carter Rose at LAX, and your quickie with him in the Rose International conference room on the morning of the Sandie Schaeffer attack. Plus the illegal stuff Har-

baugh shot inside Gillian's office the day she died—
that's in the dead file."

"I forgot about that tape in the dead file. Might be
worth revisiting. Can you print out a shot list on that
footage? If Pete okays it, I'll do a scan."

"You got it." Wendy clicked on the PRINT button and
her printer served up the shot sheet. "Want me to look at
that tape with you?"

"That'd be great. And let's ask Capra to view it with
us. He's got a great nose."

"You're dreaming."

"Yeah, I suppose so. If we find anything that might actually be something, we'll bring it to him."

"Good plan. I have to write a couple of readers for the
Noon, then I've got some time."

"Then you've got your lunch hour, you mean."

"Who eats lunch?"

"Good point. I'll reserve us an edit room. Oh," Maxi
said, lowering her voice as her eyes drifted across the
aisle to Sunday Trent hunched over a computer terminal.
"How's Sunday doing on the book rewrites?"

"Really good," Wendy said. "I can't believe she's
working so hard on the project, and doing such a great
job. She's become invaluable, doing legwork I don't have
time to do. She's researched and analyzed all the new
menu ingredients, interviewed Dr. Balthasar on audiotape, transcribed everything, pulled the pertinent quotes.
I don't know what I'd do without her."

"What's she doing here on a Friday morning? Isn't she
in school?"

"Christmas break."

"Oh, right. Well, shouldn't she be on a ski trip with her

boyfriend? Going to Fort Lauderdale with friends? Visiting her family in Chicago? Something?"

"You'd think so. Gorgeous young person . . . go figure. She's here day and night, between her internship hours and my project."

"Odd," Maxi commented. "Okay, I'm going to get Capra to give me a release on this tape," she said, gesturing with the shot-sheet printout from the dead file. "Then I'll nail down an editor. See you in a bit."

33

Some hot-looking babe," Pete Capra commented.

Wendy and Maxi exchanged disgusted glances. "She's dead, boss," Wendy said flatly. The three were sitting in an edit bay—the body of Gillian Rose was up in freeze-frame on four screens.

"Is now the time to have that women-to-man talk with Pete?" Maxi asked Wendy.

"Seems so."

"Pete," Maxi followed up, "you're sexist. And it's going to get you in big trouble."

"I'm not sexist," Capra said. "I'm Italian."

"You can't behave like that in today's business world," Wendy put in.

"Behave like what?" Pete asked, with an innocent look.

"You can't call Gillian Rose a hot-looking babe, whether she's dead or alive," Wendy answered, exuding exasperation.

"But she *is* a hot-looking babe, dead or alive," he said.

Wendy looked at Maxi. "I give up," she said.

"Don't give up. It's just going to take longer than we thought."

"And we've only booked this edit machine for a half hour," from Wendy.

"So, getting back to business," Maxi said, "what color are Gillian's eyes?"

"They're—"

"No, no, Wendy, not you," Maxi cut her off. "Of course you know what color Gillian Rose's eyes are— you're a woman. Pete, let me ask you, what color are Elizabeth Taylor's eyes?"

"How the hell do I know?" Pete tossed out.

"What about Paul Newman's legendary eyes?"

"What kind of a test is this?"

"See what I mean, Wendy? Women know that Liz Taylor's eyes are violet and Paul Newman's eyes are blue. And we know what color Gillian Rose's eyes are, because they're just as famous. Okay, Pete, you take a look at Gillian's eyes in this frame. Can you see what color they are?"

"No," Pete said.

"Can we enhance?" she asked Jack Worth, their editor. "Just the eyes."

"Sure," the editor said, and he isolated the eyes of Gillian Rose with an electronic white dotted line, then started pushing buttons. The pixels zoomed in, the image getting larger with each click.

"Hold it right there," Pete Capra said. "Okay. So her eyes are brown. With black flecks. So what?"

Wendy was staring at the image in astonishment. It

was well known that Gillian Rose had famously brilliant blue eyes.

Maxi was staring too. *This is what I saw the day she died,* she thought to herself. *And it has to have something to do with William Schaeffer's formula for glaucoma medication.*

Maxi called Richard on her cell phone. He told her he'd be right down. She was waiting in her car in front of his apartment building in Marina del Rey. It was a glossy, needle high-rise occupied predominantly by upscale singles, with a brilliant view of the Marina: inlets with hundreds of colorful boats at their moorings, and still more boats bobbing brightly on the blue Pacific. Idly she watched the Southern California "beautiful people" coming and going.

When Richard pushed out of the bronze front doors of the building—tall, angular, in tweed sports coat and chinos, sandy hair blowing, suitcase in hand, laptop bag slung over his shoulder, topcoat on his arm—her heart skipped a beat.

He spotted her Corvette and his face lit up. "Hey," he said.

"Hey," she said back. He opened the passenger door, pulled the seat forward, tossed his bags and his coat into the hatch, and settled himself inside. Maxi started the car and headed for the airport.

"That's all you're bringing for what could be a long war?" she asked him.

"What do I need? A few clothes, toothbrush, razor, camera, laptop."

Maxi chuckled, thinking about what a woman would pack. "It's freezing in New York," she said.

"Got my coat. I'll pick up a pair of gloves there."

"Do you have clothes at your mother's?"

"No. After I got back from college and got settled in an apartment there, I called my mom to tell her I was coming by to pick up my stuff. She said I didn't have any stuff. I said of course I had stuff, everybody has stuff. What stuff? she asked. And actually, I couldn't think of any."

"Simple needs," Maxi said.

"Uhh . . . about last night—"

"Yes?" Maxi interrupted, glancing over at him.

"Well . . ."

"I had a good time. Did you?"

"Uhh . . . ya, but . . ."

"Ya, but, that's all. You're going to war, remember?"

"Maxi—"

She put a hand on his arm to stop him. "It's okay, Richard. Don't worry about it. Please." Then she added, "And don't tell anybody."

They both understood that last night was a subject better left alone, and they tacitly agreed to agree on that.

"So," Maxi said, "you've got good flying weather." She gave his arm a squeeze, then put both hands back on the wheel and focused on her driving.

34

Maxi headed back from the airport as the afternoon crush on the 405 was building. Traffic was the worst on Friday afternoons.

Her car felt empty. So did her love life. But the specific logistics of the situation happened to be a blessing. She told herself again that a full-on relationship with a colleague was not possible, period. In fact, last night would definitely never have happened if Richard hadn't been going away today—far away, and for a long time. Funny, she thought, the "going off to war" analogy they'd joked about wasn't far from the truth.

She wondered what Richard was thinking, strapped into his seat in a 767 waiting to take off. Same thing, she guessed. She'd asked him if there was anything he wanted her to take care of for him while he was gone. The nurturing woman part of her, actually craving the connection. She knew the answer in advance, and didn't really expect or want a different one.

His mail would be forwarded to his business manager this time, he'd said, to be sorted, dealt with, or shipped to him if necessary. Beyond that, he didn't really need anything, and his inference was that he liked it that way. This morning he had given his four house plants to the woman next door. Mindy something, a lawyer. She said she'd take care of them until he got back. He told her to just enjoy them. Meaning he couldn't be sure they would ever have a home with him again. He canceled his cleaning lady. What's to clean? he'd said. And besides, he was more comfortable knowing that nobody would be going inside his place. When he got back she'd come in and dust. Simple needs.

Then Maxi thought about him in bed with her last night. Was it really just last night? It seemed like a long time ago. She shook it off. What was there to think about? Except, she reflected, allowing herself a slight smile as she maneuvered up the crowded freeway on her way back to the station, except it was delicious.

She pulled her cell phone out of her purse, asked Information to connect her to Schaeffer Pharmacy in Westwood, got Mr. Schaeffer on the line, and asked him if he could meet her after the Six O'clock News. He suggested that she come to Cedars, to the ICU. Sandie was talking a lot now, and he was spending as much time with her as he could. Maxi said she'd be there.

Midafternoon on Friday. Kendyl Scott was back at her desk at work. And Carter Rose was in Maui. She'd returned his call yesterday, told him that she forgave him. That was a joke. Forgive him for a huge wasted chunk of her life? But she needed to work this out from inside the castle walls. From her long-held, front-row-center seat to his life. He wanted to appease her, and she knew why. She resolved to use her leverage. She'd either get him for good or she'd make him pay.

He'd called her half a dozen times since he went to Maui. How are you? How's everything going? I'm bored out of my mind here. Today, a long, dreary seminar on the virtues and the downsides of antioxidants. You don't know how much I appreciate you holding down the fort at the company. We'll have dinner on Monday night when I get home; I can't wait to give you your Christmas present. And you know what *I* want for Christmas, baby—it's been way too long.

Kendyl was all out of illusions. She didn't believe for a minute that Carter was bored in Maui. Or that he was pining for her. In fact, if she were honest with herself, she'd admit that she'd felt the juice draining out of their relationship even before Gillian died. But he needed her now. And she would use that need for all it was worth. They were inexorably tied together, she figured, because each one would always know what the other one did that night.

Question to herself: Knowing everything she knew, did she still love him? She sighed. Fact was, that didn't really matter.

The Hawaiian evening was sultry, still, and fragrant, imbued with the lush dissonance of whispering trees, nocturnal wildlife, and the ever-drumming surf. Carter Rose reclined on the broad terrace of his suite at the beautiful Kea Lani, gazing out toward the ocean beyond the palm-lined beach, the day's *New York Times* on his lap, a vodka martini in his hand, and the sounds of Verdi faint in the background.

Everything was under control. Kendyl was back in the fold. Sandie Schaeffer was non compos mentis. And Penthe was in Los Angeles with his due-diligence team. This Maui conference held nothing for him, really; it was just a place for him to be to stay out of Goodman's way for the time being. And a pretty damned wonderful place it was.

He took a sip of his drink. Kendyl. They were certainly in bed together right now, figuratively speaking. But the way he saw it, after a little distance from all of it, he could cut the cord. Still, there was no reason to get her incensed; he'd been playing with fire that night at Spago. Or with sparks, at least. Best to keep everything calm with her, fully contained. Like with a wildfire.

The doorbell to his suite sounded its chimes. "Come in, sweet Leilani," he called. "Door's open."

35

Again, a uniformed LAPD patrol officer stood outside Sandie Schaeffer's small room in the Intensive Care Unit at Cedars. The patient was actually sitting up in bed. Her father watched her solicitously from his wheelchair. Dr. Stevens was perusing her chart, making notes. A nurse stood on tiptoes, changing one of her IV pouches.

"She's having a very good day," Bill Schaeffer said by way of greeting Maxi. "She's been talking. And making sense." He was beaming.

Maxi settled into a chair in the corner of the small ICU room and studied the patient. Propped up on pillows. Looking tired but semi-aware. Eyes focused ahead in the middle distance. Some color in her cheeks. Saying nothing. But seeming to listen.

"Maxi Poole is here," her father said.

"Hi, Sandie," Maxi put in.

No audible response, but her eyes flickered and Maxi knew she'd heard.

"You look wonderful," she said. And Sandie's gaze slowly shifted over to her.

"She does look good, doesn't she," the doctor said, a statement rather than a question.

"I'm glad to see you sitting up, Sandie," Maxi went on, encouraging the patient.

At that, Sandie whispered, "Maxi Poole."

"Yes. How are you feeling?" Maxi ventured.

"Feeling . . . fine," the patient mouthed with what seemed like great effort.

Maxi's eyes scanned the small hospital room and settled on some brightly wrapped packages on the side table. "Maybe you can open your holiday presents soon," she said, to encourage the patient to talk.

To Maxi's astonishment, Sandie launched into a halting, stream-of-consciousness riff about Chanukah and Christmas. How she and her mother and father had always celebrated both, observed the Jewish festival of lights and also had a Christmas tree. She talked about presents she'd loved. And the music, the food, the fun. Nobody in the room dared breathe. When she trailed off, she settled back into the pillows and closed her eyes. Which seemed to signal that she was finished, at least for now.

"Isn't this remarkable?" her father said quietly.

"It's wonderful," Maxi breathed.

"I'm glad you came," he said. "You seem to bring her out."

"I told you, I'll be here any time you think I can help," Maxi offered.

Sandie Schaeffer knew something. She saw something the night she was attacked, and Maxi wanted to be there when she was finally able to talk about it coherently. It would be an explosive story, and she'd have an exclusive.

"She's tired now," Dr. Stevens said. "It's enough for today. Why don't you go home and get some rest, Bill."

"Thanks, Doctor," Schaeffer said. And to Maxi, "Let's go get a cup of coffee."

The cafeteria at Cedars, on the ground floor of the sprawling medical center, was more than half filled with visitors and hospital personnel. Bill Schaeffer wheeled over to a table in the middle of the room and came to a stop, but Maxi beckoned him to keep going. He followed her in his chair, past the metallic palm trees on the wall, to a booth at the far end that had just been vacated. "A little privacy here," she said. "What'll you have, Mr. Schaeffer? I'll go fetch."

"Black coffee," he said.

"Don't you want a bite?"

"What about you?" he asked.

"Sure, this'll be dinner."

They settled on grilled ham and cheese sandwiches and green salads. Schaeffer had coffee and Maxi had tea. She'd brought the tray over to the booth and set out their food and drinks. Schaeffer had pulled his wheelchair up to the table, and Maxi scooted into the banquette against the wall. The two ate slowly, making small talk, mostly about Sandie's progress. Then Maxi got to it.

"Your formula for glaucoma, Mr. Schaeffer—"

"Please, call me Bill."

"Bill. Can it change the color of a person's eyes?"

"Yes," he said. "It can turn the iris brown. But it doesn't happen all the time. Maybe a third of the time."

There it was. "Did you ever give any of the product to Gillian Rose?" she asked him.

"Yes, early on. She wanted to do a parallel analysis with Xalatan in her own labs, make sure there were enough dissimilarities to ensure getting a patent."

"And you *trusted* her with it?"

"Well, sure. She said if we couldn't get a patent, there was no reason for her to go forward. She wanted to clear that up right away, before she wasted any time or money. That seemed reasonable to me."

"Did she tell you the results of her testing?"

"No. I assume she didn't have results yet."

"And like Xalatan, is your formula highly contaminative?"

"No, it isn't. That's one of its strong points. After a lot of experimenting I came up with a cocktail of three nearly inert elements that together render my drug much more stable than what's now on the market. When it's perfected it'll be easy to handle, which is a major hurdle with this medication."

"How much of it did you give to Gillian?"

"One vial."

"And when you gave it to her had the contamination factor already been eliminated?"

"Not fully. Not to the extent that it is now. But I did warn her about it. And she had my papers on the testing process. None of the material has been published yet, but every change has been meticulously documented along the way, and Gillian had all the literature. She knew about the contamination problem."

"Do you have any reason to believe she might have used the product on herself?"

"Why would she do that?"

"Did you specifically tell her not to?"

"No, but it wasn't necessary. It would be like giving

you a can of arsenic to poison rats in your attic and telling you, By the way, don't eat this stuff. Gillian wasn't stupid. We weren't even at patent-pending status yet, and she knew exactly what we were dealing with."

"Mr. Schaeffer . . . Bill . . . Gillian's bright blue eyes were something like a dark, inky brown when she died."

Schaeffer looked at her in silence, his intelligent eyes clouding over. "How do you know that?" he asked finally.

"I was there that morning. I saw her body less than an hour after they found her. And my cameraman shot tape. We enhanced it, and there's no mistaking that her eyes had turned a smoky, unnatural brown."

Schaeffer looked visibly troubled. "I don't know what to say. I find it hard to believe . . ."

"Could your drug have killed her?"

"No. But it could have impaired her vision if it wasn't handled properly."

"Let me ask you something. In the one-third or so cases that you say might experience a change of eye color, would that change be temporary or permanent?"

"Well, we're far from completing the double-blind studies to know for sure, but at this point I'm thinking it would be temporary."

36

Moving efficiently from place to place, Maxi produced her piece for nightside. She wrote the track in her office, voiced it in the recording studio, viewed the tape and cut it back in an edit bay, and dashed off the ins and outs at a vacant computer terminal in front of the assignment desk.

Wendy was producing the Eleven tonight, so Maxi waited for the show to start ensconced in her favorite spot out in the noisy newsroom. She'd pulled up a chair next to Wendy's desk, Wendy having the storied ability to produce the show, write the readers, monitor her crews in the field, check over the reporters' pieces, keep her eye on the clock, and gossip at the same time.

"So whaddaya think?" she asked Maxi now. "Foul play?"

"Hard to know. If not foul play, incredible negligence."

They were talking through Maxi's story, a six-year-old boy found dead in a residential swimming pool in Brentwood, where he'd attended a kids' pool party two days before. The question was, had his body been there the whole time, the result of an accidental drowning, or was he killed somewhere else and his body dumped there? The police, the homeowners, neighbors, and others said they couldn't possibly have overlooked his little body slumped in a corner of the deep end of the pool, even though the pool was murky. Big human interest. If this case didn't go to criminal court, it would most certainly go to civil court and be widely covered on local TV news, as well as on the cable channels and radio talk shows.

Reporter Laurel Baker came out of an edit room and pulled up a chair beside them. "So what's up, ladies?" she asked.

"I recut the Ayala boy for the Eleven," Maxi told her.

"Was he murdered?" Laurel asked.

"Don't know. A strange story."

"I interviewed Gregor tonight," Laurel said. "I can't believe he talked to me." Wayne Gregor was the LAFD fire captain and arson investigator who'd just been charged with setting fires in retail stores. It always amazed journalists that even foursquare criminal types seemed to love seeing themselves on television.

"What'd he say?" Wendy asked as she continued to click away at her keyboard, writing the lead for the show.

"He sez he didn't do it," Laurel said. "And he'll be exonerated in court."

"We've heard that tune before," Wendy observed dryly. "We'll lead the second block with it. A minute-fifteen total, Laurel, with ins and outs."

"You gotta give me a minute-forty-five," Laurel begged. Laurel always wanted more air time.

"He's a talking head," Wendy pronounced. "You don't

have the other side. No DA, no victims, no colleagues from the fire department, nobody. A minute-fifteen is all I'm giving Gregor."

Laurel heaved a terribly-put-upon sigh.

"Tomorrow's the arraignment," Wendy said. "This one'll mushroom—they'll be coming out of the walls to rat him out next week. You'll get your face time, Laurel."

"So," Laurel tossed out, rallying, "have you two heard the latest?"

"What latest?" Maxi asked. Laurel was consummately plugged into the newsroom grapevine.

"After yea many decades, the suits are going to take a pass on Reordan." Anchorman Rob Reordan's contract was up, and he was currently in negotiations.

"I thought they were talking," Wendy put in.

"They're asking him to take a pay cut," Laurel explained. "A huge pay cut. Less than half."

"That's the way of the business in this economy," Maxi said. "It's still a lot of money. He should go for it."

"Too much pride," from Laurel.

"Rob's gotta have more money than Oprah by now," Wendy piped up. "An L.A. icon for half a century. Since television news began, practically. He always made the big bucks. He's a hundred years old, for God's sake. He should give it a rest."

"Too many ex-wives to support, too many kids to educate," Laurel said. "He lives in a condo at the beach. Doesn't even have any decent furniture, just college-dorm crap from Ikea."

"How do you know that?" from Maxi.

"He lured me over there one weekend on the pretext of having proof about the mayor's chief of staff taking kickbacks from government contractors. He said I couldn't say who it came from and he couldn't bring his notes into the station—"

"So he got you in his crib and he tried to seduce you," Wendy finished for her.

"Couldn't believe it," Laurel said. "All I could do was laugh."

"No story?" Maxi asked.

"Of course no story," Laurel said. "But that's when I saw his beach condo, decorated with fishnet and lava lamps."

"I'm sure he likes it that way," Wendy said. "Makes him feel young."

Wendy Harris was not one of anchorman Rob Reordan's biggest fans. At this point in his life and career, Rob more or less phoned it in. He refused to cover stories, never offered story ideas, didn't get involved in series planning, didn't bother to attend meetings. He just ambled in twenty minutes before his shows, went to Makeup, had his beautiful white hair sprayed down, slid behind the anchor desk, and read the words off the TelePrompTer. But Los Angeles loved him, so the station had never wanted to let him go. Until now, evidently.

"Did he actually tell you they were going to drop him if he doesn't take the pay cut?" Maxi asked Laurel.

"Oh, yeah. Get this: He cried. Between asking me to have dinner with him. God, I'd like to take his mirror home with me for just one night, see what he sees. Talk about supreme ego!"

"So, are you seeing anyone, Laurel?" Wendy asked.

"No. As you women know, I've had two marriages and three live-ins. My new motto is: I'm dying to be intimate with a guy who'll leave me alone."

Maxi and Wendy laughed. On some level, they could relate. There was never enough time.

Sunday Trent called over from her computer station, "Wendy, after the show, check out *DBD*. I've reorganized all the menus into day plans."

"Terrific. Thanks, Sunday," Wendy called back. And to Maxi, "The book's coming along great. My agent can't believe how fast we're getting it done, and it's definitely because of Sunday—she's tireless."

"Does this big New York agent have a name?" Laurel asked.

"Robin," Wendy said, beaming. "Robin Ruell. I love her. She's so *reasonable*. Not to mention encouraging and helpful."

"Big surprise—she's a woman," Laurel said archly.

"Laurel, you've got to stop man-bashing," Maxi said.

"Why?" Laurel asked, putting on an innocent face.

"Because it's *so* last year," Wendy tossed at her.

It was exactly twenty minutes before airtime. They looked up to see Rob Reordan, the just-dished Eleven O'-clock anchor, strolling through the door from what must have been a fabulous dinner. He looked anchorly, avuncular, and trustworthy, in a well-cut three-piece suit, his complexion ruddy, a smile on his face. As usual, he would have just enough time to pick up his messages, go down to Makeup, skid across the hall to the set, sit down behind the anchor desk, and pick up the script in front of him before the stage manager pointed his fingers and said, "In five, four, three, two . . ."

"You'd think he could give us ten frigging minutes to read through the script in advance instead of bumbling through it cold on the air," Wendy groused dully to the two women.

"Yeah, then he could *ask* one of us how to pronounce Yemen instead of calling it 'yay-man' on the air," Laurel snipped.

"Give the guy a break—the viewers love him," Maxi said, though she couldn't help smiling. She knew that, say what they would, Rob Reordan was not about to change his work habits at this late date. Nor would he be happy with a contract that didn't give him a big raise and his exclusive perks, including his company Rolls-Royce and his company credit card for unlimited dinners at L.A.'s finest restaurants. With Reordan, free was good, and image was everything.

After her piece ran, Maxi went upstairs to the newsroom to wait for the Eleven to get off the air and Wendy to come up from the booth, so they could do their usual post-show kibitzing. She walked back to her office to grab her jacket and saw the message light blinking on her phone. Dropping into her desk chair, she hit the red MES-SAGE button. And was startled to hear the same raspy whisper that had delivered the last threatening message: "I told you not to pump Sandie Schaeffer—you were there tonight. This is your last warning." Click.

"My God," Maxi said aloud to her empty office, "it has to be someone who *works* there."

She picked up the phone to call Capra at home.

37

Maxi never slept this late—10:42 A.M.—but she'd been in the newsroom until three in the morning. Pete Capra had driven in from his home in the Valley, listened to the latest threatening message with her, again got a technician to lift a copy, and had an officer from the Burbank PD come over and pick it up at the station for delivery to Detective Skip Henders. After the officer left, Capra said, "You're off the story, Maxi."

"But, boss, I'm so *close*. This message just *proves* I'm close."

"Close is no good if you're dead."

"C'mon, Pete. You know I'm careful—"

"Then at least stay out of the hospital."

"But how can I—"

"*Stay out of Cedars, Maxi*. If I find out you went back there, *I'll* threaten you."

Maxi knew when Pete meant business. She left the newsroom, got in her car, drove home, talked a little to

Yukon, and went to bed. But couldn't sleep. She kept sifting through events of the story, then sifting through the players, trying to match them up. The last time she'd glanced at her bedside clock before dropping off to sleep, the digital readout said 4:52 A.M.

Now half the morning was gone. But it was the weekend. And by some miracle, Yukon hadn't tried to wake her up early. She watched him watching her as he stretched his paws in front of him, lying a few feet away from her on the bedroom area rug. Maybe he knew how exhausted she was. More likely he'd tried to wake her up but couldn't, and gave it up.

She needed to get her mind off the story and the second creepy, anonymous message that had come in last night. She pulled herself out of bed, dressed in sweats and running shoes, put Yukon on his leash, and took the boy out for a walk.

And forced her mind onto mundane concerns. Here it was, another Saturday night without a date. What else was new? Not that men didn't ask her out. She was impossibly exacting, she knew, when it came to men. She'd been married once. Didn't want to make another mistake. And didn't want to waste time with men who didn't interest her. A friend once told her that the rule was you have to go out with a man three times to know how you feel about him. Maxi knew in the first three minutes. *Call me shallow,* she thought, *but I know as soon as I look through my peephole and see the guy coming up the walk with flowers in his hand.*

Back home at nearly noon, she found a message from Richard on the answering machine in her study: "Hi. I'm here. It's freezing, but I love New York. My mother's feeding me leftover turkey. Ever hear of turkey croquettes? A new one on me. Fried cones of mashed turkey with some kind of sauce on top. Never, never order it if you see it on a menu. She's having all her friends over to show them she really does have a son. I'm taking her to see *The Producers* tonight. I did a profile on Mel Brooks back in his *Men in Tights* days, and he still takes care of me. Anyway, Mom's out doing the after-Christmas sales now, and I'm going over to the West Side to play handball with a couple of buds at the Y. So take care, Maxi, and thanks a lot for getting me to the airport yesterday."

Decidedly unboyfriendlike. But that was best, wasn't it? That was what they'd both agreed on. She had mixed feelings about it, but maybe that was because she was looking at yet another Saturday night with a glass of wine, Yukon, and a Sue Grafton mystery. *Q Is for Quarry.* In her case, Maxi observed to herself, Q was for Quiet. No bells, no whistles, zero fireworks in her life.

She allowed herself a mini-daydream about Richard, of the two of them together only two nights ago, and she felt the usual tingle in the usual places. Just checking to make sure everything was still working, she told herself, and chuckled. Then she listened to his message again.

Then she closed her eyes and shook her head and yelled at herself for being such an idiot. Then opened them wide and stomped her index finger on the ERASE button to delete his message. Then immediately wished she hadn't.

The phone rang. Gratefully she snatched it up. It was Joe Crighton on the weekend assignment desk at work. There was a William Schaeffer on the line, trying to get ahold of her, he said.

"He's okay—give him my home number," Maxi told him. She hung up and stared at the phone for a minute until it rang. *Saved by the proverbial ring-a-ding,* she thought, and grabbed it.

"Yes, Bill. This is Maxi."

"I wanted to let you know that Sandie's coming home tomorrow. The police told us about the new message you got last night. We think she'll be safer at home."

"But . . . can you manage?"

"Yes."

"How are you going to—"

"She's so much better, Maxi. She ate on her own this morning for the first time: scrambled eggs. And she kept saying she wants to go home. So Dr. Stevens said as long as someone is with her around the clock, she can go. Not to her own apartment, of course—to my house. The house where she grew up."

Schaeffer sounded determined. But he was in a wheelchair, after all, and Maxi worried about his ability to take care of his daughter in a crisis. "You're sure you can handle it?" she asked.

"Definitely. They're moving her out of the ICU into a regular room today while they process her out. I hired a private-duty nurse—she's coming over to the hospital now to spend some time with Sandie and learn her routine. She'll come to the house at noon every day when I leave for work, and stay until I'm finished at the store. And I'll come home every evening and have dinner with Sandie. Then I'll go back to the store for a couple of hours and close up."

"Sounds like you've got it covered," Maxi said, holding back the further reservations she had.

"I think so," Schaeffer said. "I know her IVs and her meds, and the nurse will too. Otherwise, there's not that much caretaking. As I said, she ate solid food this morning, and she got up and used the bathroom. Tomorrow she'll be stronger, Dr. Stevens says. And a little stronger every day."

"Let me know how I can help," Maxi offered.

"That's why I'm calling. She's said your name again. Several times since you visited yesterday."

"And she's talking more?" Maxi asked. Her subtext said, Is her brain working? And Bill Schaeffer knew that.

"Yes, she's talking more, though she has what they call selective memory loss. But here's the good news: Her tests show no brain damage, just disassociated amnesia. That's when traumatic events impair memory. She knows me, she knows people, she knows she's in the hospital, and she wants to go home. But she can't remember anything involving the night she was shot, or some of what went on before that. She doesn't know that Gillian Rose is dead. She's said a couple of times that she has to get back to work or Gillian will be way behind."

"I've heard of that syndrome, short-term amnesia," Maxi said. "Will that memory block come back, do they know?"

"Stevens says there's no way of knowing. For some patients the trauma recedes and recollections come rolling back to them, like they're coming out of a fog. It could take days, or decades. Others never recall the trauma-induced events, or the block of memory loss they produced. Whatever happens for Sandie, he says she might as well be where she's comfortable right now. He thinks she'll do better at home with me. And I'll be a lot more comfortable about her safety."

"Will they continue the twenty-four-hour police guard at your home?"

"That's their call, and they made the decision to drop

it when Sandie leaves the hospital. My address is private, and the house has good dead bolts, and an alarm system. But if anything at all happens, they'll reinstate a police guard at the house, they told me."

"Bill . . . what if something comes up that you can't handle?"

Again, he read her subtext: You're in a wheelchair. You have all you can do to take care of yourself. You can drive, but you couldn't lift Sandie into your car. There are a lot of things you can't do.

"I talked that over with her doctor," Schaeffer answered. "If an emergency comes up, large or small, I'll call nine-one-one. Get the paramedics out. And get her back to Cedars, if necessary."

"You also have a business to run," Maxi reminded him.

"Benny will open up for me, and he'll stay till I get back from dinner every night. I think we're going to do fine. Will you come visit? I live in the Palisades."

"Of course. You have my numbers. Just give a shout when you get Sandie settled in and I'll make arrangements with you to come by."

38

Saturday night. Maxi was in her Corvette headed over the hill to the sprawling San Fernando Valley, to the Cineplex on the Universal Studios lot. Wendy had called earlier and asked what she was doing. Oh, exciting Saturday-night things, she'd said. Putting together some series ideas—the February sweeps were four weeks away. The three "sweeps" months, February, May, and November, generated the ratings on which stations based the cost of their commercials to advertisers. In those months, viewers were inundated with so-called sweeps series, which were usually provocative and always heavily advertised. *Dark Sex in Southland Nunnery,* that kind of thing. Lord help us. But there was major pressure on everyone in the television news business to win the sweeps months ratings; jobs and salaries depended on it.

"How about a series on why women think they need to have a date on Saturday night?" Wendy had quipped.

"Easy. It's our nature," Maxi said. "A built-in primal drive to further procreation and keep the species going."

"But what about today's woman? Can't she suppress that, for her own *personal* well-being?"

"Don't think so," Maxi had said. Heaven knew, she was trying.

"How about we just line up some fab women—single women, like lawyers, waitresses, teachers, real estate agents, women in health care—and just ask them what's the deal here. Get their statements on this vital issue in twenty-five words or less. Why do these successful, creative, productive women think they need a man in their lives?"

"And we'll interview a bunch of shrinks on the subject to butt to their statements," Maxi put in.

"Women shrinks?"

"Women, men—*therapists*. Doesn't matter. We have to be objective."

"You know," Wendy said, "we're kidding, but this could actually be a very popular series. Think about it." It was a fact of television news that the two series subjects that always got the biggest ratings were diets and relationships. In that order.

"Want to take in a movie later?" Wendy had asked.

"Sure. What do you want to see?"

"They're rerunning *The Ya-Ya Sisterhood* at Universal. Did you see it?"

"Nope. Read the book, missed the movie."

"Well, let's go see it. Because we are latter-day Ya-Yas."

Maxi thought about that hypothetical sweeps series idea as she rolled down Beverly Glen to Ventura Boulevard. And she thought about Richard. The problem with her particular relationship status was that she wanted to be with a man who was off limits, and wanting to be with him made her not open to a nice guy who might be available to her. A Catch-22 situation. Someday maybe she'd figure it out. Maybe she and Wendy should actually do that series. Maybe they'd learn something.

After the movie, Maxi and Wendy wandered over to City Walk, Universal Studios' futuristic village all ablaze in hot pink, sunburst orange, lime green, purple, raspberry, and lemon neon—signs in motion, fountains spurting, music blaring. The place was teeming with Saturday nightlife: young people on dates, families with kids, gay couples strolling, singles looking to meet and greet. The two ducked into Dizzy's for a glass of wine.

They spotted Doug Kriegel a few tables over, sipping ice cream sodas with his wife and two boys. Wendy yelled to them over the jukebox and the general din. All four Kriegels enthusiastically waved back.

"Now *that's* a family," Maxi said to Wendy.

"Yup. Jealous?"

"A little. I envy what he has. Doug is so centered."

"So . . . someday," Wendy pronounced with a great big "maybe" smile.

"Who knows? Who knows if I even really want that. Do you?"

"No. I don't have time."

"Oh, come on—"

"No, seriously," Wendy protested. "I don't mean that I don't have time for some lovely evenings like they're having," she said with a nod toward the Kriegels. "What I don't have time for is the aggravation. And Maxi, we both know that there's *always* the aggravation."

Maxi thought about Richard for a minute. She couldn't even imagine him annoying her, or fighting with her. Would he? Would she get on his nerves? Would he bore her after a while? Not possible, she was sure of it. Ha. Beginnings were always pie in the sky.

Wendy was looking at her with narrowed eyes. "Don't even *think* about it," she said.

"About *what?*"

"You know what. Don't even think about getting into a relationship with a certain good-looking stud reporter."

"Wendy, how could you even—"

"How could I *not!*" Wendy interrupted. "You know I know you, Max—it's a Ya-Ya thing. And I repeat: Don't even *think* about it."

"I'm not," Maxi insisted, knowing that she was having a hard time thinking about anything else.

The Kriegels bopped over to their table on their way out of the restaurant. There were big hi's, air kisses, and high fives tossed around. Doug's wife Barbro was a Swedish beauty, graceful and serene, while the kids were two bundles of compressed energy.

"Maxi, let's grab a bite on Monday night after the Six," Doug said. "Barb's taking the kids to her mom's in San Francisco tomorrow for the rest of Christmas break, and I've got some interesting stuff for you on Rose International."

"You're on," Maxi said.

"Musso's?" Everybody knew that the legendary Musso & Frank on Hollywood Boulevard was Doug Kriegel's favorite restaurant.

"Okay," Maxi said. "I'll meet you there at seven-thirty."

"At your own risk," Barbro said to Maxi with a twinkle, and the kids broke out in spasms of laughter. Dinner with Kriegel was always an adventure. His appetite was as gigantic as his hearty laugh, and he usually ended up eating his, yours, and some from the next table if he could get away with it.

"I'll take care of him Monday night," Maxi told Barbro and the kids. "But otherwise he's on his own. Don't stay away too long, you guys."

"Petey will take care of Dad," one of the boys piped up, and they both dissolved into laughter again. Petey was the family's six-pound Maltese poodle.

"These kids are *so* Doug," Wendy remarked with a big grin.

"Yup. My three boys," Barbro said, laughing, her eyes full of pride and love. Maxi and Wendy watched the Kriegels as they headed for the door, Doug with his arm around Barbro, the two kids skipping in front.

"Someday?" Wendy said to Maxi.

"Sure. Someday."

"Meantime, do not even *think* about Mr. New York Cool."

"I swear to you, Wendy, I'm not," Maxi said. She glanced down at her hand in her lap and crossed her fingers.

39

Sunday. God's gift to the working girl. No wonder Sunday Trent's mother named her after this glorious seventh day, Maxi mused. She lolled at the table in her tiny breakfast nook over grapefruit juice, English muffins and raspberry jam, a pot of coffee, the *Sunday Times,* and her dog stretched out on the rug at her feet.

She'd loosely structured her Sunday. Relax, feed Yukon, jog, relax, go to the dog park, shop for groceries, relax, work on sweeps series, relax, heat up the chicken, spinach, and carrots combo she would pick up at Rosti's for dinner, watch *The Sopranos* and *Six Feet Under* on HBO, relax, shower, and fall into bed with her novel. Perfect.

For a few seconds she pondered how a man could fit into the equation, then dismissed the thought. And wondered if she would always be torn over that particular lifestyle-choice conundrum. No—she just needed a little more distance from her last marriage. Didn't she?

*   *   *

The dog park at Mulholland and Laurel Canyon was crowded, as was usual by Sunday midmorning. Yukon stood impatiently while Maxi unhooked his leash; then he dashed out onto the flats to terrify a pair of sweet, long-eared cocker spaniels. After their hasty, shocked retreat to between the legs of a young man who was reclining on the grass under a lush willow tree, obviously their owner, Yuke gave the two a doggie "Just kidding" smirk and wandered back over to Maxi.

"You're five years old," she scolded him. "Grow up."

Yukon gave her his "innocent" eyes and sat himself down to survey the scene. Figure out what mischief he could get into next.

"Just like a man," Maxi muttered to him. "Territorial, smug, put-upon innocent, a big show-off."

She put a hand on Yukon's upright back, and chastised herself for characterizing men again. But her beloved pet did have all those crazy-making male traits, for sure. Had to be a gender thing.

"Can't live with 'em, can't live without 'em, can't shoot 'em," she said out loud. Then looked up to see a plumpish woman with a big English sheepdog peering curiously at her. At both her *and* her dog, actually.

Maxi smiled sweetly at them, with the intention of conveying to the pair not to worry, it was perfectly normal to talk out loud to your dog.

"Come on, you nut ball, let's get it on with the Frisbee," she said to Yukon then, getting up and heading onto the green, the disk in her hand and her pup trotting lovingly at her heels. Just like a man. They could be so damn annoying and at the same time so wonderfully lovable.

She tossed the Frisbee out to an open space and Yuke sailed over to leap up and retrieve it. And bring it back to her, enormously proud of himself. And wait at her feet for her pat of approval. *Soooo* like the man he was.

Maxi was about to toss the thing again when she saw another dog bounding purposefully toward Yukon. *Look out,* she told herself. He must have pissed off a dog his own size this time. Then she recognized the sleek golden retriever, wavy, strawberry-blond coat gleaming in the sun, and the pooch's owner, who was running behind him: Sylvie Tran from Channel Six, the weekend anchor who wrote children's books.

"Hey, you two," Sylvie called.

"Hi, Syl," Maxi responded. "What's happening?"

Both women stopped for a beat to watch their dogs interact. Yukon and Goda had met several times before, always at the dog park on Sunday mornings. First they kind of growled, circling each other; then they closed in and did a little friendly nose-to-nose. Then they bolted out a few feet from their mistresses to cavort together.

Sylvie responded to Maxi's "What's happening?" in typical newsese. "The Arizona fires are still going—four hundred and sixty-three homes burned to the ground, can you believe? I'm sure we'll lead the March with that." The Sunday newscast always expanded to fill the time after whatever sporting event the station was carrying, and because it would often go on for longer than two hours, staffers referred to the show as "the March of Death."

"Look, our guys are making nice," Maxi said, her eyes on their two pups playing on the grass. At the dog park it was never a good idea to take your eyes off your pet for even a second. That's when the doggie war of the century was sure to break out.

"My editor told me she saw a copy of Wendy's manuscript," Sylvie said, watching the dogs frolic. "She says it was submitted under a different name. Did Wendy decide to use a pseudonym, keep her book separate from the business? I'd thought of doing that at first, but with the books I write, my news connection actually lends some credibility."

Sylvie's children's books featured animals that had been in the news, like a dolphin who regularly swims with a kids' swim class in San Diego, a Lassie dog who saved her family from a fire in Denver, a whale that got beached off Puget Sound, then with the help of the whole village, made it back to the ocean with a big smile on his face.

Maxi looked perplexed. "Funny, Wendy didn't mention that *DBD* was already being marketed. I thought she was still working on it."

"Well, this has to be Wendy's book. About short people. When she asked me about agents, I recommended Robin Ruell, so I figured Robin must have submitted it to publishers."

"How did your editor see it? She just handles children's books, right?"

"Yes, but I'd mentioned Wendy's book to her back then because I thought it was such a fun idea—Harriet is five-two. So when a colleague showed her a copy of the manuscript, she remembered it. She told me it was going to be auctioned, and she hoped her company would get it. I was going to congratulate Wendy."

Maxi held her cell phone to her ear as she steered her clunky old Chevy Blazer while Yukon, his head out the window, balanced on the passenger seat beside her. They were tooling over the ruts and potholes on Laurel Canyon on their way to Rosti's to pick up dinner.

"Wendy, I just ran into Sylvie Tran at the dog park. She told me her publisher had a copy of your manuscript. Said her editor mentioned that people were buzzing about it, it was coming up for bid—"

"Not possible," Wendy cut in. "We're not even finished with it. If we'd submitted it to publishers, believe me, Max, you'd be the first to know."

"Well, that's what I thought, but this sure *sounds* like your book, Wen. Sylvie said it was aimed at short people. How to look and feel tall. Her editor even said they were kidding on the square about getting a foreword by Randy Newman."

"God, if somebody beat me out with this idea, I'll kill myself," Wendy anguished.

"Uh-uh. That the exact same project would surface at the exact time? Too much of a coincidence."

"Then . . . what?" Wendy stammered.

"Who's got access to your home computer files?"

Silence. They both knew the answer.

"I'll call Robin as soon as New York opens for business. At six in the morning," Wendy said soberly. "She'll find out what's going on."

40

Ten to nine on Monday morning. Maxi had just come into the newsroom; Wendy was already at her desk.

"Find out anything?" Maxi asked as she pulled up her usual chair next to Wendy's.

"Not yet. Robin knew nothing about it. She's looking into it."

"So, meantime—"

"So yes, of course I changed all my passwords," Wendy said, anticipating Maxi's question. "I just hope I didn't shut the damn barn door too late."

"Are you working the Eleven tonight?"

"No. Neither are you, Max. Pete has you on the football expansion team conference live on the Noon, then on recuts for the early block. Sports will mix it for the Eleven."

"Then I'd better get downtown—that one's going to be a mob scene."

"Yeah. You know, I'm sick about this, Maxi."

"Don't be. If this really is what we're both thinking, nobody could possibly get away with it," she said. But she could see by the look on Wendy's face that her friend wasn't convinced. And neither was she.

Maxi maneuvered in the jostle-fest with the rest of the newsies at Staples Center. Her cameraman, Bart Jackson, was shooting a group of the city's wealthy, pin-striped, businessmen–sports moguls up onstage, as well as the noisy crowd of regular Joes on the floor of the massive amphitheater. The usual media crush was dwarfed by the milling Angelinos; seems everybody in L.A. wanted a professional football franchise for the city, and a lot of folks, mostly men, had taken the morning off and come to the giant arena to make their feelings known.

While jockeying to line up his live shot, the sports anchor for Channel Thirteen, Bob Avila, jammed the heel of his steel-tipped cowboy boot hard and square on Maxi's foot. Avila was an overweight, overwrought, overbearing guy whose arrogance clung to him like an aura. When Maxi whimpered in pain, he looked at her with just the slightest disdain and said, "Hey, Poole, how come they sent a chick out on a guy story? You could get hurt."

And how come you're such a sexist asshole? is what she thought. "Hi, Bob," is what she said.

Maxi had long since learned that it was a whole lot easier not to cultivate enemies among the L.A. news gang—you were going to run into these same people for years. Like most women in the business, even though their numbers were almost equal to the men's now, her MO was to just suck it up. Thankfully, the Bob Avilas of television news made up a small minority. Maxi put their swinish attitudes down to some kind of basic insecurity. Most of the men she worked alongside were respectful and professional.

She got her shots and voiced her story from Staples Center, live on the News at Noon. Then she labeled her tape and dropped it in her tote, thanked her cameraman, pushed through the crowd back to the parking structure, found her car, and navigated the downtown freeways on her way back to the station. Her day had just begun.

41

Tonight's dinner with Kriegel was work, but nice work. Doug was always a kick. Maxi parked her car in the lot behind the legendary Musso & Frank in the heart of Hollywood, slipped in the back door, and found him already comfortably settled in one of the plush red-leather booths along the wall enjoying an iced martini straight up. Musso served their martinis in generous glass cruets set in bowls of crushed ice, with condiment dishes of olives, onions, and lemon peel on the side. A cruet would fill your chilled martini glass at least twice. Just one of those and Maxi wouldn't even think about driving home. She scooted into the booth opposite Kriegel and ordered a glass of Cabernet from a waiter who instantly appeared.

Looking around the crowded room, she took a moment to catch her breath. Musso & Frank was always fascinating. Founded in 1919, as its menu touted proudly, it would be in its eighties now, a rare Hollywood survivor. The waitstaff at Musso's were actually lionized for their rudeness. It went with the territory: If you didn't get at least a small serving of abuse with your dinner, you felt a little cheated.

Their waiter came back with her glass of wine in what seemed like seconds, and slammed it down on the table in front of her.

"How long have you worked here?" she asked him.

"Fifty-two years," the white-haired gent stated brusquely, and moved off.

"I'm having the short ribs," Kriegel said. "Specialty of the house. Their homemade chicken potpie is great, too." With Doug, food was a serious matter.

Maxi raised her glass to his. "Cheers, Douggie," she said. "So what do you know?"

"Well, the villain in the Rose International stock skid would seem to be Goodie Penthe of the Penthe Group, and— ahhh . . ." He stopped as their waiter unceremoniously swatted aside their bread basket, butter bowl, and water glasses and dropped a big plate of fried calamari in the middle of the table.

"I went ahead and ordered an appetizer for us," Kriegel explained with a smile that lit up the room. Maxi knew that his beatific smile was not for her, it was for the crisp calamari garnished with lemon and cocktail sauce. He picked up his knife and fully buttered another hard roll, took a healthy bite of the bread, sipped his martini, then spooned a good-sized helping of the steaming seafood onto his hors d'oeuvres plate and tucked into it with exaggerated relish.

When he took a short breather, Maxi ventured, "Yes . . . so you say the villain seems to be Goodman Penthe. I know him."

"I figured you did when I heard a page for you the

other day, a Mr. Goodman Penthe to see you. You can bet my ears pricked up. I wanted to run out and get a look at the guy, but I was on raging deadline for the Noon. Then later that day, I happened to come up with this stuff."

Kriegel paused to help himself to more calamari. "Have some of this while it's hot," he said.

"What stuff, Doug? What stuff did you come up with?"

"Well, all of it is a matter of public record, but it's so heavily layered with bullshit it's hard to decipher. But lucky for you, I do speak fluent Wall Street ca-ca, so after about thirty thousand computer clicks I was able to translate the information into understandable English. And a recognizable cast of characters."

Their waiter pounced on the table and whisked away the appetizer platter, which happened to have a few pieces of the crispy calamari left on it. Too late for Kriegel to stop him. Wistfully, he watched after the man as he hurried down the aisle. These ancient waiters were nothing if not fast. Kreigel sighed, then resumed his story.

"Sometime back around the beginning of September, well before Gillian Rose died, a total of six entities that I could find started trading heavily in Rose International stock. All six were on the East Coast. With some digging, I found out that four of them were high-management types out of companies that circuitously traced back to the Penthe Group. Another one turned out to be Goodman Penthe's married daughter who lives in New Jersey, one Margaret Hill. And the sixth one filed under the name J. J. Ruff. I couldn't find out who that was, nothing about him or her on the Net, but I linked that one with the other five because the trading patterns were similar: large blocks of Rose International bought and sold within a short period."

"Ruff? First name Jay?"

"Just initials. J. J. Ruff."

"Could be Goodman Penthe's dog."

"Hah! Good one. And why not?"

"I was kidding, Doug. Can a dog buy and sell stock?"

"Sure, if he pays his taxes."

"Doesn't he have to have a social security number?"

"Not that hard to get. You can buy one down on Third Street for forty-five bucks."

"Jeez—could he also get health benefits and stuff?"

"For that he'd have to show a birth certificate. But the street will take anybody's money."

"Ya, but—wouldn't it be illegal to have your dog trade stock?"

"It's not that much different from having your corporation trade stock."

"But then you have to have names—"

"Hey, J. J. Ruff. Perfectly good name."

"Are you actually saying, Doug, that you think Goodman Penthe's dog could possibly—"

"You know, Maxi," Kriegel put in, "just when I think I've seen everything in this fairly corrupt business, the next nutty thing comes down. On and on, a conga line of CEOs pounding Wall Street in a wave of accounting scandals that have cost small investors their life savings. Corruption reeking at the loftiest levels. Criminal behavior by the really rich and mighty. So, did a dog buy and sell some blocks of stock? Doesn't matter. Rose stock got manipulated, and it tanked. End of story."

"And the Darth Vader behind it was Goodman Penthe?"

"Looked that way to me on my virtual travels over the money trail. Oooh . . . here come the short ribs!"

Several miles to the west, at a little-known Italian restaurant called Boccia on a quiet corner in Brentwood, another couple were having dinner: Carter Rose and Kendyl Scott. After the fiasco at Spago, Carter chose an eatery that was well off the Beverly Hills glitterati track. When the couple got there at eight, the restaurant was half empty, because either Monday nights were generally slow or the food wasn't great. Or both. But the chances of Carter Rose running into anyone he knew were slim there. And the chances that paparazzi would be staked out at Boccia were nil.

A bottle of Pinot Grigio sat chilling in an ice bucket beside them, and a small, important-looking Tiffany box lay between them on the table.

"Open your Christmas present," Rose said with an ingenuous smile.

Kendyl reached for the box and languidly removed the narrow red ribbon. And slowly rolled the ribbon neatly around her fingers, and set it down in front of her on the table.

"Come on, Kendyl, open it," Rose urged.

"I'm so used to the present being all I get that I like to make it last. Is the present still all I get, Carter? Tell me there's much more."

Though her words were delivered up in mellifluous tones and with a loving smile, they scraped across Rose's psyche like fingernails across a blackboard. Kendyl always knew how to needle him, he reminded himself, her whining usually served up with a spoonful of honey.

Barbs sheathed in scented white satin. Stifling the urge to react, he said again, "Open it, Kendyl," and sat back and sipped his wine.

In the glow of the restaurant's low amber lighting, the diamond earrings, nestled against their black velvet background, sparkled brilliantly. "They're beautiful, Carter," Kendyl purred.

"Six carats, and the stones are flawless," Carter pronounced, as if he'd know the difference if they weren't. He knew only what the sales clerk at Tiffany had told him, and he knew how much he'd paid for them. He could have got the same quality diamonds for half the price at the wholesale jewelry mart downtown, he was sure, but Carter's women were used to those little blue boxes from Tiffany. An extra fifteen thousand bucks for a fucking cardboard box, he thought ruefully. With about fifty cents' worth of Tiffany's seasonal red silk ribbon thrown in. He sighed. But in this case, a small price for keeping Kendyl happy, he conceded to himself. Promise her anything . . .

"What, darling?" she asked.

"Nothing. Just tired, I guess. A little jet-lagged." He'd flown in from Maui that afternoon.

"They're breathtaking," Kendyl reiterated in low, ice-cool tones, tilting the box back and forth and admiring the jewels as their multi facets caught the light.

"But what I really want, Carter, is a diamond *ring*," she said, glancing wistfully down at her hands. She wore her college ring on her right hand instead of an engagement ring on her left. Yes, she was smart, said the bulky, rounded UCLA ring with the big royal blue stone. But what she *wanted* to be was married.

She was not going to stop, Rose thought, still sitting

back in his chair, sipping his wine. "Kendyl—" he started.

"Really, Carter. I can't think about anything else. I love you. I always have. And you love me. Don't you?"

"You know I do."

"Then say you'll marry me. Tell me we'll be married sometime in the new year. I can wait, as long as I know we have a future together."

She looked gorgeous, sitting tall and straight across the table from him, in a dusty emerald green velour dress that hugged her body. Sensuous. Exotic. She was more dazzling than the jewels, as glances directed at her from other diners attested to. As Rose watched her across the table, he saw something more. She looked intimidating. Threatening. To Carter Rose, she looked dangerous.

"Yes, we'll be married," he heard himself murmuring.

"Oh, Carter! Sometime in the next year?"

"Sure," he said. Knowing it wouldn't happen.

42

A news breaker. Maxi heard the computer ding and watched the story roll on the wires, then grabbed her phone. It was Tuesday morning, December 31, the last day of the year.

The Associated Press had a new lead in the mysterious death two weeks ago of Gillian Rose, co-founder and CEO of Rose International. The wire story said police sources had just revealed that the late Gillian Rose was last seen alive in the company of Goodman Penthe, chairman of the East Coast–based Penthe Group conglomerate.

The story went on to report that Penthe and Mrs. Rose had been spotted together by one of the guards at the Rose company building at around two in the morning of Monday, December 16, the same day Mrs. Rose was later found dead on the floor of her office by her assistant, Sandie Schaeffer, who herself was later shot, and so on.

Maxi checked her computer Rolodex and dialed the number for Goodman Penthe in Baltimore. The nervous

Ms. Gray picked up. Obviously she remembered the name Maxi Poole and the fact that this Poole woman had seemed to be important to her boss. She put her through to Penthe immediately.

"Yes, Maxi, how are you?" Goodman Penthe asked.

"You didn't tell me—"

"No," Penthe interrupted. He'd obviously seen the news. "I didn't want that coming out, which I'm sure you can understand."

"What were you doing in the Rose building at two in the morning?"

"I was in town that weekend to meet with Gillian. She wanted to fill me in on the results of extensive testing her outside lab had done on the Schaeffer formula."

"I thought she didn't have the formula, just a letter of intent."

"Schaeffer had given her a sample of the product. She had the stuff analyzed and replicated. Simple." Poor, trusting Bill Schaeffer, Maxi thought, no match for this oily crowd. He still believed that Gillian was doing a simple comparison with Xalatan, in her own company lab, and hadn't yet come up with results.

"Anyway, she'd been working with the product, and she wanted me to see how far she'd come with it."

"You flew in for that? I understand why the two of you didn't want to put anything in writing, but why couldn't she just bring you up to date on the phone?"

"Gillian didn't trust phones. And neither do I, frankly, with all the illegal wiretaps, cloning, and the rest. This project was much too important to take even the slightest risk of disclosure before Gillian could complete her divorce and settlement."

"What *was* this all-important project, for heaven's

sake?" Maxi threw out casually, just on the off chance that Penthe would actually tell her. He wouldn't. No surprise, but it never hurt to ask.

"By the way," she said to Penthe, "this time we're on the record. Don't tell me anything you don't want on the air."

"That's fine," he said. "I have nothing to hide."

"What about the formula? And the super-lucrative product you say was at the heart of all this?"

"That's dead now. It died with Gillian."

Oh, I'm sure, Maxi thought. "All right," she said. "Be aware that I'm going to run tape on our conversation now, okay?"

"Fine. The two of us had a late dinner that Sunday night. In my suite at the Peninsula Hotel, so we'd have privacy. As I told you, it was crucial that Carter have no idea what we were doing."

"Don't you care if he knows now?"

"No. Why should I?"

"I thought you were still trying to buy the company."

"This project had nothing to do with the Rose company. Besides, Carter will sell. He has to."

"Why?"

"Well . . . and this part is *off* the record. Agreed?"

"Agreed." Evidently he trusted her, Maxi noted silently, because he didn't ask her to stop the tape. Which made her suspicious of what he was about to tell her, of course.

"Carter Rose has consistently cooked his books, and siphoned off millions into offshore accounts. Now there's word on the street that the SEC is nosing around, and the stock is plummeting."

I thought you *were responsible for the stock dive,* she

thought but didn't say. Penthe might have deliberately let that one drop to see if she'd go for it, since major accounting fraud happened to be Wall Street's white-collar crime du jour.

"And how do you know this?"

"Due diligence. My team couldn't miss it."

"Are you going to report it?"

"Of course not. I told you, I want to buy the company cheap."

Corporate sleaze, she noted silently, wrinkling up her nose a little as if to ward off a foul odor. Cutting back to the chase, she said, "All right, we're back on the record. The AP reports that one of the guards at Rose International saw the two of you in the building that night."

"Yes. After dinner we spent a couple of hours in my suite going over the research that Gillian brought. She didn't show me the actual formulations her lab work had come up with, but as her prospective partner in this venture, she outlined the steps that had been taken so far in the science and explained to me what each tier had accomplished. She was very excited about the progress to date. They were much farther along than she'd expected at that stage, she said."

"So you went to the Rose building that late because . . . ?" Maxi prodded.

"Because Gillian was so enthusiastic about it she decided she wanted to show me the product itself, and what it could do. She had vials of it in her office."

"So you *were* in her office at two in the morning."

"For about a half hour. We had a drink to celebrate the work while she did a little demonstration for me. Then we left."

"Demonstration of what?" Maxi tried again.

He gave an exasperated you-*know*-I'm-not-going-to-tell-you sigh.

"But if it doesn't matter now," she pressed.

Penthe ignored that and continued with his story. "After the guard learned the next day that Gillian was found dead, he reported to the police that she'd been in the building with a man, and what time. They checked the surveillance tapes and identified me."

"Surveillance tapes?"

"Turns out Carter Rose has an elaborate monitoring system that covers the entire nine floors of the company, including Gillian's office. The cops found it the day Gillian turned up dead. Hidden cameras everywhere. She'd never mentioned that to me. I'm sure she didn't even know about it, or she'd never have taken me into the building to show me the product. Carter always was a sneaky bastard—"

"Why are we just now hearing that you and Gillian were in the building together at that hour on the night before she died?"

"Who knows?" Penthe said. "Whatever their reasons, the police didn't make that information public, but they questioned me, of course."

"And today it leaked."

"Must have."

"So where did the detectives leave it with you, Mr. Penthe?"

"They asked me to stay in town. But as I told them, that only works in the movies. Old movies, at that. I have a business to run. They had no basis to hold me—in custody, in town, or anywhere. Just because I was *with* the lady doesn't mean I killed her."

Penthe was either an innocent man, Maxi reasoned, or

this was the story he wanted out there before today's police revelation pointed a big, bony finger at him all over
the press, not a good thing for the Penthe Group stock.
She would report his story on the Six, a straightforward
"as told to," and let the viewers be the judge. And the
LAPD.

43

Carter Rose walked briskly into his office suite, tossed a perfunctory "Hello, hold my calls, please" to Kendyl as he passed her desk, and disappeared into his inner sanctum. He'd noticed that she was wearing his huge diamond earrings. Now she wanted a huge diamond *ring,* he reminded himself sourly as he locked his door from the inside. Diamond earrings were easy. Diamond rings were hard, loaded with baggage as they were. Hell, he'd give her a fucking diamond tiara if she'd get off his back about marriage. *And* if he could be sure that she'd keep her mouth shut.

He strode over to the far wall of his inner office, which was completely lined with oak paneling in keeping with the 1920s decor. He pressed both palms on separate areas of the polished oak, then took a step backward as the entire expanse of wall slid open to reveal a bank of dozens of small monitors, each one with an identifying label above it, and each one alive with a picture of some strategic location in the Rose building, including the ground-floor conference rooms and the parking structure.

He smiled, as he always did when he "opened" this dazzling present he'd given himself years ago—better than electric trains. Incongruous, he knew, this hidden high-tech virtual citadel within the walls of his early-twentieth-century-styled space. And that's the way he liked it—no one would guess that in his low-tech surroundings he had this big, beautiful, empowering, state-of-the-art toy.

The two men who installed the system knew about it, of course; that was back when the building was being completely remodeled from the ground up for the fledgling Rose company, along with seventeen floors of outside office space to lease. The techs never questioned it—an electronic overlook of this magnitude was not uncommon for a company as big as Rose International. Gillian didn't concern herself with the nuts and bolts of framing up the space back then; her province was choosing and overseeing the interior decor, a massive job. She never knew about the wiring that snaked throughout the several floors of company space for his elaborate system of hidden video cameras, nor about the wall of hardware that was ultimately installed in his personal inner office in an afternoon. He smiled, remembering his intent back then: He could surreptitiously keep tabs on everyone. Including his wife.

Kendyl knew about the elaborate system. She was the only other person who knew it was there, and in fact he'd been able to keep it from her, too, until the day the crime-scene tape came down outside Gillian's office suite and Sandie Schaeffer did her portentous search.

Carter went over the timeline in his mind. Gillian's body was found two weeks ago yesterday. He arrived at LAX from Taiwan the next morning, and was taken directly to Parker Center for questioning. The detectives had specifically ordered him, and everyone else, to stay out of Gillian's office while the investigation was ongoing.

But he didn't stay out of her most private area at home: the built-in jewelry cabinet in her personal dressing room. It was a locked bank of eight custom-designed, felt-lined, divided drawers, locked all of a piece by a steel bolt that shot down through the entire cabinet at the turn of a key. Gillian kept the cabinet bolted down to prevent theft; a burglar would have to get into it with an ax. But that had made it physically off limits to her husband as well, and many times he'd wondered idly what secrets she might have kept in there. She didn't have *that* much jewelry. Did she? Now, with Gillian dead, whatever she owned belonged to him, and he'd wanted to know exactly what was in that cabinet in case the cops came with a warrant and searched his house just as they'd searched his building.

They never did, which he found surprising. But he'd called in a locksmith, who made a replacement key to the steel-bolted unit for him. And he was astounded at what he found inside.

The several pieces of jewelry he'd never seen before didn't surprise him. Nor did the packet of love letters, from different men. He always knew that his attractive wife must have had lovers. Sexual passion had long since seeped out of their marriage and certainly he'd had more than his own share of affairs, but that was a subject the two never broached. It was a tacit understanding between them.

And always, he'd been proud that Gillian was his wife. Proud of her accomplishments with the company. Proud to be with the dazzling Gillian Rose at business and social functions. Proud of her when she handled the media. She was his trophy, a brilliant partner in every way.

Sex had become irrelevant to their union. They'd had plenty of it, from way back when they first groped each other in his old Chevy El Camino in college, and for years later. At some point their sex life got tired, and he found sex elsewhere. And he was sure that she must have too. That was fine with him. She'd been discreet. He was totally content with the relationship they had, and he thought that she was too.

Until he found out that she was planning to leave him.

That changed everything. That meant the end of his perfect world. It meant that, to split their assets, she would tear down the company they'd created and built together. It meant the end of their upscale social status, of their prominent position as a power couple in the bicoastal community of the affluent. And it meant the diminishment of their combined wealth.

Most important, it threatened to strike a fatal blow to his personal wealth: He couldn't depend on Swiss bankers to keep those hefty funds he'd accumulated under wraps. The company was run with smoke and mirrors—only he knew that. But in today's business climate, with its microscopically powered scrutiny, the odds were high that his personal empire would be exposed in an assets search and come crashing down. And along with many of his CEO colleagues, he'd be looking at jail time.

No, he couldn't let Gillian divorce him. And now that wouldn't happen.

He had been thinking about all this while browsing through her locked cabinet, her trove of secrets, and then he saw it. The small brass key in one of the slots in the bottom drawer. He'd picked it up and examined it closely—it was the key to a safety-deposit box.

It didn't take him long to discover what it opened—that was easy. He'd called several banks in the city, asked to speak to their managers, and explained that in the course of settling the affairs of his deceased wife, his lawyers had come upon a key to a box that she'd rented, and he couldn't remember at which bank it was.

The manager at one of Citibank's downtown branches confirmed that they did in fact have a box in the name of Gillian Rose. Mr. Rose was to come in with identification, and a copy of his wife's will if she'd had one, and they would open it for him. Just a formality, of course. Most of the city knew what Carter Rose looked like, that he had just lost his wife, and that he would certainly be her legal beneficiary.

This time he was amazed by what he found. The box contained research, business memos, and contracts involving something called BriteEyes. What the hell was BriteEyes, and why didn't he know about it? When the bank official presented him with the log to sign, he saw that Gillian's box had had constant activity; she'd been in and out of it several times a week right up until her death. And scanning the documents, he noted that their dates were recent. This was an ongoing project that Gillian had been working on behind his back. He'd dumped the contents of the safety-deposit box into a gym bag and closed out the account.

The papers it yielded told him that BriteEyes was a substance in product-development stage, based on an original formulation created by William Schaeffer, Sandie Schaeffer's pharmacist father. And there was a letter of intent signed jointly by Schaeffer and Gillian, intent for Gillian to purchase the formula at a later date, at a given price. A very generous price. There was no actual formulation with the papers. Could Gillian not have had a formula? That wasn't likely, given her elaborate efforts to hide this research from him. Knowing his savvy wife, his guess was that she had the formula, had done work on it, and had found it to be valuable. Very valuable. You don't keep run-of-the-mill product-development info in a safety-deposit box. She'd kept it separate from Rose International, and specifically hidden it from her husband and business partner. This told him something. Whatever the hell it was, this was Gillian's brass ring.

The formula had to be somewhere. So where would she keep it? Not at their home, and risk that he'd find it. Not with the files in the company lab, which were open to anybody. Not even in her secret safety-deposit box. He would search her office suite, but he couldn't do that until the investigation into her death was terminated and the cops and their adjuncts had cleared out of his building. Gillian's area was overrun with police personnel at any and all times of the day and night. They badged their way in, with no prior notice. So Carter had wisely stayed out of the area as he'd been ordered. Oh, he'd thought about going in when no one was there, was sorely tempted to go in. It was his damn building, wasn't it? But he knew better. Yes, he would find this formula, find out what it was all about, but were he caught looking, he'd be questioned again. What exactly had he been doing in there? they'd want to know. What was he looking for? And why clandestinely, in defiance of police orders? What was so important that he had to find immediately, while avoiding the scrutiny of authorities? Was it something he would kill for?

There was no need to risk bringing such suspicion upon himself when everything seemed to be so nicely contained. Even if the detectives turned Gillian's office upside down and confiscated this mystery formula, it would be meaningless to them. Just some document pertaining to Rose company business. And eventually it would be returned to him, along with everything else. He could wait.

Patience paid off. On the afternoon when they announced there was no evidence of foul play in Gillian's death and removed the crime-scene tape from her office door, Carter made his plan to go in. But he would wait until after business hours, after all the employees had left the building.

He'd asked Kendyl to help him search. She was better at deciphering files than he was. They were looking for papers pertaining to a formula developed by Sandie's father, pharmacist William Schaeffer, he'd told her. It was a favor, really, that Gillian had wanted to do for her assistant's dad. A small formulation that probably wouldn't prove worth developing, but the company didn't want to just drop the ball on it, because they were already halfway through the tests. It could be labeled BriteEyes.

Since it was Gillian's baby, she'd been shepherding the project, he explained to Kendyl. She had kept him posted on the research all along, he'd lied, and now that her office space was no longer off limits, he wanted to retrieve that work in progress and hand it off to one of his managers to continue the testing. He'd explained that he wanted to look for the files after hours because staffers were still leery about going into Gillian's office. Best to do it himself, with Kendyl's help, he told her, when workers in that area wouldn't be unnerved by activity in the suite where Gillian died.

Kendyl had bought the story. The two had systematically pored through Gillian's files until nearly midnight, stopping only to eat some sandwiches Carter had asked her to order up from the cafeteria earlier in the afternoon and store in the fridge. For convenience, he'd told her, so they wouldn't have to take the time to go out to eat, and they'd finish sooner.

His real reason was different. In case they had to stay late, he hadn't wanted the guards to see them going out to dinner, then coming back into the building; better to keep a low profile, he'd figured.

Turned out that plan paid off, too. After the bloody mess with Sandie Schaeffer, he and Kendyl hid out the rest of the night in his office suite. They got some fitful sleep on the two sofas in his office, not knowing whether the woman in the next suite was alive or dead. They rose early, freshened up as best they could in his executive washroom, and changed—Carter always left clothes at the office, a couple of suits, fresh shirts, golf togs. And Kendyl kept a few outfits in her own office closet as well, in case she needed a quick change for evening outings.

Carter got himself into a different suit, shirt, and tie, and Kendyl put on a short black sheath and dressed it down with a jacket and scarf. They both took up positions at their respective desks as if they'd just come in to work. As if they'd each hopped on the express elevator, avoiding notice of the guards, which the owner of the company and his assistant routinely did. Carter was usually in his office by seven-thirty, and Kendyl in hers before eight. They'd made a show of getting on with their day's work.

Until Sandie Schaeffer was discovered in the locked suite next door.

44

New Year's Eve tonight, Maxi mused, sitting in her office. She'd turned down all invites. On New Year's Eve you were supposed to kiss somebody at midnight. Somebody you really loved. There was nobody she really loved, and she certainly didn't want to kiss just anybody to usher in another year. Somebody once said that meant a year of bad luck. No sense risking that, she thought with a smile.

Mentally, she riffled through the half dozen party invitations she'd received and imagined the respective guest lists. And what likely candidate would be kissing her at midnight at each of them. At Laurel Baker's party it would be some newsie she worked with, someone like her who had no mate. At Pete Capra's house it would be some shaggy old pal of Pete's who'd be drunk by midnight and smell of booze and cigarettes. Her attorney's bash would be uptown Beverly Hills elegant—at that one it would be some corporate type in a suit with an expensive haircut who would talk about the stock market tumble. And on down the list.

She could always leave a party before midnight and avoid the kissing portion of the evening, she knew, but what was the point of going to a New Year's Eve party if you didn't see the new year in? So she'd opted to stay home with the tube and a glass of wine and watch the ball drop in Times Square, live on cable, three hours early. Back home in New York. Where Richard was. Who would *he* be kissing at midnight?

She sighed. She'd be kissing Yukon.

Clicking on the Six O'clock rundown, she started writing today's update on the Gillian Rose story. It was a great get—everybody would lead with the disclosure that Goodman Penthe was with Gillian Rose just hours before she died, but Maxi had Penthe's own account, as told to her exclusively. She would run the man's taped voice over pictures of the Peninsula Hotel where they'd had dinner, the Rose building where they'd holed up later, and file footage from the day they'd found Gillian Rose dead.

Her phone rang. She glanced at the caller ID on the readout. A string of viewers had been phoning to wish her Happy New Year. Sweet, but if she paused to chat with each one of them she wouldn't get any work done. The caller was William Schaeffer. She snatched up the receiver.

"Hi, Bill," she said. "You got my brain waves—I was just thinking about you."

"Happy New Year, Maxi. To what do I owe your valuable thoughts directed at me?"

"Question: Do you know what exactly Gillian Rose had planned to do with your glaucoma formula, Bill?"

"Well, I assume she intended to market it to be used

for glaucoma relief. That's what it was for. What else would she do with it?"

"I don't know. You tell me. What else *could* she do with it?"

"She never talked about doing anything with it other than what it was intended for. I can't even imagine it used for anything else. Why do you ask?"

"I don't know. I can't help thinking there must be more to it. That it must represent more of a cash cow than a glaucoma medication would. And again, the Rose company was never interested in pharmaceuticals."

"I told you, Gillian was developing it to market under a new company she was going to form. Rose International isn't licensed to develop or distribute drugs, prescription or over-the-counter."

"But . . . can you think of any other possible application for your formula?"

Schaeffer paused for a moment. "No," he said then. "No, I really can't."

"Hmmm. Well anyway, Happy New Year to you, too. How's Sandie doing?"

"She's getting stronger every day. That's why I'm calling you. I'm sure you have New Year's Eve plans, but I wondered if you could drop by the house for a bit. We'd love you to have a glass of wine with us."

"Your daughter's not drinking wine!" Maxi exclaimed.

Schaeffer laughed. "No, no. I meant you could have a glass of wine with me, to celebrate the new year. In Sandie's room. I like to carry on the normal stuff of life in her presence. I know she understands it. And Maxi, she still asks for you."

"Um, okay," Maxi said. "I can duck out right after the

Six O'clock News tonight. I can be there a little after seven. Would that work for you?"

"That'd be perfect. I'll be home from the store on my dinner hour." Schaeffer gave her his address in Pacific Palisades.

Wendy came into Maxi's office and dropped down on the couch, looking visibly distressed. "What?" Maxi asked her friend, seeing the beginning of tears behind her eyes.

"It *is* my book. Robin says it *has* to be my book. And it's out there."

"What do you mean, out there? *Where* out there? What—"

"Robin called some of her literary-agent friends, and found out it's being handled by an agent in TriBeCa. The book is called *Short Sighted,* by one Sophia LeGrande, and she's . . . short. And there's going to be an auction next week."

"Well . . . so . . ." Maxi stammered, horrified, "what the hell are we going to do about it?"

"She says there's nothing much we *can* do about it."

"But . . . that's ridiculous. We can prove—"

"That's just it," Wendy broke in. "We can't really prove anything."

"But your files are all dated. You've been writing *DBD* for more than a year. This Sophia person can't get away with this."

"Her name isn't really Sophia LeGrande, the agent told Robin."

"Hah. Why am I not surprised?" Maxi threw out.

"Anyway, she asked him for a copy of the manuscript. He said sure, it was all over New York anyway, and he sent it over to her office."

"Did she tell him what she suspected?"

"No. She said if she'd told him the truth he'd never have sent it to her. She made up a reason, said she worked with a producer in L.A. who might be interested in making a movie of it, kind of like *Bridget Jones's Diary.*"

"So she's seen it."

"She's seen it."

"And . . . ?"

"And Robin says the manuscript is just different enough to not qualify as plagiarism. She says most of the concepts are the same, but there's no verbatim text. This is a nightmare, Maxi."

"Could it possibly be a legitimate manuscript?"

"No way, Robin says. This book follows the same road map as mine. She says it's a jumbled-up version of my book, all right, but she's convinced that no lawyer would take the case."

The two women looked at each other. They knew they were thinking the same thing. Sunday Trent had been spending long hours on *DBD.* And Sunday Trent was smart and creative. Was she also a thief?

"Listen, Wendy," Maxi said, "if they can't do anything about this in New York, we'll do it here. That makes more sense anyway. This is where the perpetrator has to be, right?"

"Where do we start?" Wendy ventured. They both knew the answer.

45

Maxi mellowed out with classic rock on the winding drive west on Sunset to Pacific Palisades. Rolling down her window to let in the bracing salt air, she looked down at her reporter's notebook where she'd written the address William Schaeffer had given her. She found Napoli Drive, and the pretty peach-colored Mediterranean cottage with the street number she was looking for posted on the mailbox.

She'd stopped in Palisades center and picked up two novels: Sue Grafton again. Sandie's nurse, or her father, could read to her a little, Maxi thought. Something light, fun, contemporary. Even if Sandie didn't completely understand the text, being read to might be soothing. And stimulating. It was a known fact that just like muscles, using brain cells strengthened them. Maybe the input would trigger memories. If nothing else, she mused, Sandie's nurse would get a kick out of Kinsey Millhone.

She parked out front, went up the curving stone walk

edged with a profusion of multicolored winter geraniums, and rang the bell.

Bill Schaeffer, in a red sweater and tan corduroy pants, came to the door in his wheelchair. "Maxi, we're so glad you could visit," he said. *We* again. Sandie was very fortunate to have a dad so devoted to getting his daughter well. That might just be half the battle for her.

"Come in, come in," he welcomed. "Can you believe it's another year already?"

"No. I never can," Maxi responded, reaching down to take his hand.

She followed him as he wheeled across the foyer and through a cheerful, high-ceilinged living room with Mexican terra-cotta pavers on the floor, colorful overlapping Bristol rib rugs, comfortable overstuffed furniture, and plants everywhere. Schaeffer led her down a hall and into a bright, spacious bedroom.

Sandie was sitting up in a hospital bed. She smiled tentatively when she saw Maxi come into the room behind her father and said, "Hello, Maxi Poole."

"Sandie, you look wonderful," Maxi ventured. "It's going to be a very good new year. I feel it, don't you? Happy New Year."

Sandie's expression, with the small, fixed smile, didn't change, though her gaze shifted from Maxi to her father and back again. "Happy New Year," she said in slowly drawn out tones.

Maxi put the books down on a side table by the bed, and explained her intention with them to Bill Schaeffer.

"We're already reading to her," Schaeffer said with a smile, pulling his chair up to bedside. "Thanks for adding to our trove of books."

Maxi scanned the room. A cushy, flowered love seat

nestled beneath a broad, paned-glass window, and drawn up close to the bed were two ample matching chairs. A waxed-pine lowboy stood against the wall, its surface spread with more books, a casual arrangement of yellow tulips, and several framed pictures of what Maxi assumed were family. She saw what she thought to be the touch of a woman in this house, and she remembered reading on the wires that Schaeffer's wife—Sandie's mother—had died just three years ago. How sad for this little family of two, both of them challenged now, to be without the woman Maxi imagined had lovingly created and kept this home.

Four large foil-wrapped pots of red poinsettias were set on the floor around the room, a paean to the holiday season, and a lush ficus tree stood in a corner, adorned with tiny white lights and Christmas ornaments.

The table on the far side of Sandie's bed bore the usual: a pitcher of water, a glass with a curved straw, a square box of tissues—and makeup. Lipsticks, pencils, brushes, pots of foundation, powders, and creams spread out on top. And a hairbrush, a comb, a hand mirror.

Schaeffer's eyes had followed Maxi's. "She asked for her makeup. That's a good sign, isn't it?"

"That's a *great* sign," Maxi allowed, noticing the bulging leopard-skin Gale Hayman Beverly Hills makeup kit on the table. "When we're coming out of the woods, that's the first thing we ask for after our toothbrush. Sometimes *before* our toothbrush," Maxi said with a grin, directing her chat at Sandie. The patient didn't seem to register all that was being said, but she did signal a hint of excitement in her eyes.

Maxi dropped into one of the plush chairs by the bed as a nurse in a crisp white pantsuit came in carrying a tray

with a bottle of wine, glasses, and canapes, and set it
down on the nightstand near Maxi and Bill Schaeffer. She
handed Schaeffer the bottle of wine.

"Ahh," he said, examining the label. "Au Bon Climat,
'ninety-two—a wonderful Pinot Noir. Perfect for a New
Year's toast. Go ahead and open it, Barbara Jean. And say
hello to Maxi Poole."

"I watch you all the time," the woman said to Maxi.
"Call me B.J." She took the bottle from Schaeffer,
wielded the corkscrew, poured two glasses, and handed
them to Maxi and Schaeffer.

"Join us for a toast, B.J.," Schaeffer said. "It's New
Year's Eve."

"Never on duty, Mr. Schaeffer, but I'm with you in
spirit," she said; then she let out a cheery laugh at her un-
intended pun.

Schaeffer smiled at the nurse, then raised a toast to his
daughter, whose eyes seemed to light up at the attention.
"To my girl," he said. "May the new year bring complete
health and abundant happiness for you, dear, light of my
life."

Maxi bent and touched her glass to his, and they
drank. Then nibbled, and talked, to each other and to
Sandie, who made her father glow with joy each time she
responded.

46

Carter Rose sat alone in his den in the Carolwood mansion. In fact he was alone in the house. He'd had an early supper; before she went home, Angie had prepared a honey-baked ham glazed with pineapple and cloves, an endive salad, and her special butternut squash with caramelized onions. He'd given the entire staff the night off. It was New Year's Eve; they had lives.

Kendyl had badgered him to take her to a party. See the damn new year in, as if his wife hadn't just died under suspicious circumstances, as if the whole frigging world didn't know about it, as if he and Kendyl were just your everyday couple. What was wrong with that woman? She carried on as if everything were normal and the Sandie Schaeffer night from hell had never happened.

The events of that night kept replaying in his mind like some recurring Stygian nightmare. He and Kendyl were in the office. It was almost midnight. They had thoroughly raked through Gillian's files without finding the formula, and he was giving up. His wife must have kept it somewhere else. He would come across it somewhere, he was sure, just not tonight. Carter had switched off the overhead lights, locked the doors to both the inner office and Sandie's room, and he and Kendyl had gone back to their own suite to pick up their coats and Kendyl's purse.

They'd been there for just a few minutes when Kendyl heard the noise. Heels clicking on the marble tiles, coming down the hall, then stopping at the suite next door. Kendyl had beckoned to Carter, her finger to her lips. They stood still and listened. Someone was going into Gillian's suite.

Quickly, Carter went back into his inner office and opened the paneling that revealed the bank of monitors— to Kendyl's astonishment; she'd followed him in. Ignoring her, he focused on the two screens that displayed Gillian's office suite. And watched Sandie Schaeffer look around the room, let herself into the inner office, put her purse down on Gillian's desk, and begin a thorough search there.

"What the hell—?" Kendyl started in a whisper before Carter shushed her. And the two watched, silently. Sandie Schaeffer on the video screen doing exactly what *they* had just done, poring through Gillian's files.

To conduct this covert hunt during these unlikely hours, Sandie had to be looking for something that was very important to her, Carter figured. The formula. Had to be. If Gillian had been conducting tests on her father's glaucoma formula, Sandie could have found out. She was Gillian's assistant and her father's daughter—if she'd managed to see analysis reports, she would know what she was looking at.

Even if Sandie was in the dark about the testing, the

papers indicated that Schaeffer had not yet been paid for his formulation—he'd only had Gillian's letter of intent. Just as Carter had done, Sandie might also be taking this first opportunity after the crime-scene tape was pulled to get inside the suite and search for the formula to protect her father. She wouldn't want him to lose his intellectual property to the Rose company without compensation, and she probably suspected that could easily happen in the shuffle now that Gillian was dead. In fact, Sandie wouldn't know if she even had a job for much longer.

While Sandie Schaeffer methodically searched Gillian's office, Carter had sat and watched her on the monitors. He'd figured he might as well see if the woman had any better luck than he and Kendyl had.

Kendyl wasn't dumb. Carter knew she had to be aware that they were probably searching for the same thing, and that it wasn't some papers that would most likely prove worthless in the end. Nobody put forth this kind of effort to find some inconsequential research that was done just as a favor to a small pharmacist. Not Carter. And not Sandie Schaeffer. Kendyl wouldn't have known what the grail was, but, like him, she had to realize that it must be something very valuable. That was the night Kendyl learned too much, the night Kendyl Scott had become dangerous.

When he watched Sandie discover the formula tacked behind Gillian's desk drawer, he made his move. Following the contingency plan he'd come up with over the hours, he sent Kendyl next door to scare her into giving it up. He'd given Kendyl his oversized Burberry raincoat to wear, which hung almost to the floor on her. The ski mask was an improvisation—Carter left ski gear in his closet all through ski season. A wealthy friend of his was known to call at the last minute on any given Friday to say he'd just decided to take his jet to Aspen for the weekend, did Carter want to join him at his tony lodge on Red Mountain? And Carter was always prepared to go, with skis and poles, boots, ski pants, parka, sweaters, the works. And the ski mask, the black wool hat with the eye slits that pulled down over his face for blizzard skiing.

And he gave Kendyl the blue steel Glock he kept locked in his desk drawer. Just to scare Sandie with, he told her—it wasn't loaded.

He wanted that formula.

And he got it.

Carter didn't open the envelope in Kendyl's presence. An envelope retrieved at a very high cost. "For God's sake, what *is* it?" she'd demanded to know. "Exactly what I told you," he'd said, "a formula that's most likely worthless." Kendyl would have translated that to mean it was none of her business. And she knew better than to ask him again. In fact, in view of what had happened in Sandie Schaeffer's office, she'd told him, she didn't *want* to know.

When he later examined the contents of that envelope, he did indeed find the formula inside, along with the name of the independent laboratory that had been working with it. In the days following, he visited that lab, examined their data, and authorized the techs to continue on the path Gillian had outlined, but now, with the death of his wife and partner, they were to send their work product and bills directly to him.

Upon careful study of the complex research, Carter learned what his wife had been holding out on him: a truly golden egg. The data told him exactly what BriteEyes was, and what it did. BriteEyes, in the form of an eyedrop, actually changed the color of a person's eyes for just a few hours, and with no harmful side effects. Extraordinary. A cosmetic breakthrough. Women would go crazy for it. So would men. Teenagers would be all over it. It was a slam dunk.

In the notes he'd found in the safety-deposit box, Gillian had proposed that the product be marketed in packaging of three small vials of drops that would change consumers' eyes to three different colors, colors like hot pink, vibrant purple, fiery orange, indigo blue, silver or gold, fire-engine red, even jet black. With just a couple of drops in each eye, people would have eyes to match their outfits, or their moods. Gillian had preliminarily costed the product out to sell for $29.95 per package. Brilliant.

Carter could already envision the publicity this product would generate, the *free* publicity. Newspaper headlines, talk shows, cable channels, MTV sessions, *People* magazine, *New York* magazine, *Us Weekly,* even *Time* and *Newsweek.* Why, this stuff would make the *cover* of *Time.* It would be a veritable gold mine. A lucrative, ingenious, breakthrough cosmetic eye-color product.

And now it was his. All he had to do was continue the work on it and exercise the letter of intent with pharmacist William Schaeffer. He had no doubt that he could make the deal with Schaeffer. Knowing his wife, and the secrecy with which she'd developed this product, he was sure Schaeffer had no idea what it was he had to sell.

Sandie Schaeffer somehow recognized who shot her that night—Carter had seen and heard her gasp on the monitor. But her doctor reported that his patient was suffering from a form of trauma-induced selective amnesia; she'd blocked out everything that had happened in the entire, disastrous sequence of events from the minute she'd found Gillian dead on her office floor.

Carter hoped his luck would hold. He was pretty sure no one knew where he and Kendyl had been that night. He'd sweated it big time, but twelve days had gone by. If they'd found out, the cops would have been all over his case by now. Of course they'd questioned him as to his whereabouts that night. He was home, he'd said. Alone. Went to bed early. And was back in the office at seven-thirty in the morning, as usual. They couldn't prove that any of it wasn't true. And they had never asked Kendyl anything at all.

Had he and Kendyl left the building that night, they'd have been nailed by the guards. Like Goodman Penthe, who spent Gillian's last night on earth with her. Carter had just found that out today on the morning news. The sonofabitch. *Poor* sonofabitch, Carter thought with a smirk—Goodie was on the hot seat now. But Carter and Kendyl were home free.

Unless Kendyl ever opened her mouth.

He decided to give her the damned diamond ring.

47

Ten minutes to nine. After a pleasant hour at the Schaeffer cottage in the Palisades, Sandie's father had left to go back to his drugstore and Maxi had come home. Settling in for her own little private celebration, she'd cracked a split of California red, figuring she might as well stay with wine. Curled up on the couch in her study, garbed in a comfy gray-and-white-striped Tommy Hilfiger nightshirt, her bare feet tucked beneath her, she was watching the hordes of celebrants gathered in New York's Times Square, live, and waiting with them for the silver ball to drop in ten minutes. She didn't plan to stay up until midnight to see the new year in on the West Coast; although tomorrow would be a holiday for most people, for her it was a workday. She would watch the festivities on New York time, finish her wine, and crash early.

She yawned. *Exciting, my life,* she thought, but smiled. She wouldn't change places with anybody. Okay, maybe Jennifer Aniston.

Her phone rang, and she jumped. Picking up, she answered with "Happy New Year, whoever you are."

"Maxi! What are you doing home? Shouldn't you be at a party?"

Richard! "I'm partying with my dog," she squeaked, nearly choking on her wine.

"Tell Yukon I said Happy New Year."

"Richard says Happy New Year, Yuke," she said to her party mate, bending down to ruffle his neck. "He says 'Back atcha, Richard,'" she said into the phone.

"Tell him I'm going to bring him an etzem lekelev from Israel."

"A *what?*"

"A dog bone. I've been studying my Hebrew."

"When are you leaving?"

"In the morning. El Al at nine."

"Excited?"

"Yes and no." She didn't have to ask him to explain that.

"So . . . where are you now?"

"In a rowdy bar in SoHo. On my cell phone. Wanna welcome the new year in with me?"

"Um . . . okay. Sure. Why aren't you in Times Square?" And don't you have a date on New Year's Eve? she didn't say.

"I took my mom to a party, a bunch of her pals. They're in a townhouse up the street, wearing paper hats and blowing noisemakers, and they definitely didn't need me, so I ducked out to see if I could find you."

"I hear it's snowing back there—"

"Little flurries. But it's building."

"New York is wonderful?"

"New York is always wonderful. I called your mother

and dad and wished them Happy New Year. Told Max I was wearing one of his classy jackets."

When Richard had saved Maxi's life back in October, a bulletproof vest had saved his own skin, but his Giorgio Armani jacket, the only one he owned, was slashed in tatters by an unhinged killer. Grateful, her parents had invited him to come home with her for Thanksgiving dinner, and her dad had taken him to Giorgio Armani on Madison Avenue the next day and bought him three new jackets.

"They adore you," she told him. She fervently hoped that he wouldn't read into that statement that Brigitte and Maxwell Poole would actually like her to marry him and have his babies.

"We're lucky we have our folks," was all he said. Then, "It's almost midnight here, Maxi."

"I'm watching Times Square—it's on live. I'll turn up the volume so you can hear."

"It's on in this bar, too," Richard said.

"Nine, eight, seven . . ." they counted down in unison.

"Happy New Year, Maxi. I miss you."

"Safe trip, Richard," she said. "And . . . uh . . . me too."

48

New Year's Day. Always an impossibly slow news day. Even the crooks and felons have hangovers. Maxi sat in the newsroom with Wendy, perusing the wires, surfing the Net, trying to dig up something happening somewhere.

Word was buzzing around the newsroom that this would be Rob Reordan's last week at the station. Evidently he and the company had agreed to disagree on a new contract, and, according to the newsroom grapevine, an official memo would be released later today announcing that the legendary anchor was moving on to other pursuits.

The joke was the company shouldn't bother putting out memos. The entire staff always knew everything that was about to happen within these walls well before its official release, so posting the information was a waste of time, a waste of effort, and a waste of paper. This was an organization of three hundred news gatherers, after all—you could count on *somebody* to get the advance scoop.

"Rob Reordan has other pursuits?" Wendy wondered aloud, dripping sarcasm. "He's a hundred."

"You know that's what they always write." Maxi said. "Boilerplate text that's code for dumping someone. As in, 'He/she is moving on to other pursuits.' 'He/she wants to spend more time with family.'"

"How about, 'He/she is going into independent production.' Or, 'wants to spend time giving back now,'" Wendy put in. "I always love that one."

The two were astonished to see Rob Reordan come into the newsroom. No one ever saw him in the building at ten in the morning. Since everybody was plugged into the gossip about him, the business-as-usual babble hushed when he walked in. Nor did anyone look up at him. So he knew they knew.

Rob strode over to Wendy's computer station. "Maxi, got a minute to talk?" he asked.

"Happy New Year, Rob," Maxi offered brightly, then wished she hadn't. Rob's face was pasty and drawn, actually looking his eighty-three years. Or maybe she'd never really seen him in daylight without his makeup.

"You too," he said. Then, "Hi, Wendy."

"Hello, Rob," Wendy returned glumly, making a disgruntled mental note that this was the first time Rob Reordan had been civil to her in years.

"So, Maxi, can I talk to you for a minute?" Rob reiterated. It was obvious that he didn't want to talk in the open newsroom, so Maxi led him back to her office and closed the door behind them.

She sat at her desk; Rob perched uncomfortably on her small couch. To ease his seeming tension, she started. "I hear you're leaving, Rob—"

"Ungrateful assholes," he piped up. "I put this fucking

station on the map. Now they're tossing me on the trash heap."

"But you were negotiating, weren't you?"

"Oh, sure, negotiating," he spat out. "They wanted me to take forty cents on the dollar."

"It's still a lot of money, Rob. In this economy, anybody should be thrilled to get it. It's still a lot more than *I* make," she said with a chuckle.

"It's not enough for me," he put in morosely.

"You're kidding."

"I'm not kidding. I have debts. Alimony. Child support. College funds . . ."

"And a collection of vintage cars to support. And an expensive powerboat. And the airplane. Why not just scale down, Rob?"

"Can't. And dammit, I *own* this fucking market—I'll get another gig."

"I'm sure you will. Have you talked to anyone?"

"Hitch is talking to Seven. And Thirteen. He'll work something out." Ed Hitchcock was the powerful talent agent for half the market's news personalities.

"Well, I wish you all the best, Rob," she said. "You deserve it." And he did deserve it, she reflected, if for nothing other than his longevity. It was hard to get these jobs, but even harder to hang on to them, and Rob Reordan had been a local news fixture in a major market for half a century.

"Maxi," he said then, "can you lend me some money?" The question slammed into her by surprise, cutting off her platitudes. She was speechless.

"It wouldn't be for long," he said. "Just till I land on my feet. And I'll add twenty percent interest to the principal when I pay you back."

"Uhh . . . how much money, Rob?" She couldn't fathom how a person with his income over the years, over *decades,* could be living from paycheck to paycheck.

"A hundred thousand. And I'll pay you back a hundred and twenty in six months." When she remained silent, he said, "Or fifty thou, if that's all you can do."

She still had nothing to say. Who knew if he could get another lucrative anchor gig at his age? Twenty percent interest was terrific, but twenty percent of nothing was still nothing. She had no intention of lending him that kind of money. Or any at all. He'd never been a close friend; he was a colleague. They had a professional relationship.

But how to tell him? Especially sitting with him here in her office, his watery blue eyes looking tired, defeated. "I'll talk to my business manager," she said, and was annoyed with herself for not being up front with him.

"You'll let me know?" he asked, a flood of pitiable, hopeful pleading in those eyes now. She was embarrassed for both of them.

"On Monday," she said. "Everybody's away for the holidays now."

She didn't want to look into his eyes. It wasn't just about money and his woefully inept management of the millions he'd earned. She was looking at a man who had been beloved by his fans since before she was born. A man who'd had it all—power, money, status, celebrity, a legendary run in the business, everything—and now she was looking at the end of it. And for all his bravado, she could feel that he knew it too. If he actually was able to hook up at another station, it wouldn't be for much money, and it wouldn't be for long. He was pretty much out of options, and it was sad. And it was life. This man should be comfortable now, enjoying these years, but instead she saw in him just hurt and desperation.

Impulsively, she came out from behind her desk in the tiny office and gave him a hug. And watched him go out the door.

She idled in her office, feeling a little depressed and not quite sure why. There was nothing much to do today, really. She had no story assignment, either for the early block or for the Eleven; there was barely enough going on to keep the regular reporting staff busy. She would be co-anchoring the Six with Rob, but that was nearly eight hours away.

She thought about the Gillian Rose story and Penthe's conversation with her yesterday about being with the woman the night before she died. *Late* on the night before she died. Maxi calculated that they would have been together a scant twelve hours before Gillian was found dead in her office.

Authorities had found no evidence of foul play, but they still hadn't released the body. That meant they suspected something, even though they hadn't been able to nail it down. Poison? Could Penthe have slipped some untraceable poison compound into Gillian's drink? But why? To get the formula for himself? Then why would he poison her with a slow-acting substance? The man owned two thriving pharmaceutical companies—no question he had access to chemicals that would do the job on the spot. Why wouldn't he use a poison that would fell her immediately so he could snatch the formula and run?

She hit the side of her forehead with the heel of her palm. *Hello!* Because, dummy, the guards would have seen him leaving the building alone. Then they'd have found Gillian's body. And the police wouldn't have just questioned him, they'd have arrested him and charged him with murder.

So what would he gain by causing Gillian's death the next day? Why would he want her out of the way when she was his ticket to some fabulous formula that they both seemed to believe would make them millions?

Maybe he didn't need Gillian to get his hands on the formula. He was adamant about buying the floundering Rose company. Maybe he figured that, as the CEO of Rose, he could finesse the formula one way or another. After all, Gillian didn't yet have the rights to it either, but she'd already done major testing and development on it. Maybe Penthe had figured that this small-time pharmacist in a wheelchair had to be a pushover. Penthe had seen the research documents with the name of the private laboratory doing the work clearly posted on the letterhead. As the owner of Rose International, getting control of the product looked easy—and without Gillian Rose in the picture, it would be all his.

Far-fetched? She decided to follow up on the notion anyway. Maybe she wouldn't bother chasing down such a long shot if it weren't a deadly dull news day. She picked up her phone and put in a call to the morgue, one of the few other businesses besides hers that stayed open on holidays. The business of death, she mused. It never took a day off. She gave the receptionist her name and asked for Charlie Strand.

"Yo, Max," he said when he came on the line. "You working today?"

"Sure," she said. "So are you."

"Of course so am I. I'm low man in the pecking order. It's just me and the stiffs. Happy New Year."

"Don't tell me it's just you and the stiffs—there're plenty of staff there today, right?"

"Right. I like to bitch. It clears my sinuses. What can I do ya for? Do you want my body?"

"No. I want to find out about poisons. Like how many untraceable poisons can kill you twelve hours later."

"Who do you wanna kill? Your boss? Your New Year's Eve date? You should have come with me, to this wild rave party up in the San Bernardino mountains—five hundred people, all wasted. What a blast. I am so hungover—"

"So, Charlie . . . can you put me on to someone who can answer some questions about poisons?"

"That would be our head toxicologist, Dr. Elizabeth Riker. Dr. Beth. Medical examiner, pathologist, poison expert, babe. And definitely not down here with the lowest in the pecking order—she's off today."

"When is she back?"

"Lemme check the schedule."

He paused for a beat, and Maxi could hear the click-clicking of his computer keys. "Hmph," he said. "She's in at three o'clock this morning. She's got the three A.M. to noon shift. Maybe she's not so high in the pecking order."

"Maybe there *is* no pecking order," Maxi said. "Maybe you imagine it."

"There's a pecking order everywhere. Isn't there one at Channel Six?"

Of course there was, Maxi conceded to herself. "I don't think about it," she said. "I'll call Dr. Riker in the morning."

"Wait, wait, wait," Charlie exhorted. "When are we having our New Year's toast? So I can get my New Year's kiss?"

Maxi laughed. Charlie never stopped. And she was sure he fed the same lines to a lot of women. Maybe even to Dr.

Elizabeth Riker. And he was so adorable he could get away with it; what woman would bring Charlie up on sexual harassment charges? Too young, too cute, and definitely not to be taken seriously.

"Next week," she said. "And thanks, Charlie."

She hung up and wandered out into the newsroom. Laurel Baker was sitting at her desk and called her over.

"You missed a great party last night," she said.

"I'm sure I did, but you have to forgive me. I just didn't feel like going out."

"On New Year's Eve?"

"*Especially* on New Year's Eve," Maxi said. And Laurel let it drop.

"What's new?" Maxi asked her then. Laurel always knew what was new, be it in the news, gossip, or office politics. But for half a beat she didn't reply.

"Let me ask you something, Maxi," she said then. "By any chance, did Rob ask you to loan him money?"

The question surprised Maxi. "Um . . . yes, he did," she answered. "Why do you ask?"

"Because he asked me, too, and he asked Roggin and Montoya." John Roggin and Paulo Montoya were the station's two sports anchors. "And God knows who else. Are you going to lend him money?"

"I told him I'd let him know by Monday," Maxi hedged. "Are you going to?"

"Of course not," Laurel said. "His ship is sinking."

49

Driving west on Wilshire to Kendyl's apartment, Carter Rose chuckled without mirth. He actually did have a diamond ring, and it was in his pocket. A huge, eleven-carat pear-shaped D flawless canary yellow diamond flanked by tapered baguettes and set in platinum, which had been personally designed for Gillian by Gustav Kleinberg, exclusive jewelry designer for Harry Winston. It was supposed to be a surprise for their anniversary next month. Gillian had loved the many unique, important pieces of jewelry he had given her over the years, most of which she had chosen or designed herself because her taste was so specific. And impeccable. And she'd worn her lavish jewels with great panache. She was known for them. But this year, for this anniversary, their fifteenth, he'd wanted to surprise her with a special diamond ring. That was before he'd found out she was making plans to leave him.

Back when Carter and Gillian met at Berkeley, when

she was a sophomore and he was a senior, they had no money at all, and when they married two years later, they had precious little. He couldn't afford to buy her an engagement ring back then, and she didn't ask for one. But over the years they'd made plenty of money, and he could afford to buy her all the jewelry she wanted, and did, but she'd never once mentioned that she'd like the engagement ring she never had. He would surprise her with the ring, he'd decided, as a kind of renewal of their vows, and it would be a ring that she'd love because, as usual, she would design it herself.

He had enlisted Sandie Schaeffer to make it happen. Sandie was close to Gillian, and she was happy to help him pull off his anniversary surprise. They'd cooked up a plan. Sandie told Gillian that a friend of hers was in the market for the perfect diamond ring, and that her fiancé had unlimited funds and wanted his future wife to have the absolute ultimate, a lavishly elegant engagement ring to last their lifetime together. And since Gillian was a jewelry maven, Sandie asked her to dash off on paper the ideal diamond ring, as if she were sketching it for herself.

Gillian had enjoyed the challenge. She came up with the beautiful ring design in India ink on graph paper, and Gustav Kleinberg had translated the rendering to platinum and diamonds. The piece, for which Carter had dropped half a million, was now in his office safe.

Kendyl had quizzed him about his several surreptitious meetings with Sandie Schaeffer behind closed doors. She'd suspected that he was sleeping with Sandie, he knew. The cold war between Kendyl and Sandie dipped to deep-freeze temperatures on Kendyl's side, her discourtesy extending even to Sandie's harmless invalid father, long disabled by childhood polio, who had complained to Gillian about Kendyl Scott's rudeness on the phone to him.

Gillian was adamant at the time that he should fire Kendyl, that she was an embarrassment to the company. That turned out to be a big red flag for Carter: Gillian must know for sure that it wasn't all business between himself and his comely personal assistant.

But why wouldn't she know? Carter had thought at the time. Half the company knew, the verity of their longtime affair probably promulgated by Kendyl herself, who loved to brag. He could just hear her: "Promise you won't tell anybody, but last night . . ." He'd just figured that Gillian didn't really care, that they had an unspoken understanding about such things. Later he learned how wrong he was.

Carter didn't respond to Gillian at the time. Nor did he fire Kendyl. And he wasn't about to tell Kendyl that Gillian's assistant Sandie was just helping him purchase a big-ticket diamond ring as an anniversary gift for his wife; Kendyl wouldn't have appreciated that. Carter had just put his head in the sand and continued to walk that particular tightrope. Big mistake, he found out.

He hadn't given a thought to the ring since Gillian's death. Now Kendyl would get it after all. But with no symbolism attached, at least on his part. He had no intention of marrying Kendyl Scott, but he had to let her think he did. By the time the dust settled on this entire, horrendous episode in his life, it wouldn't matter.

50

We're in a zero-news zone, Wendy," Maxi remarked
to her producer, who sat huddled over her computer terminal as usual, her small, black-rimmed reading
glasses suspended on the tip of her freckled nose.

"No kidding. New Year's Day. Nothing shaking at all.
I'm now looking into ten-year-old unsolved crimes that
we might revisit for the early block."

"How about the O.J. case—that one's never been
solved."

"Yeah, right. You want to go over to the Griffith Park
Observatory? I'll set up an interview with the director—
maybe he can talk to you about the space aliens who
killed Ron and Nicole."

"Tell you what I *am* going to do. Unless you need me
to cover some legitimate news, I'm going to spend some
time walking my fingers through computer files. *Your*
computer files. Including navigating the path from here to
your home PC. Let's see if we can find any electronic fin-

gerprints that might help us solve a *recent* crime—you know the one I mean."

"Thanks, Maxi, but it won't help. Believe me, I've thought about this backwards and forwards. I know what you're going to see. I gave Sunday all my passwords. The logs will show that she accessed my home computer about a hundred times to work on the book. For countless hours, for days on end. So what's that going to prove?"

"I don't know. Would she ever have copied the whole manuscript to disk?"

"Sure. The very first day she started working on it, she made a copy to take home and review to get up to speed. Making a copy of *DBD* takes all of about forty-five seconds on the system."

"Did she make just that one copy?"

"I have no idea, but what would it matter? All she'd need is one."

"Or two—one to make your official changes on and a parallel one to disguise as a completely different book."

"Easily done." Wendy shrugged.

"By the way, where is she now?" Maxi asked, looking around the newsroom. "She used to be here days, nights, weekends, holidays—how come she's not here today?"

"Who knows?" Wendy said cynically. "She's probably out doing her after-Christmas shoplifting."

"Right. Was she here yesterday?"

"No. Her internship is over. And I wouldn't be surprised if I've seen the last of her."

Maxi felt Wendy's dejection. "Well, I'll just take a look through your files, okay? Can't hurt."

"Okay. I'll write out my new passwords. I just changed them, but they'll get you to the same places. Or if you use the computer in my office, you won't need passwords. Curt set me up on remote access to my home computer."

Curtis Cannistra was a twenty-two-year-old technical whiz kid who was working on his computer-technology master's at Cal Tech and working part-time at Channel Six for college money. Pete Capra told people he couldn't believe how lucky he'd been to find this guy. In just a few months Curt had thoroughly updated most of the computer systems at the station.

"How do I connect?"

"Just double-click on my remote-access icon and you're in."

"Easy. I'll be in your office."

"Yell if you need me to answer any questions," Wendy said. "And I'll yell if any actual news breaks out."

Maxi walked over to the row of glassed-in offices along the perimeter of the newsroom and went into the one marked WENDY HARRIS. Wendy never locked her office door. Nobody did. Taking a seat at the computer, Maxi settled in to play cyber detective. Maybe she'd find something to indicate that Sunday Trent was doing more business than just editing Wendy's book. Maybe she'd find a trail of text going out to some New York literary agent.

Fat chance, she knew, as she clicked on Wendy's remote-access icon and prepared to rummage through her home files.

51

Kendyl sat in the living room of her tony high-rise on the Wilshire corridor, sipped grapefruit juice, and studied her long, red fingernails. And sulked. It was noon, and she was still in her floor-length gold charmeuse lounging robe. Maybe she wouldn't bother to get dressed at all today. New Year's Day, the first day of a brand-new year, when you were supposed to feel fresh and new and filled with promise. Exciting plans. Great expectations. What a crock. She had nothing to look forward to. And Carter was being a moody prick.

At least a dozen New Year's Eve invitations for her boss had come across her desk. She'd begged him to take her to one of those posh parties last night. Or out to a restaurant for a late dinner, then maybe a New Year's Eve drink at midnight. He'd cut her dead. Couldn't she see how inappropriate that would be? he'd snapped. So she'd suggested that he just come over to her place—they'd have wine and caviar and kiss the new year in. No, he'd said coldly, he was in no mood to celebrate.

She had to be kidding herself if she thought they still had a personal relationship going. Whatever they'd once had was in tatters. Gillian's death seemed to split the two of them farther apart, not bring them closer. In truth, Carter's wife's death seemed somehow to render Kendyl and him . . . over.

Her phone rang. She looked at it for a moment, then answered it with a small, hopeful, "Hello?"

"Kendyl?"

Not Carter. "Yes . . ."

"Hi. It's Claire. Happy New Year!" Claire Jenkins was a friend from the office. "What did you do last night?" she asked.

"You know, I had a raging headache and I just stayed home," Kendyl said. "I had a cup of tea and watched the celebrations on television."

"I can understand that," Claire said. "It's been such a terrible time for the company."

"Yes. Here's to the new year," Kendyl said. "Let's hope it's all behind us now."

Claire talked about the New Year's Eve party she went to, at a prominent Beverly Hills plastic surgeon's home, a colleague of Claire's physician husband. Kendyl listened with half an ear until her friend brought up Sandie Schaeffer's doctor.

"Wally Stevens was there," Claire said. "He had the best news about Sandie."

Kendyl's hand flew to her mouth. Was Sandie talking? And what was she saying? She felt her heart sinking.

". . . said that Sandie is making great strides," Claire was going on.

"Is . . . is she still in Intensive Care?" Kendyl asked.

"Oh, no. I heard she's not only out of the ICU, she's out of the hospital. Her father took her home over the weekend. I'm betting Sandie's going to make a full recovery and will be able to come back to work at some point."

Claire chattered on, about Sandie, about the party, about who was wearing what, office dish. Kendyl barely heard. She interrupted, told Claire she had to run, she was due at a New Year's brunch.

Putting down the phone, she felt her stomach contract. Did Sandie remember what happened that night? Would she tell about it? And how, Kendyl agonized, how the *hell* had she known that the person in the ridiculous ski mask, the person holding the gun, was her?

Before that night, she'd never in her life held a gun in her hand. The plan was to scare Sandie with it. But Sandie had gasped, "My God, *Kendyl*. It's *you!*" That's what had startled Kendyl so she'd inadvertently pulled the trigger and the gun went off.

Carter had told her he'd never used this gun, or any gun. That he'd had it for years and had a legal permit to keep it in the office. And that it wasn't loaded.

Wrong.

Now she was in deep trouble. How was she going to protect herself from this specter that was gaining on her, breathing down her neck? Carter was a powerful man; he would get off with a suspended sentence. He didn't pull the trigger. But she was the one who would go to prison. And in her gut, she seriously doubted that Carter would be putting himself out on a limb to protect her.

She felt dizzy. Panicky. She had to do *something*. And

she had to figure out exactly what to do fast, before her
world caved in.

Maybe she should go to the police, tell them what happened. Before Carter did. She'd have a better chance that
way. She'd break down and sob, and tell how Carter Rose
had put her up to it. Her boss. And how she had never
meant to hurt Sandie Schaeffer. It was an accident.

Her phone rang again, and she jumped. She stared at
it, and froze, couldn't pick it up. She heard her own
voice on the answering machine. "Hi, it's Kendyl—
leave a message, and I'll get back to you." Click. Then,
"Hi, darling—"

Carter! She pounced on the phone. "Yes, Carter . . ."

"I need to see you. I've got something for you."

"Um . . . where are you?"

"In your lobby. Call the guy at the desk and tell him to
let me up."

"Oh. Okay. I'll call him."

She clicked the receiver a couple of times to discon-
nect, then punched up the speed-dial number for the
lobby. Then instructed the guard to send Mr. Rose upstairs. Then ran through her bedroom and into her master
bath, and dabbed on some makeup, a little blush, eyebrows, light lipstick, a squirt of perfume. It took her
ninety seconds.

She scrutinized the results in the mirror. Pathetic, she
thought. But the fact was, Kendyl Scott was blessed with
angular cheekbones, luscious full lips, moist olive skin, a
wealth of silky brown hair that fell loosely around her
shoulders this morning, and a tall, slim body that made
strong men weak. She didn't need even a minute and a
half of primping. There was no way Kendyl Scott could
not look stunning.

She rushed out into the living room at the sound of the doorbell. Sweeping the front door open like Loretta Young in her prime, the silken gold dressing gown swirling about her accentuating every sensuous curve, she bestowed her most radiant smile on Carter Rose.

Carter came in the room and pulled her into his arms. "Happy New Year, darling," he mouthed against her neck. Then he pulled back, put his hand into the pocket of his trench coat, the one she'd worn that night, and pulled out a small, black velvet box. From Harry Winston.

In her wildest fantasy, it was the most exquisite diamond ring she could ever have imagined.

52

Maxi came back over to Wendy's computer terminal in the newsroom and handed her a sheaf of papers.

"What's this?" Wendy asked.

"It's a printout of every access made to your home computer in the last two months. Take a good look at it. Start from the end and go backwards. I'm going to run back to my office to check my messages. I'll be back."

Wendy squinted at the small type. She took out a red felt-tipped pen and started marking the papers. By the time Maxi got back and pulled up a chair beside her, she had thoroughly scanned the list.

"Okay, got it scoped," she said. "When the access hit is by the remote icon, it would be me. I'm the only one who goes into my home PC by that icon from my office, and I'm pretty much the only one who's ever in there. Occasionally Pete, once in a while a writer, but they would never use my computer."

"Do you always access by your remote icon?"

"No. I password in if I'm sitting out here in the newsroom and I don't want to bother walking back to my office."

"When you access from out here, could it be for long periods of time?" Maxi was pretty sure she knew the answer to that.

"No," Wendy confirmed her guess. "It might be to make a quick note about something that just occurred to me and I don't want to forget later. Then I'm in and out. Too busy on the job out here. If I actually do have a chunk of time to work on the book while I'm here at work, I go into my office and close the door, to escape the noise and insanity. And I access by remote icon."

"And you never use passwords from your office machine?"

"No. No reason to."

"Okay. So any of these logged time periods that are longer than, say, ten minutes, would be you if it's by remote-access icon, and Sunday if it's by password, right?"

"Yes. But I still don't see—"

"Humor me. What are these red checks you made?"

"I've marked all the hits using passwords—because, as you just said, those would be Sunday's."

"See anything out of the ordinary?"

"Nope. They start a couple of weeks ago—that's when she began working on the book."

"So, nothing unusual?"

"Nothing unusual."

"Look closer at the red-checked times and dates. Can you be sure Sunday was here on all of those days?"

"I really can't, Max. Sunday was an intern. She had a regular news schedule. After school and weekends, basically. But as you know, she was here a lot of extra hours, and at odd hours, on the book project. She was issued her own security card—she came and went freely."

"Do any of the dates look odd? Any of them days when you happen to know she was somewhere else? Think, Wendy. I'm just wondering if anyone else could have latched on to your passwords."

"No," Wendy murmured, scanning the printed sheets. "Off the top, I have no reason to question any of these dates or times. They're all within the window of her workdays here."

"And how did she leave things with you?"

"She told me she was taking a few days off to ski at Mammoth over the Christmas break and she'd be back in to the station next week."

"Even though her internship is finished for this semester?"

"Yes. She had to hand in her security pass, but she said she'd work out some hours with me, and Pete said it was okay for her to come on the lot. We were almost finished with the rewrites. We figured about another week."

"Think we'll ever see her again?"

"Not if she stole my book."

Maxi sighed. "And as you said, we'd never be able to prove that she snatched the material, altered it, and sent it off to a literary agent, anyway."

The two sat and stared at the printed sheets. "There must be a way," Maxi said finally. "Let's look at the remote accessing you did yourself."

"Why?"

"I don't know. Got a green pen? We need a different color."

Wendy dug around in the top drawer of her desk. "How about purple?"

"Fine. Get out your schedule."

"You know my schedule. I'm here every day from eight in the morning till seven, seven-thirty at night, after I archive the Six. And sometimes till after midnight if I'm producing the Eleven."

"Do you keep track?"

"Not really. I'm here when Pete needs me."

"Okay. Well, let's just look."

Maxi took the purple felt-tipped pen in hand and started from the bottom, checking off the last hit Wendy had made by remote access to her computer at home. "This morning," she said. "Ten-seventeen."

"Yup. Checked my home e-mail."

"Yesterday, three times." Maxi made three purple check marks beside the access records. "Remember these?"

Wendy did. And she was able to verify the approximate times on up the list. Until they got to one hit that made her pause. "Thursday, December twenty-sixth, one-twelve A.M. For sixteen minutes and twenty-two seconds."

"Yeah . . . ?" Maxi prompted.

"One o'clock in the morning on the twenty-sixth. That would be Christmas night. After the Eleven. I wasn't here on Christmas night. That I know for sure."

"Hmm. I was. I had Christmas dinner at Debra's, then I came back and did a recut for the Eleven. And no, you weren't here. I remember Julie Takuda produced the Eleven."

"Was Sunday here on Christmas night?"

"You know, I don't remember. She could have been."

53

Quarter to nine A.M. on Thursday. Traffic was on the light side for morning rush hour on the usually jammed L.A. freeways. Why did they call it rush hour anyway, Maxi wondered idly, when drivers were bumper-to-bumper and no one was rushing anywhere? Well, not so bad today, at least, because half the city was sitting out these last two days of the week after New Year's Day, squeezing the last ounce of juice out of the holiday season.

She exited the Golden State Freeway and maneuvered onto North Mission Road to the County of Los Angeles Department of the Coroner, the squat complex that housed the overcrowded morgue facilities for "bodies with questions"—unidentified, cause of death pending, possible homicides, and the rest.

A story that the station had aired late last year delineating a myriad of problems within the department came to mind. This morgue, sandwiched between the first floor and the basement on what was called the "service" floor, was designed for three hundred and eighty bodies, but there were usually eight or nine hundred doubled and tripled up on tables in the three large refrigerated rooms and overflowing into the outside storage bin they'd thrown refrigeration into and purloined for fifty or so more bodies. Now it was a year later and there was still no funding, still no plans to expand.

Maxi had a nine-o'clock appointment with Dr. Elizabeth Riker, poison specialist. And if she thought *she* was pooped every morning, what about Dr. Riker, who was already six hours into her shift?

The adjacent parking lot was half filled with white emergency-response vehicles displaying the red, black, and gold seal of the L.A. County Coroner's Office and the big white-and-blue coroner's vans, the so-called death wagons that transported the unlucky from the county's crime scenes. Maxi found a parking spot, locked up, entered the industrial sand-colored building, and walked through the double glass doors—where the air immediately changed to the smell of Formalin. Or maybe the smell was just her imagination in overdrive.

In the reception area, she signed in at the desk, then took a seat to wait for Dr. Riker to come out to get her. Instead, Charlie Strand bounded into the reception area.

"Yo, Max. Heard you were coming. Cool shoes," he said.

Maxi glanced down at her nothing-special J. Crew strappy brown wedge-heeled sandals. "Oh yeah? Why cool? I need to know what kids think is cool."

"I'm not a kid, which you'd know if you let me show you, and they're cool because I'm looking at painted toenails in January. Very sexy. I love L.A. But you need a toe ring."

"I need to see Dr. Riker. She in?"

"Yeah, she's here. She's got her nose up the abdomen of a heroin overdose. Ughh. Hate that skin tone—the crud-blue thing. Not a good look."

"Mmm. Do you know when she'll be available?"

A side door swung open and a tall, handsome woman in an open white lab coat and latex gloves came into the foyer. "Hello, Ms. Poole. I'm Elizabeth Riker."

"Wow! The two sexiest babes in L.A. in the same room." Charlie beamed enthusiastically.

"Charlie, Charlie, Charlie," Dr. Riker said. "Back to your kennel, boy." Charlie grinned, said, "Catch you later, Max," and scooted out the same door Dr. Riker had come through.

"Nice to meet you, Ms. Poole," the doctor said, extending her hand. Then she noticed she still had the gloves on. "Whoops," she said, and pulled them off. "Latex gloves, the way of the world today. We think they'll actually protect us from the monster."

"What monster?" Maxi asked.

"Whatever monster you're dealing with at the moment."

Maxi smiled. She liked this woman immediately. "Call me Maxi," she said. "We already have something in common. Charlie Strand's blatant sexism."

"And thank God for it," the doctor said with a grin. "Sometimes a lascivious comment from Charlie is exactly what I need for rejuvenation at the end of a hoary day."

Riker looked to be fortyish, with broad bones and an open face, very little makeup, her clear skin glowing with health, her shiny, chestnut-colored wavy hair cut short and stylish, her lively hazel eyes crinkling mischievously when she spoke—this was a woman who laughed a lot,

Maxi could see. "Come on back," she said, holding the door open for Maxi.

They settled in Riker's office, a ten-foot-by-ten-foot space jammed with a county-issue dun-colored metal desk and a creaky brown Naugahyde chair, a couple of mismatched wooden straight chairs, a bank of dented metal file cabinets, and a tall black plastic trash can overflowing with papers. Every surface was piled with files, journals, medical books, and divergent flotsam, and stored up on high shelves were jars of various sizes filled with murky liquid and globs of something. It was the jars filled with murky liquid and globs of something that Maxi tried to avoid looking at.

"How can I help you?" the doctor asked pleasantly, seeming both oblivious to and comfortable in her surroundings.

"I'm working on the Gillian Rose story. Her body is still here," Maxi said, looking around as if she fully expected to see the aforementioned body crammed somewhere among the detritus of pathologist Elizabeth Riker's cluttered office.

"Yes," Dr. Riker confirmed. "That body hasn't been released yet." She raised her eyebrows quizzically to signal Maxi to continue.

Maxi was still trying to deal with a building full of bodies and an office full of jars of parts of bodies. She straightened and pulled her grisly mental imagery back into line. "Do you know if they tested her for poisons?" she asked.

"It wasn't my case, but I'm pretty sure they would. Let's check," Riker said. She turned from Maxi to a computer terminal on top of her desk and clicked on a succession of files.

"Nothing unusual," she said finally. "Her husband gave us a list of the prescription drugs, vitamins, supplements, et cetera that she used. Aside from those, she was tested for a panel of common illegal substances—none found. But there's a note attached to the autopsy report, which means they haven't finished."

"What are they testing for now?"

"More standard stuff," she said, still perusing her computer files. "Because she was young, in apparent good physical shape, and they didn't find anything in the first go-round. Why do you ask?"

"Because someone was alone with her twelve hours before she died, at two in the morning in her office—they were drinking."

"Yes, I saw that on the news. Some big-deal eastern businessman. Were they lovers?"

"I wouldn't think so."

"What, then, at two in the morning?"

"They were colleagues. She was demonstrating some new product she was developing."

"And . . . ?"

"And . . . I don't know. I just wondered if he could have—"

"Poisoned her?" Dr. Riker finished.

"Yeah," Maxi said sheepishly. "Poisoned her."

"We could run some lethal specifics," Riker said matter-of-factly.

"Umm, even if there's nothing concrete to go on?"

"Sure, if somebody suspects something."

"If the somebody is me, and I have absolutely no basis—"

"I could go ahead and conduct a panel of specific tests

if my talking parrot told me he had a dream about it, if I wanted to."

"Oh. Well, would you want to?"

Riker laughed. "Sure," she said. "I'd like to nail something down on this case and move her out of here. We need the drawer space."

Yikes. "What'll you test for?"

"Well, let's look at this. If you were the man, and you wanted to poison this woman, how would you do it, and what would you use?" The teacher in her, Maxi noted mentally.

"Um . . . I'd use something that would not show up in routine toxicology tests. And I'd slip it in her drink when she wasn't looking."

"So it needs to be soluble, fairly undetectable in alcohol, not a substance that's routinely traced, and available to this guy."

"This guy owns pharmaceutical companies."

"So 'available' is no problem for him."

"And it would have to be something that would kill her twelve hours later, or thereabouts."

"That narrows it down. Look, I've got an autopsy at ten, but I'll get on this after lunch."

Lunch, Maxi thought. *How the hell do they eat lunch in this place?* "Here's my card," Maxi said. "You'll call me?"

"Of course I'll call you. You're my talking parrot."

54

On her way back to the Channel Six newsroom, Maxi stopped in at Security Operations on the ground floor of her building.

"Maxi Poole, anchorwoman extraordinaire, Happy New Year," director of security Jim Murphy said. "What brings you to our digs?"

"Hi, Jimbo. I need to ask you some questions about security in the newsroom."

"Sure. Come in. Sit down. Have a doughnut."

Maxi slipped through the swinging gate in the front counter and followed Murphy over to a table with a steaming twelve-cup Mr. Coffee machine, a stack of Styrofoam cups, a carton of two percent milk, and a big pink bakery box from Winchell's. She helped herself to a chocolate doughnut with colored sprinkles on top and a cup of coffee, grabbed a couple of napkins, and sat down next to Murphy's desk.

"How do I go about getting a look at a security tape from the newsroom?"

"You ask me for it."

Whoa. Twice in one morning she heard yes. So rare. Good omen for the new year. Now if she could just stick to her diet resolution. She took a guilty look at the doughnut in her hand, then took a bite.

"This was Christmas night, Jim, in Wendy Harris's office." Everybody on the lot knew Wendy. "From about one in the morning of December twenty-sixth, for the next half hour."

"What's up?"

"We think somebody hacked into Wendy's private computer files."

"Did you get authorization for the tape from Capra?"

"Not yet. I'm just getting in."

"Do that. Send me down the paperwork and I'll put a trace on the tape and have it delivered to the newsroom."

"Thanks, Jim."

"Anytime. Have another doughnut."

"I believe I will. I don't eat them in the newsroom—too many calories."

"And that one?" Murphy queried, glancing quizzically at the half-eaten doughnut in her hand.

"This isn't the newsroom. This is a doughnut in the field. It doesn't count."

Kendyl Scott had taken her lunch hour to drive up Wilshire Boulevard to Beverly Hills and have her ring appraised at upscale Harry Winston Jewelers on Rodeo Drive. She couldn't believe the figure on the document they'd provided. For insurance purposes, she'd said. "Of course," the salesman had responded with a snotty, knowing smile. "And Happy New Year to you, Ms. Scott," he'd added.

Thank you, and drop dead, she'd mentally said. And thank you, Carter. As she punched in the code for the express elevator at the Rose building, she glanced again at the dazzling rock on her finger. For about the thousandth time since Carter had given it to her yesterday. It was the absolutely most overwhelming engagement ring on the planet, she was sure. Which, unfortunately, had come with the absolutely most underwhelming marriage proposal. In fact, it wasn't a marriage proposal at all.

"Don't wear it on your wedding-ring finger," Carter had said. Actually, it was too big for her ring finger. She was wearing it on her middle finger.

"And don't tell anybody it's from me. It's too soon," he'd said. She'd told him she would have it sized later, when he was comfortable with the timing.

"Where shall I say I got it?" she'd asked, giddy with the joy of it.

"Just say it's fake, a fun ring," he'd said with a laugh. "So big, it actually looks a little fake, doesn't it? Nobody'll want to steal it."

So that's what she would tell anybody who asked her. Only nobody had asked her yet. She hadn't even set foot out of her apartment yesterday, on New Year's Day, and here at work nobody made much small talk since Gillian died and Sandie was shot. What gratified Kendyl was that Carter had bought such a huge, gorgeous ring for her. That he must have had it planned all along. And when she was given the appraisal from Harry Winston's, she nearly swooned. This was the real deal.

The question was, was she engaged to be married, or was she just newly rich?

55

Maxi put a call in to Schaeffer Pharmacy. Bill Schaeffer picked up and wished her another Happy New Year. "Thanks for coming over on New Year's Eve—it meant a lot to us," he said. "And you wouldn't believe the change in our girl today."

"Yes?"

"Yes. It's like a veil has lifted. She's speaking whole sentences. She's making sense. It's like a miracle."

"Does she remember—?"

"Still not what happened from the time Gillian Rose died until she came out of the coma. But she's talking about everything else. And Dr. Stevens says he thinks she'll get there."

"I'd like to visit her," Maxi said. "Nothing's happening on the news front—the holiday blahs. I've got some time before the Six. Is the nurse there?"

"Yes, of course. I'll call home and tell her you're going to stop by. You seem to be good for Sandie. She watched

you on the news yesterday, and she talked about it. About
the earthquake in Saugus. She put on lipstick this morning."

"Okay," Maxi said. "Tell the nurse I'll be there in
about an hour. Barbara Jean, right?"

"Barbara Jean Martin. B.J. She's a wonder—don't
know what I'd have done without her through this. I'll
call her now."

A messenger tapped on her office door, then came in
with a package. Maxi glanced at the manila envelope. The
tape from Security Operations. Wendy was busy producing the Six, and Maxi wanted to duck out to the Palisades
and back before prepping for the show. When they got off
the air, they'd view the tape. She dropped the package on
her desk, grabbed her purse, fumbled inside for her keys,
and headed downstairs to the parking lot.

As she'd expected, traffic was still light, the drive
across town unimpeded. Moving westbound on Sunset,
she thought about the Rose story. If Goodman Penthe was
the key, then who shot Sandie Schaeffer, and why? She
was anxious to hear for herself what Sandie had to say,
now that she was talking.

She felt that she had established a good rapport with
the Schaeffers. And in fact, she genuinely liked the father,
and she was rooting for Sandie. Now, with the patient's
stepped-up progress, she hoped she could get Bill Schaeffer to agree to let her videotape his daughter for the news
at some point.

"Hi, B.J.," Maxi said to the nurse, who'd answered the
door with a broad smile.

"Maxi Poole," she said. "We're expecting you. Come
on in."

"I brought the picture you asked for," Maxi said, handing B.J. an envelope. It was an eight-by-ten color photo of the Channel Six news team. "Everybody signed it," Maxi said. "Well, everybody except Rob Reordan."

"Oh, too bad," B.J. said, taking the envelope out of Maxi's hand and leading her to Sandie's room. "I've been watching Rob Reordan since I was in high school."

"You and the rest of Southern California. He's leaving the station. Going somewhere else."

"He's *leaving* Channel Six?" B.J. exclaimed, her eyes wide. "He *is* Channel Six! Where's he going?"

"We don't know yet."

B.J. wouldn't let it go. "*Why* is he going?" she demanded to know.

"Guess he thinks it's time for a change." She remembered that she had to tell Rob tonight that she couldn't lend him any money. She wondered if anybody would.

B.J. pulled the photo out of the envelope. "Oh, this is terrific," she exclaimed. "I'm going to frame it. Want some tea?"

"Tea would be great."

They reached the door to Sandie's room. Sandie was propped up in her hospital bed, her eyes locked on an afternoon soap on television. The leopard-skin makeup bag was still on the side table, along with lunch remains: a half-eaten sandwich on a plate and a glass of what could be lemonade. As Maxi entered the bedroom, Sandie turned to look at her, formed the beginning of a smile, and said, "Hello, Maxi." She had makeup on, and lipstick. A huge difference in two days—her father hadn't overstated.

"Hi, Sandie," Maxi returned, dropping into one of the flowered chairs by the bed. "You look wonderful."

"I feel good," Sandie said, and she picked up the remote off the side table and punched the button to turn down the volume on the TV. Major strides, Maxi thought.

"Your dad told me how well you're doing—"

"Gillian is dead," Sandie said, still looking at the muted television screen, her eyes clouding over.

"Um . . . you remember that?"

"Bill told me." Evidently she called her father Bill. "I watch the news."

"Yes, Gillian is dead," Maxi said, not sure if she should edit her remarks to Sandie, and if that were appropriate, having no idea what the rules were. She wished Schaeffer were here. But B.J. was in the room, bustling about, tidying up, treating Maxi like company. She was Sandie's nurse, after all, and she hadn't offered any objections to Maxi's comments. Her father always spoke to Sandie as if she were fully functional. Maxi decided that she would, too.

"You're the one who found Gillian," she ventured.

"I'm going walking tomorrow morning," Sandie said.

"Oh. That's wonderful."

"Bill's taking me to the beach."

"She walked some this morning," B.J. offered cheerfully. "And yesterday too, just around here. She gets tired fast. But her legs need using."

B.J. was Southern. A transplant from New Orleans twenty years ago, she had lost the accent but not the idiom. "Tomorrow's her first big trip," she went on. "First time in the car. It'll do her good. Right, dear?" she directed at Sandie.

"Right, dear," the patient said, with another smile.

B.J. gave Maxi a pointed see-how-great-she's-doing look and whooshed out the door to get tea.

"Sandie," Maxi said, leveling her gaze into the patient's slate-blue eyes then. "Who shot you?"

"Carter."

"Carter Rose shot you?"

"Kendyl."

"It was Kendyl?"

"Kendyl's gloves."

"Gloves?" Maxi echoed.

"Rubber gloves."

Rubber gloves. Latex gloves? The way of the world today, Dr. Riker had said. Was the assailant wearing latex gloves? "Did you see gloves, Sandie?"

"Kendyl's ring."

"Who shot you?" Maxi asked her again.

"Going to walk on the beach."

"Sandie, do you know who shot you? Did you see? Do you remember?"

"No. *No!*" Sandie shouted then as B.J. came back into the room with a tray—tea and cookies for Maxi, some crackers for Sandie.

"What's wrong?" the nurse asked, concern etched on her face. She set the tray down on an end table next to Maxi's chair and approached the bed. "Tell me, Sandie. What's wrong, dear?"

No response. Sandie had let her head drop back on the pillow and closed her eyes. B.J. looked over at Maxi for an explanation.

"I don't know," Maxi offered. "She was talking, then she just shut down."

"She's been doing that," B.J. said. "We'll let her rest."

Maxi leaned back in her chair and sipped her tea. She was glad the nurse didn't ask her what she had been talking to Sandie about. She felt a small stab of guilt for asking her the big question. But she didn't regret it.

B.J. settled into the other flowered chair, and she and Maxi chatted quietly. About Sandie's splendid progress, about Bill Schaeffer's wonderful dedication to his daughter, about today's news, about how Maxi got her job at Channel Six, about B.J.'s growing-up years in Cajun country. After about twenty minutes, Maxi made moves to leave. Had to get back to the station, she said. She got up and gave B.J. a hug.

As she turned to whisper good-bye to the half-sleeping patient, Sandie opened her eyes just a little and murmured, "Come tomorrow."

"Me?" Maxi asked, pointing a thumb at her own chest.

"Come tomorrow, Maxi."

"I will," she said. And to B.J., "Okay?"

Maxi swung her Corvette away from the Schaeffer driveway and headed east on Sunset, then south on the 405 and inbound on the Santa Monica Freeway toward downtown. Still not a lot of traffic at midafternoon on the day after New Year's; if there had been, she wouldn't have attempted this excursion downtown before rushing back to the station for the Six. She wanted to have a word with the warm and friendly Kendyl Scott, maybe toss out a veiled accusation, see how it flew. And she wanted to get a look at the woman's ring.

56

A livid Kendyl Scott couldn't believe what she'd heard. Carter on his cell phone making fucking mash plans with what sounded like some Hawaiian bimbo.

He'd neglected to punch off the intercom after she'd updated him on his next day's agenda a few minutes ago, and the system was still on speakerphone. She could have gone in and pushed the OFF button for him, but she'd decided to wait a bit, listen in a little. Not for too long, because he'd eventually figure it out, and he'd be angry that she'd let it go on knowing the sound was filtering into her outer office. If he came out in a dudgeon she'd say that she'd been in the rest room and wasn't aware. Meantime, he'd made three calls in succession on his cell.

The first was to Goodman Penthe in Baltimore confirming their meeting in Los Angeles on Monday. Kendyl could have done that, but Carter had probably wanted to give Penthe the personal touch. The second was to his mother in New York, who was taking Gillian's death very hard. And the third was to the woman.

Kendyl had been just casually listening to Carter's low-pitched conversation, all the while poised to run into his office and punch off the intercom for him. Then her ears pricked up as she honed in on his side of the call. "Leilani, I can't wait to see you. Did my driver pick you up at the airport okay? How's your suite? Did my flowers arrive? I hope you packed the red lace negligee I gave you. Sweet Leilani, did you bring me a lei?" He'd chuckled at that. "Never mind, baby—have I got a lei for you! Tonight, darling."

Her initial instinct was to march into his office and throw his damn ring at him, but that wasn't her style. Kendyl had never been hotheaded. She was definitely cool. But now she was definitely done.

She looked down at the colossal yellow rock. It didn't signify commitment; it represented hush money. In her heart, she'd known that—she just hadn't wanted to believe it.

She believed it now. Finally. He had no intention of marrying her. And even if he did, he would never stop cheating. He cheated on Gillian, didn't he? Had she really thought he would change? What a joke.

Angrily, she realized that the joke was on her. He was dangling her. Making her believe she was still in the tent. That she was the *only* woman in his tent. But the sonofabitch couldn't wait to get into another woman's red lace negligee.

Something in the deep reaches of her brain clicked off. For good, she knew. And surprisingly, she actually felt a wave of relief. Even strength. She opened the bottom drawer of her desk and removed her purse, went into her closet and retrieved her suit jacket, and headed calmly for the door.

That's when it opened.

"Hello, Ms. Scott." The words sounded like a confrontation. It was that reporter, Maxi Poole.

"I was just leaving," Kendyl said curtly.

"I want to talk to you," Maxi said. "I'll walk with you." The reporter turned and followed Kendyl out the door.

"I really don't have time right now," Kendyl tossed back at her. "You should make an appointment. Mr. Rose is in, if you came to see him." Kendyl kept walking toward the penthouse elevator.

"I came to see *you*," Maxi persisted. She jumped into the express elevator with Kendyl before the door closed.

Alone together in the small, descending car, the reporter had her full attention. Squaring off to face her, Maxi said, "Sandie Schaeffer spoke to me this morning. She remembers."

Kendyl felt her stomach lurch, but she remained outwardly cool. "And what does that have to do with me?" she asked.

"Oh, I think you know," Maxi said evenly. "Sandie saw your ring."

Both women inadvertently looked down at Kendyl's hands. She was wearing not one, but two, large, distinctively shaped rings. On her left hand, the yellow diamond. And on her right, her college ring with its heavy, round metal globe and dark blue stone.

Kendyl's eyes remained on that one for a beat, and the realization hit her: *That's* how Sandie had known it was her! On the hand that held the gun, under the latex glove, Sandie had recognized the shape of the sizable college ring she always wore.

The elevator door opened on the ground floor. "I have nothing to say to you," she said to Maxi, then turned away and hurried across the lobby. Now she knew exactly what she had to do. And she would use Carter's damned diamond ring to pay her lawyers' bills.

57

Maxi and Wendy sat silently on the couch in Pete Capra's locked office, staring up at the bank of monitors. It was six-forty, after the early block, and they were about to view the newsroom security tape Jim Murphy had sent up. Pete dropped the cassette into the VCR, then sat down behind his desk and hunkered forward, elbows on the cluttered surface, hands clasped together, waiting for the tape to roll.

The middle screen came to life, displaying a grainy, black-and-white picture of an empty room. Wendy's office.

The three watched as the minutes stretched on, watched nothing happening in the semidarkened room, lit only by lights from the outer newsroom shining through the glass windows. Then the hint of a shadow moved across the floor. They realized it was the shadow of the office door opening out of camera range. There was no sound on the tape. On-screen, they watched a figure walk into the room and move to the desk, and sit down in Wendy's chair in front of her computer terminal.

It was Rob Reordan.

All three reacted with shocked cries. Pete flew out of his chair and pounced on the playback machine, punched STOP, and rewound the tape. He yanked the cassette out of the machine and peered at the label. "Twelve/twenty-six," he read aloud. "One A.M. to one-thirty A.M." He shoved the tape back into the slot, punched PLAY, fast-forwarded through the first ten minutes of inactivity, then stood to the side of the monitor.

This time they watched the tape play through. Watched Rob Reordan clicking on computer keys, bending down to insert a floppy in the disk drive, glancing periodically at his watch, drinking from a bottle of water he'd put on the desk, clicking on the keyboard some more—for the next sixteen minutes and twenty-two seconds. Then he popped the diskette out of the drive, got up from the desk and slipped it into his coat pocket, picked up his water bottle, walked across the screen, and disappeared out of frame.

Pete reached over and punched STOP, then REWIND. Then leaned his elbow on top of the monitor system and silently faced the two women, his expression a mask of compressed rage. Very unlike Pete Capra, who wasn't given to holding back fury. But this affected his station and everybody who worked for him. When this scandal got out, and of course it would, it would be national news: Veteran anchor steals book written by colleague and attempts to have it published. It was the kind of story that would be all over the local and network news, all over the wall-to-wall cable programs, all over the radio talk shows, all over the country. With pictures. And interviews.

"Stupid motherfucker," was all Pete muttered, almost under his breath.

"I can't believe this," Maxi whispered, her hand to her mouth. "Didn't anybody see him go into Wendy's office?"

"One in the morning—everybody on nightside had probably left by then," Wendy said.

"Besides," Capra put in, "Reordan's the five-hundred-pound canary. Nobody would ever question him."

"But . . . how could he turn the book over so fast?" from Maxi.

Wendy had tears in her eyes. "Easy," she said. "It was all laid out for him. Riff through it on the disk and change half the wording. Switch some chapters around, cut and paste. Maybe he hired somebody to do it for him, passed it off as his own work. Or got one of his kids to do it. Everybody knew we'd be finished with it soon and my agent would be sending it around. He had to beat me to it. And," she finished mournfully, "he did."

"I have to call Skip," Pete said. Detective Skip Henders.

When Maxi had gone to Pete in the morning for his okay to requisition the tape from Security Ops, she'd filled him in on the whole scenario of the suspected theft of Wendy's manuscript, including both women's suspicion of Sunday Trent. But this, the station's longtime, revered anchorman as common thief—this was a cannon blast.

"Maybe there's another way to deal with this," Maxi offered halfheartedly.

"I don't think so," Pete said with a quick shake of his head.

"If you talked to him . . . ?" she persisted. But she knew she was making futile stabs. It was too late. Rob had taken it too far, getting his tossed-together version of

Wendy's book to a literary agent, who had already taken it to market.

"What happens now?" Wendy snuffled.

"The police get a warrant and search his condo, confiscate his hard drive, any pertinent correspondence—"

"And if we don't go that route?" Wendy questioned. "If we *do* talk to him first?" Even Wendy wanted to spare the station this.

"Then he'll deny it, he'll make up a reason why he was hacking your files after the Eleven O'clock News, his computer will end up at the bottom of Lake Castaic, and there'll be no case."

"And my book?"

"Who knows?" Pete said.

"There'd be a cloud over its authorship," Maxi put in. "That would probably make publishers back off it."

"I gotta think about this," Pete said.

58

Propped up against a mountain of plush, satin-covered pillows in the custom king-sized bed he had shared with his now dead wife for a decade, Carter Rose stretched luxuriously and sipped from his cut-crystal tumbler of Courvoisier. He had just sent the exotic Leilani Harwood, Miss Hawaii, back to her suite at the Bel Air Hotel in a limousine. Best of all possible worlds, he thought to himself, and smiled.

She'd whimpered a little, said she wanted so much to spend the night with him, but he explained that it wouldn't look good when the help arrived in the morning, so soon after the death of his wife.

That was a crock. The fact was, not one of his household staff had much liked Gillian, to put it mildly. Especially Angie, their longtime housekeeper and cook who ran the house and the rest of the staff. A few years back Carter had had all he could do to keep Angie from walking out after Gillian had actually slapped her. For using cream instead of nonfat milk in the crepes. Other than Gillian's personal driver, a young bodybuilder whom she'd rewarded with probably more than hefty yearly bonuses, none of the rest of the staff had attended his wife's memorial service, nor had any of them offered him their condolences. After being told of her death they'd all just carried on, business as usual.

It was Angie who had tipped him off that Gillian was planning to divorce him. The first time she brought her suspicions to him, he didn't believe it. You're wrong, Angie dear, he'd told her. He and Gillian had a good marriage and a solid partnership. So he'd thought. But Angie told him what she suspected again, then again—and the third time she'd produced evidence.

Her first inkling came while Gillian was working in her office at home and Angie had brought in her lunch. Angie told Carter that she found his wife sitting at her computer printing out copies of some research on the Internet. Angie had idly glanced at the oversized screen and saw that the Web site Gillian was visiting was the California Bar Association's, and the specific page she had opened up dealt with details regarding the state's community property laws. Angie had gone through a painful divorce herself—she knew what she was looking at, she'd told Carter.

Carter had laughed. "Your imagination is working overtime," he'd told Angie. He'd been well aware of Angie's dislike of Gillian, and of her loyalty to him.

A few weeks later, Angie presented him with a sheaf of real estate brochures for multimillion-dollar, Upper West Side apartments in Manhattan. Gillian had just come back from a few days in New York, where she'd attended an industry trade show, and Angie had unpacked her luggage for her. And found the brochures. To Angie it was proof that Gillian intended to leave Carter and move to New York. To Carter, again, it was nothing; his wife had probably been gathering some New York real estate information for a friend. "Just leave the brochures on her desk," he'd told Angie.

The third time produced what Carter finally had to admit was the smoking gun. While he was away in Chicago on a business trip, Gillian had had a visitor to their Carolwood home, Angie had reported. A short, middle-aged, balding man in black-rimmed glasses and a dark suit, carrying a briefcase. He and Gillian had disappeared into her home office and closed the door. And stayed in there for the better part of an afternoon. At one point, Gillian had called Angie in the kitchen and asked her to bring them a pitcher of iced tea. When she went into the office with the tray, their conversation immediately ceased. The two were seated on opposite couches, the coffee table between them strewn with a voluminous amount of papers and files. Neither spoke while Angie was there setting out the tea things. Later, after the man had left and Angie had gone into the office to tidy up, she saw a business card that had been left on the table. When Carter got home, she brought him the story, and the card. It read: MORT MOROKO, ATTORNEY AT LAW.

Carter had called the number printed on the card. "Hello," he'd said to the receptionist who answered the phone. "This is Solomon Greenberg. I'd like to speak to one of the attorneys handling the Gillian Rose divorce.

I'm her accountant, and I'm working on some files for the case."

"That would be Mr. Moroko," she'd said. "I'll transfer you to his office."

Carter had hung up. There it was.

Now there would be no divorce.

59

Friday morning in the newsroom at a little after nine o'clock, the final day of the final week of the long holiday break. Not many people would be working today, Maxi knew, as she listened to her phone messages. Then she heard the familiar voice of Dr. Elizabeth Riker on her Audix, early-bird pathologist from the L.A. County Morgue. Business as usual there.

"Hi, Maxi. Call me," was all she'd said.

Maxi dialed the number and Dr. Riker answered. Must be her private line, Maxi realized and made a note of it while she said hello.

"It was selenium," Riker said. "We took a set of electrolytes and found that Gillian Rose had a heightened selenium level."

"And that would kill her?" Maxi asked.

"That *did* kill her," Riker said soberly.

"Um—what exactly is selenium?"

"It's a chemical element. Not a compound. It's a crystalline nonmetal with semiconducting properties. In concentrated form, it's used in some shampoos, paints, as a vulcanizing agent for rubber . . ."

Maxi flashed on the fact that the Penthe Group included a tire manufacturer. "Well, where could it have come from? In Gillian, I mean."

"Selenium is a naturally occurring element in our diet," Riker went on like the scientist she was. "We all maintain a certain level of it in our bodies. Selenium is sold as a dietary supplement in health stores, as needed to maintain normal levels. But a blood level of over two thousand micrograms per liter will definitely kill you, usually within twenty-four hours."

"And that's what Gillian's blood showed?"

"Actually, we didn't test her blood, though we do have frozen samples. We tested her hair, which is an accurate indicator. Gillian Rose's selenium values were well into toxic range."

"Could someone have poisoned her with selenium?"

"Someone would have *had* to. We've notified the LAPD."

"Could someone have slipped enough of this selenium into a drink to kill her?"

"Absolutely. A gram and a half of sodium selenite would do it. I suggest that you call the detectives on the case and tell them what you know."

"I will—"

"Or they'll be calling you," Dr. Riker added quickly. "We made a note of your connection to this matter in our report."

60

Kendyl Scott sat stiffly in a small, dingy interrogation room on the third floor at Parker Center. Officer William Murchison, one of the detectives working the Sandie Schaeffer case, sat in a chair pulled up to a scarred wooden table but he had waved Kendyl away from the table, and positioned her uncomfortably on a metal folding chair against the wall.

Audiotape was rolling, and Dan Black, Murchison's partner, sat behind the two-way mirrored wall opposite Kendyl, listening in. Also auditing the interview behind the glass were Sergeant Carlos Salinger and Officer Donald Barnett, the two primary detectives on the Gillian Rose case.

Kendyl had sobbed quietly as Murchison read her Miranda rights off a card, which was probably not necessary since defense attorney Robert Hanger, her newly hired high-powered criminal lawyer, sat beside her, but these days, in the world of legal technocrats like Johnnie

Cochran et al., the police were operating under the mandate that they couldn't be too cautious. Now, under the watchful eye and keen ear of her attorney, who stopped her at several points, Kendyl was outlining, for Murchison and his hidden colleagues, the broad strokes of exactly what had happened in the Rose building on the night Sandie Schaeffer was shot.

Hanger had already ascertained that a plea bargain would be structured for his client. The terms of the deal were as follows: Kendyl Scott would plead guilty in L.A. Superior Court to criminal charges of conspiracy to pose a physical threat and attempted involuntary manslaughter.

"What the hell is attempted involuntary manslaughter?" Hanger had bellowed in his private meeting at the district attorney's office the day before.

"The victim isn't out of the woods yet. If she dies, we strike 'attempted,'" was the response he was given.

Bottom line, in return for having to serve no prison time, Kendyl Scott would give testimony that would lay the groundwork for the prosecution of Carter Rose in the shooting attack of Sandie Schaeffer in the early-morning hours of December 20.

And tying Rose to the attack on his wife's assistant would give the DA's office the opening they'd been looking for: It would justify revisiting the case of the death of the man's wife and business partner, Gillian Rose.

61

Maxi was rolling across town to a lunch visit with Sandie Schaeffer, as she'd promised yesterday. This time she'd brought with her a bouquet of sunny yellow daffodils that she'd picked up at a flower shop on Sunset Boulevard in the Palisades.

She'd also brought her mini tape recorder. It was in her purse, a loosely crocheted fabric purse through which a tape machine would pick up sound. A little bit illegal? she mused as she drove through the intersection at Bundy Drive. Hmmm. Was a little bit illegal like a little bit pregnant? she asked herself. Not in this case, because it was illegal only if she actually used what she secretly taped on the air, which she had no intention of doing. But if Sandie happened to say anything that was worth reporting on the news that night, Maxi wanted a verbatim record of her exact words.

She had had a conversation earlier this morning with Sergeant Carlos Salinger about her suspicions concerning

Goodman Penthe, the man who had been alone with Gillian the night before she died, and about her subsequent conversations with Dr. Elizabeth Riker at the county morgue. Salinger said they were in touch with Mr. Penthe. Whatever that meant. He'd given her zero information, thanked her laconically, and hung up.

Oh, well, she had heeded Riker's warning and done her civic duty. Which did absolutely nothing to further the story, as it happened. But which most definitely, she knew, stirred the pot.

She parked in front of the Schaeffer house, reached into her purse and turned on the tape recorder, got out of her car and locked it, and scurried up the walk. As expected, B.J. greeted her at the door. The nurse ushered her inside the house and exclaimed over the flowers.

"Just let me get a vase for these beauties," she said. "Then lunch will be served. You poor girls," B.J. said with a twinkle. "I'm not much of a cook. It's chicken sandwiches and lemonade—a menu that even I can't ruin, right?"

"Chicken sandwiches sound wonderful," Maxi said.

The nurse chatted on. "Bill doesn't seem to mind that I'm a less than competent cook. He says that's why God invented gourmet delivery. He has dinner sent in almost every night for the three of us. Isn't he the most wonderful man?"

Maxi noticed the rosy glow that lit the woman's cheeks when she mentioned the name of her employer. *Interesting,* she thought.

She followed B.J. into the small kitchen and watched her arrange the daffodils in a vase. "I think I know why Sandie always asks for you," the amiable nurse said then.

"Really?" Maxi asked as casually as she could muster. "Why?"

"Well, I think it's because she watches television all day long and she sees you on the news. They kept the TV on when she was in the hospital in a coma—it's a common technique, to try to break through to the patient's unconscious. And now she sees you reporting Gillian's story, and her own story. I think she reaches out to you because you could be a key to the part of her world that she's trying to remember. Trying to put the pieces back together. And she feels that, somehow, you can help."

Makes sense, Maxi thought. She went with B.J. into the cheerful living room, where Sandie was sitting on the couch in a jogging outfit. This was the first time Maxi had seen her out of bed and dressed.

"Maxi is here, Sandie," B.J. said. "She brought you some gorgeous flowers." She set the vase of daffodils on the coffee table.

"Hi, Sandie," Maxi said, as she took a seat a couple of feet away from her on the couch. She laid her purse down on the seat between them.

"Hello, Maxi," Sandie said with a smile, and with strength in her voice.

"I'm going to serve lunch right here in the living room," B.J. said, and she went off into the kitchen.

"Did you go on your walk today?" Maxi asked Sandie. "On the beach?"

"Yes. It was wonderful," Sandie said. "I didn't even realize how much I love the ocean."

Whoa! Maxi mentally exclaimed. Complete sentences. Totally coherent. You've come a long way, baby. "You're so much better today," is what she said.

"And getting better every day, I hope," Sandie replied.

"I need to get to where I remember everything. And I want to go back to work."

"You know that Gillian is dead," Maxi said quietly, in case she'd forgotten that since yesterday.

"Oh, yes—I know. I don't remember it," she said, as if reading Maxi's mind. "But I know it from the news, and from Dad, and the newspapers."

"You're reading the newspapers?"

"Yesterday, for the first time," Sandie offered, and she broke into a proud smile. Then she immediately sobered. "I read the story about Goodman Penthe being with Gillian the night before she died. The story gave you credit for reporting what he had to say about that night, on Channel Six. I saw you on that report, Maxi."

"Did you know Goodman Penthe?"

"He'd come in to the office to meet with Carter and Gillian a few times."

"Sandie," Maxi said, spurred on by the nurse's conjectures as to why this woman whom she hardly knew kept asking to see her, "maybe I can help you remember. Tell me what you do know about everything that's happened."

"All I know is what I've been told, and what I've read or seen on the news," she said. "The last thing I actually remember is going out to lunch on the day Gillian died."

"What do you remember about that lunch?"

"I went to the cafeteria downstairs in the building and had a tuna sandwich and a Diet Coke. Then I walked over to Ninth Street, to a button shop I know in the garment district. I like to walk on my lunch hour, and I needed a new set of buttons for a suit jacket."

"Then?"

"Then I remember walking back to the building and taking the express elevator to my floor. Gillian's floor.

And that's all. Isn't that weird? I am so clear on everything that happened up to that point; then it's a complete blank."

"It's not weird, Sandie. It's not that uncommon after what you've been through."

"That's what they're telling me. Dr. Hamatt says don't sweat it. It'll come. Or not. And if not, it doesn't mean there's anything wrong with my brain, or that it'll haunt me all my life. If it doesn't come back to me, just forget about it, he says, and move on."

Forgetting about it and moving on was not going to advance the story, Maxi mentally flashed, then inwardly chastised herself for such thoughts. The curse of the journalist.

"Do you remember anything about being back in your office after lunch?" she asked gently.

"No. Not a thing." Sandie sighed. "I know what happened, of course. I know that I'm the one who found Gillian's body. That I must have screamed, and somebody called the police, I guess . . ."

Maxi's heart went out to Sandie for what she must be going through. Poor woman was trying so hard to remember that she'd resorted to *guessing* what must have happened in order to piece things together. She waited, letting Sandie fill the silence.

"I know Gillian's beautiful new crystal award got broken. And the police came—"

"Award?" Maxi asked.

"The award the chamber of commerce had given her just the week before, when she spoke at their luncheon— she was so proud of that one."

"Do you remember the award breaking?" she asked.

"Of course not," Sandie said, frowning. "I saw it on the

news. And I know they didn't find any foul play involved. That Gillian died of natural causes. Probably a congenital heart defect, I heard on one report. Tragic. She was so young, so brilliant. I can't imagine what it's like at the Rose company now, without Gillian."

B.J. came in carrying a tray and set it down on the coffee table. A platter of chicken sandwiches on whole wheat, cut in quarters. A dish of sweet midget pickles. A plastic deli container of cole slaw. A pitcher of lemonade. She set out plates, forks, glasses, napkins, salt and pepper. And all three women dug in.

62

Carter Rose was perplexed. More than perplexed, he was nervous. Kendyl had left work yesterday afternoon without even letting him know, and she hadn't come in at all this morning. He'd tried phoning her, at her apartment and on her cell. He'd left messages. After work he'd stopped by her apartment building and asked the guard on the desk to call upstairs, but he was told she wasn't answering. "Well, is Ms. Scott in?" he'd asked. The guard said he didn't know. Of course he said he didn't know; it was the Remington, the premier snooty high-rise in the Wilshire corridor, a mega-discreet security building. Very expensive. He knew, because he was paying her rent.

Now he was really worried. This morning he discovered that he'd left the intercom line open and the phone on Speaker. He did that sometimes, and Kendyl always caught it. He tried to remember what went on in the office yesterday afternoon after he'd gone over today's agenda with Kendyl.

Then he remembered. Jesus Christ, could she have overheard his call to Leilani? Fuck. That meant big-time damage control.

He'd sent Leilani packing this afternoon, back to Maui. She had intended to stay in town for a few days after completing her photo shoot for a pineapple company this morning: Wholesome Miss Hawaii looks like this because she grew up eating fresh pineapple. Yeah, right.

Carter had planned to pick up the cost of her stay for a few extra days. Now that was much too risky—no telling what Kendyl was up to. He'd told Leilani that something had come up and he had to leave the country, and he had his driver take her to the airport. He'd make it up to her next time, he said. And he made a note to himself to have Mrs. Paul at Tiffany send her a classic stainless Rolex watch. All women loved them.

The door to his office opened. Damn, the temp at Kendyl's desk was an airhead, letting somebody in without checking with him first.

It was the police.

63

"Poole, get in here. You too, Harris!" Pete Capra yelled from the door of his office. Maxi had just come in from lunch with Sandie Schaeffer; Wendy was sitting at her computer terminal in the newsroom, producing the Six.

"Can it wait?" Wendy yelled back. "I'm jamming."

"No, it can't fucking wait!" Pete bellowed across the newsroom for all to hear. Wendy rolled her eyes, got up, and followed Maxi into Pete's office. He slammed the door shut behind the two of them.

"Henders is on his way over here to pick up Rob Reordan," he said tersely. "Maxi, you'll anchor the Six alone."

"My God, this is his last day," Maxi said. "He's supposed to be doing his big good-bye-to-the-viewers speech—"

Pete cut her off. "Two Burbank uniforms are waiting for him outside the door to his condo," he said. "He knows something's up—and I'm sure he knows exactly what it is."

"So he won't be dumping his hard drive in the L.A. River on his way in?" Wendy asked.

"Nope, the cops have orders to follow him here."

"Why not just take him in from his place?" Maxi asked.

"Yeah, I don't want to look at him," Wendy groused.

"I don't like the idea of him being carted off the lot, either," Pete said. "Jesus, we're a news organization. This arrest is big news, and we have a fucking exclusive on it. If we're responsible journalists, we've got to cover the fucking story."

The two women knew that beneath the bluff and bluster, Pete Capra was at his core a responsible journalist.

"Skip wants to pick him up in Burbank," Pete explained. "Reordan lives at the beach, and that's LAPD. But he did the theft here in Burbank. Skip says if we keep it in his jurisdiction, he might be able to contain it a little better."

"He's dreaming," Wendy said. All three of them knew there'd be no containment once this one got rolling.

"What made you decide to do this?" Maxi asked Capra.

"I thought about it for thirty seconds—it's the right thing to do. Reordan is a public figure in a time when a rogues' gallery of public figures—CEOs, politicians, priests—are just so many Humpty Dumpties. Well, our Humpty Dumpty's gonna have to take the fall. We're not gonna hide him, and we're not gonna save him. And since this is his last day at the station, it's our last chance to nail him here."

"I'm sorry, boss," from Wendy.

"Not your fault, Wen. A thief's a thief. Get back out in the newsroom and produce the show."

"Do you want me to pull some tape on Rob and put a story together for the Six?" Maxi asked.

"Christ," Pete muttered. "Yeah."

Sitting in the backseat of a squad car rumbling downtown to the Men's Central Jail, Carter Rose used his cell phone to call a powerful lawyer he knew socially, Robert Hanger. Up until now, he hadn't attempted to hire a criminal attorney because to him, doing so would seem to suggest that he was guilty of something—it would be all over the news. He was told by someone in the law office that Mr. Hanger would call him back.

What had happened was clear. Kendyl had gone to the authorities. Foolish woman. He wasn't the one who pulled the trigger. The publicity would be bad, but he would walk away from this, he was sure. He would survive.

Goodman Penthe was close to closing the deal to buy Rose International. After he sold the business he'd dump the house and forget about the sophisticated penthouse apartment in downtown Los Angeles; he'd go to plan B. Move out of the area completely. Somewhere big and anonymous, where business was business and nobody cared about your past, just your net worth and your business prowess. Texas, maybe. And he'd launch BriteEyes and laugh all the way to the bank.

These thoughts kept his spirits buoyed as he was put through the ignominious booking process: the fingerprinting, the mug shots, the strip search. As he was taking off his watch his cell phone rang. He looked at the booking officer, who shrugged, so he took the phone out of his pocket and answered it. It was Robert Hanger.

"Thank God it's you, Bob!" he said. "I'm at Parker Center. I'm under arrest, can you believe it? For shooting my wife's assistant. I didn't do it and I can prove it. They're booking me right now. I need you to get down here right away. Hurry."

"I can't," Hanger said. "I have a conflict of interest."

64

Pete Capra was holed up in his office with Detective Skip Henders. Wendy sat at her computer in the newsroom, producing the Six. Maxi was back in an edit bay, viewing tape of Rob Reordan anchoring, accepting an award, coaching a Little League team. She'd pored through dusty jackets that had been stored in the tape library for years and was scanning cut stories from back when the man was a young, slim, dark-haired reporter covering the famous Baldwin Hills Dam break back in the fifties. Her editor had asked what was up. This was Rob's last night on the air, she'd said, and she was putting together a retrospective reel for the close of the show.

Maxi built a four-minute piece, then wrote the track but didn't record it, because Rob hadn't shown up at the station yet and nobody but herself, Pete, and Wendy knew what was going on. If her voice track tipped an audio engineer at this point, the news would be all over the station like wildfire. In minutes they'd have the story in Cleveland, and everywhere else in the country where L.A. newsies had pals. She would voice over the pictures live.

She labeled the tape, slugged it ROB REORDAN, put it on the playback shelf for the Six, then duped an intro with a roll cue, along with a tag, to Wendy's computer. If the arrest went down while they were on the air, Pete would call Wendy in the booth, Wendy would alert Maxi via the Telex in her ear, and Maxi would read a copy of the intro she'd slipped into the pocket of her suit jacket. Wendy would call for the tape, and the tech in playback would find it on the Six O'clock shelf where Maxi left it. Wendy would give him Maxi's two-word roll cue from the booth, and he'd roll the Reordan tape on the air. Staffers would hear the story at the same time L.A. viewers heard it.

Six o'clock, and Rob Reordan still hadn't come into the station. Maxi slid into Makeup, then onto the set. The Six O'clock open played, then she led with the arrest of Carter Rose that afternoon in connection with the attack on Sandie Schaeffer. That bulletin had rolled on the wires just before they went to air; newsroom staffers were upstairs digging for the details.

On the set, Maxi was reading an intro to business editor Doug Kriegel with the show's second lead, another Enron arrest, when Wendy's voice blasted in her ear. Anchors were used to talking and listening at the same time.

"Pick up the phone," Wendy was saying. "It's Capra."

When the Enron tape rolled, Maxi snatched up the phone that was blinking on the set. "Yeah, boss."

"I'm yanking Kriegel's tape. Rob Reordan was just found inside his condo—dead. Gunshot to the head. Self-inflicted."

"Jesus," Maxi hissed.

"Report it," Capra ordered. "Now." The phone slammed down in her ear.

She looked up and saw herself in full close-up on the monitor. "We interrupt this report for breaking news," she ad-libbed. "We have just learned that veteran Los Angeles anchorman Rob Reordan has been found dead, inside his home, the victim of an apparent suicide. We'll have details as they become available. Reordan, who anchored the Six and Eleven O'clock News, had been with Channel Six for more than four decades. . . ."

She felt tears forming behind her eyes, but she swallowed them, and kept going.

65

Saturday morning, no alarm set to wake her, and Maxi straggled her way up to consciousness feeling an ominous foreboding, a blackened, musty cloud that seemed to put a stranglehold on her soul in that zone between half-sleep and wakefulness. Then she came fully awake and remembered: Rob Reordan.

Her station, as well as all the other L.A. stations, had run with the story—right through prime time and on into the Eleven O'clock News. Other news operations showed paramedics rolling the body out of Rob's condominium building. Reporters speculated on the cause of suicide by a man whom the city revered. It came out that this was to be his last day at Channel Six; he was scheduled to do farewell speeches on both the Six and Eleven O'clock News. A journalist at one of the independents had unearthed a fairly recent investment scam where Rob Reordan had lost a lot of money. Another station had a live interview with Reordan's doctor, who cited several ailments. Failing health could have been his reason, said the physician, who came off as shamelessly grasping at his fifteen minutes of fame.

Other reports showed all his wives, his children, his vintage cars, his cigarette powerboat, his Piper Cub. All of them aired footage from his long, illustrious career. And they all played glowing sound bites from family, friends, colleagues, and luminaries—the governor, the mayor, local pols, movie stars, heads of business, a couple of kids at schools he'd visited—all of them Rob Reordan fans.

Nobody had the real story. And nobody ever would. Maxi actually felt some guilt about Rob, though her rational mind knew that it was misplaced. She consoled herself, knowing there was one thing that she, Wendy, and Pete could do for him: They would forever keep the secret that he was facing arrest, scandal, a possible trial, no chance of ever getting another job, and the ruination of his stellar lifelong reputation. Detective Henders had assured Capra not just that the book was closed, but in fact it was never opened. There'd been no arrest, no charges, no case. Rob Reordan died with all of Los Angeles adoring him.

Details in the new lead in the Rose International story got buried: Carter Rose being arrested for conspiracy in the attack on Sandie Schaeffer, Kendyl Scott turning State's evidence against him—a bizarre twist. This had to be a big crack in the Gillian Rose case, she thought. Rose was out on bail but the police would be all over him now, looking for a connection to the death of his wife.

Maxi pulled herself out of bed feeling sluggish, world weary, and sad. Something else was bothering her, something hovering around the periphery of her consciousness, pushed away by the long, emotional night of covering her colleague's suicide.

She brushed her teeth, pulled on some sweats, socks, and running shoes, and thought about it some more.

Yukon was panting by her bedroom door. Count on him to be cheerful, always. She bent down and ruffled the fur around his neck; then they padded into the kitchen to get the guy some breakfast. They took a brisk walk up Beverly Glen, and around the corner onto Mulholland Drive, down Nicada, back to the Glen, and home.

On their walk, she'd remembered what was bothering her: something Sandie Schaeffer had said. She dropped into the desk chair in her study, picked up the phone, and dialed Pete Capra's home number in Tarzana.

"Capra," he answered brusquely, even at home.

"Hi. It's Maxi. How're you holding up?"

"Whaddaya gonna do?" he said mournfully.

"I wish I knew. If only I hadn't gone into Wendy's computer—"

"Hold on," Pete shouted. "Don't go there. Do *not* beat yourself up, Maxi. This wasn't your fault. Or Wendy's."

"Or yours," she said, knowing he needed to hear that.

"Crazy fucker," Capra muttered. "You know, maybe he was just done. Guy had a helluva life up till now and maybe the rest of it wasn't looking so good to him. Maybe he just didn't want to go down that road."

"Yeah. Listen, Pete, is there any way I can get into the dead file? Today, I mean?"

"It's Saturday, Max. Take a damn break, will ya?"

"Something's bothering me."

"*Everything's* bothering *me*, for Chrissakes. Kris is dragging my tired ass to the Rose Bowl swap meet. I'd rather take a beating."

"Oh . . . well, you have to come in on the Ventura Freeway to get to the Rose Bowl, right?"

"Yeah. So?"

"So how about you meet me at the station, which is right on your way, and open up the dead file for me."

"Do you ever quit? Even a bus stops."

"This is important, boss," she said. *Maybe,* she added to herself.

66

Saturday in the newsroom. Quieter than the weekdays. Capra had come and gone after an inordinate amount, even for him, of whining—that he, as he so elegantly put it, had to haul ass into this dump on a Saturday morning just to open up the frigging dead file for an overwrought, PMS-riddled reporter. *Whatever,* Maxi thought but didn't say. She was going to *have* to continue that talk with him about sexual harassment, perceived or otherwise, and how one day, at the wrong time and in the wrong circumstance, it could get him into a mess of serious trouble.

Ensconced in an edit bay with one of the weekend editors, she sat viewing the tape Capra had pulled out of the dead file for her. Apart from the video and still shots made by the forensic team, she was positive that this was the only commercial tape ever shot of the body of Gillian Rose. She knew that she was the only reporter who'd been able to get inside the Rose building that day, and it had been by subterfuge, at that. Her cameraman and his camera had been summarily tossed out. So they had this exclusive footage, but it was virtually useless. The station had never aired any part of this tape, couldn't use it; it had gone directly into the dead file the day it was logged in and there it had stayed, except for the couple of times she had taken it out for viewing.

The scene was as she remembered it: Gillian Rose lying lifeless on the carpet next to her desk. Crime-scene personnel with grim expressions processing the scene. She asked the editor to rewind the tape and slo-mo it forward from the beginning. When it came up on a wide shot that included Gillian's desk, she said, "Stop here, please," then asked for the picture to be enhanced. Just the desktop, she told her editor.

The picture enlarged, and in the foreground on the mostly clear desktop, close to the right front corner of the black slate surface, she saw what looked to be a crystal bowl.

"Can you enhance just that object?" Maxi asked, using the back of her ballpoint pen to point to the bowl on screen.

The editor drew an electronic dotted line around the object she'd pointed to, and as it zoomed larger, they could make out enough of the wording of the three lines of lettering engraved close to the lip of the bowl to piece together what it said: LOS ANGELES CHAMBER OF COMMERCE, BUSINESSWOMAN OF THE YEAR, and the name GILLIAN ROSE.

So there *was* a crystal award. On Gillian's desk. But it *hadn't* gotten broken when Gillian fell to the floor. It was intact as Gillian's body lay prone beside her desk. Was the broken crystal piece just part of a scenario that Sandie had dreamed up? She'd said she remembered when Gillian received that award. And she'd have seen it there on her boss's desk every day for about a week. Trapped in a world of denial, her mind blocking out a period of horrific events, plagued by elusive memories she couldn't access, could Sandie's imagination create such a happening? Since her mind wasn't able to own the actual events, had she imagined Gillian's brilliant accomplishments as symbolized in a crystal award, then fantasized that it was shattered that day, as was the woman's life?

Wait a minute. Now who's fantasizing? Maxi chided herself. She checked her Palm Pilot for a number, picked up the phone in the edit room, and put in a call to the Schaeffer house.

B.J. answered.

"Yes," she said to Maxi's request, "do stop by to see Sandie on your way home. My patient is dying to know the inside scoop on Carter Rose being arrested. With poor Rob Reordan's suicide, that story seemed to fall through the cracks," B.J. said.

Driving across town on Sunset, Maxi thought about Sandie Schaeffer's physical and mental condition. Doctors had removed a bullet that had lodged in the frontal area of her skull, dangerously close to the soft cerebral cortex of the brain. Fortunately, it had missed her brain stem and any of the major vessels in the brain. That she had escaped permanent brain damage was pure good luck, her doctors said. As for the emotional and traumatic damage, that was not so easy to get your arms around, as Sandie's father had put it. That aspect of her injuries remained a wait-and-see situation.

Maxi still felt that Sandie was the key to unlocking the baffling Rose company riddle, but now she wondered just how reliable the woman's memories actually were. She flipped on the tape recorder inside her purse again and rang the Schaeffers' doorbell.

This time Sandie came to the door. She was wearing tailored gray slacks and a short yellow sweater, and was in full, light makeup. Hair combed. Looking ready to go shopping, or to work, or whatever the day might bring on.

"Hi, Maxi. Come on in. Hey, I'm feeling good. Don't I look it?" the woman chimed.

"You look it and sound it," Maxi said, marveling at her vitality. "Where's B.J.?" she asked.

"Dad let her have nights off. I really am functioning on all cylinders now," Sandie said brightly. "Except for the gap. I think my head is programmed like that Nixon tape with the legendary gap. Call me Rose Mary Woods. By the way, they never did retrieve that one, did they?" she lamented with a half smile.

"Maybe you don't need to get those memories back, Sandie," Maxi offered. Though she profoundly hoped she would.

The two women walked into the living room and Maxi sat on one of the couches. Sandie went over to the triple bank of windows and adjusted the blinds, filtering out the late-afternoon sunlight. When she came back to the middle of the room, she dropped down on the opposite couch. Maxi's tape recorder would not pick up clearly across this much space, she knew, but it didn't matter; she felt, now, that she couldn't really depend on what Sandie remembered of those traumatic events anyway. This patient seemed completely healthy except for the time lapse of unwanted memories.

"You *are* operating on all cylinders, Sandie," Maxi said. "I'd like you to go on the air with me and tell what you do remember, and what you don't remember, and why. Show the world that you're ready for it. And talk about your reaction to the arrest of Carter Rose in the attack on you."

She didn't expect Sandie's quick and positive response. "Okay," Sandie said. "Let's do it."

67

Monday morning, in the living room of the Schaeffer house in Pacific Palisades. The lights were set and the camera ready to roll on Maxi's interview with Sandie Schaeffer.

Maxi had spent a good chunk of the day before in the newsroom, surrounded by the weekend staff preparing the Sunday so-called March of Death that was to air after the Saint Louis Rams' playoff game. They'd expected a huge tune-in spilling over from the game, since a big chunk of Angelinos still rooted for the guys who used to be their L.A. Rams. While the hustle of the daily news prep went on around her, Maxi had prepped for today's interview with Sandie Schaeffer.

Instead of going in to the station this morning, she'd driven directly from her house in Beverly Glen out to the Schaeffers' bungalow near the beach. This was the exclusive Maxi had worked toward and waited for. Still, since Sandie's father so adamantly opposed exposing his not-altogether-stable daughter to the glare of television news, she told Sandie several times that she didn't have to do this, even as they were ready to start rolling tape. But Sandie was just as adamantly determined to do it. They'd settled on an agreement that if Sandie became uncomfortable at any time during the shoot, they would call a halt and never air it—a concession that Maxi had never before granted to an interview subject.

Bill Schaeffer had Benny filling in for him at the drugstore this morning so he could be on hand. Maxi had scored cameraman Rodger Harbaugh as crew, for which she was grateful. Sandie Schaeffer was in full makeup and dressed in a dark, lightweight wool business suit with a crisp white blouse, her look signaling that she was on top of her game.

The camera, set on a tripod, was focused on Sandie. Harbaugh would zoom in and out, from close to middle ground to wide, to give the static "talking head" shot some movement. Maxi cupped her hand to her eye and took a look at the image in the viewfinder: Sitting erect in the corner of the silk chenille-covered couch, Sandie looked healthy, radiant, and springtime pretty. Then Maxi took her own seat at the opposite end of the couch, a technique to ensure there'd be no chance that she'd obstruct the camera's view of the interview subject from any angle or inadvertently get into Sandie's frame with a head or hand movement of her own.

When the interview was finished, Maxi would do her reversals, voicing questions on camera that Sandie had already answered. In the editing process, those questions would be dropped in and followed by Sandie's previous answers to each, a stock process in television news. Maxi would lay B-roll over the sound where it was appropriate, using extant footage of scenes from the Gillian Rose case and the attack on Sandie. When they were finished here, she would rush the tape back to the station, write her ins and outs, track her voice-over, edit it all together, and air the cut piece on the Six O'clock News.

The room was hushed, steeped in the routine tension that precedes the start of a news interview. Harbaugh checked the viewfinder, then said, "Rolling."

"Sandie, how much do you remember about Gillian Rose's death and the attack on you?" Maxi started.

"Nothing, really. I remember everything up until, I'm told, I discovered Gillian's body, as well as everything since I came out of the coma," she answered, strength and clarity in her tones.

"And nothing in between?"

"And nothing in between."

Maxi went on with the interview, occasionally glancing over at Bill Schaeffer in his wheelchair, who looked progressively more relaxed. She verbally walked Sandie through what she remembered, what she had later learned about the events, and her feelings about all of it.

"And tell me about the crystal award that was on Gillian's desk that day," she said.

"Um . . . award?" Sandie asked, looking perplexed.

"The crystal bowl that the chamber of commerce had awarded her at their recent luncheon, the one you said she was so proud of. The crystal piece that you told me got broken when Gillian fell," Maxi clarified.

"Gosh, I don't remember anything about that," Sandie said, then gave a sheepish smile and a little shrug. "I'm afraid I'm not a hundred percent yet. But I'm getting there."

Sandie was charming in her confusion. Viewers would

applaud her courage, Maxi knew. And her own theory about the crystal award must have been correct: The image of it shattered had been a fictitious analogy to Gillian's death conjured up by Sandie's still troubled mind, and now she didn't remember it at all.

Maxi moved on to the big topic. "How do you feel, Sandie, about your boss, Carter Rose, being arrested in connection with the attack on you?"

Sandie's eyes darkened. "Shocked," she said. "And sad. If it's true, I have no idea why he would have wanted to hurt me. After all my years there . . ."

She pulled a handkerchief out of her jacket pocket and fumbled with it, and Maxi was afraid she might break.

"You're doing beautifully, Sandie," she reassured her. "I'm finished with my questions." Mentally, she decided she'd just edit out Sandie's words, *After all my years there* . . . and let her answer stand without it.

"Is there anything else you'd like to say, Sandie?" she asked then.

"Just that . . . it's been a very rough time for me. And for my dad. I never would have made it without him." With that, she beamed a small, grateful smile over at Bill Schaeffer, who was sitting close by in his wheelchair. Maxi made a mental note to make sure Rodger got an ISO shot of Bill Schaeffer later, so she could edit it in for reaction after Sandie's loving tribute to him.

"But I think it's done me a lot of good to tell my story," Sandie went on. "Thanks for the opportunity, Maxi. And now I'm looking forward to getting on with my life."

A perfect closing button for her piece, Maxi knew, and she signaled Harbaugh to stop tape. She was satisfied with what they got and was ready to do her reversals.

"I'm going to sit closer to you now, Sandie, while

Rodger shoots over your shoulder at me asking what we call reverse questions. That's just so I'll get a little face time in the piece, to prove I was really here. Otherwise they might not pay me," she said with a wink, and Sandie laughed.

Harbaugh picked up the camera and tripod and carried them over to a spot behind Sandie, then he set up to focus on Maxi's face. He knew to include a little of the back of Sandie Schaeffer's head and shoulders in the shot, another one-camera television news trick to show the viewer that interviewer and interviewee were indeed both in the same room. After he shot Maxi's reversals, he would come around to the front of the couch and widen out to a two-shot, handheld. Then he'd shoot the two of them walking into the living room and sitting down on the couch together, closer than they actually had been sitting during the interview—this would be the establishing shot that would begin the piece, with Maxi voicing over her setup to the story.

When they finished getting all these elements on camera, Maxi said she had to run; she had a lot of work ahead of her to get the piece cut for the evening news.

"Thanks, Sandie," she said. "You came off like a star. And thanks, Bill," to Sandie's father, who looked relieved that it was over. Maxi took the tape cassette that Harbaugh handed her and hustled out to her car, leaving her cameraman to get final cutaway shots, feed them in from the truck for her editing process, then gather up his equipment, pack up the Channel Six News van, and move on to his next assignment.

In her car, rolling back across town eastbound on Sunset Boulevard, Maxi started mentally planning her work. The first thing she would do when she got the tape back to the station would be to lift a few salient sound bites from the interview to use on the air as teases all afternoon, leading up to the Six O'clock News. She started choosing them in her mind.

Maxi led the show with her Sandie Schaeffer interview, which ran almost a full five minutes, under a Channel Six EXCLUSIVE banner. She knew that television news operations and newspapers all over the country would pick up her story and credit her and Channel Six in Los Angeles for it. She felt good about that. But still, something bothered her. That business about Gillian's crystal award. The more she thought about it, the more it nagged at her that it had seemed to come out of nowhere. She was too busy before the show, jamming to get the piece done on deadline, to look into it, but after the news was off the air she intended to put a call in to Detective Salinger or Barnett and ask if they knew anything about a crystal artifact being broken at the crime scene.

She went on with the show, moving into other stories, the business news, the weather. About twenty minutes in, while she was intro-ing the sports reporter, Wendy's voice sounded frantically in her earpiece. At first Maxi was annoyed that her producer hadn't waited until Roggin was into his sports report, knowing that Maxi would then have a break for a few minutes, but then she was shocked as she processed what Wendy was yelling into her ear. "Maxi, Capra is pulling you off the air! He's sending Tran down to replace you."

Before Maxi could ask why, she saw weekend anchor Sylvie Tran, who worked as a reporter during the week, come in through the studio doors and rush onto the set.

"We have to swap out during sports," Sylvie whispered to her while the cameras focused on Roggin in the next chair giving the sports scores.

This was unheard of. Maxi had never witnessed a shift of anchors during a show. She wasn't about to make a scene while the show was live—she removed her mike, disconnected her Telex, and got out of the chair, which Sylvie quickly filled. Curious and indignant both, she picked up her purse from the floor beside the anchor chair and strode off the set, out of the studio, up the stairs, into the newsroom—and into Capra's office.

"Explain this," she threw out, standing squarely in front of his desk.

"What the hell is wrong with you, Maxi?" her boss asked, looking hard at her face.

"What's that supposed to mean?"

Capra paused for a beat, still scrutinizing her face. Then he said, quietly, "Sit down." He indicated a chair in front of the bank of monitors, one of which was tuned to Sylvie Tran, now anchoring the Six, the others tuned to other stations, monitoring the competition.

"What do you—" she started indignantly.

"Sit down," he said again.

Capra walked over to the screens, bent down, pushed the STOP button on the VCR that was recording the station's Six O'clock News in progress, then pushed EJECT. He grabbed the tape as it was sliding out of the machine, jammed it back into the VCR, pressed the REWIND button, then let it play. Maxi dropped into the chair and watched the opening credits roll, still pictures of herself and the other personalities featured on the Six as the announcer intoned their names, then watched herself on-screen leading off the Six O'clock News with her exclusive interview with Sandie Schaeffer. Capra fast-forwarded through it, and through a succession of other stories, then let it play from a few minutes before he'd yanked her off the air.

"Look carefully," he said to Maxi.

"What am I supposed to be looking for?"

"Just watch."

"What—"

"Shhh. Wait a minute, till you're on in close-up."

Maxi watched the end of a story on a local robbery. When the tape ended, she saw herself come on screen in close-up. And gasped.

She bolted out of her chair and over to the twenty-five-inch color screen that electronically transmitted her image. "Good God," she whimpered, clutching her face in her hands. "I . . . *I'm going to die!*"

Her two eyes, larger than life size in close-up on screen, were a bright, glittering, shocking pink.

68

The realization had hit her immediately. Maxi knew exactly what the chimerical eye color meant, and she also knew that she couldn't take the time to explain it to Pete Capra. Snatching her purse, she'd run out of his office, raced across the newsroom and out the security door, taken the stairs two at a time, blasted down the wide, ground-floor corridor, causing people to start and jump out of her way, and exploded out into the parking lot, all the while crying aloud, *"Oh-God-oh-God-oh-God . . ."*

Gillian's eyes had dramatically changed color. And then she died. It was poison, Dr. Riker had confirmed. Someone had to have deliberately poisoned the woman, the doctor had said.

Sandie Schaeffer!

Maxi unlocked her car, jumped in, and gunned the motor. Saint Joseph Medical Center was just a few blocks away from the station. She sped out of the midway, trying to stay focused on getting to the hospital—she had no idea how much time she had for an antidote to be able to successfully reverse the fatal effects of the poison she knew had to be in the experimental cosmetic eye-color product.

Jockeying her old Corvette up Catalina Street then down Alameda Avenue toward the Burbank hospital, pieces of the puzzle, unbidden, came rocketing at her consciousness as if shot at her from a cannon.

Sandie Schaeffer had poisoned Gillian. It wasn't Goodman Penthe, and it wasn't Carter Rose. It was Sandie, the only person in the entire dismal cast who had been in a position to poison both of them: Gillian and now herself.

How did she do it? Gillian kept samples of the fledgling BriteEyes product in her office. Sandie had access to that office every day. All she had to do was slip poison into the product vials, knowing that Gillian, not wanting anyone to know what she had, had been testing BriteEyes on herself. Sandie knew it was just a matter of time before Gillian would use the product again. And she did, of course—on the night when she wanted to show Goodman Penthe how fabulous it was.

How did Sandie Schaeffer know what kind of poison would be readily soluble in liquid, hard to detect, and not routinely traced? Easy. For eight years she had been the right hand of Gillian Rose, product-development chief of Rose International—as such, she'd worked continually, on a close-up basis, with elements and components in the Rose product line. And the reason she'd got that job in the first place would probably have been her background, her working knowledge of drugs and supplements: she was the daughter of a pharmacist and for years had worked in the family drugstore. And she no doubt still had access to the pharmacy. Figuring out what to use, and getting her hands on the substance, would have been easy for Sandie Schaeffer.

The harder question was *why*. Why would Sandie poison her longtime friend and boss? And why Maxi?

With the clarity often spawned in panic, some answers occurred to Maxi, but before she had time to think them through, she'd arrived at Saint Joseph Medical Center. Screeching to a stop in front of the Emergency Room entrance, she parked illegally behind a pair of ambulances and ran up the steps and inside the door.

"Help me," she gasped, grabbing the arm of the first white-coated staffer she ran into, a young medical intern working the ER.

"You're Maxi Poole," he said, recognition lighting his eyes. Then he saw the color of hers. "My *God*—"

"I've been poisoned. With selenium. If we don't hurry, it's going to kill me."

He knew what selenium could do. He grabbed her by the arm and led her quickly across the wide waiting room. When they passed the admissions desk, a white uniformed nurse said, "Excuse me, Doctor, this patient has to be processed in—"

The intern waved her off, and pushed Maxi ahead of him through the double doors of the ER. *"Testing, stat,"* he bellowed to anyone and everyone, and three white-coated staffers immediately appeared. They got Maxi into a treatment room and up onto an examination table.

"Get me a full panel of electrolytes," the doctor ordered tersely, then set about checking Maxi's vital signs.

"It's not the pink eyes," she babbled while he worked. "That's something else. But trust me on the selenium, Doctor."

A technician tied a tourniquet around her upper left arm and injected a syringe into the inside of her elbow to draw blood. Maxi winced, turning her head to the side, and squeezed her eyes shut. She was in capable hands now. She was going to be all right. She'd made it in time. They would save her.

Twenty minutes later, the doctor again stood over her. "Maxi," he said. "Maxi Poole."

She opened her eyes and looked up at him.

"Your electrolyte values are normal," he said.

"Wh-what?"

Putting a hand on her arm, he said, "It's not selenium."

69

Exceeding the speed limit over bumpy Coldwater Canyon, Maxi felt herself driving light-headed, almost in a trance. Was she getting sick—was the poison kicking in? Or was she just panicked? Nerves frozen with fear? She willed it to be the latter.

The young intern at Saint Joe's, Dr. Gotler, had chased her out the door of the ER to the entrance rotunda, trying to hold her back. "Wait, Ms. Poole!" he'd called. "We need to send a specimen to a reference lab to be sure. We'll have the results back in twenty-four hours—"

She didn't have twenty-four hours. As he looked on helplessly, she'd scrambled into her car, which was still parked illegally among the ambulances at the entrance. It had been there for half an hour—thank God it hadn't been towed yet.

If it wasn't selenium, then what? Only one person knew the answer to that. When she emerged from the cellular dead zone that she knew from experience stretched all the way down through the long canyon, she picked up her phone and punched in 911.

The bright lights of Sunset Boulevard flashed and glimmered just ahead. The clock on her dash read 7:52 P.M. Calmly, she told the dispatcher who came on the line that this was a life-or-death emergency, and that she should alert the paramedics to bring as many poison antidotes as they could get their hands on.

"What kind of poison?" the woman asked.

"That's just it—I don't know. But I've been poisoned with something, and I know it's something that will kill me."

She told the woman who she was, Maxi Poole from Channel Six, hoping that would lend her some credibility. And she gave her William Schaeffer's address in Pacific Palisades.

"Stay on the line with me," the woman said.

As she drove, Maxi gave her a sketchy account of what was going on and prayed that the dispatcher wouldn't think she was some kind of wacko impersonating newscaster Maxi Poole and making a wild crank call.

A light shone through the three front windows at the Schaeffer house. No fire-department paramedics van out front. She'd beaten them there. God, she fervently hoped that the dispatcher had believed her story and they were on their way.

Walking briskly up to the now familiar front door, her cell phone still to her ear, Maxi rang the bell. When she saw the doorknob turning, she folded the phone and dropped it into her purse.

The door opened and Sandie Schaeffer stood backlit in

the archway, still dressed in the clothes she'd had on for their interview that morning.

"Maxi Poole," she breathed, and made a quick move to slam the door. Maxi hurled herself over the threshold, pushing Sandie back into the foyer before she had a chance to shut her out.

"Tell me what it is," Maxi said through clenched teeth, slamming her two hands on Sandie's shoulders. "Tell me what poison you used."

"Like your new eye color?" Sandie asked. "It certainly sparked up the news for a few minutes."

Maxi slapped her face. *What poison did you use?* she demanded again. She was six inches taller than Sandie, and strong. Sandie was weakened from surgery, a duration of coma, lack of exercise. She was frail. Unarmed, this woman could not get the better of her, Maxi knew.

"Telling you that might defeat my purpose," Sandie said, almost tauntingly.

Was this woman deranged? Maxi wondered. Then she flashed on the reality that anyone who did what she now knew Sandie Schaeffer had done couldn't be entirely sane.

"Even if I told you," the woman went on, "you don't have enough time to do anything about it."

"Where's your father?" Maxi rasped, nudging Sandie backward into the living room.

"Not home yet. He doesn't close up till ten."

And there was no B.J., Maxi knew—she had nights off. Sandie Schaeffer was alone in the house.

She wasn't afraid of Sandie, but she was terrified that she would run out of time. Giving the woman a mighty shove, she pushed her down into one of the wing chairs in the living room and stood menacingly over her. Hurting her would do no good, Maxi knew; she had to find a way to make her tell what poison she'd used.

Keeping her eyes on Sandie, Maxi reached into the bag on her shoulder and fished out her cell phone. She hadn't committed the number for Schaeffer Pharmacy to memory—she punched in 411 and asked Information to connect her. William Schaeffer answered.

"Bill," she said, "it's Maxi Poole. I'm at your house. Get home immediately. It's Sandie—she's in trouble."

She broke the connection before he could question her. She reasoned that the man would rush home faster having heard that message than if she unleashed the whole unbelievable story on him over the phone. He'd probably think it was a bogus call to the drugstore by some nut who'd seen his daughter on television earlier tonight.

Maxi felt her eyes twitch reflexively, and suddenly half a dozen Sandie Schaeffers wavered in front of her. Behind Sandie, the entire room was out of focus. Images started moving in elliptical circles and melding together. She felt a sudden, sharp catch in her throat and felt her face inflame.

This wasn't lost on Sandie. "Having trouble seeing? And breathing?" she asked.

"What did you do to me?" Maxi gasped, dizzying, clutching at her throat now, dropping backward onto the nearby couch.

"I slipped a little Botox into your BriteEyes," Sandie said with a malevolent smile.

"Botox?"

"Yup. Everybody's favorite wrinkle remover. Even my manicurist is giving Botox shots these days. Every drug salesman in the country carries a supply of it in his case.

I ordered a few milligrams through the drugstore, as a backup in case the selenium didn't work."

"Your father will know—"

"Nope. I used Benny's name, had it shipped to my apartment address, and I paid for it in advance with my credit card, so there'll be no invoice on the store's account. I even burned the paperwork that came with it. Nobody will know. And," she added, "I get frequent-flyer miles." Sandie chuckled at that.

Maxi felt tears forming in her eyes and running down her cheeks. Botulism. The most poisonous natural substance on earth, a toxin that paralyzes by attacking nerve cells. And now so readily available in cosmetics circles. Please hurry, paramedics. Hurry, Bill Schaeffer.

Maxi's mind flicked back to a short reader she'd had on the show about the development of a new botulism antidote. When the deadly 9/11 terrorist strikes were followed by an attack of anthrax distributed by mail, countering bioterrorism had become a national priority. This highly effective botulism antidote was one of a slate of new therapies that had been developed fast. That's all she could recall about the story. She couldn't remember what the antidote was called.

"Why did you do this?" was all she could manage. She was having trouble seeing now, and was barely able to sustain steady breathing, but she was fighting to maintain control. Had to keep the woman talking . . .

"Gillian ripped off my father's glaucoma formula just to distill out its eye-color properties, purely for its cosmetic potential. Dad had agreed to sell because she said she wanted to market it for glaucoma relief. She never paid him—said she couldn't yet, for business reasons.

But she had other plans for his formula, *big* plans. And she stood to make millions."

"So you wanted the formula for yourself—"

"And for my father. Gillian was so secretive about this project that nobody knew what she was really up to. Not even Dad. But I figured out what her lab was doing. I could read the equations. I'm the only one who knew."

"Goodman Penthe knew. He was going to be her partner."

"Too late for him. His plan died with Gillian."

"Carter Rose must have it by now. . . ."

"Carter's looking at prison time. He won't be developing anything."

Maxi's head was spinning and a gurgling rattle came from her throat.

"Can't breathe?" Sandie asked. "That's what one milligram of Botox will do—cause respiratory failure. Complete pulmonary collapse. I didn't know when you were going to use your eyedrops next, but when I saw your eyes turn pink on the news, I knew you had."

My eyedrops! Sandie must have added the poisoned formula to the small container of Visine she kept in her purse. She always put in drops before she went on the air, to ease the harshness of the bright studio lights on her eyes. But where would Sandie have kept a vial of poison in her father's house? Then she flashed on a mental picture of the leopard-skin makeup bag on the table next to Sandie's hospital bed. Perfect hiding place, among a woman's usual jumble of bottles and jars and pots of beauty products.

"When did you—?" she started, but the words again caught in her throat.

"This morning. I had a vial in my pocket. I saw you

use your eyedrops just before we went on camera. Then, when the interview was over, you left your purse on the couch while you used the powder room. When your cameraman went out to his truck to get a new battery, I asked Dad to go to the kitchen for some water. Nobody was around. That's when I went in your purse and spiked your Visine."

Using sheer force of will, Maxi straightened up in the chair. The movement helped her rally. *"Why?"* she asked.

"Because I've been watching the news. I've seen you all over the story from the day Gillian died, except while I was hazy for a couple of days after surgery. I knew you weren't about to stop nosing around."

"H-hazy?" Maxi forced herself to squeak. "You . . . weren't in a deep coma? You never had amnesia?"

"Of course not. I was in and out of consciousness at first, but I understood you perfectly in the ICU that Sunday morning you barged in. I knew you were just trying to get a story out of me. And then all those visits. You're all heart, aren't you—that's what you had my father thinking."

"But . . . you were asking for me—"

"Sure. You gave me the idea to ask for you the first time you popped in that Sunday morning and tried to grill me. I figured you'd put whatever I babbled to you on the news. I could hand-feed you my own version of events, hint that Carter shot me, and you'd buy it."

Maxi groaned. Reporting the ongoing story, she *had* put Sandie Schaeffer's "babblings" on the news.

"And I knew when the police saw your reports they'd take a good, hard look at Carter Rose. If he was the one who shot me, maybe he murdered his wife."

"But . . . the break-in at the hospital. Somebody tampered with your IV bottles—"

"*I* did that. I just reached up and ripped them out. I did the phone messages, too. All while you people thought I was blitzed."

"You were supposed to be out cold—how could you get to a phone in the ICU without being seen?"

"Dad spent hours in the hospital with me. And he would leave his cell phone on top of his book on the bedside table when he'd go down for coffee. I made a couple of quick calls."

"And blocked them, and whispered, so we'd think someone wanted to silence you. Like Carter," Maxi gasped, putting it together.

"Like Carter. Or Kendyl," Sandie went on. "As long as everybody thought I was in danger, no one would ever suspect that I was the one who killed Gillian."

"But . . . the police must have found the poisoned vials in her office that day. . . ."

"I got rid of them as soon as I discovered Gillian's body, before I screamed and supposedly fainted. I knew where she kept the box of vials; she was always playing with them. When I saw that they'd served my purpose just fine, thank you, I wrapped them up in a plastic bag and tossed them down the waste chute. Down into the furnace with the rest of the crap that oozes out of that place. Nobody ever looked there."

"But if you tossed all the vials—"

"All except one. In case I needed it. Smart, huh? Only problem was, I couldn't find the formula that day."

"So later when you went back in to search, Carter and Kendyl nailed you . . ."

Maxi was down to a raspy whisper now, but she

needed to keep Sandie talking. Her chest and throat were on fire. Images swirled in front of her, the lights from lamps magnifying, multiplying, and half-blinding her. She was too weak to get up off the couch, and she knew that Sandie knew it.

"I realized it right away when I slipped up about the crystal bowl," Sandie said with a smirk. "That big windbag Nagataki broke it, swinging his arms around, showing his underjerks how important he is. I saw him do it. But I forgot that it was never on the news. Of course they'd never let the big cheese's stupid mistake get out to the press. They had someone sweep it up fast."

The *coroner!* When Maxi had left the crime scene he was still there. It would have happened after she and Harbaugh were gone. Sandie was right—the broken crystal bowl had never got on tape and had never been reported, on television, radio, in print, anywhere.

"You were beginning to get on to me then," Sandie droned on. "I changed my story in the interview today, but I knew you weren't totally buying it. I knew you'd go digging and figure everything out. You're too smart for your own good, Maxi. You're going to die here. I'll say that you showed up to visit, and you keeled over. Just like Gillian. I'll be heartbroken, horrified. I might even stage a little relapse. They never suspected that I poisoned Gillian, and they'll never suspect that I poisoned you. A heart defect—"

"But . . . my boss saw my eyes," Maxi forced with guttural breaths. "The ER docs saw . . . A million *viewers* saw my eyes. . . . The nine-one-one dispatcher has . . . the story on tape. They'll . . . put it together—"

Maxi stopped, realizing that she was arguing with an insane person. Sandie wasn't hearing. Head tilted, the woman sat fixated on her with hollow eyes and a thin, determined smile.

"Why Botox, Sandie? Why not just use the selenium?" Useless question, Maxi knew, but she was buying time.

"Gillian applied a whole vial of the formula with each use. I knew you'd only use a drop or two of your eye-drops, and there wouldn't be enough selenium to hurt you."

"How . . . how much time do I have—"

"With Botox? Oh, you don't get twelve hours like Gillian got, Maxi Poole. Maybe twelve *minutes* left before you strangle.

"In fact, let's get this over with now," she said then, getting up from her chair and picking up a throw pillow. Quickly, she closed the distance between them, pushed Maxi's head back on the couch, and smashed the pillow into her face.

With a burst of strength coming from pure adrenaline, Maxi reared up and grabbed Sandie by the throat. Thrown off guard, Sandie dropped the pillow and clutched at Maxi's hands around her neck. One woman frail, the other barely breathing, the two went at each other with everything they had left.

Through the still open front door, Maxi heard a car pulling up. It wouldn't be Bill Schaeffer, she knew. He had to maneuver in a wheelchair—it would take him much longer than this to get home from his drugstore in Westwood.

Sandie heard it too. With Maxi distracted for an instant by the car, she pulled out of her grip and lunged at her. Eyes scratchy, vision distorted, Maxi miscalculated the body coming at her. Sandie landed on top of her on the couch and pulled her down to the floor, and ground the pillow into her face again.

With literally the last reserve of breath she could muster, Maxi curled her knees up to her chest, and with a hardy two-legged kick, hurled Sandie off her body and several feet across the room. That's when she became aware of the team of L.A. County paramedics bursting into the room. There were three of them, but to her dystopian vision it looked like twenty responding to the shouts and thuds of the two women in a fight for their lives.

Maxi's head fell back to the floor. All she managed to utter was, "Botulism . . . toxin."

70

Fitting for a January funeral in Southern California, the sky was gray and heavy with drizzle; the mourners were in basic black. A great outpouring from the City of Angels was on hand to bid farewell to Rob Reordan, L.A.'s premier news anchor for most of their lives.

Maxi stood with Wendy and Pete Capra at the edge of the throng at the legendary Forest Lawn Cemetery in Glendale, archetypal burial place of the region's famous. They'd positioned themselves on the perimeter of the crowd so they could make an inconspicuous getaway back to work if the ceremony went too long. And it probably would. There had been no church service prior to the interment—Rob had professed to no religious affiliation. So eulogies were being spoken here, and the number of friends, colleagues, family, and celebrities scattered through the crowd portended that there would be many.

As Rob Reordan's boss at Channel Six, Capra had spoken first. Eloquently, for him. Then Maxi. Glowingly.

Wendy passed; besides the fact that the man tried to steal her work, it was fairly well known, though she had the grace not to mention it today, that she never liked him anyway. Now, while others spoke, the three stood apart from the crowd, chatting softly with each other, waiting for a graceful time to make their exit. As was the case every day, they had a full slate of news shows to put on the air.

Dominating the news all week was the aftermath of the scandalous Gillian Rose case. Sandie Schaeffer was in custody, facing a murder trial. Her distinguished father, in his wheelchair, had been showing up on every channel, standing by his daughter, arguing for the insanity plea. Beside him always, her hand on the back of his chair, was Barbara Jean Martin, B.J. They were obviously a couple now. Maxi felt very good about that.

BriteEyes was dead. Bill Schaeffer would never sell his glaucoma formula for the purpose that Gillian had intended, and the story was too widely publicized now for Carter Rose to be able to steal it and proceed with the lab work that Gillian had done. Besides, Rose was facing prison time on a conspiracy rap.

Goodman Penthe got out of his deal to buy Rose International on a contingency; since the company was now tainted with both murder and fiscal corruption, he successfully took the position that consumers would no longer support the Rose brand. Only Maxi knew that the real deal breaker for Penthe was the demise of BriteEyes.

Beautiful Kendyl Scott was free on an immunity deal, and was making the rounds as a prominent guest on the national talk-show circuit. So far she'd been offered a cameo role in a Bruce Willis movie, a recurring part on a daily soap, and a regular panel slot on a revival of *The Gong Show*.

This story wasn't going to go away soon. The media were pouncing on every angle and sidebar—even the supermarket tabloids were full of it—and the country was getting to know all the players well. As is always the case when a story grabs the attention of the nation, news viewership was up, and the saga in all of its ramifications was on everybody's minds and lips, including those of the three Channel Six News journalists. It was all anybody in their circles had been talking about since the Sandie Schaeffer meltdown last Monday.

Reporter Maxi Poole had since declined all offers to do print interviews, or go on local or national radio and television shows and talk about it. She told each editor and producer who called that she didn't march in the parade, she just reported on it.

"We should get going," Wendy said.

"Yeah," Maxi concurred. "I'm doing a piece on the availability of the new anthrax and botulism antidotes for the Four."

"I still can't believe how lucky you were that most of the paramedics in the country have been carrying them as staples since nine-eleven," Wendy marveled. "I hate to think—"

"Then don't," Pete squelched her.

"Gracious, as usual," Wendy groused, tossing him a sour look.

"What *I* can't believe is that the nine-one-one dispatcher didn't think you were one of the usual nuts who call in and make them crazy," Pete put in.

"I talked to her yesterday," Maxi said. "To thank her. And I asked her why she didn't just hang up on me with my insane story. She said she recognized my voice, so she knew it really was me. Lucky break."

"Why didn't you call *me?*" Pete asked. "You just went running off into the night with your devil eyes and I had no idea what the hell was going on."

"I was so crazed to find out what poison it was I couldn't much think about anything else. And I thought everything would be okay if I got to Saint Joe's on time."

"What did your mother and father have to say?" Pete asked. Brigitte and Maxwell Poole had been hip-deep in Maxi's last deadly imbroglio, and Pete remembered well that they had not been pleased.

"Oh boy. I thought I'd just spare them this one," Maxi said. "I should have realized they couldn't escape the story. Dad was majorly ticked that he had to hear about it on the news."

"Yup. Their well-bred daughter in yet another tabloid catfight." Pete smirked.

"Speaking of Sandie the cat, here's something I still don't understand," Wendy said. "Explain to me again why she faked a coma and amnesia. And how the hell do you fake a coma, anyway?"

"Easy," Pete tossed out. "You lie there, you keep your eyes closed, and you don't talk. I have reporters who fake comas all the time."

"She did it so no one would suspect her of poisoning Gillian," Maxi said. "And nobody did."

"And Carter Rose completely staged that would-be attack on himself, and even called a news conference about it," Wendy said.

"Because he wanted the police to look for a murderer," from Maxi.

"But he didn't *do* it! He didn't kill his wife. So why would he pull a stunt like that?" Wendy asked.

"Good question. You two know that since my insane bout with Sandie Schaeffer I've had many hours of conversation with the detectives, and I asked them about that. They told me they knew from the get-go that Carter Rose was lying about that attack. There was no forced entry, no sign of a struggle, none of the help saw anything. . . ."

"So why didn't they nail him with it?" from an incredulous Wendy.

"My question to them precisely. Salinger said they actually suspected Rose of murder because Gillian's divorce lawyer came forward and told them she was divorcing him. That gave him motive. And that faked attack made them suspect him even more. So instead of tagging him with falsifying a crime report, which they couldn't prove anyway, they decided to wait and watch him."

"He *knew* they suspected him of murdering Gillian?" Pete asked.

"Evidently from the morning he got in from Taiwan, when they interrogated him for three hours at Parker Center. They got from that session that this was definitely not a grieving widower, and they let him know that."

"So he faked an attack on himself to throw off the blame. Does he think they're all stupid?" Wendy asked.

"Actually, yes," Maxi confirmed. "Salinger and Barnett told me that's how this kind of man thinks. He's extremely arrogant."

"I say he's a nut-ball. That whole crowd deserved each other," Wendy tossed out.

Pete was thoughtful. "You know," he said then, "Sandie Schaeffer almost pulled off the perfect murder. If

Maxi hadn't stumbled on the clues, no one would ever have suspected her of killing Gillian Rose because she wanted the patent on the BriteEyes product, and—"

"Excuse me, boss," Maxi interrupted adamantly. "*Stumbled* on the clues? That was not *stumbling,* sir. That was solid investigative journalism."

"Yeah, yeah," Pete conceded grudgingly. "And there'll be a little something extra in your paycheck."

"Right, like always." Maxi sneered.

Wendy was still thinking about the fascinating case theory. "And if the police *did* suspect murder, Sandie wanted the blame thrown on Carter Rose," she said.

"Yes," Maxi agreed. "She knew about the lab work that Gillian had done on the formula—that's how she knew this product was going to be the golden goose. She had every intention of running with it, and it would have been even easier with Carter totally preoccupied. Like in prison."

"And she kept tossing *you* some bones so you'd put her version of things on the air, reinforce it with news credibility, right?" Wendy finished.

"You've got it. It almost worked, too," Maxi mused. "If it hadn't been for the dead file—"

Maxi looked up just then to see Sunday Trent making her way across the grass toward them. "Well! Look who's here, Wendy," she said.

When Sunday caught up with the trio, she was grabbed in a bear hug by both the women, which totally surprised the young intern. "Wow!" she said when they let her go. "What did I do to deserve this?"

"Hey, Sun, good news," Wendy said. "I got you a job."

"Huh?" This from Sunday, still overwhelmed by the

enthusiasm directed her way by her two women news idols.

"First, we finish up my book next week. Then you report to Channel Nine—to news director Nancy Bauer. You're their new editorial assistant on the weekend news. If you work out, there's a full-time slot on the writing staff waiting for you when you graduate in June."

Sunday was beaming. "Oh, don't worry. I'll work out. I'll work my butt off—you both can count on that."

"We know," Maxi said.

Pete was gaping happily at Sunday, who was dressed in a thigh-high, skintight black miniskirt topped with a cropped, black fur-lined jeans jacket, black pantyhose, and high-heeled black suede boots: her funeral attire.

"Terrific body!" he said to her with a leer.

"*Pete!*" Maxi and Wendy wailed in unison.

"You can't *say* that to a woman," Maxi admonished.

"It's *sexist,*" Wendy said.

"It could be construed as sexual harassment. We have lawsuits like that on the news all the time. For God's sake, don't you *see* that, boss?" Maxi pleaded.

"Sunday, tell him," Wendy said. "Maybe he needs to hear it from someone else besides the two of us."

"Tell him what?" Sunday asked.

"Tell him when he makes a remark about your body, you're offended."

"Offended? I *love* it," Sunday fairly squealed. "Why do you think I kill myself in the gym at six o'clock every morning? To hear guys tell me I have a great body, that's why. Thanks, Pete," she directed at the man. "You're such a teddy bear."

She flashed Capra a megawatt smile as she turned to continue on her way. Capra watched her retreating backside admiringly, then responded to Maxi and Wendy with an I-rest-my-case palms-up and a big, self-satisfied grin. The two women could only roll their eyes. Sunday was no help, and Capra was hopeless.

The appearance of Sunday Trent had reminded them of the shameful saga of Wendy's book. Since it had been brought to light that *Don't Be Dumpy* was in fact the intellectual property of Los Angeles television news producer Wendy Harris, that the author called Sophia LeGrande did not exist, and that her alias was no longer among the living, the other literary agent had dropped all claims to it.

Maxi looked out toward the flower-bedecked casket and murmured to both her companions, "Do you think Rob actually thought he could get away with it?"

"Sure," Pete said. "All Rob had to do was hide behind the fictitious skirts of Sophia LeGrande, who was a very shy author, or maybe an extremely busy one, because she would never make any personal appearances. It was a beautiful scam, if you think about it." Clearly this was a subject that intrigued Pete Capra.

"And where would the publisher have sent the fictitious Ms. Sophia's money?" Wendy asked, a subject that intrigued her.

"To Sophia LeGrande's bank account, wherever Rob set it up," Pete said.

"What about her taxes?" Maxi asked.

"Ha! The IRS would never find her," Pete said, "because she didn't exist. It was beautiful."

For a couple of moments of contemplative silence, they all looked over at the coffin again.

"What a guy," Pete finally said.

"What an asshole," Wendy muttered.

71

Friday night. Home from work. The end of an emotional day. The end of a bizarre and dangerous week. The end of a roller-coaster case that had spawned a blockbuster news story. Maxi was completely drained. She was curled up on the couch in her cozy living room in Beverly Glen, in sweats and her comfy sheepskin slippers, with Yukon stretched out on the floor at her feet. Too tired even to get up and go to bed.

When the phone rang.

It was Richard Winningham, calling from Tel Aviv.

"Capra told me your eyes were shocking hot pink on the air," he said. "You've just gotta get more sleep, sweetie."

"Um . . . well, actually, what happened was—"

"I know, I know—I got the whole story. About a dozen people e-mailed me about it, including Pete. And I read all about it in the *International Herald Tribune*. Are you okay, Maxi?"

"I'm fine. Are you coming home, Richard?" she heard herself asking.

"Yup, one of these months. Dinner at Spago?"

"You're on."

Acknowledgments

MAXI POOLE AND I WANT TO THANK SOME VERY IMPORTANT FRIENDS OF OURS WHO HELPED GET DEAD FILE "BANGED OUT AND ON THE AIR," AS THE HARDWORKING FOLKS IN THE SWEATY NEWSROOM AT FICTIONAL CHANNEL SIX NEWS WOULD SAY:

My thanks to dynamic NBC-4 News producer *Wendy Harris,* the soul of the newsroom and my longtime friend, who plays herself in all my books.

And to my former news director *Tom Capra,* who would jump on the desk in the newsroom and point and scream, *"You, get a vest on and scout the riot area! You, get downtown and smoke out the mayor!"* (and who would get severely cranky every time he gave up smoking); and my former managing editor *Pete Noyes,* who was known to punch out a reporter for burying the lead (before they put you in jail for that). Together these two inspired my character, Maxi Poole's boss, Pete Capra. Thanks, guys, and don't get mad.

I'm indebted to **Dr. Paul Khasigian** of the California Poison Control System, Fresno/Madera division, for teaching me how to poison someone and get away with it; to **Detective Sergeant Richard Longshore** of the Los Angeles County Sheriff's Homicide Bureau for shepherding me through two weeks of "murder" school; to **Assistant Chief Juan Jimenez** of the Los Angeles County Coroner's Investigations Division for a tour of the morgue, with lunch (yes, they do that!); and to **Dr. Rick Gold** at Cedars, medical adviser to me and all the doctors in *Dead File*.

I owe *Dead File* and Maxi Poole's very life to my editor **Sara Ann Freed,** the sage of Warner Books' Mysterious Press and America's undisputed queen of the mystery genre.

Special thanks to the irrepressible **Susan Richman,** the patrician of New York Public Relations; and **Kim Dower** of "Kim from L.A.," Susan's counterpart in La-La Land.

And to the wonderful women of Warner Books: publisher **Maureen Egen,** the mother of us all; editor-in-chief **Jamie Rabb,** the first to read Maxi Poole and run with her; production editor **Penina Sacks,** who went to the mat with me on the minutiae of grammatical correctness (she won); and astute and exacting **Karen Thompson,** who dazzled me with her canny input.

To my literary agent **Robin Rue,** who brought Maxi Poole home to the women of Warner, and who guides Maxi and me on our adventures.

To my super-readers: author/screenwriter **Linda**

Palmer, social conscience of *Dead File;* brilliant comedy writer *Gail Parent,* my partner on the TV show *Kelly & Gail,* who loves brainstorming plot twists over a bottle of wine; and gorgeous *Gale Hayman,* cofounder of Giorgio, Beverly Hills, Maxi's arbiter of taste and fashion.

Hugs to playwright *Marvin Braverman,* who feeds me ideas along with Maxi's (and my) favorite veggie burgers.

Eternal gratitude to *Shawn Kendrick* of Borders, who walks behind me with a wheelbarrow full of my books at outlandish events (on the Santa Monica Pier during an afternoon cloudburst, on the pitcher's mound at Dodger Stadium during seventh-inning stretch) and manages to hang on to both his aplomb and his cash box.

I am indebted to NBC-4 News editor *Bart Cannistra,* my ever-patient computer guru; *Terry Beebe* and the gang at the NBC Credit Union for letting me monopolize their copy machine; actor/screenwriter *Bob Factor* for helping me out of some deadline jams; *Jim Alvarez,* head of NBC Wardrobe, for suitably dressing both Maxi and me; and *Patti Hansen,* head of NBC Travel, for keeping Maxi and me flying between the palms of Los Angeles and the publishing canyons of New York.

My gratitude to restaurateur *Ron Salisbury,* who throws me book parties and feeds me besides; to *Barbara Jean Thomas,* the *real* B.J.; and my voice-over agent *Sandie Schnarr,* who actually likes having Sandie Schaeffer named after her.

Special thanks to *Dr. David Walker* of the Los Angeles Church of Religious Science, who teaches calming metaphysics to Maxi and me; and to wonderful *Vera Brown,* the grande dame of TV's *Shop NBC,* for mentoring me in life and literature.

And my profound adoration goes out to Maxi Poole's spiritual family, my fascinating sister **Ellie Poole,** and the whole **Poole** clan. And always and forever, eternal love and gratitude to my sturdy bookends, **Kelly Lansford,** my princess daughter, and **Alice Scafard,** my incredible mom.

IF YOU LIKED DEAD FILE, AND YOU'D LIKE TO SPEAK TO ME OR MAXI (WE'RE VERY CLOSE), VISIT OUR WEB SITE—WWW.KELLY-LANGE.COM. BOTH OF US WOULD LOVE YOUR COMMENTS AND INPUT FOR OUR ON-GOING "MAXI POOLE" SERIES. (IF YOU DIDN'T LIKE DEAD FILE, IN THE WORDS OF THAT GREAT NEWSWOMAN ROSANNE ROSANNADANA, "NEVER MIND.")

More
Kelly Lange!

Please turn this page
for a preview of

GRAVEYARD SHIFT

available
Spring 2005.

1

I don't get it," Maxi said, scowling at her boss.

"What part of 'you're working graveyard starting next week' don't you get?" the man asked, scowling right back at her.

The disgruntled two were Channel Six anchor-reporter Maxi Poole: dedicated, hard-working, popular; and her managing editor Pete Capra: crack journalist, irascible hothead, grouch. The two sat in his glassed-in office in the newsroom at Channel Six, the Los Angeles flagship station for UGN, the United Global Network.

"I haven't worked graveyard since I was a cub reporter, that's what I don't get, Pete. And you've got seven reporters junior to me, that's what I don't get. And Kittridge has been working graveyard for the last year, and he's actually weird enough to like it."

"Yeah," Capra mused, leaning forward, dropping both elbows onto his desk, resting his chin between his fists. "Kittridge does seem to like it. Never bitches. Think he's dealing drugs at night?"

"Probably. So why mess up a fine arrangement for him, a

fine arrangement for you because he doesn't complain, and a fine arrangement for me because I have a life?"

"You don't have a life, Maxi."

"*Excuse* me?"

"You're not married, you have no kids, you don't even date anyone. What life?"

"I have a dog," Maxi said indignantly. "And I happen to anchor your award-winning *Six O'clock News*, remember?"

"You'll keep that show, at least for now. You'll come in at four, anchor the *Six,* take off for dinner till nine, then go out on the street. Your shift will end at six after you edit your stuff for the *Morning News.* If you're needed on the set you'll stay a little longer. Then you'll go home and have your life."

"Then I'll limp home and feed Yukon."

"Whatever."

"And then I'll go out and do my run, come home, shower, fall into bed, try to sleep till two in the afternoon, get up, get dressed, and come back in to work by four."

"That's right," Pete said, smiling benevolently.

"And that's going to be my *life*?"

Ignoring the question, Pete said, "So you're reassigned. To graveyard. Starting Monday. Got it?"

Maxi considered the alternative. On-air talent in any television news market makes up a very small club. She could refuse the assignment, but then she'd have to bring in the union to engage in a fight with the company on her behalf, and thereafter she'd be branded a troublemaker. These industry brawls become juicy gossip topics for everybody in the business, including execs at other stations whom she just might need to hire her down the road. Most media bosses won't hire a troublemaker. So in the television news business, refusing an assignment is called eating a death cookie.

"Okay, that's all," Capra said. He'd already turned back to his computer screen.

Maxi gave a *you're-pathetic!* shake of her head and walked out of his office.

Tom McCartney hefted his bulging black canvas back-pack up the stairs to the back door of the Channel Six newsroom and leaned on the VISITORS bell. His lanky frame was clad in worn jeans, a blue work shirt, a faded olive green safari jacket that looked like it had been through wars because it had, and scuffed-up Nike running shoes. His dark hair curled over his collar, not because it was a style choice, but because he tended to go too long between haircuts.

McCartney didn't have security clearance at Channel Six, or at any other station. That's because he was a member of that most oddball of tribes—McCartney was a stringer. A stringer is a newsie who works for no company, belongs to no unions or guilds, is a member of no professional groups or clubs, and has no loyalty to any news outlet, radio, television, or print. A stringer, for the most part, is a journalist who can't get a job.

And they almost always work at night. All night. On the graveyard shift. Stringers can't compete on daytime stories because broadcast stations and print media have their own reporting staffs out in the trenches all day. But come the dark of night, media outlets usually have just one reporter—read: one poor sucker—out there, who cannot possibly cover every sordid middle-of-the-night happening, let alone even find them all. So out from the low-down sludge of the City of Angels emerges this aberrant army of stringers to prowl the nightside and ply their trade. They peddle their tape from station to station. If they land a taker, or more than one if the story is hot, it was a worthwhile exercise. If they don't, it was a losing investment of time and money. Sometimes you eat the bear, and sometimes the bear eats you.

In general, stringers are regarded in the news business as a notch below pond scum. However, Tom McCartney was much more highly regarded in the industry because McCartney had a history in legitimate news, and a higher than usual average of delivering the goods. Tom McCartney was regarded as a notch *above* pond scum.

McCartney had been a correspondent for CNN. He was bucked off the skids of a chopper hovering over a land skirmish in Kuwait, and when he hit the ground, he'd broken what seemed like most of his bones. During months of recuperation he took to washing down Vicodin with vodka to lessen the pain. He got back to work, but he never got off the pills. Or the juice. After one too many somewhat slurred on-air deliveries CNN fired him, and nobody else would hire him. And now he was forty-two years old and prowling for news in the seamy underbelly of L.A. after midnight, like a vagrant digging for day-old bread in back alley dumpsters.

He rang the bell and pounded on the back door to the Channel Six newsroom for ten minutes before a writer, rushing by with a script in his hands, happened to hear him and let him in. He could have avoided all that hassle if he'd made a call in advance, or announced himself at the guard desk down in the lobby. Not his style. McCartney always parked on the side street east of the sprawling United Global Network complex and came in through the back loading docks opposite Studio Nine, where they shot a long-running daily soap. From there, he would eschew the bank of elevators and take the stairs two at a time to the back entrance of the newsroom, then wait for someone to heed his banging. That was because he was never entirely sure that his calling card would get him in the door. Anywhere.

"Hi, Tom," the young writer said. "Got something good?"

"The fire at PriceCo. Capra around?"

PriceCo was a discount store in South El Monte, an industrial city east of Los Angeles, where a fire of mysterious origin had broken out during the night.

"He's in his office," the writer said.

McCartney took long strides down the back hall and out into the open newsroom, nodding to a few acquaintances as he passed their computer terminals. McCartney didn't really have any colleagues that he could call friends. He didn't cultivate friends. Didn't drink with newsies. He could have. They'd have welcomed his company; McCartney was nothing if not interesting. But he was a dedicated loner.

He tapped on the glass of Pete Capra's office door, and walked inside at the managing editor's bidding.

"What?" Capra blurted from behind his desk, not inviting him to sit.

"The PriceCo fire."

"We were all over it on the morning show," Capra said. "We're recutting it for the *Noon*, and we'll have a reporter out there live for the early block."

"Do you have the new top?"

"What new top?"

"They're calling it arson."

"Last I checked, that was a speculation. We reported that."

"They have a suspect. I've got him on tape."

This got Capra's full attention. "The wires didn't say anything about a suspect," he said.

"I know." McCartney rummaged in his backpack. "That's why this one's expensive. Want to see it?"

"Talk to me first."

"I rolled on this guy at the scene because he looked squirrelly. Nervous, but enjoying himself. Having way too good a time."

Capra got out of his chair. "Show me," he said.

McCartney popped the tape into Capra's playback machine, and the two stood back to watch. Establishing wide shots showed flames shooting through the roof of the sprawling structure, firefighters on the scene dragging hoses and hoisting ladders, and a small group of lookie-loos hanging around the action. McCartney fast-forwarded to a zoom-in on one of the bystanders: a white male, mid-forties, of medium build, pale thinning hair, wearing a somewhat rumpled tan suit and wire-rim glasses. He was standing alone, a little apart, watching the flames.

"What time was this?" Capra asked, not taking his eyes off the figure on the screen.

"Three in the morning, around there. Guy looks like he went to a bar right from work, and went to the fire scene right from last call."

"Doesn't mean he set it. Coulda stopped on his way home to have a look."

"Guys in suits don't stop, park, get out of their cars, hike over to the fire lines, and slouch around watching a fire at three in the morning."

The picture cut to a close-up of the man's face. Sweat beaded his high, bony forehead, his eyes shone in the firelight, and the beginnings of a smile flickered at the corners of his thin, gray mouth.

"A computer programmer for Dinex, a small software company in West Covina. Been there eleven years. Nerd type," McCartney said. "Name's Bernard Peltz."

Capra narrowed his eyes. "How much?"

"Three thousand."

"You're insane, McCartney."

"I've been called worse," the reporter said with a humorless chuckle.

"You *are* worse," Capra said. "Fifteen hundred. Tops."

"Twenty-five, bottom."

"Two thousand. And I must be nuts."

"Twenty-five," McCartney reiterated, rewinding the tape. He punched the EJECT button, snatched the tape out of the machine, walked over to the chair where he'd set his backpack, and tossed the cassette into it.

"Okay, okay, twenty-five. But for chrissake don't tell anybody—they'll commit me. And needless to say I've got an exclusive on it. I'm not shucking out two-and-a-half large for you to peddle this tape all over town."

"Needless to say," the stringer echoed dryly.

"So," Capra said then, "what's going on with the Nodori arrest?"

Gino Nodori was a second-tier actor in a weekly network cop drama who'd been arrested after midnight on a lewd conduct charge in a public park the week before.

"What's going on with him? You know what's going on with him, Pete—it's on the wires. How come you didn't air my tape?"

"Nodori didn't make my lineup."

"You paid for it. Everybody else aired it. Two, Five, and Nine bought it from me."

"Like I said, Nodori didn't make the cut. Doing any follow-ups?"

"Why would you want follow-ups when you didn't even air the bust?"

"Just asking."

"Nodori's out on bail. You can cover the court procedures with your regular staff," McCartney tossed out with a pointed *you-know-this-as-well-as-I-do* look.

Capra looked over at the wall for a beat, then back at McCartney. "I'm thinking follow-ups at the scene," he said.

"Huh? It's a gay hangout in MacArthur Park. What goes down in the men's john is the same ol' same-ol'. With an occasional police bust, which nobody gives a damn about, and a one-in-a-million celebrity arrest like Nodori."

"How about shooting some tape out there for me? A couple of cassettes every night for a while."

McCartney looked puzzled. "What did I shoot at the Nodori rout that I don't know I shot?"

"So how about it?" Capra asked, ignoring the stringer's question. "Get me some long-lens CUs of the dirtbags who hang there. Five hundred a night."

"A thousand a night."

"Get outta town," Capra snapped back. "Five hundred, take it or leave it."

"I'll take it," McCartney said, his news nose telling him that Capra had to be looking for something big in MacArthur Park for that kind of video surveillance.

"And in return for the easy bucks, I need you to do another job," Capra said.

"That pays money?"

"No."

"Why does that not surprise me?" McCartney said, taking the arson tape out of his backpack and laying it on Capra's desk. "You want me to brief your writer on this?"

"Of course. The other job is to watch Maxi Poole."

"Nice job," McCartney said with a droll expression. "I already do."

"I mean on the street. She's working graveyard starting Monday."

McCartney raised his eyebrows. "No kidding. She on your shit list, Pete?"

"Just show her the ropes on the overnight," Capra said, writing a check.

Capra waved the check back and forth as if to dry the ink even though he'd used a ballpoint. "So you'll help Maxi get her bearings for a few nights?" he asked.

"Sure," McCartney said, reaching out and snatching the check. He folded it in two and tucked it into the upper flap pocket of his jacket. "But, Maxi Poole on graveyard? I don't get it."

"You don't have to get it," Capra said. "I'll see you in the morning with my MacArthur Park tapes."

"You want me to start out there tonight?"

"Jesus, yeah, I want you to start tonight. It's money for nothing!"

Tom McCartney smiled. He knew that Pete Capra never paid money for nothing.

ABOUT THE AUTHOR

KELLY LANGE is the author of *The Reporter,* the novel that introduced Maxi Poole, along with *Gossip* and *Trophy Wife*. A former news anchor and reporter for KNBC-TV, Ms. Lange is the recipient of numerous honors and awards, including an Emmy for Best Los Angeles News Anchorperson. She lives in Southern California.